CHAOS REALM

the immortals

S.E. Bellian

PublishAmerica
Baltimore

First printing

ISBN: 1-4137-2476-0
PUBLISHED BY PUBLISHAMERICA, LLLP
www.publishamerica.com
Baltimore

Printed in the United States of America

Dedication

This story is thanks to the people in my life that have kept so much inspiration flowing with their unending support and boundless enthusiasm.

My Dad:
Everything I could possibly say to you, you've already heard. I hope you find this novel dark and twisted enough for your liking. Thank you for treating even my earliest attempts as bestsellers. Someday in the future, I hope to prove you right... but for now you'll have to settle for this little embarrassment.

KJ, my best friend:
Thank you for always being there for me, no matter what. I owe you more than I can probably ever repay. Thanks for the Pepsi, the anime and everything.

Candy/Mouse:
Behold! You now have a starring role! I want you to know that no matter what you choose to do with your life, you can do it. You are mighty.

Amber-san:
What's life without a few laughs? If it wasn't for you and your bewildering sense of humor, this entire book would be one sappy sob story.

Megan:
Though we haven't spoken in years, I want you to know that none of this could have happened if it were not for those lunches we spent in the art room of PVHS.

Chris:
My shameless fanboy. Regardless of what happens in the future, I want you to know that you've changed my life, and I am grateful for it. It is you who makes my dragons possible.

But, most importantly, for Tiffy:
Thank you for believing in me, even when I had a hard time believing in myself. I may not always understand you, and sometimes you make me crazy, but your passion for this work is what saved it when I was about to throw everything away. Truthfully, if you hadn't slapped me when you did... this book would still be in my closet.

No failure, no matter how great, is ever truly a mistake... and no amount of time, however long, is ever truly wasted, not so long as you are doing what you love.

Thank you,
Sarah

Prologue

"Hello, Bruno."

The sound of my name jerked me from sleep. Gasping for breath, I searched the darkness nervously for any signs of an intruder. Familiar faces greeted me from the many framed photographs scattered across the room. Despite the visible stillness, I still felt as if I was not alone. I sighed heavily and pushed my glasses back up onto my nose.

It was the third time in the past two hours that I had dozed off at my desk. Wiping my lenses clean of ink smudges, I discovered that my nose was slightly blackened from where I'd rolled my face onto an incomplete stack of tax forms.

"Bruno?" a voice wondered, almost hesitantly. "Can you hear me?"

I stopped short.

Though I couldn't see much, I was certain that I had heard someone speak. Remembering that my wife, Patricia, had gone to bed early, I immediately felt guilty for forgetting to lock the doors. We didn't exactly live in the best of neighborhoods.

Uneasy as I was, I knew at that moment that my worst fear had come to pass.

There was an intruder in my house.

"Bruno…" The strange yet powerful voice surrounded me like a blanket, whispering my name. Very much afraid, I staggered back against the wall and looked up to the ceiling. It was a dark night and somewhat cloudy, but more than the potential storm that had me paranoid.

A feeling had come over me then, a sensation that I couldn't quite place. In an eerie, distant way, it was almost familiar. And yet I couldn't help but wonder. Why… why would a burglar call me by name? Why, if it were only a common housebreaker… why would I feel as if there were a thousand icy spiders crawling up my back?

"Who are you?" I shouted, not sure whether I should expect an answer.

Thunder cracked, and for a split second, a flash of light lit up my surroundings.

"Ah." The voice laughed softly.

I could see no one, but the sheer power that filled the room was electrifying. It was not the energy of any human being. Worse still, I knew, somehow, that whatever paranormal force had invaded my study was not something my wife had conjured with her occult hobbies.

It was real, in the horrific way that her little spirits never were real enough to touch.

"Who are you?" I repeated, begging for a response.

The question I had posed took advantage of the acoustics of the room. You? You? My voice repeated.

For a moment, the echoes fell silent and above my head the skylight began to open. A shadow, virtually invisible in the darkness, peered down into my dim study. The shadow was a figure of a woman.

"Who am I you ask?" She laughed softly, swooping inside and landing crouched like a cat in the shadows near my fireplace. "Ah, Bruno!" She shook her head. "Don't you recognize me?"

Absolutely petrified, I only shook my head and mouthed the word "no."

If we had ever met, I was sure I would have remembered her... because that was the impression she gave. Her attitude alone seemed to suggest that she was the kind of person that most people wouldn't forget easily, and her physical appearance only gave support to that fact. She was tall, easily six feet, with skin as white as milk, long blue-black hair and brilliant, dark eyes that seemed to burn with a strange inner glow as if they had seen entirely too many things in their time. There was something very Roman, almost aristocratic, about her profile. I supposed she was around thirty but her exact age was difficult to place, especially taking into account her steely gaze.

"Mr. Fargrove..., " my visitor sighed heavily, pulling a chair from the corner of the room into the faint light of my desk lamp. She smiled in such a way that I felt a sudden chill and I poured myself a glass of wine from a bottle she carried under her arm. My initial instinct had been correct, I realized, as I watched her move, lithe like a dancer and incredibly fluid in her step, across the floor. Whoever the woman was, one thing was certain, she was not human.

"You're wiser than you give yourself credit for." The woman grinned, absorbing my expression of shock as she filled another glass with wine, taking a drink herself. "But I am afraid that I must tell you now, as I have told you before… I cannot answer such a question."

Though I was still terribly confused, I nodded obediently and allowed her to continue the speech she had begun, sensing that it wouldn't be wise to argue.

"Who I am is so drastically overshadowed by what I am, what I have been, and what it is that I yet hope to become," she explained, leaning over my desk and looking at me directly in the eyes with a frighteningly ancient glare.

Perhaps recognizing that her teeth were about a quarter-inch from my throat, she composed herself instantly, still eyeing me almost hungrily. The scent of old leather and lavender was overpowering.

"Currently, I am a traveler." The woman stared at her pale, thin hands as if she were ashamed of herself. Her fingers moved slowly in hypnotic patterns as if she were contemplating some obscure memory. "At times I can be a stubborn fool, and there are those who would consider me a selfish, miserable beast not half-deserving the countless gifts I have been given. I am many things... but perhaps my most remarkable attribute is that I…" She paused and looked up, her hypnotic eyes meeting my own. "I am immortal."

"Immortal?" I wondered, awed. I could not doubt her words for a moment, not with the certainty in which they were spoken.

"My name, if you would be so kind to remember it... is Ireval Ithraedol, but please… call me Artemis."

It was then that I remembered a warning that a friend had given me. Perhaps "friend" wasn't the right word. He was simply… Eric, or at least that was the name he usually went by.

It was strange for me to suddenly draw a connection between my housebreaker and the vagabond who often appeared in town on a moment's notice. The more I thought about my last encounter with Eric, the more everything began to make sense.

I remembered our conversation that night, not long ago. We had been sitting at the bar a few blocks from my house when he had drunkenly rambled off yet another one of his ridiculous stories of time travel, dragons and magic spells. Though his identification claimed he was twenty-six, I sincerely doubted he was really old enough to drink at all with the way most liquor seemed to affect him.

His general attitude and physical appearance reminded me constantly of a boy not quite out of his teens... and though he always seemed to find ways of paying me back for his stays at my house, I was simply not willing to believe that he was really the bastard son of a deity... as he often claimed. He was a lunatic, albeit a harmless one.

As it was, it took about twenty minutes of my listening to Eric attempt to explain how dimension travel "really works" for me to lose my patience. I pulled him out the back door of the bar by the arm and demanded to know what he was thinking. After a moment's hesitation he had asked me, completely serious, if I had ever met a demon before.

I yelled at him to get lost.

"She's on her way at last! You'll see her soon!" Eric had promised, staggering his way across the empty parking lot. "You watch out for Artemis Ravencroft!"

In a flash of recognition, I returned to the present. The woman across from me grinned.

"Artemis... Ravencroft?" I wondered, sensing that the name itself did beg repeating.

"Yes indeed." She laughed strangely and stood, bowing and saluting in a peculiar manner.

"What do you want from me?" I whispered, hoping that Patricia was still asleep. The last thing I needed was my wife attempting to test her magical "knowledge" of plants and stones against the limited patience of a real demon.

I was beginning to believe Eric more by the minute.

"Why are you here?" I asked.

"I am here to tell you a story," Artemis began. "You are one of the few writers I have met that I like... and I have not the patience to complete my memoirs alone. You see, Bruno... I have lived for many centuries, and I have done things so terrible you could not begin to imagine them. It is a lonely business compiling what I remember, and it leaves me increasingly frustrated as the hours pass. I need someone with a true writer's patience."

"Why me?" I demanded, still shaken. "I've never even been published. I'm not a real author. I'm a nobody. Why not go find Steven King?" I suggested.

"Because I do not wish to confide in your King Stephan." She scowled, the expression on her face serious enough to keep me from laughing at her ridiculous mistake. "Bear with me, fool, and I will make you a rich man."

Certain that I wouldn't live much longer, let alone become "rich" if I didn't at least attempt to appease the demon in my study, I pulled my tape recorder out of my desk and brought a yellow legal-pad and pen from the kitchen.

"All right," I sighed heavily, returning to my chair. Artemis's glare made me increasingly uncomfortable. "You win. Let's hear it," I finished awkwardly.

"First I must warn you," she pointed at me, shaking her head heavily, "I do not wish for you to harbor any misconceptions about my nature. I am not a hero, and I am not a God. I cannot grant you wishes. I am not good… no, not by any means, but nor am I truly evil." Artemis paused, producing a folded page of loose-leaf from a hidden pocket.

She squinted at the words written there and grinned. "This tale I am about to tell you is my true story. A story of a confused and tormented creature wrapped in fate. It is a story of a thousand years, three wars, countless exiles, desperation and betrayal. A tale of love, jealousy, regret, fear… but most importantly hope. Hope for all of us."

"I like that," she laughed. "You ought to use that phrase somewhere. My friend Ruveus helped me write it. Do you have any friends, Mr. Fargrove?" Artemis wondered.

"A few," I admitted, shrugging sheepishly.

"Friends are…important. They make the time pass," she admitted. "After seven-hundred years you would think that each day would end quickly and meaninglessly… that days would fade into weeks and weeks into years, ceaseless, repetitive, eternally unbearable. But… there are some days that are more vital than many centuries. There are some moments that shake the very foundations of the universe."

It was then that I knew I was about to hear something truly remarkable.

"If only you could imagine, my friend," Artemis smiled faintly. "Your future is not set in stone. Your dreams may one day change your world."

"In the Beginning," Artemis sighed, making herself comfortable as I pressed the record button on my tape-player. "Those three words mark the first chapter of a book I read long ago. I never quite understood it. Raised as I was, I have a rather difficult time understanding your human concept of the divine. He seems rather… weak."

"We like him," I admitted feebly, following her biblical reference with the best comment I could muster. She ignored me completely, obviously lost in her own thoughts.

"I borrow that phrase now for lack of a better one," Artemis continued. "In the Beginning," She mused. "Certainly, nothing was before "the beginning," though much did come after it."

Casually, she stood and began pacing the length of the room. "I have read some of your world's literature, friend. It is not unlike the tales of my own people. We have much in common, our two races. We are both powerful in many respects, and we are both capable of some kindness, but more often, we are petty and cruel to others as well as to ourselves.

You may know a little of what I am about to explain to you," Artemis yawned and stretched, moving once again with her oddly feline grace. Her teeth were much whiter than they ought to have been, and though they were not precisely pointed, there was something visibly demonic about them.

"The tribes that you call Greeks, Hebrews and Egyptians believed that all things arose from darkness and chaos. 'In the Beginning' as they say, there was no light."

With her clawed finger a quarter of an inch from my nose, she grinned suddenly and resumed her speech.

"That concept of theirs was what intrigued me most, really… the idea of a world without light. A world lingering eternally in the shadows and chaos of the time before all time began."

"A world like the one you came from," I interrupted, somehow knowing what she was getting at.

"Yes, precisely," Artemis muttered, eyeing me suspiciously. "I have thought about where I started out incessantly as of late." She sat down. "And I think I am beginning to understand. I was nearly a hundred years old the first time I ever saw true daylight," she admitted. "Perhaps… in such a place as the one where I was born, it is that absence of light, that absence of sight and clarity that breeds…" Artemis paused, as if searching for the proper word. "Evil," she finished abruptly.

Not waiting for my response, she took a long drink from her glass and spit the wine on the floor, shuddering.

"Perhaps it is not," Artemis admitted. "But having no better excuse, I shall blame all of my many wrongs on the darkness… not only the darkness that existed in the universe before any sun, but on the darkness that still exists within me."

I was very much afraid of those words. As clouds drifted to cover the moon, the room became filled with shadows which only seemed to aggravate Artemis further.

She closed her eyes, breathing in the cold night air.

"We are all imperfect, but my flaw is one that runs far deeper than most. Like a mirror marred by a crack that spiderwebs outward in all directions... I am torn to pieces by my own hateful memories. I have little empathy for others. I cannot feel as they feel. The guilt that sometimes overcomes me passes so quickly that it seems inconsequential. I can never pity. I do not know fear… and only once have I ever been loved."

There was a certain sorrow in the way that Artemis spoke, and I wondered momentarily how much emotion she had artfully concealed in that one final sentence.

Lightning flashed overhead and in an instant, she was feral again. "That impossible depth of emptiness was all I knew for nearly a millennium." Artemis shook her head. "Though I would much rather move on to the story that concerns itself with my nobler pursuits, I will not. Without knowledge of my origins, you cannot imagine the power of the journey I have taken… and I want one soul, at least, to know the truth. My tale begins in a world and time not so distant as it might seem."

As she whispered those words and made a strange motion with her hands, a remarkable sphere of light appeared hovering in her palm. It was a tiny window that seemed to play out pictures, almost as if it were a visual recording of the things that so obviously weighed heavily on her mind.

"Imagine, if you will, a plane of darkness, cold and unchanging," Artemis whispered as the images appeared within the globe. "A golden sun burned above the tortured land once, but all that now remains is the ruby flicker of that dying star. Salt beds span for miles, windblown and dry, where once great oceans lapped against rocky shores. Skeleton forests of wraithlike trees, and shadows of once-greater things burned flat into the gray rubble of the soil… are few and far between, a poor distraction from the endless wastes."

I had never considered that there might truly exist a place as desolate as the one she showed me, the desert at her fingertips. Instantly I fell silent, resolving to let Artemis continue her story without interruption.

"Truly, such a world is one of infinite misery," she sighed wearily. "I know not what age it lies in, whether it be your past, your present, or your future. In a sense, it is as eternal as its creatures. The few and far-reaching ones, the Traversers, have given it countless names in all of their many tongues. Each title illustrates some new terror or timeless curse, but for our purposes I shall refer to it as Magog.

For Magog is what it is called by its inhabitants, my people, the I'Eloshir."

As she spoke that final word, something stirred within me, a fragment of recognition. Though I couldn't comprehend how it was possible, I suddenly saw myself, for a moment, as she saw me, experiencing for a split second how it felt to be… what she was.

It was only Artemis's voice that brought me back to my own body as she sternly pushed a pencil into my hand.

"Forgive me if my musings simply provoke more questions in your anxious mind, Mr. Fargrove. The only way I know of to relate an epic of such magnitude to an audience is to allow the spirits of the ages past to speak for themselves."

Tossing the globe of light into the air, she grinned in such a way that I realized I had been somewhat misled as to what my writing her memoirs would entail.

As the spell spun wildly out of control, I felt myself being absorbed into the strange light completely. My whole self was overwhelmed by the energy that was hers and I forgot everything I had ever known and melted completely until "I" no longer existed.

There was only Artemis… and her story. Consciously, the last thing I saw was my tape recorder sitting on my desk which I laughed at almost contemptuously. Why should I record my own voice speaking words that were so very clearly already within my head? Artemis's memories were as poignant as my own and as the white light from the globe cleared, the world took shape again before her eyes… my own eyes.

Unlike all of my childhood fantasies trapped in the yellowed pages of long forgotten paperbacks, I would not simply read this story as I had so many other great tales. I would experience this legend first hand.

The Creature

"The soul is a seed of infinite potential."

One

In the dead forests a woman was running. Her robes, once fine, were torn beyond recognition, and her feet were bare and bloodied from thorns, melting ice and sharp stones. The rain and the wind posed obstacles to her and the weight of the child she clutched in her arms was almost more than she could bear, but the beast that pursued her never faltered. She could catch glimpses of him, tall, pale as death and terrifyingly inhuman, through the trees. The fiend, the creature, whatever it was... it wanted her daughter.

From every possible angle, I watched, but I would not interfere. I sat, disconnected and unfeeling, on an insubstantial pedestal and allowed the events to occur. It was not my duty to meddle in the balance of life and death, but at the same time as the scene unfolded before my all-seeing eye, I was overwhelmed by the sudden wrongness of the hunt. Somehow I knew that there were greater stakes involved and I sensed distantly that I would soon become part of the terrible ordeal, whether I wished it or not.

Yet I, being what I was, cared nothing for the mortal and even less for the demon that pursued her. To me, they were insignificant. Trivial.

Still, drawn like a moth to their meager light, my eye followed them to an ancient temple dedicated to some long-forgotten deity. The light inside was gray and cold, and the walls were damp and crumbling, reeking of age and bloodshed. A few skeletons of men in armor lay rotting on the stairs, and a scattering of abandoned red silks revealed that the unfortunate human guards had fought something worse than infidels in their last great crusade.

Those were the scarlet flags that lingered like open wounds for centuries on battlefields throughout Magog. They were the colors of the greatest warriors of any world, the indestructible hellspawn known and feared... as the legendary I'Eloshir.

The woman clawed hopelessly at the wet vines that covered the door to the inner sanctum, but her hands were numb from the cold and clumsy. The child in her arms cried softly… weak, exhausted, and frightened. Even the young one was wise enough to feel the evil within the place. It was a sadistic, cruel and senseless apathy. The storm was strong, the chill was biting, and the temple, despite its history, was nothing more than a mound of lifeless stone.

Yet the monster that hunted the woman and her child was not hindered by such inconsequential forces of nature. What was temperature to him? What was sacred, sanctuary? Holiness was a mortal creation of humankind, not of any divinity. Blessings and curses died with their believers.

He... and yes, even I myself had no concept of such things.

The demon stopped, hovering above the woman as she slowly turned. He grinned, savoring the fear she radiated. Her innate goodness would have made her death all the more enjoyable for him, had he been allowed more time. But his mission had not been to toy with an insignificant human female. The child, that... that was what the beast sought.

The woman looked up into his cold, pale eyes and slumped to the ground in one motion. The demon had but to force his will upon her and her feeble, wildly beating heart had stopped. All ended… so quickly.

The woman's body he kicked down the stairs without remorse, but the child he pulled up from the ground and held for a moment, almost curious as to why such a helpless, screaming little creature was so powerful and worthy of such protection.

And then all at once I knew. I KNEW! Even in my omnipotence, I had overlooked the obvious, failed to recognize the place and failed to see that only one soul still lingered in the ruins.

The Wanderers were mocking me and laughing arrogantly amongst themselves as the demonic creature spoke in the Old Tongue, words of a High Priest, a spell of summoning.

I was drawn down quite suddenly with a force unlike any I had ever experienced. I was drawn down and flung into the small near-lifeless body and felt so many parts of my consciousness locked off like dark and terrible doors. I knew cold, knew hunger, and knew fear. But the mystery of where I had come from, who I was... what I was... in that instant was lost to me.

I felt only confusion as the spell warped and changed my child's form, lengthening the limbs and stretching the features. I had grown, aged, and changed twenty years in a few short moments, but my mind was still that of a new-born being.

Truthfully, I couldn't comprehend what was happening for my thoughts had been wiped clean of all knowledge of self, of identity.

I lived. I breathed. And, standing on my own two feet, naked and horrified by the ordeal, I faced the demon eye to eye.

He smiled in such a way that I knew I was desirable to him, but I knew also, with the way he flung me a filthy robe, that he would not harm me.

"Ireval," he grinned and gestured as if that were my name.

It was not. I had another... but no... I could not remember it.

"Ireval Ithraedol," he repeated.

I couldn't speak. To form words... that was beyond my ability, but to understand them...

Ireval. In the tongue of the demon-kind the word meant One-Without-End.

I reached up and touched my own face realizing that in my transformation, I had become more than a mere adult. My teeth were sharp enough to draw blood from my own skin, my ears and the bones in my face arced in such a way that I recognized suddenly what I had become. A demon. I'Eloshir.

At this thought, my back suddenly exploded into a mess of pain. I doubled over and watched almost as if I were outside my body. I was shocked and awed all at once as I realized that I had wings.

The beast... the beast that was no longer a beast, gave me his clawed hand.

"It is less painful if you stand quickly," he advised.

I wanted to reply. How did he know... who was he? Had he too gone through what I had just experienced?

The question that was so pressing immediately deserted me. I felt only hunger and, again, fear. Yet still, I desired to speak, wondering if I could.

"Wh...," I began, amazed at the sound of my own voice. Only one word could encompass all that I wanted to say at that moment, only one word.

"Why?"

The demon reached out and placed his hand on my chest. I could not scream, struggle, or even so much as breathe. He who had been nothing was now everything... and I, who had been everything... The thought vanished.

Silently, I lost all control of my limbs and slumped to the ground as if in death. Yet the rain fell still and the wind still blew. I knew and I remembered thinking with an almost cosmic arrogance how ironic it all was.

Two

My earliest real memory of my life with the I'Eloshir was of the day that I first reached Tirs Uloth. From the temple in the forest where I had awakened, the demon, I had learned was called "Geruth,"carried me slung across his back over leagues and leagues of death-pale countryside.

Jostled back and forth by his startling pace on foot, I bit my tongue dozens of times. Though I often wished to speak, he only removed the wooden bit he had forced in my mouth long enough for me to drink water, which I needed desperately each and every time he offered it.

I couldn't fathom why I was forbidden to talk, or why my arms and legs were tied and my eyes were covered, but that first experience caused me to hate my captor with an incredible passion.

The fact that he called himself my father and said that he was a king only made the rage burn more deeply.

Yet finally after what seemed like an eternity, Geruth set me on the ground, made me spit out the wood and untied my hands and feet. Taking off the blindfold that I had worn over my eyes for so long, I caught what felt like my very first glimpse of the world.

We were standing in the shadow of a great monolith hundreds of stories high. It was a mountain burnt black by centuries of smoke and fire... with the ruins of a fortress high atop the rocks. All around us was a barren, flat desert smoking faintly in the darkness as if the scorching sands had only just begun to cool after the setting of the sun.

We were not to ascend up the cliff, however. At first I had anticipated that Geruth would hit me and tell me to fly as he had once before, tying a rope around my neck to be certain that I would not run away. Yet he did not. Instead, he led me towards a massive gate at the foot of the black pillar.

It was not the ancient castle that was our home... it was the caves below the mountain. Despite our wings, we I'Eloshir were denizens not of the heavens, but of the hells.

Reaching the borders of his kingdom, Geruth entered through a secret door, virtually invisible in the stone and ordered me to follow him.

The rock melted closed behind us and we were in darkness; not the darkness of the night sky, but a pure, black dark more impenetrable than the shadows I had seen through my blindfold.

Yet my eyes adjusted immediately and I soon found that I could see.

A haggard, stinking old woman waited there by the entrance for us, reading the future in bones. Though her robes were red and made of fine silk, she was a dark, filthy creature hobbling about in a rotting body that should have been laid to rest many centuries ago. Only her pale gray eyes gave any glimmer as to what power she held.

I remembered Geruth speaking about her once as he waited for me to finish drinking at a spring. Before either of them uttered so much as a single word, I knew who the old woman must be. Without a doubt, she was Geruth's most trusted advisor, his own mother, oldest of the I'Eloshir. He referred to her simply as "The Grandmother."

No mortal could have guessed how many millennia she had lived through, and no immortal dared to. Even Geruth, who honored no man or God save himself... bowed low before her, but I did not.

It had never occurred to me that I would be expected to.

"You," The Grandmother glared at me. "Show some respect! Have you no fear?"

"Why should I fear?" I asked innocently.

"You must know I may kill you," she hissed.

"You may try," I shot back, arrogant despite my inexperience. How dare they toy with me, I thought to myself snarling. How dare they treat me like an inferior... when it was they who were so much less than I?

Despite my having no memories, my instinct alone told me that I was unique, at very least special if not blatantly superior to the rest of the I'Eloshir.

The Grandmother paused and then quite suddenly she laughed. It was not altogether as unpleasant of a sound as I had imagined it would be. "And who is this young one, Geruth?"

"They call me Ireval," I replied.

The ancient creature squinted at me, pacing. The sound of her claws on the stone floor was repulsive. Annoyed, I tried to step in front of her, but surprisingly, although I suspected that I should have had her in my grasp, my hands passed through the old woman's body as if she were nothing more than air. In the next instant, her solid form returned.

"Will you stop circling like a vulture, you ugly wench," I growled. "I am not a prey animal."

"Insulting me, are you?" She shook her head.

"Do you not know who she is!" Geruth demanded, grabbing me by the hair and tearing me to face him.

"She is no one," I shot back, though I knew that much was a lie.

"Indeed," The Grandmother stepped closer, reaching out tentatively as if she intended to touch me with her hideous hands. With Geruth holding my hair, I could not struggle too far, though I desperately wanted to pull away. The old woman's claws and her awful half-rotten skin was altogether something I couldn't bear.

"DO NOT TOUCH ME!" I screamed, and then clutched my throat, wondering if the sudden explosion of power I felt had really come from the sound of my own voice. It echoed remarkably through the cavern with a force that was almost visible.

"The Order," Geruth stared in awe, backing up a few paces. "Indeed... I was mistaken about you. No warrior will you be. We must deal with you immediately."

"You can't mean…," I choked, suddenly very afraid. "You wouldn't kill me?"

"Kill you?" Geruth shook his head heavily. "I could not kill you even if I desired to do so," he whispered. "You are much more than a mere soldier. You are destined to rule."

"Ah," I grinned very broadly, suddenly understanding why I had felt so subjected. They had been treating me like a slave when in truth I was queen. "Is that it?" I wondered. "I thought so."

Without paying attention to my so-called elders, I turned and headed down the nearest corridor with my head held high despite the fact that I hadn't the faintest idea where I was going.

"You knew she would be strong," The Grandmother chided Geruth.

"I had not imagined she would be so difficult to control," he admitted, his voice trembling a little.

Control? Me? The mere idea was ridiculous to imagine.

"Try to control me," I interrupted, stepping back into the room, enjoying the expression of horror on Geruth's face. "I dare you!"

Laughing maniacally at my own rash behavior, I skittered off into the shadows and waited for the old man to chase me, but he never came.

I realized then, sitting alone in the darkness, that despite my power, I was only a tool to Geruth, a simple pet, nothing more and that no matter what I said or did, the truth remained that I would never be more than a possession in my father's eyes.

Despite the futility of the entire situation, I resolved to fight. My determination was my one true weapon, the one thing that he could not take from me, even if I were bound and gagged and led about on a leash.

I may have come to Magog as a slave, but I would not remain one for long.

That encounter was only the beginning. The mere fact that I possessed "The Order," a power to bend lesser creatures to my will with no more than a word, kept most of the other I'Eloshir a good distance away from me. Yet as I soon discovered, my dead mother's strange blood was at work within me in ways I could never have imagined.

Three

I came to the gates of Geruth's kingdom alone on horseback after a short hunt one night. The sun was just beginning to rise in the distance and I knew I had to reach the safety of the caves before it cleared the mountain tops. In Magog, the sun was a cruel and terrible thing that could pull the very flesh from one's bones, so hot and merciless it was.

The shadow of the mountain began well before I could see the entrance of Tirs Uloth, and the ground beneath my beast's pounding hooves was littered in shards of steel and bone. The stench of the dead hung heavy in the air.

Perverse as it may sound, it was a welcoming smell.

The black monolith of the ancient castle on its decaying mountaintop towered above the windblown sands, rumbling in its own quiet way, drums ever-pounding below the ground. A wave of searing heat blew past me as I approached and my horse reared back, stung by the flurry of stones that followed. Pressing on, the winds parted and the gate of the cavern loomed before me.

As I rode closer, I realized that I was not arriving home unannounced.

My cousin Zaethe Eylchaur sat on a rock on the other side of the gate, grinning insanely. Her one lop-sided wing made her recognizable, even from a distance, and by the time I reached the bars, I could see her crooked mouth and ever-squinting beady little eyes.

Most often, the imperfect of the I'Eloshir were killed, unless they were the children of nobility. And… as my father's sister's daughter, Zaethe was one of those fortunate few survivors. Her handicaps hardly made her bitter, rather, she seemed proud of the fact that she was superior to most of the other warriors in battle, even without the ability to fly.

The power of flight may seem like a glorious thing, to those who cannot imagine how difficult it is. As a race, we I'Eloshir preferred to avoid anything requiring much effort, which is why the demons of Magog, though winged, were most often seen riding horseback.

I looked over my shoulder, knowing already that the sun had begun to rise.

"Let me in Zae," I demanded.

"Perhaps I will, perhaps I will not," she taunted.

I jumped off my horse and it fled into the desert. "Let me in," I growled. "If I am burned again, I will kill you."

It was no idle threat. As ruthless as I was then, I had no objections to tearing anyone… even a relative, to pieces. I would not be punished for fighting either, because I was special.

Zaethe winked and turned to walk away, ignoring me. Furious, I grabbed the bars of the gate just as the first ray of sunlight hit my back, searing through my whole being. The rattling and sparks alone were enough to send Zaethe fumbling for the locks, but then, something amazing happened. The pain I suffered was nothing compared to the shock of seeing the iron melt beneath my grasp, my hands glowing in purple flame.

I stepped inside over the melted wreckage and Zaethe crept warily towards the light. "Did the sun do that?" she wondered, awestruck.

I shook my head. "No… I think I did."

Zaethe reached out hesitantly and touched my arm, jumping back as an arc of energy shot towards her face. "How are you… what is wrong with you?" she demanded.

Curious, I punched the wall. The granite crumbled, as my "power" rose to the surface. I… felt it.

Zaethe stared, her eyes wide and her crooked mouth breaking into a grin. "Do that again!" she hissed.

I hit the gate, kicking through and searing the metal with the strange wave of heat I found I could suddenly control. The element of fire was mine to command, and it was exhilarating!

Then… we heard, footsteps echoing down the corridor, wondering what the commotion was.

"Fix it!" Zaethe screamed, as voices approached us. "Fix it!"

"I can't! Damn you, Zae!" I cried, scrambling for the melted bars, knowing I had done something terrible. Zaethe glared at me. It had been her fault I'd broken the gate in the first place… and she expected me to use my new magic to make the problem go away.

"You've got to," Zaethe ordered. "You must or we'll both take a beating."

I clenched the cold iron bars in my fists and squeezed as hard as I could, willing them to melt back together. The metal obeyed me, though by the time I had forced it all back in place, whatever unnatural wizardry I had experienced a moment ago dissipated.

"That's better," Zaethe grinned. I think I scowled at her.

"DAUGHTER!" my father's voice rumbled throughout the tunnels. He never called me by my name…and especially not when he was angry with me.

"Do you think he knows about the gate?" Zaethe wondered.

"If he knew about the gate…," I snarled. "He would be tearing you apart… not shouting for me. We do not kill our own, Zae. We open the gates for them when the sun rises."

She ignored my chiding, her gaze drifting from the twisted bars back to where I stood. "So what else is there?" Zaethe pressed.

"Nothing at all," I lied.

It wasn't nothing. The night before I had departed on my hunt, I had directly disobeyed my father and done the one thing that even I, the chosen one, was not permitted to do.

I had forced my way through the locks and into the Great Hall during the sunlit hours, instead of remaining in my room as I should have, and I had seen something that I couldn't explain. I knew not what it was at the time… but I knew that, despite whatever punishment my elders could come up with, I would be out and searching for it again as soon as they weren't looking. A… a something that moved and changed and stung my eyes. Something… I guessed the word was white.

"Inapsupetra, help me," I whispered, passing under the statue of the Goddess. She smiled at me in a certain strange way and I felt instantly comforted. Many of elders of Magog called themselves gods, but they were not like Inapsupetra. None of us were. Sometimes I wondered if my father and his foolish companions really believed they were the creators of the universe.

I shook my head, resolving to work harder at controlling my dangerously drifting thoughts, and entered the hall.

The Great Hall of Tirs Uloth was a cavern easily ten stories high. Open passages and doors from floor to ceiling gave the mottled black stone an almost honeycomb appearance, and in the center of the room was a massive staircase of five steps. Around the staircase, pots of molten fire bubbled, lighting and warming the cave with their ever-burning flames, and on each step I'Eloshir sat, feasting and fighting amongst themselves.

The bottommost level was full of tables reserved for the youngest of our kind, those who possessed little or no rank, the second step up was the place of the warriors, the third step of the elders, and the fourth step reserved for the royal family and the red-robes, our generals.

At the very top was the Warlord's high seat, an immense gold and red chair stolen centuries ago from some legendary court. Though we possessed excellent metalworking skills, we I'Eloshir forged none of our treasures, save our swords, preferring to loot the wealth of humans and elves instead. The riches surrounding the throne were obvious proof of that, and as approached the fifth step, I could see that Geruth was somewhat preoccupied with a new oddity, what appeared to be a gold breastplate so ridiculously tiny that no I'Eloshir could possibly wear it, least of all Geruth who was twice as big as most

"Warlord," Rath Iekuh, one of my father's stewards interrupted. Geruth looked up suddenly and upon catching sight of me, his grin broke into a terrible scowl.

"Where were you this morning past when you should have been sleeping?" my father demanded. His younger brother, Elhilom, the shape-changer, snickered and I knew immediately who turned me in.

Elhilom sat, not on the fourth step where Rath and I stood, but at the foot of Geruth's throne as if he were his brother's favorite dog. Rolling onto his back, he kicked off the wall and flipped over our heads, landing soundly on his feet behind me.

"Bastard!" I turned and glared at him, baring my fangs.

Most of the younger warriors shrank back in terror, or even jumped under the table... but my father, Elhilom and The Grandmother were unfazed. Zaethe winked mischievously from the edge of the third step. She had been part of the conspiracy as well.

"Give me your bracers," my father ordered, gesturing to the golden bands I wore on my arms.

"No," I shot back, "they're mine."

"Do not argue with me, Daughter." He frowned.

The Grandmother had given me the magical bracers as a gift and I knew well that once they were off my arms, someone... most likely Elhilom... would steal them before my father remembered to return to me. Still, fighting with Warlord Geruth would get me nowhere.

He struck my face and sent me flying into the wall. My bracers clattered across the floor, out of my reach. Elhilom twitched his claws out, reaching for the golden bands, but The Grandmother stepped on his foot.

"I shall hold them," she promised, glaring at Elhilom. "God Malkali the Troublemaker must have killed my son and left you in his bed," The Grandmother sighed. "You shame me, Elhil. Now resume your rightful place." She scowled at him and he slid down to the fourth step obediently... though if looks could kill, the old woman would have been dead where she stood.

I sighed with relief. At least I would get my bracers back, but probably not until after I'd been beaten senseless by ever warrior of the I'Eloshir. The bracers possessed a strange magic that deflected most of the blows I would have received on a daily basis, by allowing me to move with even-greater supernatural speed. It was that particular power that had made me extremely difficult to fight against, and somewhat unpopular with the others who were near my own age. They were all deformed and hideous, while I had not a single scar.

"Prepare yourselves," my father ordered to his men. "Sleep if you must, but we leave in three hour's time. You will all ride with me."

I moved to follow the warriors as they left the hall. Although I had just returned from hunting and wished to sleep, I wasn't about to leave the protection of my father's shadow. And then, knowing that it was daylight outside in Magog... there was that hope I still held, that Geruth would take me with him and his army across the world's barrier to a new realm.

Demons are renowned for their uncanny ability to be everywhere and nowhere at once, an ancient and secret art that focuses on the moving of Tears, temporary disturbances in the fabric of the cosmos. It is difficult to explain the concept of there being multiple dimensions to a soul who has never seen but one sun in the sky. Still, that is, as has always been, the true nature of the universe, a many-faceted diamond of realities and possibilities.

I stood in line behind the last of the grumbling warriors as they waited to find their weapons and mounts, but, as I had feared he might, my father barred my path before I could slip back into the hall with them.

"All... except you," Geruth pushed me away. "We hunt outside Magog."

"But why is it that I am never allowed to see other worlds?" I demanded. Geruth shook his head. "You would not understand."

"Why would I not understand?" I begged. "And how would you know that I would not understand if you won't ever tell me anything!"

"Prophesy," he replied stiffly. "You are the beloved of Inapsupetra... your mother knew before you were born. The sickness you suffered... the sickness that took your memories was the wrath of the God Aryun. He knows that someday you will be greater than all of the warriors of all the I'Eloshir..." Geruth paused briefly as he recited the now-familiar tale for the hundredth time. "That day must not come too soon," he said no more to me but disappeared into the shadows.

I watched him mount his horse before the throne, a black ripple appearing in the far wall on his command. Following Geruth, the warriors drew their swords and galloped through the open Tear, disappearing as if they had never been.

I turned to The Grandmother. "Why does he do that?" I demanded.

"You have your answer there," she chuckled. "Because you ask."

"What do you mean?" I frowned.

"It is your intelligence that makes you dangerous," The Grandmother explained. "You dare to ask why. You need a reason. The strongest rule in Tirs Uloth... for it is our way, and the way of the Gods. But it is not the only way."

"Is he afraid I won't come home?" I wondered.

"More than that," she cackled. "Your father fears that you will destroy him."

"I could not," I argued. "He is too powerful. I could never."

"So you say," The Grandmother shook her head. "So you say."

Four

The heat of the day came swiftly… The Grandmother retreated to her rooms, and still the warriors did not return. I woke near the fall of the sunlit hours, when the mists of the cavern were still pale and close to the floor.

And I knew, at that instant that I had to have my bracers back. Something was happening… something I couldn't understand, but could sense all the same.

I crept down the hall towards The Grandmother's chamber and carefully slipped through the door. The bracers were on the table, but The Grandmother was nowhere to be seen. I could smell blood everywhere. She had been eating rats again, too weak to kill anything else. Their tiny bones lay scattered across the floor, crushed to dust beneath my feet.

A breeze rattled the draperies above her bed, a slight wind where no movement should have been. I looked down into her seer's pool, a dark abyss of stagnant water at my feet… and saw a shadow behind me. A feeling came over me then… I wanted to run, flee, hide… anything… now… now…

Breathe. I ordered myself, though I still struggled against the overwhelming panic. The treasure I had sought was within reach. I grabbed my bracers and snapped them onto my wrists, turning to attack whatever man or beast had dared to approach me in such a fashion.

And I found myself immediately… face to face with a strange, towering creature dressed entirely in the glowing color of the light I had seen in the hall.

He appeared human but like no human I had ever seen. He was much too tall, tall enough to have been I'Eloshir, save that he bore no wings. The man's age was impossible to determine. His body was young, but at the same time, he seemed to radiate an elder's wisdom as well as a Warlord's unnatural power.

I stepped back, stretching my wings to make myself seem larger and hissing at the stranger through my clenched teeth. Backed against the cavern wall, I dug my claws into the stone and called up a flicker of my purple fire, which seemed to surprise the intruder considerably. Yet the flames died quickly and I found myself reduced to pointing a sharpened leg-bone at the white man. It was all I could do.

"Don't be afraid," he whispered.

"Dogs! Dogs!" I shrieked… but no dogs came.

"I dispatched them," he admitted, pointing to a black pile of immobile fur in the corner. "I hadn't intended to, but they attacked me."

"Who are you?" I stared into his strange eyes. "How did you get in? You speak our language, but are you human? Why are you here? Why do you look at me?"

"I see myself in you," he laughed softly, answering only the last of my questions. "You think you should be afraid and yet you are not. To answer your question… I am Ardain Ravencroft. A Traverser."

"Traverser?" I wondered… a chill running down my spine. Traversers were the creatures of every I'Eloshir's worst nightmare, beings that had once been our kind, but through a terrible magic had been made like the humans we preyed upon.

"Traveler," Ardain corrected quickly, obviously noticing my expression of horror. "A traveler," he repeated. "Yet now that I have told you my name, would you be so kind as to give yours?"

"Ireval," I shot back, still uncomfortable in his presence.

"Can it be?" He squinted. "Are you truly?"

"GO AWAY," I ordered. The entire room shook briefly and then quieted.

To my surprise, Ardain laughed.

"That's quite an Order coming from such a young noble as yourself, Ireval," speaking my name, he smiled faintly.

"I have always liked that name," he admitted. "I never had any daughters of my own."

"My Order didn't work?" I took another step back and tripped over a skull on the floor.

"Certainly not." Ardain laughed. "No more than it would have were you to use it on your own father."

"Impossible! My father is an Immortal…," I argued, though I distantly sensed that there was far more to the white man than I could have imagined.

Ardain lifted his sleeve and I gasped. Burned dark and true in his left arm near the shoulder was the triple moon mark worn by only the eldest of the I'Eloshir, the elite red-robes... the Gods of Magog, often called "The Immortals."

"As am I," he whispered. "You may know me as Arduh Ithraedol," Ardain explained. "I myself was once Warlord of Magog. I was defeated in battle by Aruna Iekuh, the same king that your father Geruth killed to earn his title. I wanted to end myself, rather than live in such disgrace. But then... I came across a most extraordinary world." Ardain grinned. "It is called the Chaos Realm."

He placed his hand against my shoulder and sent a flood of images into my mind.

"Why do you show me this?" I wondered, overcome by his vivid pictures of all manner of things, schools where people could learn to make gold from stone... and forges where they crafted remarkable artifacts, like my mysterious bracers. Forests full of trees that still lived, and wide-open stretches of water that reached as far as one could see. All races lived together there, without fearing the light of dawn.

"I tell you because it is your right to know," he explained. "I am a member of your clan, though I cannot be sure how closely we are related... especially if you are who you say. But I can promise that if you were to come with me now, to this world, you would grow to be like me."

His speech was halting, as if he were holding back a cry of pain. I stared still. I wanted to be like him, to travel endlessly without fear, to be subject only to my own whims. He was easily the most remarkable being I had ever met.

"They would call you a Traverser, and they'd fear you a bit at first... but if you could convince them your intentions were good..."

"Good?" I scoffed, remembering what The Grandmother had said and feeling perhaps more than a little guilty. "Why in all the many hells should I want that?"

Ardain shook his head. "Because it is the most rewarding thing in the cosmos," he admitted. "Believe me... I've looked."

I wasn't sure I trusted him, but the man's prospect was somehow less repulsive than it had been, though the mere idea of my becoming a Traverser still made me feel somewhat ill.

"So maybe I believe you...," I began, and then stopped short. I could smell on the air a certain scent which filled me with uneasiness, a familiar stench that at that moment seemed to me the most terrible thing I could possibly imagine.

A grotesque, hulking figure loomed in the doorway of the room, one that it took me a moment to recognize.

The Grandmother. Her face was contorted into a hideous mask of rage as she growled at Ardain and drew from the folds of her red robe a long, twisted knife. Before I could stop her, she flew at us in a whirlwind of claws and feathers, still wielding her curved dagger. The Grandmother plunged its blade into the back of the white man, stabbing him again and again. Ardain fell.

"Grandmother, stop!" I begged, not knowing why I wanted her to leave him, except that his death filled me with a terrible and incomprehensible sense of loss.

She looked up at me, snagged the chain around my neck and glared, blood in her wretched teeth. "Do you know what this man is!" She snarled, glaring at me. "A fool Traverser… a wretched bloody Mage… a deserter of his own family! Damn you, Arduh!" she howled.

"Arduh?" I pushed away, suddenly feeling quite cold. "How is it that you know him?" I demanded.

"He was my husband," The Grandmother fell silent and turned away from my gaze. "My first husband."

"And you killed him?" I was horrified. "But we do not kill our own kind!" I argued feebly. "We do not kill our own kind!"

"He was not our kind," The Grandmother interrupted, throwing her bloody knife at my feet. "See how he bleeds!" She pointed. "So much blood in him, don't you think? It is more red than black these days."

I did not know how to reply. Seeing the man's corpse fading away into a sparkle of silver light made me doubt her all the more.

"Go to bed, Ireval," The Grandmother growled, abruptly changing the subject. "Take your bracers and go. Tell no one of this, least of all Geruth… or I shall be forced to kill you as well."

"But how did he get here?" I begged. "If he was banished, how did he survive? Where did he hide, Grandmother?" I pressed. "HOW DID HE GET HERE!"

"That you do not need to know," she spat, kicking the glittering robes and ignoring my weak command. "Your father does not want you to know."

But I knew… I knew already. Through the hall was the gateway my elders did not want me to find, and daylight was the key.

31

Five

It was another dull, ordinary evening some decades later that brought about my third remarkable experience. Try as I might, I could not reveal half of what happened from night to night in those dark times, for it was nothing that either intrigued or affected me in any way. So many years I lingered, with so few memories. It is a rather sad thing when one considers it.

"We hunt within our realm tonight," my father announced, being the first to pass around our wine, a yellow liquor humans sometimes call "ambrosia." The true name of the substance is thoroughly unpronounceable in any mortal language, and the properties of it have been misinterpreted more often than not.

It does not really grant immortality. The scent of ambrosia alone is often enough to make even strong-stomached humans quite ill, yet they come in search of it regardless, seeing what is merely a drink as a source of godlike power.

I drank as much as I could, and ate more than my fill, near starving and knowing there was no way I could smuggle enough provisions out of the hall to keep me well fed for more than a few days. There was always hunting, but unless I came across a human village, it was unlikely that I would catch anything.

The strongest part of darkness fell as the clocks chimed the thirteenth hour, and we rode out... a shadowy parade of hooded warriors on black horses with horrific masks.

Such was our way. On some worlds they call the skull-faced leader of the hunt and his consort "Death" and "Death's Army." It is ironic, being so very true. We I'Eloshir do not believe in taking prisoners... unless we intend to eat them later.

It took me quite a few miles to reach the head of the army where my father rode and more than three hours to speak to him. We broke slightly away from the main group and slowed our horses to a walk.

"I heard about something," I admitted, not knowing how to begin. "Though I swore on my honor I cannot say where."

"It does not matter. If there is trouble it will root itself out in good time. You need not break your word," Geruth announced, watching the dim gray horizon.

"I heard that there is a world with green trees and oceans," I muttered.

"There are many such worlds," he sighed, his eyes still on the sky.

"I heard that our kind doesn't live in underground there... and that the races don't hunt each other," I continued.

"That is a lie," he said it so calmly that I doubted him. "Did the one you cannot betray give his fantasy a name?" Geruth wondered.

"The Chaos Realm," I admitted.

My father laughed softly. "Daughter, that place is a myth! A story the elves and the humans invented when the waters dried up and the sun turned black. They lost everything when Raedawn fell."

"Oh." I looked down at my hands. A lie then?

I knew the tale of Raedawn well. Ages ago in my world, the humans had been powerful, stepping above and beyond their proper place as slaves. They had built a great city with a wall a thousand feet high, the "White City" as some called it, and placed it high in the clouds, daring others to attack them.

Some of the I'Eloshir had joined the humans of Raedawn. Lead by an exile, a blind seer named Kyura, they learned magic and science, avoiding the divine retribution of Inapsupetra and the gods by hiding in many dimensions until they became known as "Traversers."

The gods grew angry, but instead of simply striking down the foolish mortals who had gone beyond what arrogance could be forgiven, they showed them how to build a dangerous weapon with which they might bring ruin upon themselves.

Disguised as a holy gift, such a creation could only destroy its wielder.

It destroyed Raedawn. And then, in the wave of fire that followed, the sun became blocked by a dark cloud that would last five-thousand years. The world broke into three parts, the first two pieces flying off into oblivion, and the third, Magog... sinking into an eternal shadow. What survived was changed irreversibly. Most of the mortals died, being so dependant on things like water, plants and sunlight... all luxuries I'Eloshir could do well without. And thus... we began to rule.

"I don't understand," I looked up to my father. He seemed so distant. "Why would anyone make up such foolish things?"

"Humankind has a great love for legends," he explained. "They must believe what is not true, for they find in their fantasies the strength that their bodies lack. You will understand all in good time. Let us return to the men."

No sooner had he spoken than a flaming arrow soared overhead. "The signal!" Geruth gasped. "We have been attacked!"

Another arrow whizzed past, a mere hairsbreadth from the top of my head... this one glowing with a cleric's unnatural blessing. Such a weapon could wound or even kill us. My father roared in pain as the blessed shaft caught him in the shoulder.

I wheeled my horse around to face the fool who had fired it and dismounted, flying skyward. The winds were unruly and refused to give me any sort of balance whatsoever, but I did not return to the ground. From above, I had the edge.

The archer fitted another arrow to his bow and I shot down at him, throwing a wall of acidic flame from my fingertips.

My hands burned at the sudden energy, the magic I'd practiced with so little... as a wave of power, not unlike the sensation of my "Order" rippled through my body. The fire tore through the ground and then shot back up again, catching the archer in the chest. I did not know what I should expect, but the sight of the man bursting into a cloud of ash certainly awakened a little more of my barbaric nature.

Amazed by how easily I had killed him, I threw another spell, this time aimed at the cleric who had been blessing the weapons.

The second human crumbled into nothingness and his three companions ran.

All I could see was blood and fire. Even greed meant nothing to me... and discipline was for the weak. I fired another mammoth spell, focusing what energy I had, and somehow drawing more from the dark sky above. Only one man remained, only one still running.

By that point, I was too far withdrawn from myself to stop, had I even wanted to.

All around, the I'Eloshir gathered, watching my effortless display. Though Elhilom could change his shape and some of the other demons had the ability to make pictures out of air that could deceive the eyes, no one, my father included, had witnessed the kind of magic that I possessed, not in many centuries.

Of all of the elements, fire was our most favorite. To be blessed with the ability to manipulate the power of the flames in such a way was another clear sign, even more obvious than my unsettling Order. I was more than a mere legend given flesh. I was indeed the "Beloved" of Inapsupetra.

I remember chasing the human at a distance, knowing I could catch him. That was what the hunt was, I finally understood. The simple feeling of power, knowing that each of your footsteps was life and death. The human screamed in terror, and begged, goddess or devil, whichever I was, to spare him.

Finally I came close enough that I slammed him in the back, throwing him to the ground. His neck did not snap, and I was overwhelmed by a sudden strange instinct I had never before experienced. Like bloodlust… perhaps, but far more violent.

I pressed my open hand over the man's bruised and bloody face. A shock of pale energy I had not known I possessed drew forth something smoky white and powerful from the man, something I knew that I wanted immediately. A soul.

I took it, held it in my hand and crushed it, watching in amazement as the silver lines raced through my own dark veins. The feeling was like having a cool drink of water after running across an empty, parched desert. I felt instantly rejuvenated and more powerful than I had ever been. It was addictive. I had to have another. I… had to.

A shadow hovered over me, and I looked up blindly, listening to the beating heart and watching the tiny, faintly flickering spirit of the creature rippling up and down within its body. The shadow was too strong for me yet, but if I could stop its heart… Almost too late, I realized who I was looking at, and immediately regretted even considering what I had almost done. The dark blur with the little soul was Geruth.

My father smiled, so ignorant, so oblivious to the terrible danger he was in with me by his side. "Well done, Ireval." He applauded. "Well done."

Six

More than four hundred years went by. In my due time, I was branded with the mark of a warrior and made a full member of the I'Eloshir, and as more time passed, I was given all of the due honors of a red-robe, save the third moon on my shoulder.

I lead many hunts on many different dimensions... all of them equally dark and hateful to me.

For a time I convinced myself that Ardain had been lying to me about his beautiful world, untrustworthy Traverser that he was... and then gradually I forgot that we had ever spoken. My life was a whirlwind of excitement, hunts, wars, and the death I savored.

I was given a fine black sword, a god's weapon, decorated with gold and emeralds. I broke tradition in refusing to kneel before anyone, not the Warlord himself or even the powerful black-robed priests who were the most terrible and ancient of all our kind. Rumor had it that I would be named a true Immortal soon... and after that I would be entitled to challenge my father for his title.

I often imagined being a female Warlord, the first in all of history, and more often I dreamt of killing Geruth, who had become just another soldier to me. For a time I had seen him as a minor threat, but as I grew stronger and he began to soften in his position of prestige, I began to think even less of him.

I was invincible, untouchable. I had a thousand names and even more deaths. I would cry my name aloud with the force of my Order, sending entire armies into retreat.

"Ki met'tha udorai... edu'ne nakoh!" The words, they had a certain music to them, a kind of sense that seemed to trandenscend any language. "For I am the death of five-thousand worlds."

My famous maxim became more than an ignorant boast as I continued to push myself harder, refusing to accept any limitations, even the light of day.

I began riding in the sun, always summoning a thunderstorm to follow after me, and I became known and feared, revered by some. Those who did not know my name called me "The Demon Queen," a perverse blending of my dark nature and my ethereal, often regal appearance... but most remembered me well, for I blazed each of my paths across the realms that I knew... nine times, in sets of three years each.

It was my game, an obsessive one at that, but it also became my legend. Every three years... I, Ireval, would return.

I stole many souls, bringing my path of destruction full circle for the twenty-second time, when finally... I and my army returned to Magog, and to the iron gates of Geruth's kingdom. The darkness that loomed before me was not comforting... despite the fact that I knew the merciless sun would soon rise.

I turned my horse around. "We ride west!" I commanded.

My hundred warriors shrugged, looking to one another, not questioning my Order but nevertheless concerned by it. Zaethe, my cousin... who had remarkably kept herself alive galloped up from the right flank to face me. Though I outranked her still, her influence in my army grew stronger each time she dared challenge my command.

"The sun will soon be up," she announced. "You may have no objection to riding forever in rain, but the rest of us would prefer to sleep. I vote that we spend this dawn with the armies of Warlord Geruth."

"And I second that." Her lover, Orin Saede, dismounted from his horse.

"Very well," I sighed, knowing there was no way I could save face. "If none of you are god enough to continue... we shall spend the daylight hours here. Bring me the slaves!"

Two of the younger warriors drug forward a chained line of thirteen humans, all covered in sand. Our breakneck pace had killed the rest of our captives, but those few had escaped temporarily... only to be caught again as we neared the desert.

"A fitting gift for Lord Geruth," Elhilom smirked, surveying the new slaves. Looking like a great dark hawk, he sat crouched on the stones above the gate, picking his teeth with a shard of bone. I had not seen him at first, but once he opened his mouth, he became visible. Elhilom snapped his claws and the gates parted. Jumping down from his perch, he disappeared into the shadows ahead of us, presumably to announce our arrival.

The drums beneath our feet pounded incessantly and a young warrior came forward to collect our horses as we dismounted before the throne.

Surveying my army with a disinterested snort, from his pedestal, Geruth threw a bone to one of the dogs and motioned for someone to pour him more wine… his eyes finally coming to rest on me.

Visibly disturbed, he smiled awkwardly and excused himself from the high seat. Without hesitation, I proceeded up past the fourth step, which was my place by official rank… and sat in my father's chair. From the throne, which was where I preferred to sit, I could still sense Geruth nearby. Slaves moved to attend the both of us.

Though Geruth would not challenge my unofficial rule, my victory was still incomplete. I had the full support of the warriors. They feared me like no other, and in our world, fear was the truest form of respect. Yet so long as Geruth remained Warlord, even if it was only in name… he would still be watching over me… my silent, terrible shadow, the burden that kept me shackled, inches away from my true potential.

I was home at long last. It was not a pleasant thought.

"Another round for the Warriors of the Demon Queen!" Orin laughed and threw a handful of rubies onto the table. Slaves quickly refilled the goblets round the hall. The new captives were especially willing and able… perhaps out of fear, for the older slaves had surely told them that those who did not please their masters would become the main course of our feast.

"Quite a loot you've gathered there," Geruth remarked, surveying the gems and the slaves from his place looking over my shoulder. "How long of a hunt was it?"

"Two days," I sighed, sharpening the blade of my sword. "It would have been a few hours less, except that some clerics interfered."

"Elves? Those slaves of Fyeris?" Geruth asked with profound distaste.

"I think they were humans," I admitted.

"Small and fat, with lots of sick ones, and a few sheep," Zaethe nodded. "They were not even living in the city we sacked, they were outside of it, in the hills."

"As if they didn't beg 'God help us' enough!" Orin sighed. "With all that screaming my headache will never go away."

"Pah!" Elhilom laughed. "You're in pain from a few words? Weakling! At least the elves provide challenge and sport. The humans are pathetic. They have only one god to call upon and he doesn't even have any magic to give them. I remember the days when we fought Traversers!" Elhilom grinned, taking another drink. "Those were the days!"

"Then these were mages, not clerics. They threw spells… and good ones. We lost thirty of our warriors," Zaethe muttered.

One of her friends had been killed. I couldn't have cared less. I had planned to take the bastard's soul as he slept anyway.

"Wearing strange robes, were they?" Geruth wondered.

"Some," I nodded, suddenly interested in the conversation. "Some in pale robes, some in long cloaks."

"Red cloaks?" he pressed.

"Why… yes." I couldn't fathom what he was so afraid of, but I was beginning to become a little concerned myself.

"May we move somewhere without so many ears?" Geruth hissed in my ear.

"If you feel we must," I agreed. Seldom had my father ever requested that we speak alone.

We walked off into a dim corridor. Water dripped from above into the empty eyes of a molding skull on the floor. I ignored the temptation to kick the revolting thing away, instead composing myself. I would face Geruth not as a fearful and easily distracted child, but as an equal.

"Those men you confronted were Priests of the White Cross," he whispered, almost as if he feared to speak the name. "As we hunt humans… they hunt demons."

"They certainly made a poor showing," I laughed.

"How many were there?" he demanded.

"Seven," I admitted. "We slew them all."

"Seven to your army, and they still killed many more than their number before you were able to destroy them."

"True," I admitted. As I thought back to the battle, I realized just how strong the strangers had been, even in their small group. If such clerics were to form an organized force as the elves were known to, they would be able to slaughter all the I'Eloshir.

"But… how were they so powerful?" I wondered. "What world do they come from that I have not seen?"

Geruth shook his head. "I have known for many hundred years that this day would come. I feared to show you. Few know of its existence, and fewer still are capable of reaching it on their own. It is a world of infinite bounty, ready for the taking… but it is also very dangerous."

"Danger?" I almost laughed, but somehow sensed there was nothing funny about the situation. "I fear nothing," I argued.

"Not even the loss of your magic?" he pressed. "If you are not strong enough, the Goddess will take your powers from you when you cross over."

"My powers?" I scoffed at the ridiculous thought. "Are you blind? Have you not seen what I have done? Are you deaf? Have you not heard that they are screaming my name across a thousand realms? Mortals flee from I'Eloshir as none have since the days of Raedawn! And this I have done myself! Tell me that is not strength enough!"

"We shall see." Geruth turned back to the table. "Give me a day and a night to meet with my warriors… and then you and I shall depart for the Chaos Realm."

I shuddered, flashing back to that long ago day when the white man, my grandfather had spoken about the place. So it was true. All those centuries I had believed Geruth's lies, believed that the place I had often imagined was nothing more than a fantasy, when all along... it had been there, waiting.

"E'Nara!" One of the warriors shouted. "Rath Iekuh killed one of your slaves! Do you want a new one?"

I did not respond.

"Are you well?" Orin wondered, as he passed by in the hall, obviously sensing my anger.

"Well enough," I replied, clenching my teeth. "I will be in my chambers."

"Should we save one of the small ones for you?" he asked.

"Don't bother," I muttered, fading out of visibility down the hall.

I may have been heartless all my life, but for the first time then, I felt the cold.

Ardain... Ardain had spoken the truth.

I went to sleep and slept all that day. I had never been a heavy sleeper, but something had overwhelmed me and exhausted me to the point I couldn't keep open my eyes. And I had a dream.

Dreaming is a mortal phenomenon, perhaps one of the best things about being at least partly human. True demons dream rarely, and never so vividly as mortals do.

I had never dreamt at all before that night. In my own mind, that first experience of dreaming was something rather like being truly awake.

I saw myself standing alone on a yellow plain of wheat, underneath a turbulent sky. Behind me was a tree, a bleeding tree stabbed with many swords. Before me were three riders… but they were not I'Eloshir.

Fast as the wind they rode, coming to stop on the front steps of some great and marvelous house. I stood on the stairs and watched in amazement as the riders folded up into three paper-thin cards and soared away.

I walked inside and down an increasingly narrow hall until I came to a door, a door concealed by a large mirror. My reflection I recognized, though I felt much older than I appeared. I opened the door and crept carefully down into the empty cellar. A single beam of blinding white light came from somewhere up, casting an unearthly glow on the white painted wall. My eyes drifted towards one brick in particular.

I went to pull it free, but with all my strength and all my mage-powers I could not. Bits of plaster fell from above, and finally the stone obeyed me. I looked inside the dark hole, desperate to see what I had found... and promptly woke up.

I was breathing heavily, but fortunately all of the sleeping bodies around me were too drunk on blood and wine to even notice that I was stepping on them. I went where instinct lead me, to the empty hall, knowing I was looking for a door.

Or perhaps... it was not a door at all.

Pulling aside the red velvet draperies behind the Warlord's high seat, I found a mirror, and not just any mirror, but the most extraordinary piece I had ever seen. It was easily six feet tall and framed in solid gold. I did not know how I had missed it... living so close and yet so far away for so many centuries, but somehow I had. I reached out to touch the flawless glass and it rippled beneath my fingertips. The fiery torches in the room all exploded in unison and a blazing white light flared out from the mirror itself. I staggered back, shielding my eyes and then gasped in amazement at what it revealed.

"The Chaos Realm...," I whispered.

"Who goes there?" my father's voice demanded.

I grabbed for the curtain to recover the mirror when all at once, three sharp ropes of blue light cut through the glass and twisted around my neck and wrists, flinging me forward through the mirror. I could hear it shatter and I squeezed close my eyes as I shot through space and time, bound by another's magic.

I could hear the drums of the I'Eloshir in the far off distance, but as I flew closer to whatever had called me, I could hear something else too, the sound of waves crashing on rock.

The sun burned brightly, but my eyes were unhurt. I gazed in wonder at my almost three-hundred-degree view of the strange world for a moment, overcome with a profound sense of recognition, and then choked, flung forward with even more pressure directly through the upper story window of a tall white tower.

I struggled, pulling away and clenching my teeth, but it was useless.

More glass shattered. Completely unable to control my own body, I slammed into a wall. I collapsed onto the floor, kneeling in shards of glass, black with my own blood. Breathless and awestruck, I looked up.

Across from me sat a young boy, human in appearance, and perhaps a little older than thirteen. His hair was a peculiar shade of blue, and he was dressed in gray robes much like the clerics of Magog. Still, I knew from his scent that he was no God-Summoner. He was a mage… like me.

I had never heard of a human mage, let alone one who could pull an I'Eloshir through a disturbance in space. That was the stuff of mortal fairy-tales…

The boy slid backwards across the floor a few paces and looked up at me, bewildered. He swore in some language I did not recognize and kissed the amulet around his neck, retracing his green powder circle and muttering something unintelligible.

Arrogant little beast… thinking it would keep me from him!

I lunged forward and struck my head on something that felt quite solid. Stepping back, I was amazed at the sudden appearance of a shimmering pillar of energy surrounding the young apprentice.

Clearly, I had met my match.

The Magician

"Wise is he whose every waking moment is an expression of the greater joy."

Seven

We stared at each other for a long while until finally, content in knowing that I couldn't reach him, the mage-child broke the uneasy silence.

"Did I... summon you?" he wondered.

Part of my magical gift was the ability to understand any spoken tongue. At first, when he had called his spell, I had not been listening carefully, but then, suddenly, his words began to reshape themselves.

"In a manner of speaking," I admitted, speaking to the boy in his own language. "I was looking for trouble."

"But you're ..."

"A demon?" I supplied.

"Not like any demon I've heard of," he argued. "For one thing... you've got no wings."

No wings? I bristled... and then realized he was right.

"Perhaps not," I shrugged, though that in itself would take me some getting used to. I felt my back over, wondering where they had gone to.

Somehow, I had changed. My eyesight seemed permanently blurred, and the bones in my face had shifted, becoming more rounded, my teeth blunt and my nails small and incapable of tearing through even the thinnest of fabrics, let alone metal and stone.

I wished desperately that could find a mirror. I was terrified... I had to see if it were true, what I feared... the mere possibility that I might be helpless... that I might be human.

"And you're... pretty," he stammered. "Demons are supposed to be hideous. You look like an elf."

"An elf?" I snarled, swearing under my breath. "Accursed, wretched..." Lacking the proper words in the human's language, I slipped into my own familiar demonic tongue. "Shifak etu nys'kaa nyesh." I fought the urge to rip

45

the boy apart, reminding myself that I couldn't enter his circle anyway. For once in my life, I would have to use my wits.

"Now you sound like a demon," the boy observed.

"Shut up, brat," I growled, attempting to sound as appeased as possible. "I promise I won't kill you if you help me. Have you got a mirror?" I asked.

The boy frowned. "I'm not stupid. You could be a Traverser."

"I'm afraid you have named me in truth," I laughed, suddenly understanding what had happened. Though I was still uneasy, I would not sacrifice my upper hand to a mere child, and a mortal one at that. Traverser... that was a term I recognized. Whether I had been transformed into one or not, only time would tell.

"You are?" he stammered. "A real Traverser?"

"My name is Ireval Ithraedol," I explained. "Of the I'Eloshir. Now what do they call you, Mageling?"

"Phineas," The boy replied stiffly. "Phineas Merlin."

We stared for a few moments longer, until a knock came at the door. I jumped to my feet as an old man entered the tower room, another mage, possibly the young Phineas's teacher. Instantly on my guard, I felt my bones crack and shift as my body changed and my wings re-formed. A well of strength flowed through me, and I gasped in amazement, feeling as if I had just taken my first breath. The boy gasped and the old man nearly fainted when he saw me.

"Dddeemon!" he stammered, pointing. I smiled as terribly as I could. It was a wonderful thing to be recognized.

Hours passed as I related to them bits and pieces of what I knew, the worlds I had been to and the spells I had learned. I gathered quickly that neither of them approved of my moral standards, as I scoffed at theirs.

The old man was called Silas Galwick, and "Young Merlin" as he took to calling the boy, was his apprentice. The world I had stumbled upon was indeed the mysterious Chaos Realm I had been warned to avoid, and the kingdom I had landed in was known as Ardra, the Duchy of Celedon.

It was a sane, pleasant place where wars were a great deal less frequent than in Tirs Uloth. There was not much of any treasure to be stolen, and as far as I could tell, no plausible reason to hate and kill mortals... if Phineas and his teacher were any sort of example at all. What was even more perplexing was the strange ability I suddenly possessed to disguise myself in a human body. Since it seemed to set the wizards at ease, I adopted the form without coaxing, although the relative dimness of the senses and the pathetic lack of physical strength made me extremely uneasy. However, as I soon learned, in the Chaos Realm, I'Eloshir were exceedingly rare. It was not surprising to me in the least. The only things traded were secrets and spells, bits of wisdom and sometimes money, never lives or slaves.

Overwhelmed with so much potential intellectual stimulation, I decided almost immediately that I could grow to like it there very much.

"Are there many of my kind here?" I wondered.

"Not particularly," The old man admitted. "At least not on this continent."

"There are six countries in the Empire," Phineas recited, counting on his fingers "Ardra is where we are now and Accoloth is where Master Galwick was born. Eldar is the kingdom of the Elves and Istara is full of mountains and castles. Ranlain is where the Emperor lives, and the Badowin Isles are where the pirates and the Demons come from," he finished proudly.

"Demons? Like Traversers?" I wondered.

Phineas shook his head. "Like the kind you don't want to be around."

"You ... want to be around Traversers?" This was news to me.

"There's a difference between the I'Eloshir of Magog and those of Raedawn," The old wizard explained.

"Raedawn?" I tried the word out. I knew of the city and its legend, but I had never suspected that there were I'Eloshir that had survived its supposed destruction.

"The Etone Brotherhood, the Ravencrofts, the Falchons, the Heroes of Gelthar and the Good Emperor himself. They are all your kind. Immortals."

"You... respect them then?" I was still in shock. "They don't hunt you?"

"Certainly not," The old wizard replied in a slightly injured tone. "They're a bit frightening, but that's only because they're so powerful. Overall, the Errida Dynasty is the best government I've seen on any of the realms I've visited, and that's saying a lot."

"Could I meet this Emperor of yours?" I wondered, intrigued by the new possibility.

"If you wish," Galwick shrugged. "It's not as if we can keep you here."

"I rather think your apprentice can," I whispered, pointing to Phineas who was petting a small herd of cats near the fire. "He drug me here, after all."

"Stay with us then," The old man offered. "I just may be able to learn how to create that... "ambrosia" you speak of. I know they're quite fond of it in Ranlain, and it's quite possible that the recipe is in one of my travel books."

"I accept your offer," I nodded. "There seems to be much that I do not know… and that is troubling. I wish to know the truth. I tire of being made to believe things that are not so."

"I suspect we've been misinformed about you as well," Galwick admitted.

"Unlikely," I shook my head heavily. "What most say of us is true, save that we have no honor. Honor is our very foundation. We simply define it differently."

"You'll do what you say you will?" Galwick wondered, glancing at me almost fearfully.

"Of course," I nodded. "I am nothing but my word."

"You will not harm Phineas or myself," he spoke slowly, perhaps suspecting I would refuse. "And no… killing any of the neighbors," he added, almost on afterthought.

"Never fear," I promised, and realized that I meant it.

For perhaps the first time I didn't feel the urge to wreck anything at all. I smiled conceitedly. Was I really turning good, or I was I just biding my time?

Either way, it promised to be interesting.

Dusk fell and morning came. Seven long years passed, and I grew to love my new home, rarely even dreaming of returning to Magog. All my old aspirations to lead the I'Eloshir seemed foolish. Phineas and Galwick gave me a new name as well… Artemis, ironically, a Goddess of the hunt, and Ravencroft, after my grandfather. I liked it a good deal more than I had ever liked being called "Daughter" or "Beast."

And yet my own name still held a certain flavor, in its sound. Every so often I would hear it as I lay asleep, a soft voice whispering to me, gently repeating my name. Yet as soon as I opened my eyes, the speaker I had sensed would be gone.

I had turned soft, I realized with grim certainty, but it did not bother me as much as I suspected it would. As the years passed, I taught Phineas the way of the sword, and in return, I learned the fine art of controlling my radically unpredictable spells to a small degree.

There was something about the old wizard Galwick I never could place. I recall clearly the last conversation we had, though it was ages upon ages ago. The white tower on that hill in Celedon is little more than a pile of rubble now, and the name of Silas Galwick has long since been forgotten.

Yet, every so often, I remember our sitting in the warm study that cold winter morning. A blizzard had nearly buried us the night before, a storm that Phineas had carefully worked away from our home with moderate success.

Still, we were very nearly snowed in, despite what sorcery he could manage.

I craned my neck to peer out the tiny wax-paper window and then finally pulled the covering down entirely.

In the center of the icy courtyard, Phineas stood, in his bare feet, spinning about in the drifts and gazing skyward like a madman as the snowflakes continued to fall around him.

For the life of me, I could not comprehend what he was doing.

"Artemis!" Galwick coughed. "I understand that you do not feel the draft you are letting in, but have some mercy for my old bones, will you?"

"Forgive me, sir," I muttered, still staring at the spectacle in the snow.

"What are you gawking at?" Galwick demanded, hobbling over to my side.

"It's Phineas," I admitted. "Is... is he ill?"

Galwick chucked softly and returned to his seat.

"I don't understand. Isn't he supposed to be training? What can one possibly accomplish by standing out in the snow?"

The old man grinned. "Artemis, do you remember what I told you about the nature of magic?"

"I remember that you told me I would never be a real sorcerer," I admitted grudgingly, "because I think too much."

"Precisely," Galwick sighed. "Look at the boy. To him, magic is a joy. It is in the very air he breathes. He does not know why the snow falls, he will never ask... because to him, it simply is... and therefore is good."

Snoring softly, he slumped forward and fell asleep. After moving him to his bed, I sat for a few twilight hours on the roof of the stable, looking out over the snow-covered fields and farms. And I felt a strange loneliness, a feeling that I had never before experienced.

I had changed so much in such a short time. To Galwick and Phineas, my conditioning for the world of men had been a long and arduous process, but to me... the many hours I had spent were of no consequence. I felt as if we had only just met, yet already I was sensing the mortality, the impending death that lingered in the both of them.

So little time we had... so little time.

Eight

The next morning I awoke to find that the miraculous winter world had melted completely, leaving the ground green and muddy with the crisp scent of an early spring.

After marveling for a few short moments at the sudden change in the weather, Phineas and I returned to the solar, only to discover that Master Galwick had passed on quietly in his sleep. We buried him near the oak tree, as Phineas assured me was proper, though I much disliked the idea of a body that did not immediately disintegrate.

Phineas was twenty with plenty of talent to become quite famous and an aura about him that seemed to compel complete and total trust. I was just nearing eight-hundred, and ready, I supposed, to start my life.

After Galwick was safely seen-to and the tower quietly locked and warded, we gathered our meager possessions, three horses, a cow, and a fleet of cats, pigs and chickens and headed for the city that lay to the west.

Phoenicia, gem of the kingdom of Ardra. Each of the royal clans, which numbered four, possessed a magical stone, a brilliantly colored gem with mystical elemental powers. The Etharel-Wells family, longtime kings and queens of the continent, ruled over the element of fire, and their leader was a man named Jahmed.

Phineas was hoping to seize the recently vacated position of court wizard. I was hoping to find my way, somehow, sooner or later to the capital of the Empire, the city of Zenith.

"Over this next hill," Phineas pointed to the map.

I stood in my stirrups, but I still couldn't quite see ahead. The horses whinnied anxiously and I sniffed the air. "Smoke." I shook my head. "I'd recognize that smell if I were dead. It seems that your peaceful royals are having quite the conflict down there."

"A battle?" Phineas wondered. "But why?"

A young man came running up the road towards us, coughing and dragging a half-lame mule behind him.

"There's your answer," I pointed.

"Sir!" Phineas shouted. "Sir!"

"Can't stop now!" the man shouted. "And I'd turn around if I were you! The cavalry's here but they're too late!"

"Too late for what?" Phineas demanded.

"Them demons," the man shook his head. "The Republic's found themselves a whole new world of beasties… an they just opened up a Tear to bring em' here. Four day past. Think they was called I... ellow-sheer or somethin'."

"I'Eloshir?" I wondered. "Here?" A sick, cold feeling came over me. I bit my own lip and closed my eyes, knowing he spoke the truth.

I had been found.

"Let's hope not," Phineas finished.

"They are here," I shook my head. "I sense them." The peasant looked at me doubtfully. "Who leads the army?" I demanded.

"There's two, from what it looks like," the man admitted. "I seen them only from a distance, so I'm not real sure, but they say one's a tall, pale one with yellow hair… and the other's a real ugly dark one with one wing. Think the second one's female... maybe. Anyhow, the both of em' are dressed in red."

"Orin Saede and Zaethe Eylchaur," I snarled, certain of my guess.

"You know the demons?" he wondered.

"We've met," I admitted, cursing viciously under my breath.

"Say! The man brightened visibly. "You're a Traverser, aincha?"

I nodded… disturbed.

He shook my hand almost insanely, and I took off my glove, disliking the smell he rubbed onto it. "I'm Edgar Dunharrow." He grinned.

"Artemis Ravencroft," I replied.

"A Ravencroft!" Edgar beamed shamelessly… as if I'd just revealed myself to be his patron Goddess.

I was in no hurry to face my father, but even from Edgar's vague descriptions, I knew it had to be Orin and Zae in the lead of the warriors. I'd had seven years to practice my magic in the realm, and evidently, from the mess they were making, they'd only just left Magog.

"Four days to flatten a city? Ridiculous," I snorted, certain that, had been in the lead, there would have been nothing left but ashes, gold and chained slaves within the first hour.

Phineas somehow guessed I was drifting off. "Do you want to turn back?"

I shook my head. "I am no coward."

"I don't know about this." Edgar eyed our third horse, hopping from foot to foot in a paranoid sort of dance. "But if you're riding down there…"

"He wants a piece of the action," Phineas rolled his eyes. "Hero-worshipper."

"Hero," I muttered. "A hero to darkness perhaps, but no one you want your children looking up to."

Phineas smiled. "That may change."

I spurred my horse and galloped down into the fire-scarred wreckage. Phineas and Edgar close behind me. The I'Eloshir had vanished without a trace, as they were well trained to do, and all that remained was the bare bones and scars of what surely must have been a beautiful city. How many like it had I destroyed over the course of my disastrous centuries?

I didn't care to count, but suddenly, I felt a considerably worse about being a convert.

The streets still ran red with blood, and though I reminded myself again and again that what had happened was wrong, some far-off part of my consciousness, the part that I had worked so hard to contain, was slowly breaking free from its mental trappings... and it was disappointed that there was nothing left to kill.

A high pitched shriek in a nearby alley sent a chill of excitement racing down my spine. Intrigued and overwhelmed by nothing more than a single scream, I leapt from my horse and raced through the rubble to the scene.

Distantly, I could hear Phineas shouting for my attention, but I ignored him. I could smell that I was getting closer.

I turned the corner into a little courtyard where rainwater pouring down the gutters mingled with blood and spilt wine in the grass. The bodies of several men and women lay mangled in the bushes, dead where they had been thrown, but I still sensed life in the ruins of the villa.

And then I saw him, a thin, white-skinned beast with a gray brown mane and a jaw that was crooked enough to look like the muzzle of a dog. His smoke-gray wings hung heavily across his back giving him the relative appearance of a waterlogged rat. At first, I scarcely recognized what he was, and then it hit me. He was a young I'Eloshir, of low rank and questionable parentage… but a demon nonetheless.

He did not notice my entrance as he stood there, in the faint shadows, gloating over a human woman and her two small children.

For a moment, I nearly let him have his way with them, until I remembered, quite suddenly, where I was... and what I was not.

"Get out of here," I growled, dismissing him in the common tongue.

For a moment I suspected that he would turn on me, but he did not, instead squinting as if he saw something in my face that he remembered vaguely.

"No!" he gasped suddenly, his eyes wide in terror. "Ireval? It is impossible!"

"GET OUT OF HERE!" I ordered, tearing at him in a crazed fury. Completely out of control, I ceased commanding him in the common language and began screaming words I knew he would understand, the same two words over and over again.

"Ki euto! Ki euto! Ki euto!"

Caught off-guard, he barely evaded my first awkward assault, and the second thrust that I made ran him clean through the chest.

Bewildered by the sight of his own blood and a blade through his body, he stared up at me and whispered in our language what I feared he would say all along.

"How could you? You have betrayed your own..."

I collapsed into the ground, fighting tears... over the body of the beast that had already begun to fade away.

"Ki euto," I whispered. "I hate you." But who did I hate, really? Not the warrior I had killed... I hated the part of me that was like him. I hated myself.

At the last possible moment, I realized that I knew the boy, and felt even more terrible. Though I had seen him as a beast when I had first attacked, now he was only a child in my arms, scarcely a century behind him. He was Ruhk Saede... one of my youngest warriors, a protégé if I had ever had one. I had killed one of my own. As Rukh's body faded into nothingness, I looked up.

Still uncertain, the demon's victim took her daughter's hand and gazed at me with a look that was relief and fear rolled into one emotion.

"You there!" a voice shouted, interrupting my strange, startled confusion. "You in the shadows. Name and rank!"

"I'm not one of your soldiers!" I shouted back, forcing myself to my feet, wiping the tears from my eyes. The intense pain had already begun to subside, and I was thankful for that. I had trained myself for centuries to kill other l'Eloshir, to fight the terrible agony that came from feeling your victim die.

I could put another death behind me now.

The woman and her children had vanished, and it was a man that now demanded my attention, not Phineas or Edgar... but someone, something else entirely.

He stepped into the light, a waterfall pouring off the roof in front of him, so that at first I could not see his face. Following the sound of my voice, he stepped out from behind the rippling screen and we stood across from one another, face to face. The man was tall, perhaps near seven feet, and attired entirely in dark purple and silver, a remarkable contrast to the whites and gray-greens of the courtyard. His dark eyes glowed with power, while his long black hair, blown by the wind, revealed his human-like features.

But he was no mortal, that much was certain. I could feel it in my bones that he and I... we were a kind of kin. Not relatives, no... but two, lonely, ancient creatures in a young and foreign world.

Never in all my many years had I encountered a single soul who radiated such a powerful sense of balance as that stranger did. And I knew then, as I had seldom known anything, that I was indeed face to face at long last, not with a demonic convert like Ardain, but with one of the true children of Raedawn... a real Traverser.

"Who are you?" the man demanded. "I've never seen you before."

"Surely you don't know everyone in the Empire," I began, trying to work my way out of the situation.

"The Errida Dynasty is not like the Warriors of Magog," The man replied. "There are too few of us Traversers to miss a single one. What is your name?"

"Artemis," I replied. "Artemis Ravencroft."

"A relative of Ardain?" The man frowned, recognizing my name instantly. "Surely not!"

"And why might that be?" I glared at him, though the look in his eyes left me unsettled. "He must have many descendants you haven't met. With ten wives at very least and dozens of children..."

"It is too long a tale for this place and time." He shook his head. "Perhaps you should go to the capital." He gestured towards the sky. "This ship is headed back to Zenith."

"What ship?" I wondered.

The mist cleared, almost as if on queue, and before my eyes was the most magnificent vessel I had ever seen, not floating on the water, as I had expected, but hovering in thin air.

"The Spellcraft Dogma." The man smiled. "Pride of the Imperial fleet."

"Who are you?" I asked, turning to face the soldier, who had miraculously vanished, leaving in his place a tiny shattered mirror.

"Hooo boy!" Edgar grinned, rubbing his hands together in anticipation. "I always wanted to hitch me a ride on one a' these things!"

"Think we'll be able to lose him?" Phineas wondered, jerking a thumb at the villager.

I didn't respond. Apparently neither of them had witnessed the man's disappearance, or else they were unmoved by it. But to me, it was thoroughly impossible. In my minds eye I still saw that beautiful, familiar stranger. "Do I... know you?" I wondered. The breeze mocked me, carrying with it the faintest sound of laughter.

Nine

The ground beneath our feet rumbled as the Spellcraft descended and we hesitantly climbed aboard. Though the design was familiar to me, reminiscent of the sailing vessels of many realms, something about the ship itself was vaguely unsettling.

The crewmen stared as we boarded, most of them human. Bouncing about and whistling as he paced the deck, Edgar saluted awkwardly and waved to the helmsman.

Phineas and I, despite our ragged attire, must have carried some sort of unspoken importance. The quartermaster of the ship introduced himself only with his rank, and did not even dare to ask what our business was, escorting us directly to the captain's cabin instead.

The captain of The Dogma was a gray-haired human man, short of stature, yet with a fighter's build and a gleam in his eye of one who had seen many inexplicable things, obviously a seasoned military man rather than a merchant sailor.

His age was impossible to truly determine, though if I was asked to guess, I likely would have placed him between the years of forty-five and fifty.

Though we had not requested an audience, he sat very still and said nothing, as if he expected Phineas or myself to supply the conversation.

"My name is Artemis Ravencroft...," I began.

The captain silenced me with a wave of the hand. "I know what you are," he growled, in a gruff and somewhat disgusted manner. "My name is General Maurice Auderrauk, and I am Grand Vizier to the Lord Errida. Nothing in this Empire escapes my notice. I know you... and your kind well. I know that you have come from Magog, and I know that your companion here summoned you. Correct, Master Merlin?"

"Y...yes." Phineas blinked, somewhat startled at hearing his own name pronounced with the addition of a title.

"By accident, seven years ago, in the south of Celedon," The Vizier continued.

Phineas straightened himself up in his chair and took a deep breath.

"Indeed," he replied gravely.

Though the situation was somewhat unsettling, I fought the urge to laugh, recognizing his sudden change in demeanor as his Galwick impersonation.

The Vizier was not amused. "I know, yes, I know," he muttered. "I know also that you possessed rank in the demon's society, and that you are far older than you appear. I know that you are a spell caster... and that the name you seem so fond of tossing about, Artemis Ravencroft, is not really your name at all. What I do not know, however, is your true identity... nor why is it that you have come."

"I... have changed," I admitted, not sure how to explain. "You were right in your assumptions, I was indeed a leader amongst the l'Eloshir. But none of it matters to me now. I cannot return to Tirs Uloth. My coming here alone was an act of treason in the highest degree. I have nothing left in the demon's world. If you require their secrets from me, I will give them to you, and gladly, if only you will take me to your capital city. I want to go to Zenith," I finished. "I want to meet the Emperor."

"Quite a few Traversers have been in and out of Phoenicia in the past few days. Lord Errida himself was here last night, and his brother arrived this morning," The Vizier admitted. "Though I confess I don't know where either of them have spirited off to. Those damnable glass-breaking Traversers are impossible."

He looked to Phineas for support on the matter... but Phineas only shrugged.

"The Court will find your proposition interesting at any rate," The Vizier sighed. "Imagine an actual l'Eloshir... you say, an exiled noble willing to expose the darkest reaches of the lawful evil world."

"Now that you put it that way, I don't know that I will tell you anything," I muttered.

"The way you carry on, one would think whatever you've got to tell could be the secret to their final undoing. So you led a few raids. It's not as if you're The Ireval," he argued.

I smiled broadly despite myself. "Just who is it that I am not?"

Phineas grew very pale, and I recalled suddenly that I had never told him that the common name "Ireval" and the legendary "title" were both my own.

"The Ireval," The Vizier repeated. "Oh come now!"

"Continue," I shot back, grinning insanely and searching the Vizier's eyes for emotion. He was afraid... and that fear energized me.

Phineas stared, with an expression I guessed was brought on by pure terror, but I was having too much fun. I had a sudden urge to tear the old man's heart out through his eye socket... and taunt him with it.

"So who was this Ireval?" I asked, tapping my nails on the desk, imagining how much fun it would be to hear him scream a little. Humans made such amusing sounds when they were frightened... like pigs.

"A beautiful demon," The Vizier shook his head. "The Traversers tell stories about her when they pass through this realm. Those who saw her face seldom lived to tell the tale, but the legends... they've reached farther than the Demon Queen herself. Though she never made it to our lands, we feared that she would come. For hundreds of years, she was the worst thing any world had ever seen... and then, quite inexplicably, she vanished."

I was lost in my own memories, sword drawn in my mind, and then, quite suddenly, I was back in the cabin. From across the room, I could sense The Vizier's uneasiness, and I thought arrogantly how satisfying it would be to jump out of my chair and take him down.

He was a fighter, and he was on his guard, his hand drifting towards a heavy battleaxe mounted on the wall behind his desk. He would be a challenge, a real struggle, even stronger than the demon I had killed in the alleyway. I could hear his heart pounding, and I wanted to take his soul.

A pain raced through my back, tearing wide where my wings had been... or were. Were. My teeth drew blood from my own lip, and the bones in my face stretched, cracking as they reformed. It was a glorious feeling, shedding the human body I had worn for so long, yet it came also with a price. All that remained was for me to...

"Snap out of it!" Phineas shouted.

Where was I? Who was I? I?

I jumped back and stretched to my full height, standing on the very tip of my right foot. Muscles I hadn't used in ages were suddenly at my command and a spill of black feathers pooled on the floor. I had wings again.

Despite what I had nearly done, I still felt smug, until I saw Phineas's face. The look was one of intense pain... and fear. He had his hand wrapped around the door pull so tightly that he'd cut into his own palm.

What I had been, even for an instant was so earth shatteringly wrong, that he looked as if I had killed him. I rolled my shoulders and the wings fell to pieces, the bones shifting back to nothingness with a painful twist.

"Sweet mother of mercy," The Vizier swore, looking very ill. He stood clutching his axe.

Though in my own shape-changing agony I had not felt the blow, I realized then that he had struck me in the chest... and that my skin had chipped his blade. I pulled the small piece of metal out of my neck, wincing, and awed that I had reverted completely from frail human I had become to my time-honored immortal power in little more than the blink of an eye.

"This... this has never happened before," I admitted, slumping down in the chair, trying to breathe calmly, although visions of savagely tearing the man apart still lingered in my mind. "Phineas, get me some of that..." I pointed to my wineskin in the corner. He did as he was asked, filling his mug with the bubbling yellow liquor, and I drank heavily.

The ship rolled on across the clouds towards a sparkling light on the distant horizon. I stood out on deck in the darkness and savored the strong breeze, longing to simply fly away. But I knew what that meant, and as much as I desired to run forever, I knew I could not. Phineas had already lost two families and a teacher. I would not cost him a friend as well.

The days wore on. I had assumed, incorrectly, that because I could see the light, it was near, but that was hardly the case. It was on the eve of our third day at sea that disaster struck.

"Storm rolling in!" one of the sailors shouted. "Hurricane!"

The peals of thunder and flashes of lightning only caused me to become more unapproachable. I locked myself in my cabin to be sure that I would not harm anyone, and as an extra precaution, I chained myself to the barred window.

I'd have to tear half of the ship to pieces before I could kill any of the crewman, but what sickened me more was that I knew what I was... still capable of. I looked out over the night sky. Far off to the west, in the direction of the storm, I caught sight of a small sliver of pale blue where no such light should have been. The sailors saw it as well.

"Tear!" the lookout roared. "Betwixt opens to the west! All hands on deck!"

I knew what a Tear was, as did all l'Eloshir, including the Traversers. There were two forms of dimensional travel. One, apparently, concerned mirrors. The other was the fine art of moving Tears, small disturbances in the fabric of space-time. An open Tear allowed one to travel in the dark and dangerous paths that lay between dimensions. A closed Tear could trap an individual indefinitely. The creation of such a Tear, a Tear large enough to move any sizeable attack force, was a complicated and difficult process.

I had been quite good at it in my day.

"Tear!" The call echoed throughout the ship... and then all at once the porthole burst open and several flying contraptions soared in, laying down balls of fire on the Spellcraft immediately.

"Republic fighters!" one of the men shouted. "They're firing on us!"

More explosions whistled through the air, and the entire ship shuddered, dropping ten feet. I hastily reached for the key to my manacles but instead dropped it through a crack in the floorboards.

The Spellcraft sunk low again. We returned fire... sorcery from the Mages on deck and blasts from the cannons, but even the most powerful spells had little effect on the strange nearly invisible "fighters." They were entirely too fast-moving to follow.

Two of the fighters crashed into the ocean, but more replaced them, and they were far more maneuverable than our lone ship.

I dug for my sword and sawed furiously at the chain I knew I could not break, and the Spellcraft took a third hit, spiraling through midair and splashing into the water.

My window was open. I gagged as the room began to flood and struggled furiously with the locks, shaking the bars from the window and finally just ripping them loose altogether. I raced up the stairs, near drowning and slid right over the edge of the sharply tilted deck.

Though fire was not something that I feared, and though heights were of no consequence to me, I was panicked. For all of my power, I cannot swim.

Not far away, I could see two flying lifeboats shooting off towards the silver speck. My own impending doom seemed inconsequential, so long as Phineas was safe.

I fumbled through my pockets for the mirror fragments I had picked up in Phoenicia. I didn't know what to expect, but I knew it was my only chance. I concentrated on the mirror, half-willing a Tear and half-expecting to be pulled through the glass. Neither happened.

Visions raced through my mind of deep blue-blackness, of struggling for air and sinking into the abyss. Water, cold, dark, all-encompassing...

I screamed, terrified, though over the sounds of the battle, no one heard me. And then, I scoffed at myself. It was fitting that I should die. Fitting... that no one should come to my rescue as I begged and pleaded for the mercy that I... in my monstrous centuries, had never granted to any of my victims.

Though far from devout, I panicked, crying out all of the names of the Gods that I knew, wondering whether any of them even existed, begging Malkali and Eamos, and especially Inapsupetra… my guardian, my guide.

And then, when I felt that I could scream no more, the rail I held cracked, and I plunged headlong into the dark and forbidding sea below.

The Knight

"She needs no champion. She alone is mistress of her destiny."

Ten

When I regained consciousness, I found myself lying curled up in a round sort of basket bed, dry and warm as I had not been in some time.

The room seemed to be a sort of hospital or dormitory, all white upon white.

Even I myself was dressed in a simple gray smock with several bronze buttons, each in an obnoxiously poking place. Someone had dared take my clothes!

Though I was far from modest, the idea of being unconscious and vulnerable in the presence of humans was not something that appealed to me.

"Morning to ya!" a voice laughed. Unaccustomed to waking up in such a state, I was immediately on my guard.

Which meant, seeing as I was unarmed, that I was standing in a position that probably looked more foolish than threatening, growling through my barred teeth. Had I been a demon, my expression alone would have most likely would have achieved my desired result, but human growling tends to be moderately ineffective.

As I was, I got a good laugh.

"Now that's no way to behave," the voice sighed, clucking, apparently at me. "Girl, you are an absolute positive ship-a-wreck! Literally."

I turned towards the sound, finding myself face to face with a grinning young human woman, perhaps only a few years older than I appeared to be. Her skin was near the color of honey and her many-colored hair was braided and tucked up under some sort of cap. Then, as if to defy all logic, she wore a white robe and a shimmering red jacket with heavy, knee-high black boots.

"Hate the kilt," she admitted, gesturing to her dress. "But it's uniform around here... y'know."

"Where am I?" I wondered, looking around the empty room.

"White Cross HQ. On the isle o' Safehaven. Home to every religious sanctu'ary in the Chaos Realm."

"You don't look like a priestess," I squinted, though I realistically had no right to protest. What I knew about otherworld religions was minimal, limited to whether the priests were male or female, what sort of defenses they had, and whether or not their faith made them prone to martyrdom.

"That's cause I'm not!" She laughed again. "I'm here visitin' my friend Sikara. My name's Terry. Terese Elonwyn Mack. I'm a Chaos Knight."

"A what?" I wondered.

"Kay –oss Niiii hhhttt," she drawled. "Yeah, I know I look young an' I act kinda dopey but I threw around some pretty good stuff before the Imperial Court when I was your age."

"My age?" I muttered under my breath.

"So what's your story?" Terry wondered, slumping down in the nest across from mine.

"If I were to tell you, you'd have me thrown into the sea," I argued.

"Nah… not me. Us Chaos Knights are pretty tolerant folks. But don't you let them monks hear if you're anything other than a human serf, I'll tell ya! They found out that I got some magic in me and right off they was tellin' me I was gonna go to hell."

"Sounds pleasant," I smiled slightly at her exasperated expression.

"Yeah, but it's all in a day's work," she sighed. "I'll tell ya, Friend, sometimes I just wish I never got it in my thick 'ead to come all the way here. There's noplace to even get a decent drink on Safehaven."

"With so many priests, why would there be?" I wondered.

"Holy-ness is overrated," Terry yawned. "This isle's a fairly dull place, when all's said and done. After the suns go out of the sky, everybody goes to sleep or locks im'self up in a library somewhere. Now, when I'm home, I got plenty of stuff to do whenever I just need to kick back, not-includin' tending bar at Mad Mack's… that's my family place. All us Macks are born crazy, y'know… gamblin', parties, fightin'… the works. Guess it comes from some Etone blood way back, if ya know what I mean." She winked. "You know what they say about the Etone."

"I'm afraid you've lost me," I admitted.

"Etone Brotherhood of Raedawn. You oughta know, you must be a real sister," Terry paused, as if she were considering going into detail, and then reverted to her previous line of questioning. "If I tell you about me, you gonna tell me about you?"

"I'm not going to win at this, am I?" I sighed, leaning back in my bed and unbuttoning the sleeves of the gray smock I was wearing. It was at least four sizes too small for me.

"Durn straight you ain't," Terry grinned. "Aw c'mon, It'll be like girl chat... y'know sleepover stuff!"

"Don't you have anyone else to bother?" I muttered, not sure whether I was impressed by her fearlessness or annoyed by her tenacity.

"Now thatcha put it that way... nope. This isle's full of a buncha stuffed-shirts prayin' to stuff that don't exist for things they ain't gonna get anyway," Terry sighed heavily.

"You don't believe in a God?" I wondered, amazed. I was aware of many religions, but I had never encountered an individual who actually professed a complete lack of faith. It was preposterous to imagine. How could the many worlds and races exist if there were not gods to create them?

Terry shook her head. "Well, not exactly. There's lots of folks upstairs all right. Take my Good Old Boys for an example. They're real strong, and they done given me some great things, don't think I'm not thankful, it's just that they ain't Gods, y'know? I never met one bein' I ever thought was really big enough to create the entire universe. No, there ain't no God for me." She sighed. "What about you, hunh? Whose blessed stars are you under?"

"I don't know," I fell silent. My abandonment of the I'Eloshir had been the most unforgivable treason. I had heard that many Traversers became followers of the sun god Arion, choosing to live eternally as humans. Though I feared my demonic side, I did not see it as something I could entirely part with, being none too fond of pain. Yet if not Arion, then who would have me? Certainly not my goddess. I had abandoned her.

"What about that on your arm?" Terry pointed. There was something in her eyes I recognized, a sort of uncomfortable, almost fearful respect.

On my left arm above my two, almost three moons, was a black tattoo of Inapsupetra's mask. No one had mentioned it in so long that I had almost forgotten it was still there.

"It's nothing," I lied, though I remember clearly the day I had accepted that mark. I wore my red robes without sleeves for that specific reason, not so much to show off my bare shoulder, one moon short of an Immortal's rank... but to remind everyone of who it was I served.

"Looks like somebody likes you," Terry grinned.

"Who?" I wondered. Terry pointed to the tattoo again, tracing something evidently only she could see.

"Looks like Inapsupetra if I'm not mistaken. Now she's a doozy. She's got some power, and better than that, she's got the guts to use it. I never met her face-to-face afore, but I like her all right, s'far as I can tell. The Goddess of Chaos."

"How did you know that?" I demanded.

Terese winked. "Seventy-six years. I been around."

"You don't look seventy," I argued. What she looked was human.

"And you don't look a day over twenty," she shot back. "But I'll bet my gold tooth you're at least twice as old as me."

"Much more than that," I admitted, laughing softly.

"How long you guys live anyway?" Terry wondered, searching me with her eyes. "Traversers, I mean. Six hundred years or somethin' wasn't it they said?"

"Few could answer that question," I shook my head. "Some think we never die... unless we're killed."

"Gimme somethin' to gauge it on." She tapped her fingers anxiously. "Say, you look about five and twenty. How old are you?"

"I don't know precisely," I shook my head. "My people count centuries, not years. I was born shortly after the destruction of Raedawn."

"Really?" Terry stared. "And that makes you what?" She countered. "Almost eight-hundred?"

"About," I nodded. "Seven centuries... six or eight decades. I'm not quite sure."

Terry shuddered. "That's just weird. And how come you was covered in feathers when we pulled ya out of the drink, if you ain't got no wings? Ya get tarred and pitched overboard?"

"I don't remember," I sighed, thinking back to the wreck. I remembered falling into the sea and sinking, but nothing after that.

Terry pulled a white feather from her coat pocket. "Yeah, well they's some real nice feathers. Soft, but like steel. Can't figger why they'd dump em' off a ship."

I reached out to touch the white feather in amazement. It was not one of my own. Even after I'd ran away and betrayed the I'Eloshir, someone was still looking out for me.

Perhaps... as Terry had suggested, I still was the "beloved" of Inapsupetra.

In any case, despite my human form, I still carried myself a bit too distinctly to be mistaken for a mere mortal. Terry, apparently knew this, as she evaluated me with a critical eye.

"You seem surprised that I know what you are," she muttered. "Girl, everyone's gonna know what you are."

It was an uncomfortable thought. "Can you help me?" I wondered, but before she had an opportunity to reply, a knock came at the door.

"Open up!" a man's voice demanded from outside. Terry winced.

"I'm just helpin' our rescue-ee get dressed Brother Lacchus," she sang in an almost comical voice.

Terry turned to me. "Now I'm gonna cast a spell on you," she explained. "Even though you look almost human, some wizards and priests especially have a way of smelling... I guess you'd say." Terry whispered. "He don't know you yet and it's better if he don't, y'understand?"

I nodded, a little afraid but more comfortable trusting a fellow Mage than a creature of the "cloth" that I... in my former existence, had only seen fit for food. She clapped her hands very hard, directly in front of my face and blew something silver over my eyes.

The stench was repulsive. Holding my breath, I sank back into the comforters.

The door opened. Terry bowed. "G'day Brother Lacchus." She grinned winningly.

"And good day to you also, Miss Mack." The man who entered the room nodded thoughtfully in her direction. He was moderately tall and thin with shoulder-length blonde hair and an uneasy look about him, as if he were somewhat uncomfortable with his own awkward body. Though I couldn't fathom how or why, I felt that I should recognize the priest.

"Missy my arse... I'm a Knight, Brother," Terry muttered under her breath.

I bristled immediately as "Brother Lacchus" turned in my direction. His robes may have been convincing and his face, decidedly human, but he seemed to radiate an aura of something I recognized all too well. The man was I'Eloshir. He had to be.

"Have we met?" Lacchus inquired, staring at me the same way.

"No," I reply. "Not that I recall," I lied. I knew this stranger... somehow. But I wasn't about to let him get the upper hand.

"Are you well enough to walk?" he asked.

"Well enough," I replied stiffly, fighting the sudden urge I had to growl at the priest.

"We've had your clothes washed," he whispered, a faint tremble in his own voice.

"Thank you," I answered, knowing not what to say.

I followed Brother Lacchus down the white mirrored halls, slowly, watching the murals painted across the ceiling. Some I recognized, the ancient legends of the "Traverser" Gods, the god of Order... Arion, and his eternal enemy, the goddess of chaos... my own Inapsupetra.

Other tapestries told tales of a man who healed the blind, a poor carpenter God who summoned fishermen to him with the power of faith alone. And still more spoke of foreign deities with many arms, heads of animals and even stranger powers.

"Here on Safehaven we support all good faiths," Lacchus explained. "I serve the God Arion. Others are entitled to what they choose. Is there any particular temple you would like to visit to give thanks for your rescue?"

"Not that I can think of," I muttered. Now, at least I knew why the priest had made me so uncomfortable, though that knowledge did little to relieve my paranoia.

"The kitchens are that way," he pointed. "The gardens are down the stairs to the left. Feel free to explore the grounds on your own. I have work to do."

Without further explanation, Brother Lacchus disappeared. I went in search of Terry but she was nowhere to be found. Wandering the paved walkways and museums, I discovered more about the world I had stumbled upon.

The White Cross were indeed the demon hunters that Geruth had warned me about, priests and priestesses of the God Arion.

Despite my attempts to be civil and force my past behind me, I disliked them almost immediately, knowing that it had something to do with their enigmatic leader, the one known as Brother Lacchus.

Fortunately, perhaps, for my conscience, they seemed to find me equally repulsive, as if they sensed that I too, was not what I seemed.

A few short weeks passed as I recovered, more mentally than physically. I bided my time, not willing to wait for Terry's ship to arrive. I gathered my things, intending to journey to a secluded spot I had chosen on the north face of the island, where, if Inapsupetra was willing, I would create a Tear.

Eleven

Night fell, and I went out for my customary prowl around the garden. As much as I had grown to appreciate the beauty of the daylight hours, a small part of me still knew what I was, and still savored the supernatural calm of darkness and moonlight.

I sat down on a park bench and let my thoughts wander. For a moment I was in the tower with Phineas and Galwick, and then I went further back. I remembered my last hunt… the one that had led me home to Geruth's cavern. I smiled slightly, and then took a long draught of sour wine before I went feral.

"This has got to end," I muttered to myself, longing to flee the island so seeped in religion that one hardly knew how to breathe without offending some God or Goddess. Yet I reminded myself that I still had two days left before my plan could be put into action.

And then I heard it, the sound of drums underground. I fell to the grass and listened to the heavy beat… the drums of Magog. The source of the magic grew closer still… as I crawled through the bushes, looking up… only to discover that the pounding that matched my very pulse was indeed coming from the direction I had suspected… ironically enough, from deep beneath Arion's temple.

I knew who was behind it, no doubt, and I knew that I ought to warn the keepers of the isle lest some danger was approaching, but at the same time, the drums drew me in.

Almost unconsciously I pushed a carefully concealed white stone peg in the God's foot and drifted down a flight of dark stairs. The music compelled me… it had been so long!

Something silver rubbed off my face as I descended into the sweaty, smoky pit. I guessed it was the spell that Terry had cast. It did not matter. Nothing

71

mattered to me, save that I find the source of the driving beat.

Kill and ride. Ride and hunt. Hunt and kill. Kill and ride.

Firelight danced off the walls, pulsing in unison with the drums. The bones in my back stretched out again, and I regained my full demonic form.

Inapsupetra had called to me.

I turned the corner and stepped into the yellow glow of the fire. Several young humans, priestly adepts I recognized from the White Cross, played the drums as if under spell, and in the center of the room, beneath the watchful eye of the Chaos Goddess, Brother Lacchus, or rather, Orin Saede prepared the sacrifices.

The pieces of my puzzle had fallen into place at last. My old adversary had somehow, despite his arrogant front… become a "Traverser" as well.

Yet before I could think to stop Orin from killing his victims, he stabbed the first girl, letting her drop to the floor in a pool of blood. The earth rumbled as the statue moved.

I had never known stone to breathe before. Some great power was indeed at work. Frozen at the sight of such a miracle, I gasped in awe.

The drummers stopped playing and even Orin seemed terrified. The Goddess stepped forward and snarled, hurling Orin on his back with a single earsplitting roar. Dodging behind a pillar, I struck a vase in the alcove. The china fell, ever so slowly, and then shattered into a million pieces.

Inapsupetra paused and turned in my direction, no longer fierce.

Orin stared. I could see my own reflection in the blood on the floor. My appearance was stunning in a way that I had not known it could be. The fire in the cave surrounded me in an almost godlike ring of light. "It can't be!" Orin hissed. "Ireval? But you're dead!"

I stepped forward, into the Goddess's shadow, by this time sure I was not the target of her aggression. She laid her hand on my shoulder… tracing the mark of the mask and smiling all the more. I shuddered as a mysterious sensation raced up my back. Inapsupetra bent on one knee, face to face with me, and began to remove her mask.

Orin grabbed the second two of the young girls and began to flee. The Goddess roared again, wheeling to face him… and then froze, stone once more. My state of shock broken, I stole a weapon from the wall and shot after Orin through the underground labyrinth and up the stairs into Arion's temple.

"You let them go," I snarled, pointing the blade of a ceremonial sword at his throat. Orin held one of the humans before him as a shield, whimpering like a coward.

"Let them go," I repeated. "Or so help me Inapsupetra I shall kill you and take your soul."

"We do not kill our own kind," he recited, though he apparently guessed that I would probably gut him anyway.

"You are not my kind," I glared.

Lanterns approached, followed by the pounding of feet and horse's hooves. "Ho…. halt!" Voices muttered amongst themselves in disbelief.

"What is the meaning of this?" an old priest demanded, stepping into the torchlight of the temple.

"IT WAS HER!" Orin ordered, pointing at me.

Startled, I dropped my blade. I had not known he held such power. The temple columns rumbled under the force of his Order… I dared not use my own to defend myself.

Panicked, I did the only thing I could do. I ran past the baffled guards at the door and leapt into the dark sky.

"Things are not over between us," I warned, my muscles aching as I strained to lift myself into the still air. "I will get you one day, Orin Saede. You may lay your life on that!"

"Not so fast!" a woman shouted from below me. Sensing that she was calling for my attention, I turned sharply and glared at her.

Below me stood a white robed human Cleric with a red cape, emblazoned with the insignia of the White Cross. Yet it was her cold eyes that gave no doubt as to what she was. A demon hunter.

"You want a monster, go get your Brother Lacchus!" I growled, pointing a claw at him where he stood, flexing his wings nervously as if he were contemplating whether to fight or fly. "Ask the girls… they know what they saw!"

"And I know what I see. I cannot allow you to leave," the woman replied with a sneer.

"You're welcome to try to stop me!" I pulled away, but something held me back.

"I am Sikara Ruth-Mary, defender of the innocent," she announced. "In the name of the God Arion, I bind you, demon!" A silver chain of energy shot forth from her hands, snapping around my neck.

Another clasped my arm. The dark-haired woman wasn't the only priestess in the garden. Ten other red capes all stared up at me, pulling me down with what felt like freezing metal ropes. I struggled futilely, hissing and snarling, terrified at their incredible strength.

It had taken less than that many to slay a third of my army, but it took all of them to simply hold me.

Still I fought, snapping two or three chains, until at last Orin emerged from the temple in his Lacchus guise, adding his own bit of magic to the trap.

Death was one matter. Deception was another entirely.

The mere thought of the bastard Orin masquerading as a friend to the innocent sacrifices he herded sickened me. We were a proud people, barbaric, but proud nonetheless. No self-respecting predator would put on the skin of a sheep in order to attack the flock. It… was not our way.

I fell from above, bound by the unbreakable chains, the force with which I landed shaking the ground. A few of the more cowardly priests scurried behind the White Cross clerics as I folded my wings and staggered to my feet with one final growl. Beaten, but far from dead, I followed my captors obediently. The clerics lead me to a dank cell in the heart of the main hall, a place that had been a prison before it was converted into a convent. The stench of mold and age was sickening to me, and the chilling draft nearly tore the soul from my body, but I did not struggle. I simply followed the lead of the priests, fighting the thoughts that were welling up in my mind.

There were times when I cursed my vivid imagination.

The door to the cell slammed shut and locked with a magical click.

Despite my exhaustion, it took me quite some time before I even began to fall asleep.

"Hey?" a voice whispered, as I had just begun to close my eyes. "You in there?"

It was Terry. I climbed to my feet as best as I could, though I was shackled to the wall with obviously magical chains.

"Lacchus told them what you are," she whispered, awed. "They're working on a way to kill you, but they don't know nothing about vanquishing big demons," she paused, "the real Ireval. I can't believe it, honestly. My mum… she was a White Cross. She use'ta tell me stories about chasing you to scare the crap outta me when I was little."

I had never even guessed I had been hunted.

"You said it yourself. I'm the spawn of the Chaos Goddess," I shook my head.

"Yeah… but chaos isn't necessarily black," Terry argued, though she was obviously nervous. "The whole world came outta chaos… and it ain't all evil."

"I suppose I've never thought of that before," I admitted.

"There's a first time for every great idea," Terry grinned. "Anyway, I don't think you're really so terrible as they keep on about. Sounds crazy, don't it? I believe you're Ireval all right... there ain't never been another with eyes like the ones you've got... but I don't believe you're all bad."

"Oh believe it," I muttered. "They can't imagine half of what I've done. The best stories have never been heard by mortal ears. I am undeniably evil."

"No you're not," she countered, with a startling sincerity. "I've got an instinct for knowing people, and it's never off. You're confused, and you're troubled... but you're not flat-out-bad," Terry sighed. "As a matter of fact, it's that Lacchus who really creeps me."

"He's fooling them all," I whispered quietly. "He isn't a priest at all... he is I'Eloshir."

"But ... how do you know that?" she wondered.

"I feel," I hissed. "I sense what he is as easily as he recognizes me. His real name is Orin Saede and he is a warrior of Tirs Uloth. On my honor, I swear it."

"I believe you," Terry nodded. It was the last thing I expected to hear.

In the uneasy silence that followed, I could hear the faint creak of a door opening above us.

"Someone's coming," Terry announced, passing a business-card through the bars in a streak of blue light. "If you ever get out of here and make it to Zenith... look me up at this address."

The card was blank.

"Terry, wait!" I shouted, but she had already gone.

Twelve

I shuddered, listening to the sound of footsteps above, so even in tread that I knew they had to be artificial. Only one person I had ever met disguised his approach in such a fashion, and that was my egotistical uncle Elhilom.

He had spent centuries perfecting his thief-tricks, throwing sounds and shadows where there were none, vanishing inexplicably and disguising himself to look like a number of different people, most notably Geruth and on one memorable occasion, The Grandmother herself.

Yet even as I was watching the room, somehow anticipating his approach, I laughed at my foolishness. Elhilom would never leave Magog. He may have been a talented trickster, but he was also a coward.

"Awake, Ire'?" a voice wondered, speaking in the common tongue. To my amazement, a flat shadow of a catlike man, twitching his tail and smoking a cigar, appeared against the far wall.

And as I stared, the shadow gradually became more substantial. The silhouette of the cigar dropped some ash on the ground, and a black-gloved hand reached out of the wall towards me, followed by the rest of the stranger's body, which was suddenly solid.

Whatever I had been expecting to see, it was not who I saw. "Who...," I began.

"I thought you'd never ask," the shadow laughed. And as he stepped into the dim light, his vaguely feline features morphed in such a way that I recognized him before he even completed the change.

I had heard tales of my uncle and his shape-changer's powers, but I had never known that he could pull off such a terrifyingly convincing illusion.

"Elhil?" I was amazed.

Grinning, Elhilom resumed his cat-like form, "In this world, the name's Panther." he explained, twirling a golden set of keys absentmindedly. "I am he and he is I, that is... His honorable Lowliness, Prince of Cutthroats and Thieves... God of the Jailbreak."

"Panther?" I wondered, recognizing the name instantly. Of all the Traversers that the l'Eloshir cursed, his was a name near the top of the list. Apparently, my grandfather and I were not the only traitors in the family. "Elhil, when did this..."

"Geruth may be vicious and powerful but he's not quite as sharp as he thinks he is," Elhilom snickered. "I've been traversing the Chaos Realm for five centuries behind his back and he's yet to suspect what I'm up to."

"Surprising," I muttered, though there was something about his familiar eyes watching out from the strange face that he wore that frightened me considerably. "So what are you 'up to'?" I asked. "What do you want?"

"Amore, Ireval," he sighed. "Love. It's what everyone wants."

"Down to business, Elhilom," I glared, sliding down against the wall, still held by my bonds.

"I have a proposition for you," he explained, grinning maliciously.

"I won't return to Magog," I countered.

"It doesn't require that," he snarled in our language. "Now will you shut your half-mortal trap and listen to me!"

I fell silent, knowing he was quite serious.

"Good," Panther sighed. "It's a business venture... if you will."

"Go on," I nodded obediently, though I desperately wanted to throttle him.

"I need someone to kill a few people for me," he explained casually.

"No," I growled. "Why don't you do it yourself?"

"Because I don't want to get my claws dirty," he shot back. "And furthermore, I have a certain reputation, one that happens to get blown ridiculously out of proportion on a regular basis. Besides, I'm not about to get any more cards pulled with the other Traversers... they can be a tough crowd sometimes, and right now they are looking for a reason to pitch me out of this realm. There's this code they have about no stealing and no killing... and all of this other stuff I can't seem to remember not to do. The Good Etone think I'm picking favorites... The Coven of Darkness thinks they're losing money, and I'm really in no position to start a war with the Brotherhood."

"So I'm a debt-collector?" I shrugged, beginning to understand his dilemma. "I keep a few mortals under your thumb, and in return..."

"I set you free," Panther smiled, "and maybe I show you how to use the mirrors in this backwater plane."

"Fair," I agreed, knowing that anything Panther might expect of me would be nowhere near as terrible as the treatment I would likely receive from the White Cross in the morning. "Let's go."

Grinning at my change of heart, he held up a small shard of glass. "This is how it works. First you concentrate," he explained. "You hold it up to light so that it reflects, and you picture where you want to be. That place has to have a mirror too."

I concentrated, and sure enough, the mirror began to reflect the interior of Galwick's tower. Panther rubbed the palm of his hand over the glass and the scene changed to a dark, somewhat shady-looking establishment, presumably his home.

"Then you jump," Panther pulled the mirror away. "After you swear to me."

"I swear on my honor that I will fight for you… until it suits me to go elsewhere."

"Until it suits me to release you," Panther corrected.

"A mortal year," I shot back. "No longer."

"Three years," Panther pressed, though he apparently guessed I would refuse.

"Two," I finished. "My final offer."

"Taken."

I bit my own palm so that the blood welled up, and Panther did the same, a traditional gesture. We clasped hands, elbow to wrist, and all at once, he uncovered his mirror.

This sensation was eerie. Panther raced like the wind, dragging me in his wake as I gasped for air, wondering why I could neither see nor hear… nor even breathe in this strange space. Then, when I thought I would most certainly die with Elhil's claws in my neck, the terrible journey slowed to a dreamlike stop. We spiraled through unknown depths of space and fell into the dark room in a sudden smash of glass.

"Well, well," Panther grinned. "Here we are–Home."

The Barbarians

"In manners of war, they are beyond mere numbers and without equals."

Thirteen

At first, I was hesitant. Though I did not trust my uncle, I had put a small amount of faith in his intentions. It would not have surprised me in the least if I were to wake up one night only to discover that he'd sold me back to the I'Eloshir, into the hands of the highest bidder. That idea alone was sobering enough to make the death that waited for me at the hands of the White Cross almost appealing. Yet I never saw another demon in Elhilom's company, and he never spoke about Magog, not even in casual conversation.

Still, I hoped that I would not live to regret the bargain I had made.

I had never particularly liked the old Elhilom, but I found that I could tolerate his alias, the Traverser "Panther." We shared a common past, and some sort of bond, though not a particularly strong one. I soon discovered that, while I had come to the Chaos Realm seeking answers of a philosophical kind, Panther was purely a capitalist.

Although simply hearing him admit that we shouldn't have killed so often and so mercilessly helped strengthen my developing conscience, I found that the road ahead of me was still uncertain at best. Never before in all of the illustrious history of the I'Eloshir had any creature succeeded in repressing their barbaric instincts and terrible powers as I myself was attempting to do... not even my grandfather, Arduh himself had been able to remain calm and sane when in immediate physical danger, even after he became a priest of the White Cross. More things could throw us off as well, lust, hunger, and pain. But nothing was as terrible as a true fight. Panther avoided his own battles with the same fear that I felt, even after five centuries of fine-tuning his emotional control.

Sometimes from my place in the ring, I would see Panther's eyes flicker slightly as he rose from his chair, vanishing into his chamber. If he was able to restrain himself, he often returned in a few minutes time, grinning and calling for wine, yet there were frequent occasions when "His Honorable Lowliness" would suddenly take ill and not be seen for weeks.

Only I knew where he hid. Through the sewers, a mournful howl would echo, and in the catacombs, the floor would be spattered with blood.

Fortunately, those few years that I served my uncle soon passed, and I quickly became accustomed to the rigors of fighting for the entertainment of the idle rich. For the most part, I did very little, but whenever a new warrior grew particularly arrogant, the doors in the center of the pit would open, I would "theatrically" rise from the depths of Magog... smash a couple mirrors and impress the paying customers by pretending to be "The Ireval."

To them, it was quite the beautiful show, but nothing more. If only they knew.

It became so that I could no longer count the number of times I woke underground, surrounded by clerics and chained to walls. In a perverse way, it was those hours of torment that reminded me ... just how serious the game we played was.

"You have made me quite a rich cat... you do know that, Ire'," Panther commented, on the last night before our contract was up. It had been a flawless performance. "I think I will buy a Spellcraft, eh?" he mused, sipping his ambrosia.

"Why?" I wondered. As far as I knew, Panther hadn't legally purchased anything he owned in all of his thousands of years.

"To have one," he admitted.

"Why not steal one?" I asked. "You've stolen or gambled for everything else you've ever wanted."

"True," Panther nodded. "But I want a nice one," he complained... with a terribly over-dramatic sigh.

"Then steal a nice one," I muttered, turning to walk away.

I stopped short, suddenly realizing what had sparked our conversation.

Sitting on the ground in the repair yard across the street from our place of residence, an inn called "Lady Mercy's" was a ship that I almost recognized. It appeared at first glance to be a copy of The Dogma, only a smaller, faster model.

I had seen dozens of Spellcraft since the day I arrived in Chaos Realm, but not one that was so flawlessly made. The red sails and green and gold accents of the glass windows, combined with the dark wood of the ship's body and the shimmering white and chrome of its engines painted a picture that was almost painful to look at, an absolutely beautiful ship, remarkable in every way.

I smiled. "Should we, Elhil?" I asked, knowing well enough what my uncle was about to suggest.

Panther shrugged, grinning... and fished a set of wire cutters out of his belt pouch.

"How can we not?"

Fifteen minutes later we were cruising through the skies at nearly seventy miles per hour... on the ship, which the previous owner had dubbed The Cadillac.

"Needs a better name," Panther mused, as we landed in a copse of trees on a tiny desert island. "Something from this book, perhaps."

After hearing the tale of how Galwick had dubbed me "Artemis Ravencroft," he had become obsessed with the subject of mythology, determined to choose yet another title for himself.

"What sort of a creature is the face on the figurehead?" I wondered, examining the white and gold carving with its green-glass eyes.

Panther shrugged. "I believe it is supposed to be a dragon, but in my 'humble opinion'." He coughed on purpose, presumably to draw my attention. "In my opinion.....," Panther repeated, a little louder. "It more closely resembles a cow. What do you think? Doesn't it?"

"A cow?" I stared, running my hand along the smooth, curved horns. He was right.

Panther leafed through another of the books we had found in the cabin of the ship. "There!" He pointed.

I squinted at the page. It was a picture of a white cow in a field of reeds, a golden disk balanced on its head.

"A cow?" I wondered, not sure that I was seeing whatever it was that Panther saw.

"A cow, is it?" I mumbled, attempting to read the passage below the drawing. The concept was so ridiculous it did beg repeating.

Panther slapped me hard in the back of the head. "Not just a cow, stupid. An immortal cow! The goddess of all cows... The Legendary Hathor!"

"The Hathor?" I mused. The more one repeated it, the better it began to sound.

Fourteen

And that was how The Legendary Hathor came into being. If nothing else, I have always been proud of my ship. Perhaps I no longer believed in senseless killing, but a new treasure… and especially a theft as artful and painless as the crime we committed that day, gave me a little of the rush my life was lacking.

In a way, the many events that followed led me to believe I was meant to have the craft.

Sometime later, after making sure we had not been followed, we took off again, hovering to a stop over the shimmering white-sand beaches of Ranlain, watching the twin suns set in a flare of color.

It was a moment that seemed to lend itself to the discussion of the past, which was something I had seldom dared to ask my uncle about.

"Do you ever miss traveling with the I'Eloshir?" I wondered, attempting to spark a conversation.

Panther had fled Tirs Uloth shortly before I had, the very same night I was summoned by Phineas. It was largely thanks to his customary carelessness that I had been fortunate enough to discover the hidden mirror at all.

"Never," Panther sighed, pouring himself another drink. "Magog's a dump. This place… now this is a world worth exploiting."

"It is," I agreed, watching the moons rise. "Our world was like this once. What did we do?"

"We did nothing," Panther muttered. "It was the human's fault."

"Oh, come now!" I groaned. "Surely you don't believe that they could have possibly been responsible for everything. We have a great deal of sins to atone for, uncle. You've said so yourself."

He did not respond.

"Is there something the matter?" I wondered, sensing immediately that I had touched on a sore issue.

"I'm going back," Panther dumped the bottle he drank from on the deck, sighing dejectedly. I had expected that it should be filled with ambrosia, or at very least, sickening expensive wine, but all that poured out was some water with a few pieces of ice in it and a faint brownish tint.

Something was seriously wrong.

I was startled, not only because my uncle was actually carrying around a bottle of water, but because he had just announced that he planned to return to Magog. I could scarcely believe my ears.

"Why?" I demanded.

"Ashes if I know," Panther admitted. "I always leave, always for the last time... and then I always return. I guess I'm a glutton for punishment. Perhaps they'll brand me again for cowardice. Three times earns an extra fifty lashes." He paused, wincing at the thought, and then suddenly brightened. "You want this ship?" he wondered.

"But I thought you said that you hated Magog," I began... somewhat awkwardly. "And you've made yourself a fortune. We've just stolen this Spellcraft. You've got everything you've ever wanted here!"

"One last fling, Ire'." He closed his eyes.

"What is it, Elhilom?" I pressed.

Panther would not respond, not even to his given name. Whatever was troubling him was serious indeed

"I'll tell you what," He grinned, suddenly brightening. "You play me for The Hathor."

"A gamble?" I wondered, suspecting that there would be either cards or dice involved.

"What else?" Panther drew a deck from his belt. "One game. I win, you do me a favor... you win, I give you something. We'll start with the Spellcraft for the bet."

"So what is this favor?" I asked. "You seem to be fond of the high stakes this evening, Uncle."

Panther shook his head. "You better hope you're lucky. There's a girl up north I'm supposed to marry."

"Marriage?" I laughed. "You are quite possibly the last man in any world that I thought would fall into that trap. Blessings to you and your unfortunate betrothed!"

"Ireval, you're missing the point!" he muttered, avoiding my eyes. "I cannot go through with it."

"Why not?" I wondered. "It isn't as if you couldn't still have some other women."

"Believe me, I couldn't! My... wife-to-be... her father's one of the Immortals who survived Raedawn," Panther sighed. "And she's as smart as he is... which is even more terrible. She would figure out in a day that I was leading a double life and then she'd have my wings clipped so that I couldn't leave her sight. Brandings are nothing... she would have me gone so long from Magog that if I returned, Geruth would have me beheaded."

"So?" I sighed. The look on his face said it all. I would have guessed that he'd fallen in love again, even if I didn't know of his terrible weakness for women.

"Fair enough," I agreed. "Deal."

He laid out the cards.

I glanced at my hand, knowing it was impossibly good, and Panther dropped his, suspecting he had me beaten anyway. Remarkably, we'd both been dealt the exact same cards.

"Elhil...," I began. "There is something suspicious about this."

"This deck had a habit of doing that," Panther muttered. "It looks to me like you take the ship and do my favor."

"Where does this Goddess of yours live?" I asked, grinning slightly.

Panther did not even look up. "Coast of Accoloth. Around the Gelthar area," he mumbled.

"She isn't a... dragon, is she?" I wondered.

"You'll wish she was," Panther laughed suddenly. "Her name's Ejora. She's the 'Goddess' of the Barbarian Hordes."

"A Barbarian?" I glared at him skeptically. "How did you end up engaged to a Barbarian?"

"Lost a bet," he admitted. "Actually, I won the bet, but then her father found out I cheated and he..." Panther winced at the memory. "It wasn't something I'm fond of remembering."

"I'm sure," I agreed. "Who is the father-in-law anyway?"

"His name's Ordo Iekuh, but I wouldn't mention his clan to his face." Panther shrugged. "These days they call him the Storm-Bringer. I've never met a Traverser of his like."

"I believe you," I nodded respectfully.

Panther stood up and stretched, placing a mirror on the floor. "Anything in particular you want me to fetch for you while I'm in hell?" he asked.

"My black sword, some good ambrosia, and those bracers I used to have if you can find them," I sighed. "But Elhil...," I argued feebly. "Are you sure you..."

He did not give me the opportunity to finish my sentence.

"See you in a few years," Panther winked. In a shattering of glass he was gone, and I was alone, on my way north... to Accoloth.

Fifteen

The continent of Accoloth was, at one point the most powerful country in the Chaos Realm, before the Ardran court visited and sunk half the civilization into the ocean over dinner, royally angering the locals, who in turn summoned the dragons and set fire to the four of them, jewelry and all. History had been a favorite subject of the wizard Galwick, and compared to the dark and largely forgotten past of Magog, the legends of the Chaos Realm were interesting to me too.

I had begun, incidentally, to compile a guidebook for new Traversers at about the time that Panther and I stole The Hathor... and aboard that ship I found more than enough manuscripts to satisfy my curiosity on the fifteen-hour trek north.

Perhaps on that very journey was the first time I ever heard mention of a certain book, the pursuit of which would become a substantial part of my life's work. The Archives of Teyme.

The strange artifact was created by one of the few humans who had escaped the long-ago destruction of Raedawn, a man known as Teyme. Legend had it that he was a powerful mage, if somewhat insane. The Archives he left to his apprentice, "The Architect"... as a sort of dying joke.

And what a joke it was.

On the surface, The Archives of Teyme appeared to be an ordinary book, except for one small... almost inconsequential little enchantment. Far beyond the known dimensions, in the remains of the ivory city of Raedawn, atop the highest tower of the temple, and only with a very specific pen, one of royal blood could write in that book words... words capable of altering the very fabric of time itself.

I did not know what I would do with such a power, I only guessed, in a childish way, that it would be something I would very much like to have.

The hours passed quickly, and before I realized exactly how long I had been reading for, the ship stopped entirely, alighting on a cliff-face above the green, rocky shores of the kingdom of the dragons.

I dug through the closets on board and finally came to the conclusion that whoever had sailed The Hathor before we had relieved them of it was no one important enough to have anything of interest.

Golden plates and portraits of some man with unnatural hair... and many oversized over-glittered white suits and capes filled every available space. I threw all of it overboard and set about renovating, which simply meant knocking out quite a few walls, unnecessary pieces of furniture, and any ceilings that were low enough to be bothersome.

Digging through a strange, built in cabinet, I found something quite fascinating, a sort of stationary Tear that evidently had been used as storage space. Hours passed and I failed to reach the bottom of the drawer, pulling out all manner of strange things, until finally I decided it would be safer to keep the cabinet closed until I managed to figure out exactly where the Tear ended.

"Well, Master Elvis," I mused to myself, gazing up at the one portrait I had decided to leave on the wall. "I must say, I am enjoying your ship."

I took a sip of ambrosia and surveyed my reflection in the full-length mirror. Presentable... maybe regal? I could pull off a very convincing spokesperson for my poor uncle, I decided, opening the door and emerging out onto the deck.

A small crowd had already gathered on the cliffs. It was a group of dirty-brown dwarfish humans, who were attired in leather smocks and armor. All the inhabitants of the village had apparently dropped their work simply to be the first in line to witness my spectacular arrival. Accompanying the craftsmen were their wives and children, as well as several soldiers, who stood wielding their axes and clubs impatiently as they watched my ship. True to form, a flock of immense, golden-skinned dragons soared lazily overhead, taking no notice of anything below them.

In the distance, a tall, cold mountain stood, its spire surrounded by lightning.

The crowd parted as an old, bent warrior came forward, adjusting his eye patch.

"State your business!" he demanded, his axe a few inches away from my chin.

"I come to speak with the Gods of that mountain, on behalf of the one they call Panther," I announced, stepping off the deck of The Hathor. The gathered backed up several paces with a collective gasp. I was not sure whether their hesitation was thanks to the deeds of my uncle... or of my own strange appearance. Both fears were justified. Afraid to spark any sort of conflict, I said nothing.

After a long pause, an equally decrepit shaman stepped forward and pointed with his crow-skull staff to the strange mountain in the distance.

"You are in luck then. Tonight is a great feast in the Hall of Gelthar."

Without further questioning I found myself thrown headlong into the business of loading carts with food, bolts of coarse fabric and fine-crafted weaponry. Not long after the final preparations were made, we set off along the narrow stone-paved road, passing through the town and into the heart of the thunderstorm.

The shaman and leader of the party was a demon of sorts... a half-mortal beast known as Belgaor, an old friend and sometimes foe that I had known in my days as Ireval. The near-hundred years since we parted company had changed us so that even Belgaor did not recognize me, nor did I know him at first.

It amused me to see that, despite his history, even Bel the Dragon-Killer seemed content enough with his duties as a crackpot "witch-doctor." The trek continued as we marched past... and kept our distance from, the caves of several particularly ferocious dragons, and across a bridge that seemed to be built entirely out of bones.

The sky was gray by the time we reached the point where the stone road met the great gates of the mountain hall, the north face of the cliff carved as far up and as far down as I could see in the shape of an immense tree. Two burly guards barred their spears in front of us.

"Who dares to enter the Hall of the Heroes of Gelthar?" they demanded in one voice.

"I am Belgaor, Protector of the Barbarian Horde, and these are my people. We bring gifts for the Storm-God and the Mountain-Goddess," Bel answered.

"Proceed," the first of the guards growled.

The men marched beneath their spears. Quietly, I attempted to join in near the end of the parade.

"Halt!" the guards shouted, slamming the doors shut before me. "Who are you?"

"I am Artemis Ravencroft," I replied.

"You say that name as if we should recognize it," The first sneered. "Are you god or mortal?"

"Neither," I snapped back, deciding immediately that I did not like his tone.

"We cannot allow you to enter," The second guard frowned. "We do not know you, and you have not brought a sacrifice."

"A sacrifice? Why should I have brought a sacrifice?" I glared. "Your gods are simply Traversers, are they not? Who are they to be taking sacrifices... when they are no more divine than I myself?"

"Let her pass!" a great voice roared from behind the closed doors.

The gate that it had taken four large men to move blew open with unnatural force and I suddenly found myself eye to belt with a giant of a man whose sheer bulk filled the entire cavern door. The energy surrounding him was unmistakably familiar, the scent of a Traverser... though by physical appearance alone I would have called him human. At his side he carried an immense, dangerous-looking war hammer, but his smile was unmistakable.

"I am Ordo the Storm-Bringer, Lord of Gelthar. Your name speaks well of you, Lady Ravencroft. Welcome to my kingdom."

Hours of drinking and merriment passed in the magnificent mountain palace. Ordo introduced his wife, Jedera, and his daughter Ejora, Panther's betrothed.

Ejora was easily the ugliest creature I had ever seen, but her heart was good... which was more than I could say for myself, despite my looks. She was a woman of few words, but when she spoke, it seemed as though everyone listened. Always Ejora was heard, without ever raising her voice. I wished enviously that I had learned to do the same, to command respect without having to force my magic upon the weak-willed.

I could understand why Elhilom wouldn't marry her as well. Ejora would certainly tie him down... but worse still, she would restrain him in such a way that he would have had no desire to leave, to steal or travel. He would be provided anything and everything he desired. It was simply waiting within Ordo's mountain for him to claim.

The end of his unending immortal conquest. The coward had fled from his last great prize. That didn't surprise me in the least. I suspected once he worked up his nerve... in a few years, he'd be back for a visit.

But then, after the Storm-Bringer finished his tales of the old days when he, Jedera, Teyme, a man they called "The Prophet" and my ever-elusive grandfather Ardain had wrecked havoc on the realm, the question I had feared came.

"So what brings you to us?" Jedera asked.

I hesitated, suddenly realizing that I hadn't told them anything.

"I am afraid it is not good news," I admitted. "My Uncle has returned home. He sent me to tell you that he can't marry your daughter."

The look on Ejora's face was one of complete and utter desolation.

"I'm sorry," I replied. "But I can do nothing on the matter."

Jedera took Ejora in her arms and the two of them left the room. Ordo stared at me gravely... and I began to feel terrible.

"Damnit, Elhil!" I cursed.

"This is ill news indeed," Ordo muttered. "Did he give you a reason?"

I nodded solemnly. "He did not simply say it, but my guess is that he fears his brother."

"And who is your father?"

A familiar sensation raced down my spine, and I felt instantly cold.

"A name I dare not speak," I replied quickly, with some degree of hesitation. No response was necessary. I almost blurted out the truth, though from the pale that had crept across the Lord's face, I guessed that he already knew.

"It is no mere coincidence that the Demon Queen no longer rides... now that there is a new Ravencroft in the Chaos Realm, is it?" he whispered.

I shook my head, overwhelmed by an uncomfortable silence. A strange coldness weighed heavily upon me as I waited before Ordo, completely still and biting my lip until I could taste my own blood. And still, he stared.

"I do not know whether it is an honor or a misfortune to meet you," Ordo stood.

Yet it was Jedera who spoke, standing slowly and stepping towards me, her blue-velvet gown rippling down the stairs like water.

"As you know, the barbarians who live here in Gelthar and in the forests and mountains that surround us are no strangers to darkness. They are exceptional warriors, all of them, and they have both fought against the I'Eloshir and served them. But in the end, they choose peace over violence."

I could not respond.

We faced each other for a long while until finally Ordo broke the silence.

"I have a plan," he explained. "If you wish to see your Uncle out of his current dilemma as much as I would like to see him married to my daughter, perhaps you can help me."

He opened a dark wood case near his throne and produced an instrument so delicate I almost feared he would he would break it between his two fingers.

It was not so small as it had seemed when he brought it down for my view.

"Across the sea to the south on the Island of Lethos there lives an old enemy of mine, the Goddess Beyoni. She has a servant, a man who goes by the name of Ruveus of Accoloth. Ruveus is the only living soul in the Chaos Realm who can play this mandolin... and the magic of this instrument is so potent it can even cause gods to fall in love. All you need to do is give it to him and ask him to play... within a mile of your Elhilom. Once your uncle hears the music he will come running back to me... and I shall handle the rest."

"I will," I replied, and almost immediately hit myself.

Another quest... another favor? Was I ever going to reach the Imperial City?

Sixteen

After a short night's sleep I made my way down the mountain and back to my ship with a good deal of provisions from the barbarians, not to mention some fine new clothes woven of a lightweight and virtually indestructible fabric made by Ejora.

I thanked all my new friends and set a course south to the Island of Lethos.

Before I reached the coast that night, I could already hear music playing. From the sandy shores of the beach into the deep green forest, skull totems and animal skins lead the way to a plantation house high on the hill. Rivers of lava ran through the never-ending party, and the dancers simply leapt over them, as if the idea of being burned or killed was thoroughly ridiculous.

Bird-faced demons, young red dragons and flower-bedecked human natives seemed to make up the population of Lethos Island. Though I was an obvious newcomer, few of them paid me any mind, seemingly unfazed by presence.

"Hey, I'll buy you a drink!" A man with a crown of pink flowers and a woman on each arm waved to me.

I smiled... perhaps a little maliciously and he scattered into the crowd without another word. I found myself almost wondering if in all the Chaos Realm, no Traverser had ever given a thought to doing anything other than celebrating.

Reaching the door of the manor, I stopped for a moment. There was a power inside that I sensed I should avoid. I very nearly turned away from the door, but then I reached across my back to where I would have worn a sword and remembered that, although it had been a long while since I had possessed a good blade, I still carried a dagger at my side. Perhaps more fortunately still, my greatest weapon was one that no opponent, no matter how powerful, could ever completely disarm. Calling up a small flicker of flame to my fingertips, I took comfort in its purple glow and stepped up to the door.

I sighed, wondering when I had suddenly developed such an acute sense of paranoia, and reached for the knocker.

Yet before I had knocked even once, the door was flung open by a large gorilla-like human dressed entirely in black. He ushered me in, slammed the door, bolted it, and disappeared.

"Hello?" I wondered. As loud as the island was, the Goddess's house was oddly silent.

I walked into the living room, which was full of old furniture buried under a collection of dusty red sheets. A glittering red velvet couch sat uncovered in the center of the room, apparently one that was recently occupied.

But nothing moved. The room was entirely devoid of life.

"Why hello, chyl'," a voice laughed.

I turned in shock, feeling a sudden warmth behind me. A short, rather matronly woman in scarlet silks, gold and furs smiled. She was almost dark enough to blend into the shadows completely, except for her glowing orange eyes and sparkling white smile.

"Have a seat." She pointed, and the couch skittered up behind me, its clawed feet racing across the floor as if it had a mind of its own. Accustomed to such odd furniture, spending so much of my time with wizards, I sat without question.

"Now whatchu here for?" Beyoni grinned. "You got to have come for somethin'?"

I did not have a plan, I realized quite suddenly. I actually couldn't fathom why I'd even been admitted to the house. I'd given no explanation to any of the guests or even to the butler, who I could glimpse unmoving in the darkness of the hall. Finally, I settled on the truth.

"I was sent to look for a man named Ruveus," I admitted. "I have heard that he works for you."

"In a manna of speaking," Beyoni snickered.

"I need him," I demanded.

"We all need somebody, chyl'." She grinned.

"It isn't like that," I sighed. "I've never even met him... will you trust me on this?"

"Fair." Beyoni nodded. "So... whatchu gonna give me if I give you, Ruvi'?"

"My services," I offered. At one point I might have bribed her with gold and gems, I remembered, or even slaves... but I was poor and insignificant now, no longer the noble I had been. Though I had legally won The Hathor, I did not see the ship as something I could part with, and I honestly had nothing else.

"Services from a lone woman with a nice Spellcraft," Beyoni considered.

"My Spellcraft? How did you...," I began.

"Oh, my people tell me when you arrive." She shrugged, nonchalant. "They say you come from Gelthar, and that you fly a good ship, but they know nothing of your position or powah. What exactly can you do?"

"There's very little I can't," I admitted. "I have no rank to speak of, but I have ways of influencing people. Simply name your price, and I shall consider."

"Consider?" Beyoni frowned. "No... you donna consider. You donna ask no questions! You do!"

"Will you listen...," I began, sensing that I was quickly losing the argument. But what terrified me more was that I felt something else in the room as well, a certain energy that to me was like a drug. I knew instinctively that I had to get out of the house. I had to leave, and quickly, or there would be hell to pay... in a literal sense. "I am trying to bargain," I hissed between my clenched teeth.

"Cheeky little mortal! I am a Goddess!" Beyoni snarled, slapping me across the face. "I donna make bargains, I give orders!"

I snapped. The moment her hand struck my face, I felt all the warmth drain from my body. Whatever sense of diplomacy I had possessed departed immediately... and I knew what I had feared. There were spirits in the house... wandering souls that I could very nearly grasp. I could see them hovering above Beyoni's head, gazing at me solemnly from a distance as if they knew what I was. They knew I could tear them apart, though they were insubstantial, and what was more, they knew that I wanted to.

My bones cracked and reformed as I grew taller once again, stronger and inhuman. The wings came first, followed by the change in my face. I pulled my unruly hair out of my eyes, running my claws across the back of my skull, grinning in satisfaction as I looked down at her, smelling her faint breath and hearing the furious pounding of her very mortal heartbeat. Despite her grand illusions, she was most certainly not a deity. I could feel her sense of inadequacy as she stood in my shadow, staring up at the even darker curtain of my black-feathered wings.

"What...," Beyoni stared. "What are you?"

"I am Ireval!" I roared, realizing too late that I had used my true name. "I do not take orders. I consider them!"

Then, my conscience returned. My body I recognized... my telltale wings and sharpened senses. Arrogantly, I grinned, knowing that the "Goddess" who stood before me would break like a handful of twigs in my grasp. Then... the guilt hit.

"The Ireval!" Beyoni's eyes lit up. "You exist?"

"If you must know, yes," I muttered, shifting down to human form, ashamed that I had lost control so easily. "I have been called by that name."

"My–my–my–my–my!" Beyoni clapped softly. "First a dragon prince now the Demon Queen."

"You sound like you're making a collection," I glared.

"Oh I am," Beyoni grinned. "Avoon Baiah!" she screeched, causing magma to shoot up from every red sheet in the room.

Though I am powerful in my own right, I had never even imagined such incredible sorcery. Even had I been my demonic self, I was sure the spells would have frightened me.

I tried to jump out of the way, wherever instinct led, but I was already trapped within Beyoni's deadly circle. The room became immense around me, and before I had fully come to grips with what had happened, the Goddess picked me up in one hand, and threw me into her jewelry box... turning the key with a click.

I was small.

At first I could see nothing but the man-sized pearls I had been tossed on top of, but then I climbed down onto the red velvet floor. Wandering for a few moments in the darkness between large gems and tiny scattered bones, I finally caught sight of a small fire burning in what appeared to be the interior of a gold snuff-box.

"Hello?" I wondered. "Hello?"

A shadow near the fire jumped. "Wha' the hell!" a man's voice demanded.

"A friend," I reassured him, though I couldn't safely make out the shape of the person I had startled. It seemed to be changing somehow.

Yet as I approached I began to make out more of his figure. He was of average height and moderately well-built with strangely fine features and long, near-gold hair. He wore a pair of small green glasses on the tip of his nose... as well as a slew of multicolored beads and a heavy leather jacket.

The man held out his hand to me.

"Hey babe. I'm Ruveus. Current lord of the box. Welcome to the Prison of Lethos."

"Ruveus, is it?" I asked.

He nodded.

"I was sent to look for you." I admitted. "By Lord Ordo of Gelthar."

"Really?" Ruveus grinned. "I knew that dude would forgive me… someday. He got quite a catch in Jedera, even if I did magic the two of em' together. Ordo gave you my mandolin, right?"

I nodded, producing the instrument from its case that had been slung across my back and handing it to him. He plucked a string, and the note that echoed throughout the velvet walls was perfectly remarkable.

"Mmmm…," he sighed. "How sweet it is. By the way…"

I turned.

"D'you know how we might get out of the collection… Miss?" Ruveus wondered.

"Artemis Ravencroft," I supplied. "Honestly, I don't know how I got in here in the first place. I'm fairly difficult to catch."

"So am I," Ruveus laughed. "From what I hear, the Mistress likes a challenge. She seems partial to catchin' people she thinks might kill her if they escape. I'm serious, babe."

"Delightful hobby," I sighed, but then caught my eye on something that glimmered around Ruveus's neck. "You wouldn't happen to have a mirror, would you?" I asked, knowing already that I'd found a way out for the both of us.

"This piece of crap?" He laughed and handed it to me. "Yeah… I just use it for when I put on human face. So I don't screw up, y'know. Walk around lookin' like a friggin Frankenstein."

I took the small glass and held it up to the firelight, my hand shaking.

"What's up with you?" he demanded, glancing over my shoulder.

"Take my hand," I ordered, concentrating intently. "I can make this work!"

"Hey hold up!" Ruveus stared. "You're a Traverser? For real?"

"Is that really so extraordinary?" I eyed him suspiciously and then shook my head.

In the mirror, I could see the interior of The Hathor forming, and something else as well, a reddish-gold shadow. I didn't care what it was. I jumped. Pulling Ruveus after me, I soared across the purplish space between the mirrors, amazed at how much easier it was to do the "Traversing" and not be dragged as Panther had to me.

The glass of the tall mirror shattered and then strangely melted back into place.

Ruveus choked and fell to the floor. I twitched, overcome by the rush, and Beyoni fainted, clutching her heart.

"Man… I think we killed her," Ruveus mused, staggering.

Weakly, Beyoni clawed at the rug near my feet as she regained consciousness, slowly looking up until her eyes met my face. Hysterical she screamed, jumped to her feet and raced up the stairs. There was a heavy slam, followed by a large splash and the sound of furious paddling.

"She swimmin' to shore?" Ruveus grinned. "Think she might sink with all that clothes she's got on?"

"Good riddance," I shrugged. "Though I would like to…," I trailed off into silence, clenching my fists and biting deeply into my lip.

Reading my expression, Ruveus laughed softly. "Spose' we ought to let her have a fighting chance, eh?"

Once the Beyoni was on her way back to her isle, I set my sights toward Zenith once again. Three calm days passed, and then finally, at long last, the dream of the silver speck that had kept me moving through so many disasters was finally real.

At dawn on the third day, we approached the most remarkable city I had ever seen. The green rolling fields stopped abruptly at the perimeter wall of a never ending expanse of tall glass buildings, castles, white bridges and hovering Spellcraft. Far off in the distance… a great palace floated above the open sea, and beyond that, the world simply cut off into space.

Three pale moons shone faintly in the sunrise as the twin suns rose in a glorious display of light. Pink and gold clouds rolled through the sky with supernatural speed, nearly touching the clear blue waves of the sea, yet never in the same place for more than an instant. Altogether, it was a spectacle to be remembered and a once in a lifetime experience, it was an orchestra of all the glory and beauty in the universe.

"It's just the edge of the world," Ruveus grinned. "Looks like this every morning. You're starin' like you never seen it before."

"I haven't," I stared, aware that my jaw was still dropped at the sheer majesty of the scene.

"Wild." He laughed. "This must be your lucky day."

Seventeen

We approached the harbor, flying slowly between a dazzling array of towering wooden docks stacked one atop of another. They were painted in a variety of colors that gave the entire port the general appearance of a rainbow made solid, constantly raising, lowering and rearranging themselves.

A lighthouse stood on the cliff-face of a small island below us, the white tower spinning on its own accord, the green crystal atop its spire flickering in the sunlight.

"Identify yourself," an almost-artificial voice demanded, as we approached a high-level red landing pier.

"It's me, dude. Number four-thirty two," Ruveus interrupted before I had a chance to speak. I had not even realized the voice was coming from a small radio aboard our ship. "Open the gates, Phil."

"Permission granted," the voice sounded considerably more enthusiastic. "Enjoy your stay, Prince Ruveus."

There was the word "Prince" again. I had a hard time picturing the under-dressed musically-inclined wanderer I had "rescued" from Beyoni's jewelry box as a dragon prince, but I said nothing. Our arrival seemed almost unnoticed, except by a few workers unloading oranges on the level below us. Ruveus waved cheerfully to them and they returned the gesture without any sort of formality. We continued down the boardwalks of the aerial marina and into the city.

I fished through my things for the business card Terry had given me when I was imprisoned on Safehaven. The words had a habit of changing, disappearing and reappearing at random. I could only hope that the card actually read something useful now that I needed it.

"Mad Mack's Magic Users: Fine drinks, fine women, fine weapons. 46135 E. Gandalf, West Quarter, Zenith 10430 Ranlain, The Chaos Realm. 000.

Owners and profiteers: T. Mack and P. Merlin."

Phineas? I wondered. It had to be coincidence. Though I could not remember precisely when, I could've sworn the card had said "M. Joseh" at some point.

"Have you ever heard of this place?" I asked, handing over the business card to Ruveus. Ruveus grinned.

"Tch…yeah! Who hasn't?" He laughed. "It's only the most famous bar in any dimension, past, present or future!"

"A friend told me to meet her there," I admitted.

"Well what are we waiting for!" Ruveus whistled. "I could use a drink. Taxi!"

In an instant, a screeching yellow monstrosity that it took me a moment to recognize as a car… screeched up to where we stood on the curb. Following its abrupt stop, both doors fell off, and a cloud of strange-smelling smoke suddenly overwhelmed the street. The driver turned down her music and glanced at us, seeming disinterested.

She was vaguely demonic in appearance, except for her red plastic "horns" and her long, blonde hair that seemed to be styled in the most ridiculously impractical buns possible. The expression on her face was somewhat troubling. I couldn't place precisely how old she was, or even whether she was human or not, but I somehow sensed that this woman was at least moderately dangerous.

"Hey Ruuuveeeusss!" she grinned, swinging out of the driver's seat with a practiced flair. The clothes she wore bordered on ridiculous, red and black vinyl with little metal spikes and massive, impractical holes in awkward places. "Long time no see, baby!"

"Lucy!" Ruveus grinned. "What are the odds?"

Yet the woman was not alone in the cab. Noticing Ruveus, the front seat passenger unbuckled his seat belt and climbed out to fetch the battered yellow door. Looking somewhat out of place in broad daylight, he wore white makeup, a leather bodice, and tight breeches with flames embroidered on them. Furthermore, the second occupant of the cab carried a different unnerving aura about him that I had learned to recognize as the trademark of a wizard.

"If it isn't my sweet and scaly baby boy!" He laughed, nearly choking Ruveus in a tremendous bear-hug.

"Master Jeo!" Ruveus gasped for breath. "You're breaking my ribs."

"Weakling," the one called Jeo clucked in mock disapproval, and then caught sight of me, standing slightly aloof. "Who's the chica?" Jeo wondered.

"She your new lady?"

"If she's his girlfriend then I'm a saint," the driver muttered, opening up the trunk of her taxi and shoving both doors into it. They fit, but only barely, and with a heavy metallic crunch.

Yet no sooner had she closed the trunk than time itself seemed to pause. A bird in mid-flight hovered mere inches from a speeding car... which had also stopped inexplicably. I lifted the creature a few feet higher, placing it again in thin air, awed by the strange magic, and then turned to the cab driver, who was smiling, as if she alone controlled the silent plane.

"I may be one of the few great unholy ones, but you, m'dear, are a living legend." Lucy sighed and reached to shake my hand. "Well met, Ireval."

Jeo and Ruveus seemed unfazed, frozen as if they hadn't even heard her speak my name.

"It's a talent," she whispered. "Kinda like post-hypnotic suggestion." Dancing backwards to the point where she had stood when the city froze, Lucy snapped her fingers.

The real world blared to life in an instant, and I pulled away in shock. "How did you know?"

Though they were obviously blissfully oblivious, Jeo and Ruveus linked arms... and then Jeo began to sing, softly at first, growing louder and bawdier as Ruveus joined in at the chorus.

"She sees with whom you're sleepin,' she knows when you're awake... she knows if you've been bad or good, so be bad for goodness sake! Cause Lucifer's a runnin' this tooowwwnn!"

"Is this getting somewhere that I'm not aware of?" I asked.

Ruveus smiled. "The devil is like Santa Claus. She knows where everyone's at."

"Wonderful," I sighed, climbing into the back seat of the taxi. As I had suspected, I had encountered another Traverser... and she had a fan club.

Lucy hit the gas. I flew forward into the window, pulled myself back, snapped on my seatbelt and then... we were there.

Soft music drifted out the open doors as Ruveus and I stood on the curb, facing a somewhat unimpressive brick building, standing in the smoke of the tires of the yellow cab. Over the street-facing window were large gold letters painted on the brick reading "Mad Mack's Magic Users."

Approaching the bar, a smaller, whiteboard sign inside the glass proclaimed "No duels after two on Sundays. Check weapons at the door. Etone welcome."

We went inside.

The bells on the door chimed and I surveyed the place. To the left, an open door marked "Pool room" led off into a maze of video games and card tables. To the right, along the window, was a row of booths. The brick façade that made up the back wall was graced by a painting of dogs playing poker and a fully stocked bar.

Terry was wiping down the counter as we entered. I recognized her immediately, even from a distance.

"What the…," she began, and then stopped abruptly, unable to finish her sentence. "Hi."

"Well, I honestly don't see what the problem is. You've had two weeks to pay us," a familiar voice argued from inside the wall, behind the picture of the card-playing dogs.

The wall slid open and two figures stepped out. One was a thin, pale man in a brown pinstripe suit. The other, considerably shorter… was all the more recognizable.

Phineas.

He seemed slightly older and more like his Master Galwick than he would have cared to know, despite his patched leather coat and paperboy cap. I noticed with considerable amusement, that he wore Galwick's monocle as well.

"Tomorrow morning that check had better be in the mail! We're Knights, not Etone… we don't work for Favors!" Phineas shouted.

The businessman took no notice of him, or of either of us standing in the doorway, but simply walked right through Ruveus and out onto the street where he vanished in a beam of yellow light.

"Offworld ass," Phineas muttered… and then caught sight of me. He stared. "Artemis?" Phineas gasped. "Is it you?"

I nodded, smiling despite myself. "Took me a while to get here," I admitted. "Sorry."

The elevator screeched and the floor beneath us rumbled as another character I recognized came up from behind the wall.

The red-cloaked priestess stared. "God grant me… is it possible?"

"This is Sikara," Terry gestured, "and this is Artemis."

"I thought you were someone else," she admitted awkwardly.

I knew very well who she thought I was and I didn't care to explain, so I said nothing. The bells on the door rang yet again, as two more figures entered the bar.

"Scuse' me, Ruveus," the first muttered, dunking under Ruveus's arm and then stopping short. He was somewhere between the ages of ten and twelve, wearing a white robe over a pair of grubby jeans and a black t-shirt.

"Ruveus?" he gaped.

"Well, well… if it isn't Ira the Kid!" Ruveus grabbed the boy around the neck. "Why don't we start where we left off?"

"Before or after the werewolves came after you?" Ira grinned… prying his way free and slinking into the corner. "Bro Heathcliff sends his apologies," he finished, winking mischievously.

Ruveus sighed and shook his head. "Forget it kid. Forget it."

"Pardon me, sir," the second stranger, a pale man in a wide-brimmed hat and trench coat entered, dunking through the doorframe and pulling shut the blinds with a flick of his wrist. The bar quickly became dark, which was more to my liking than the sunlight, and the stranger sat down in a booth and threw off his hat, kicking his feet up on the table.

"Carpe Diem!" he proclaimed triumphantly… as if he'd had quite a bit of practice. For a moment, no one so much as breathed, and then the man turned slowly, staring at me.

We both recognized each other at the same moment.

"You're…," I began, futilely trying to remember his name… if he had given one at all that day we met in Ardra.

"And you're…" Evidently he was having the same difficulty.

"Tongue-tied?" Phineas laughed, stepping between the two of us.

"Raph… Artemis Ravencroft. Artemis… Raphael Errida. Emperor of the Chaos Realm."

The Emperor? I stared for what felt like an eternity, searching his eyes as carefully as he watched my own. At close range… perhaps too close for comfort, he appeared even more familiar. Compelled by some strange force, I found myself wanting to reach up and just touch his face to be sure that he was real and there before me.

Equally hypnotized, his hand drifted towards my own and our fingertips met.

"Eh, Raph?" Ruveus's voice interrupted, and the two of us froze.

"What?" Raphael wondered, grinning awkwardly and pulling on his own ear as if he were vaguely embarrassed.

I wasn't quite sure what I was expected to think, and suddenly found myself laughing.

"Hey… is this day screwed up or what?" Ira shook his head, fishing a few coins out of his pocket and heading for the video-machines.

Hours later, once our entire company of not-quite strangers was somewhat friendlier and considerably less sober, we began to talk about just what had led us to where we stood.

"I can fix your problem," Raphael admitted. "Honestly, I can do whatever I want... but you have to realize there are politics involved. There are many people that won't be ecstatic to find that suddenly there's another Traverser in the realm, and a descendant of High Commander Ardain, no less. That makes five of us now."

"Five?" I was amazed. "But in Magog there are hundreds... thousands!"

"There were more in the Chaos Realm at one point too. Before the destruction of Raedawn." Raphael shook his head.

I fell silent. Raphael took a drink and continued. "The Etone Brotherhood is mostly composed of humans, mages and shape shifters, realm-travelers that run in packs. They would seek to establish themselves somewhere if they were powerful enough... but they're not. They aren't full-blooded l'Eloshir, which means they aren't "natural" Traversers. They travel by technology, and sometimes by magic, but it isn't as simple for them as it is for us. Other than Ordo, there's Ekbatah, also known as Lucy... your uncle Panther, my brother Kieran, myself, and now you. We are quite possibly the last."

I counted, reciting the names over in my head. So few...

"We'll probably have to pretend you're a lot younger than you are," Raphael added, his mind apparently moving a little bit faster than my own. "When you've got more than six centuries behind you, people always want to know what you were doing... believe me! My dear Aunt Kaora got herself killed in a Spellcraft crash when we all though she would reign another two hundred years. So the court found me and I spent the next decade just trying to explain that I lived most of my time in southern Ardra on a rice farm where absolutely nothing of interest ever happened."

"It does sound nice," I admitted.

"Until the press got hold of it." Raphael laughed. "A flock of damnable dirt-hungry harpies... the lot of them! Soon I was sacrificing virgins and creating Tears in my basement."

"Do they really make up that much?" I could scarcely believe it.

"That much?" Raphael shook his head. "That was the tame stuff."

"I never knew it was so difficult," I sighed.

"To what?" Raphael wondered.

"To be good," I admitted. "When you're intentionally causing trouble it doesn't matter when people spread malicious lies. The most I had to fear was the threat of being seen as soft or weak... and if you've heard any of the tales, you can imagine that not many dared to confront me with such an accusation."

"Yes, I see your point." Phineas nodded. He hadn't spoken much, but at least he was still listening.

Everyone else had long since fallen asleep or gone home.

"Well, as I was saying," Raphael began again. "We'll set up a day where we can have a whole entrance before the court... and then we'll "test" you and give you something to do."

"Must I have something to do?" I sighed. "I am not accustomed to working."

"Even the devil has a day job," Phineas pointed out, nodding off.

"Look at your friends here. Two of the finest Knights in the Empire and all they do is pour drinks and play pool all day."

"It's a good bar," Phineas argued, half asleep.

"A damn good bar," Raphael corrected. "The point is, we've little, if any trouble. The Chaos Realm isn't like any other world. We've some petty crime... but it's all minor business for the police and occasionally a few Chaos Knights. There hasn't been a civil war or world war... realm war or anything like that in the last seven-hundred years. Since the fall of the Raedawn we've had nearly perfect peace. Even the Gods have settled down and raised families by now."

"Are you married?" I wondered, and then paused, realizing it was a somewhat impertinent question.

Raphael shook his head. "No, and I'm the most eligible bachelor in this dimension. Can you imagine how much trouble that is!" he sighed, stirring his drink and glancing up at me. "Children want my autograph."

"Believe me, if anyone knows, I've been there," I sighed... sipping my ambrosia. "When I was given an army of my own to command, one of my students, Orin Saede decided that it would help his "rise to power" if he managed to convince me to marry him. Orin may have been born royalty, but he was also sixteen at the time, while I was closer to four or five hundred."

"That sounds like the little problem I had with Bianca Wells," Raphael laughed softly. "After my brother Kieran married a human, Lady Bianca got the idea in her head that we might do well together. She wasn't content being second-in-line for the Ardran throne... that woman was a power maniac! But, by the time she turned seventy... I guess she finally figured out that I wasn't interested."

"It seems we've got something in common." I smiled. "Eternally young and beautiful... but somehow incapable of having any sort of meaningful relationship. The curse of the Traverser."

"Too true," Raphael sighed. For the first time, I supposed, we actually saw each other closely. He smiled at me briefly and then suddenly, almost awkwardly... he turned to look out the window.

I watched him, drawn in completely by the expression in his eyes. They were full of an incredible wisdom, but they were tired nonetheless.

Though Raphael was, in many ways, what I hoped to become, he still remained almost painfully unfulfilled, as if he lacked the one thing he most truly wanted. A knock came at the door and I jumped, startled.

"Who is it at this hour?" Raphael muttered.

I recognized the silhouette all too well.

"Elhilom...," I hissed. Remembering the look on Ejora's face, I debated even letting him into the bar, but suddenly he collapsed to the pavement... and I ran to the door despite myself.

There was blood everywhere. He had been beaten to the point where he had been rendered unable to shift into his usual cat-form, a dozen bones broken and an open bloody gash across his back from his shoulder to his thigh. I raced to his side. "Elhil... are you?"

"I'm fine, Ire'." His breathing was shallow. "It isn't all mine."

"What happened?" I demanded.

Panther shook his head.

"It's over... the game is over!" he muttered, babbling mindlessly as he attempted to lick his own wound.

"What game?" I shook him. "Elhil, you're not making any sense."

"The game, Ireval," he whispered, pointing to the ceiling. "The beautiful game, it was so much fun, wasn't it... but it never really happened at all." He stopped short and shook his head, perhaps trying to understand his own terrible words. "The Warlord has gathered all the I'Eloshir. Not just Tirs Uloth, but Nebatna and Nyehsa...," he rambled insanely. "Every red-robe in Magog and every warrior!"

"What are they doing?" I asked, though deep inside, I knew all too well.

"They ride for war," Panther coughed. "They ride to destroy the Chaos Realm."

It took a moment for the reality of what I had just heard to actually set in. Never before had any demon made such a threat. Orin disguised as a priest was only the beginning. I couldn't imagine what horrors awaited the Dynasty.

For a moment I wondered why I'd decided to become involved at all. I could not face my father. No mortal could.

Panther took a sip of ambrosia, brushed himself off and pulled a mirror from his pocket. "I love the sound of breaking glass," he admitted, rubbing it on the leg of his tattered pants and then wiping his filthy claws on my clean shirt.

"Hold on! Just where do you think you're going?" Ruveus demanded, reaching for his mandolin.

"Got someone to see, amigo," Panther grinned, pulling himself to his feet. "If the world's coming to an end and all."

"How long do you suspect we have?" I wondered.

Panther shrugged.

"A few months maybe. No longer." He paused for a moment and then threw me several vials on a chain. "Here's some stuff for you. The rest is outside."

I threw the ambrosia back.

"I've got plenty," I admitted. "You take it."

Panther smiled. "Thanks, Ire'. We make a good team, eh?" The mirror shattered and he vanished.

"Elhil! Say hello to Ordo for me!" I shouted... but Panther was already long gone.

The Emperor

"Books might be written of his secrets, yet none question his judgment."

Eighteen

A few uneventful months passed as we carefully set up my entrance into politics and quietly prepared for the threat of The I'Eloshir.

Though the Emperor spent his days at the palace while I wandered the city, lurking in the library and avoiding the White Cross, we spent our nights together at Mad Mack's drinking, talking, and reminiscing about centuries so far past.

All in all, I could not have wished for more... but Raphael wanted me to appear at court so that we could travel together. I guessed he was leaning towards our "friendship" becoming more of a relationship than a potential scandal.

I couldn't argue, and beyond that I couldn't fight the urge, the strange sense that told me a city was too small a place... the instinct that Raphael shared, the desire to run, through hundreds of worlds and keep traveling indefinitely.

We had agreed that the first opportunity we found, we would take The Hathor to Silver Point, Raphael's island retreat... and stay for more than a few short hours. The lighthouse had quickly became our favorite hiding place.

I would sit on the rocks near the beach and occasionally wade up to my knees in the water, but only when I was feeling especially brave.

Often, I was tempted to throw off the limitations of my human body and soar in the cool, salty sea winds... but I feared that I could not trust myself. The bloodlust that my demonic side harbored was entirely too powerful and overwhelming.

Raphael taunted me endlessly. He argued that he had never seen what I really looked like and occasionally begged me to fly with him. He had not taken to the sky in over a century, not since the death of his father, and he was not even entirely certain that he could still change, but he offered to try

... for my sake.

Yet I would politely decline, saying always that I was content to watch him... riding his horses and sitting up on the roof of the lighthouse tower, the wind in his hair.

He was the single most beautiful, intriguing individual that I had ever met, and with all of my dark secrets and flaws, I felt unworthy of his attention.

I may have been a queen in the eyes of the l'Eloshir, but I had been a deluded, petty queen who ruled by fear alone, building a place for herself in a society of lies by breaking the backs of others.

Finally, after what seemed like ages of preparation, the day arrived when I would make myself known and become something more than the mysterious shadow that often lingered near the Emperor in impromptu photographs.

I would be introduced at court.

"Taxi!" Phineas waved, hopping up and down on the curb. It seemed to me that he was perhaps the only member of our group that could not immediately get the devil's attention.

Yet as soon as I thought of Lucy, the same doorless smoke-filled disaster that had greeted me on my first day in Zenith pulled up to welcome us, with the addition of yet another strange passenger... a small, stony-faced gray creature that most closely resembled the common perception of a gargoyle.

"Morning Jeo... Morning Lucy," Phineas sighed, jumping into the back seat.

"Guten Morgen!" The gargoyle grinned, stuck between the two of us. "Ich... mein name ist Igor." He paused, perhaps contemplating a translation. "Who is you?"

"Artemis." I shook the creature's claw.

"Where'd you pick him up?" Phineas hissed at Lucy, jabbing a finger at Igor. The gargoyle blinked.

Lucy grinned. "Oh... me an' Jay'O here went on a little joyride round' this place called Paris last night, you heard about it... to France in Earth Realm. We pulled him off the roof of Notre Dame an' brought him to life. It was wild."

"Ja, ja!" the gargoyle laughed.

"I'm sure," Phineas seemed concerned. "But if you pulled him off the cathedral in France... why does he speak German?"

Lucy incinerated a cigarette in a single breath. "We don't know," she admitted. "Weird, isn't it?"

Mostly because I did not know what they were talking about, I nodded in agreement.

"So where can we take you today?" Jeo wondered.

"The Imperial Palace," Phineas supplied. "And make it quick, we're already running late."

"It's always fast, love," Lucy grinned. "Try the speed of thought."

And we were there, inside the building itself. The cab vanished suddenly as a few servants entered the hall, bowing to Phineas and glancing at me with a sort of silent bewilderment.

Fortunately, I had become accustomed to precisely that reaction.

The Imperial Palace of the Errida Dynasty was an immense, white-marble building, hovering over the ocean on the nearly invisible threads of some long-forgotten energy source.

Within the monolith was an oval, five-story chamber with thousands of seats and a ceiling high enough to comfortably accommodate even the largest of dragons, though oddly enough, the delegates from Accoloth preferred to attend in human form.

A group of them sat gathered on the marble floor as if they had no concept of chairs, playing little hand-drums and guitars, listening appreciatively as a young girl with silver hair accompanied them on her flute.

Aside from the serene dragons, the remainder of the council chamber was in uproar as we entered. The argument apparently was focused on the rumors of war with something called the Interdimensional Republic... the IR and l'Eloshir of Magog, not on the sudden appearance of a strange new Traverser.

"Master Merlin!" A voice laughed. I turned sharply, and realized that Phineas was being drawn away by a young, dark-skinned woman with green hair who wore a white velvet dress and a large emerald stone set in gold around her neck.

"Artemis... this is Rosalind," He choked.

"Duchess of Celedon." She smiled winningly, releasing Phineas from her vise-like grip. "Green Opal of Ardra."

Rosalind gestured to the two men that accompanied her, one a foot taller than me... abnormally tall for a human. He was dark too, his skin so deep a brown that it was almost purplish. Something about him bothered me vaguely, but I shrugged it off, my eyes drawn to the glimmering blue sapphire he wore around his neck.

The second man was quite ordinary, of average height and build, hair combed and clean-shaven, dressed in old clothes that seemed to be generally brown everywhere, with an aura about him that I recognized immediately as a warrior. He wore a yellow opal.

"This is Octavian, Count Avencourt of Aquara..." The dark man bowed. "And this is Sir Xane Tradewind of Orienca..." The second man waved, seeming a little distracted.

All three of the noble's gems flared to life as a short, red-haired woman stomped into the room, carrying a loaded crossbow and followed by a large black cat.

"Don't... talk!" She glared at Rosalind and then slumped into an empty seat in the first row on the floor. "Gossiping biddies," she cursed.

"Who's that?" I asked.

"That woman is Baroness Gloria Etharel," Rosalind sighed and turned to Xane and Octavian, presumably for moral support or additional gossip. "And as if it isn't terribly obvious, she's the one that inherited King Jahmed's fire opal when his daughter Hazel refused it. They call her the powder-keg of the Ardran Court for more reasons than one, let me tell you that! Why, once she wrecked an entire inn... all because some man made a pass at her at the bar! I'm sure that everyone's heard about that little incident by now, it was absolutely dreadful! And speak of the devil! There he is! That's the poor soul I was just telling you about. Just watch how the Baroness scowls when she sees him!"

Rosalind pointed at yet another figure in the crowd, an unimpressive and homely-looking individual whose only point of interest was his exceptionally fine sword. Other than that, he appeared to be a social disaster; quite out of his element.

"Who is he?" I wondered.

"Remember Edgar Dunharrow?" Phineas asked. "The peasant we met on the road to Phoenicia? The one with the mule?"

I did... but only vaguely.

"Well as it so happens, that bumbling idiot managed to stumble upon this legendary sword... unwittingly fulfilling an ancient prophesy which naturally lead to his becoming King of Istara." Xane interrupted Phineas before he could even blink.

"Don't bother, wizard," Octavian advised, noticing the troubled look on Phineas's face. "Leave the intrigue up to these professionals."

"We'll tell you anything you want to know about anyone," Rosalind smirked. "And it's all absolutely true."

"Is there anyone else I should recognize?" I wondered hopelessly, knowing

I couldn't possibly keep track of more names.

"Just up there," Phineas pointed to the chair nearest the throne where a man in a brown suit sat playing checkers with a fox-tailed creature dressed in rainbow silks.

"The human or the fox?" I wondered.

"The human!" Phineas sighed, exasperated. "The fox, her name is Zephresi. She's a nice woman, but she's only one of the thirty librarians at Alexandria. The man is General Maurice Auderrauk, Raphael's Grand Vizier... and, coincidentally, former captain of The Spellcraft Dogma."

"Coincidentally, we think they've got a thing going on." Rosalind winked. "If you know what I mean... "

"Enough coincidences," I muttered.

A gong chimed and some of the obviously less distinguished members of the Imperial Court raced for their seats, including the Ardran Opals who all sat in the same row with three or so people between them as if wanted to remain near enough to whisper but feared being seen together.

The doors to the hall opened, and Raphael entered, walking with a tall black staff. His appearance had changed little from our previous meetings in the bar, except that he wore a dramatic, flowing purple robe and heavy silver crown. The crown alone made all the difference in the world.

This wasn't the man I'd spent hours drinking with and teasing about his former loves and unfortunate accidents, this man was Emperor of an entire realm, and certainly no fool. He winked in my direction. I smiled to myself. Despite Panther's grim tidings, I still felt near weightless.

"Artemis?" Phineas wondered, obviously sensing my distraction.

I snapped out of my daydream. The Emperor was about to make his speech.

"People of the Chaos Realm. I have called you all here with very grave news indeed."

I stopped short, suddenly very afraid. This was not the piece that we had rehearsed.

"The rumors of the past months have been confirmed," Raphael continued. "The attacks on Ardra and the recent outbreaks on the Island of Safehaven are indeed, no mere coincidence. We have always been advocates of peace, but now it seems that we are under attack. A mere three-hundred worlds away... the armies of the Warlord of Magog are mobilizing, intending to combine their power with that of the Interdimensional Republic."

"I have just spoken with President Fairfax of the Republic," Raphael announced. "He believes that our honorable council has outlived its usefulness. He seeks to overthrow the Dynasty."

A murmur of shock raced through the gathered nobles like wildfire, but I knew Raphael was far from finished.

"Together, these two armies make up a force powerful enough to destroy us completely, but only if we are not ready for them. I will not allow Zenith to follow in the footsteps of Raedawn. We may advocate peace, but we cannot hide behind it, for as the past has taught us, those who practice the dark crafts will spare none of us. Therefore, with no choice but to fight... in order to save as many lives as we possibly can. I move for a Vote of Defense."

The room was silent, possibly in disbelief, until at long last General Auderrauk stood, "I second that."

Then the commotion began.

"We hate the Republic," a woman in the back of the room stood. "We'd like nothing more than to show them a thing or two... but fight demons?"

"How can we fight demons?" Zephresi argued, accidentally knocking the checkerboard over with one of her twitching tails.

The man next to Baroness Gloria shook his head heavily.

"I fear this vote, milord. There is very little difference between strengthening our defenses and arming ourselves for battle."

"I wish to preserve this Empire by any means necessary," Raphael announced solemnly. "If we do not prepare ourselves for the worst, I assure you, we will suffer it."

"War!" Octavian shouted. "Are you mad, Lord Errida? We may hold off the Republic but we cannot fight the Warlord himself! I have seen what his fiends did to Phoenicia! I will not allow my city to suffer the same fate. We stand to lose everything!"

"Then what do you propose that we do?" Raphael glared. "Sit and be slaughtered? Safehaven saw no fight... and it fell from within!"

"Bargain!" Octavian argued. "Give the Warlord whatever he's come for and send him away! Buy him off and he'll leave us in peace!"

"That cannot be done," Everyone stared. I stopped short, realizing that I had spoken aloud.

"It cannot be done," I repeated, with more certainty. "The Warlord rides for the sheer joy of death and destruction. No bounty can satisfy him."

"And how would you know this?" Octavian sneered.

"I have served him," I shot back, not giving up an inch. "My name is Artemis Ravencroft... and I have ridden with the Warriors of Magog."

Silence again, and then a third man stood... Xane. "I, Xane Tradewind, so move."

Baroness Gloria followed. Her cat growled.

"Five," Raphael counted.

"Six!" Phineas stood. "I so move."

"I, Prince Ruveus, move on behalf of Accoloth." Ruveus came to his feet. "We've been chasing those demons and their hunting parties out of our mountains for the past fifty years, and that's been difficult enough. I'm not willing to take the chance that they might be able to organize."

"They organize," I shook my head. "And with the Warlord Geruth riding in the lead, they are capable of things you cannot imagine."

"What about The Ireval?" Rosalind demanded.

I froze at the sound of my name and Raphael looked visibly ill. He of course, knew the truth, but it was an issue that we both avoided. Whenever he spoke to me, Raphael would call me Artemis.

"Is the Demon Queen with them?" Rosalind repeated. The entire room fell into an uneasy silence.

"The Demon Queen is dead," Xane frowned, attempting to shatter the cold fear that overwhelmed the court. "Or else we would have been brought to ruin long ago."

"What if it was all a plot? To take us now, when we've let our guard down?" Gloria argued. The red stone she wore flared brilliantly as Octavian turned to glare at her.

"Aquara will not fight demons," he sneered.

"Then Aquara can burn in hell," Gloria hissed, grabbing Octavian by the shirt though she could not see higher than his chest.

"Phoenicia ought to calm herself,." Rosalind muttered.

"Celedon can join Aquara," Gloria glared. Xane stood as if he were about to interrupt her, but she clapped her hand over his mouth. "Shut up," Gloria ordered. "I'm in the middle of a…"

"The delegates from Ardra will return to their seats and close their mouths," Raphael interrupted. "You would think that after so many centuries, the failings of your ancestors would have at least taught you something about self-control. Yet every generation of the Aquara family is full of greed, every Tradewind is so sure of himself… every ruler of Celedon obsessively paranoid and every single Gods help me… every single Etharel-Wells is more obnoxious than the last! I tell you good people, and believe me, as your Emperor… we need not fear the Demon Queen."

Immediately, the four bickering fools returned to their chairs.

"We will continue to take vote. Keep in mind that this vote will only permit the court to form a committee in the interest of our defense," Raphael announced. "Seven have spoken. We have more than half that which is needed. Any others, please rise."

"Eight," Maurice counted, as Rosalind stood without speaking.

"Nine," a young girl stood on her chair... despite her mother's clear opposition. "I so move," she announced confidentially.

"Brin of the Falchon House," Raphael smiled, ever so slightly.

Another stranger rose from the crowd, an Elvin man, who, from the reaction of the gathered, was obviously a figure of great importance.

"I, Rowanoak, King of Eldar, so move," the man announced solemnly and then returned to his seat.

"Ten." Raphael surveyed the room. "Three are still required."

"Three you have," a strange voice announced... as the doors to the hall opened. Ordo entered, looking solemn, but it was not he who had spoken.

His wife, and a young boy that I did not recognize accompanied him... Jedera dressed in khaki clothes and a hat that made her look as if she had just returned from a trek across the desert, while the boy was wearing a flowing orange robe that made him appear even smaller than he actually was. The child carried a chessboard under one arm and some sort of red cup in the opposite hand. All three of the newcomers seemed obviously exhausted from what must have been a trying journey indeed.

"I, Lord Ordo of Gelthar, so move," Ordo announced.

"And I, Jedera Blanche, so move." His wife sat down in an open chair, her gaze drifting from floor to ceiling.

The third, the boy, only shook his head.

"The winds of change are upon us," he warned, his voice full of some unquestionable power. "This war will not end in my time... nor in yours." He pointed to Raphael, counting on his fingers and glancing skyward from time to time, scribbling on a little notepad as if he were taking shorthand from the divine.

"A great army will arise, with seven leaders, one who represents each continent in the realm... and a bunch of bad stuff will happen... What is with the doom and gloom all of a sudden? Damnit, ok!" the boy demanded... and then stared up thoughtfully as if he were absorbing an inaudible response from his invisible conversation partner. "Oh? Yeah, I get the idea," he sighed dejectedly.

"I'm sorry it's not terribly creative, but these "epic-prophesy-things tend to follow a certain pattern, you understand? Seven leaders, one from each continent, okay?"

I nodded, completely baffled. Fortunately, much of the room seemed to be as utterly bewildered as I myself.

"That makes six," Raphael counted. "Prophet Deiunthel, what seventh do you speak of?"

"A High Commander," The prophet announced. "One who possesses The Third Sight."

"No such person exists," Octavian argued. "That staff is locked away where it belongs!"

"I am the Prophet here... am I not?" the boy glared.

Octavian fell silent immediately.

"Such a person exists," he continued, grinning slightly. "And I'll prove it to you."

The young girl, the one called Brin, made her way down the stairs somewhat awkwardly, tugging on her sleeves nervously and brushing her hair away from her face in an attempt to seem more presentable.

All eyes remained on The Prophet.

"The daughter of the Falchon House will bring forth the crystals from the Vault," he announced. "And the test shall commence."

Brin walked slowly through the open doors at the end of the hall and returned with a black box. Opening it, she produced two round white crystals and stepped up into midair, closing her eyes in concentration. She held a glowing white sphere in each of her outstretched hands and a third crystal hovered in the air above her head.

Hours passed as warriors and sorcerers of all races and ages lined up, each approaching the girl who stood frozen in time.

Some chose the left hand, others the right, and still others both... or none at all. But the light above her head no hand dared approach, until I began to doubt that anyone even saw it.

"What's the trick?" I hissed.

Raphael shook his head. "No one knows," he admitted. "Except Teyme himself, I imagine, and perhaps your grandfather as well. But they've both been dead several hundred years."

"Why do some walk away?" I wondered.

"Some see nothing," he admitted. "Others see only one sphere, some see two. I see both myself, because I am both a warrior and a mage... a healer, but that is the same." Raphael paused. "The right is the sphere of Wisdom...

the left is the sphere of Valor."

"Both?" I stared.

Sure enough, there were only two.

"And then there's that shadow of a third sphere," Raphael sighed. "No one knows what it is. Some reach for it... only none of them ever quite manage to pick it up. I dare not touch it myself, though I feel its presence. Being Emperor is more responsibility in itself than I have the heart for."

He pointed down to the floor where a man stood, his hand passing through the nothingness over Brin's head.

"Emperor, we have gone through every last soul in this court!" Maurice announced. "The Prophet has spoken false."

"There are those who have not been tried," the boy whispered, looking as if he had begun to doubt his own speech.

"I for one," Phineas admitted. "Though I confess I only see one crystal." He scratched his head. "This is a strange enchantment. I sense that there is more to it but I ..." he trailed off into silence.

"You," the Prophet pointed to me.

"I thought I saw three," I admitted. "But it was a trick of the light, and now there are only two."

"Come down here," the boy ordered.

I sighed. "Regardless of what may happen, I assure you that I am most certainly not the sort of person you want leading your armies."

"Arion speaks through me," he argued. "It isn't my choice."

"If your God thinks I am a hero... then he is a fool," I snapped, stepping down to the floor.

The child Brin stood frozen and I shuddered involuntarily. The spheres were not really stones at all! The crystal on the right was a human man, weather-worn, a man of the land and many mysteries... Though I did not recognize him, he carried a sort of solemn, orderly importance in the way that he stood entirely still, never blinking.

Yet it was the crystal on the left that truly had me mesmerized. The stone of Valor had taken the form of a woman, a demon woman wielding a sword and a wearing a mask, her eyes burning with magefire: Inapsupetra.

I fell to my knees, blinded by the miraculous sight. They were not supreme, no, something greater was above them, but in all my travels, not one immortal I had ever met had come so close to what one might truly consider a God.

I looked skyward to where the third sphere hovered, a brilliant and perfect white light. The room was irrelevant.

I reached forward and took it in my hand. It had no shape. It was warm, like the energy of a spell, and cold as steel.

And then it changed, morphing in my grasp into a tall, curve-bladed staff. A weapon, but a gift of magic as well.

The light cleared and I opened my eyes, shocked by my own reflection glimmering in the steel of the thing... whatever it was.

In all my years I had never encountered a weapon of its like, so flawlessly designed and light to the touch. It was a deadly, powerful creation indeed.

Around the hall thousands of faces stared, all bearing the same expression of awe.

The Prophet stood with his jaw dropped. I turned to him for an explanation, but any trace of Godly wisdom he had possessed was gone completely.

"Damn," he grinned, "do that again."

Nineteen

And so… I became the High Commander.

King Rowanoak, thanks to his knowledge of the arcane, and his never-ending supply of young sorcerers, was designated the "hero" of Eldar and lord over the mages and wizards, with Phineas as his chief advisor. Phineas loved the elves and their culture, and I was glad for him, though I myself couldn't help but feel uneasy in the presence of their King. His sharp features and green, lucid eyes reminded me all to clearly of the vast numbers of his kindred I had slaughtered. In my darkest years, there was nothing I had loved to hunt more than elves.

Ruveus would lead the forces of Accoloth, and General Auderrauk the armies of Ranlain. The dragons amused me with their antics… and General Auderrauk had won my respect the day he had attempted to kill me on his ship.

Baroness Gloria of Ardra and King Edgar completed the mix with Terry Mack the Chaos Knight thrown in to represent the shiftless sea-going lords of the Badowin Isles, the kingdom in which she had been born. The three of them seemed to play off one another at court gatherings, switching sides sporadically. Every so often, Terry and Gloria would launch into rants about the foolhardiness of men, but on an equal number of occasions, Edgar would join forces with the Chaos Knight in order to mock the Baroness's ridiculous "grooming" requirements.

There were many others involved too, though it would take centuries to list all of their names and brave deeds. Still, although I was surrounded constantly with admirers and critics, in my heart, I was alone. All of the warriors, even the ones who had lived several centuries seemed like children to me.

I suddenly felt as if I were not the commander of an army, but the mother of a very large and most unusual family, all of my charges wrapped in their little fears and problems, all expecting me to care for them...

There was one person, however, that to me was neither subject, servant, nor slave... one person perhaps, in all of the many worlds that perceived things as I did, living in the hours of dawn and twilight, dreaming of ages long past, envying mortality yet remaining untouched by time.

Raphael.

Though Raphael continually reminded me that I was bad for his image, there was always an element of humor in his rants. He would send servants scurrying up and down the stairs with "urgent messages" that turned out to be nothing more than obnoxious cartoon sketches of some of the less-liked members of the Imperial Court. Gloria breathing fire was one of his favorite subjects, challenged only by the number of times he drew Count Avencourt in various embarrassing positions.

I tried to remain as aloof as I possibly could, reassuring myself that the less I reacted to Raphael's teasing, the less he would bother me with it, but my stern behavior only seemed to intrigue him further.

He followed me almost incessantly whenever he could escape his more serious duties and lost no opportunity to overwhelm himself by adding to his already ridiculous schedule the additional burden of whatever research I was busying myself with.

The two of us spent a considerable amount of time in the library.

"You're telling me THIS is the only written history of the Chaos Realm?" Raphael muttered, skimming through a worn old book. "It's less than a hundred pages!"

"Makes for great bathroom reading," Jedera snickered.

She and Ordo, and their companion Deiunthel "The Prophet" planned to resume their quest for a certain missing relative they referred to as "The Architect" rather than support our cause, wars being classically "not their thing," but they were helpful nonetheless... especially when it came to finding out all we could about "High Commanders" and their general purpose.

"I've got something on our friend Deiunthel here." Raphael grinned, holding his book out of The Prophet's reach. Dei lunged for it furiously but missed, stumbling into a chair, and Raphael began to read aloud with great enthusiasm.

"Let me first say this. Of all the positions of the Imperial Court, The Prophet is the most generally disliked, not because of his temperament... in this regard he is quite amiable... but because he is largely predestined to be the eternal bearer of bad news. It would appear that you were damned the day you were born, my diminutive friend."

Deiunthel scowled. "Well it says here in this newspaper that the High Commander and the Emperor... well, well!"

"Well well... what?" Raphael turned suddenly, his grin vanishing.

Dei coughed dramatically and then tore the paper in half. "I can't read it, it's too dirty."

"Let me see that!" I demanded, grabbing the pieces and putting them back together.

"How to make your own gold. A Kalyzar recipe?" I glared, ripping the paper in half again and throwing it on the floor. "That isn't what it says!"

Then it hit me. "Make gold?!" I jumped for the scattered pages.

"It doesn't work!" Raphael laughed.

I climbed to my feet and frowned at him. "How should you know?" I demanded, trying to save face.

Raphael smiled. "I've tried it. Several times." The expression on his face was more than just the mad grin I had become so accustomed to. I avoided his gaze almost continually around the palace and especially at court. It seemed that every time I looked into his eyes felt like the first time, I realized then why I felt so terribly incompetent around him.

Trained as I had been, my life before entering the Chaos Realm had been one devoid of commitment. I cared little for most of my relatives and nothing for my father. In my army, I replaced those who might have been friends with warriors who were more obedient and asked fewer questions. I did not have attachments, much less relationships. My own emotions baffled me. Feeling a strange burn creeping up across my face, I immediately turned away and absorbed myself in my book.

Hours later and thoroughly exhausted, Jedera and Dei retired for the evening while Raphael finished book after book and I pretended to read. I would not speak to him, or look him in the eyes, but I couldn't bring myself to leave the library either.

Every so often, I glanced up at him when he was turned the other way.

"You can look at me, you know," Raphael announced suddenly.

I froze momentarily and then returned to my book.

"You've been on page three-hundred for two hours now," he interrupted, running his finger down the page and up to my chin, turning me to face him. "Is it really so interesting?" he wondered, with a faint grin.

"I'm through with reading," Raphael sighed heavily, rocking back in his chair. "I'll go cross-eyed if I look at another book. Why don't we talk?"

"About what?" I asked, not paying much attention.

"About us," Raphael suggested.

I gasped, wondering if I was hearing things. "What do you mean?" I whispered, almost too faintly. "There isn't any 'us'."

"I know that now," Raphael closed his eyes and collapsed facedown the table.

"But I can't help myself," he continued, not looking at me. "You have this invisible wall that surrounds you. You walk around like you're on a mission every day. It's absolutely unbelievable." Raphael sighed heavily. "I've tried everything I can think of... and yet there you are, ever present and always untouchable... like an angel looking down on me."

"I am not an angel, Raphael," I argued.

"No you're not," he paused, "you're a Goddess."

"Raphael!" I turned away toward the window. I couldn't explain precisely how I felt at that moment. Since the day we had met, the mere thought of Raphael had compelled me in ways that I had never imagined. I wanted nothing more than to be with him, and yet I could hear myself mercilessly crushing his hopes... as well as my own.

"Artemis," Raphael begged. "I've sent you gifts, I've taken you places... I'm working a dozen times harder than I have ever worked in my life just hoping that you might look in my direction. What do you want from me?"

"Nothing," I lied, attempting to seem emotionless, though tears were welling up in my eyes as I saw the expression on Raphael's face, the desperate pain that lingered there. And although I told myself repeatedly that I was being merciful by saving him from the cold darkness that I carried with me, my own heart cried out violently in protest of my words.

"You know, Raphael," I shook my head slowly. "You know what I am!"

Without a word, Raphael stood slowly and opened the window. Sighing heavily, he took off his coat and bowed his head, breathing slowly and muttering quietly under his breath.

"I know," he paused. "Is my charade really so convincing?" Raphael shook his head. "It's been so long... a hundred and eighty-six years." He sighed, glancing skyward. "But I have to do this. You have to see."

In an instant, he collapsed to his knees, his face contorted into a mask of pain as he struggled to remain conscious and slowly, slowly changed.

One moment he knelt on the floor in a pool of sunlight, completely human, and the next... a shudder rippled through his entire body. Wings that were a pure, snowy white speckled with a deeper blue-gray exploded out of his back and his jaw shot forward, his face twisting into subtly familiar new shapes until finally he fell to the floor, utterly motionless. I couldn't tell if he still breathed, but as I stared at him lying there on the floor, a pain struck me.

"Oh goddess." I jumped to my feet, no longer caring what anyone thought, or even what was best, wanting only to be sure that Raphael still lived. Suddenly thrown to the ground by a terrible shock that overwhelmed my own body, I gasped in horror. I was shifting, I realized, though I couldn't fully comprehend what had triggered it.

Yet even as I felt my wings again, the mindless rage and arrogant contempt for all life that I had associated with my demonic form did not surface. Instead, I was compelled by a completely pure, equally mindless instinct.

Raphael could not be dead. I simply couldn't accept the possibility. I wanted him. I needed him… and despite the trouble that I knew such feelings could cause, I… loved him passionately.

He opened his eyes and stared at me in bewilderment.

"My god," he whispered, almost awed, "you're beautiful."

Ashamed without knowing why, I drew my knees up to my chest and turned over on my side, hiding my face with my hands and rolling my dark wings around me like a blanket.

"No, no, no!" Raphael sighed, pulling me up off the ground with an incredible strength. Helplessly, I collapsed to the floor again. It was so strange to be weak, yet not trapped in my mortal form. No one had ever dared touch me in such a way.

"I cannot," I argued futily, pushing my way free of his arms. Yet as I looked up… and our eyes met.

"So?" Raphael wondered, kneeling down and running his fingers through my hair... touching the back of my neck gently with his claws.

"I did it," he winced. "It hurt… but I've done it. What do you think?"

I knew what I thought, but I wasn't about to admit to it.

"This isn't a good idea," I whispered, and Raphael grinned, reading my expression effortlessly.

"Why not?" His response was almost childlike in its simplicity.

"We… we'll get caught!" I argued.

"So?" Without giving me time to respond, he kissed me.

Logic was futile. All my many centuries of training to feel no emotion, succumb to no foolish temptations… I forgot them in an instant. Weeks passed. We met, always under the cover of darkness, in the library, the rose garden, on the roof.

And I felt fulfilled in such a way that I never had before… loved maybe. Or it wasn't love. I wouldn't have known the difference anyway…

But still, part of me wanted to believe that it was possible, that I could be a gem to someone, that someone might find me something more than my terrible legacy.

One thing led to another, and finally, morning came.

"Ammano loa!" an old maid screeched, opening the doors to the library.

"Jeezus," another servant stared.

Soon there was a crowd gathered in the hall, all staring at the tattered pillowcases hanging from the ceiling and the piles of gray goose-down that covered the floor. The many sheets and blankets that had been drug into the room were shredded and full of holes.

"I canna imagine where so many feathers come from!" The old maid shook her head slowly. "Some of those is not pillow-feathers," she muttered, glancing to the other servants suspiciously.

I guessed I must have looked smug because Phineas immediately turned to me. He held a blue-white plume in his left hand and a raven-black feather in his right.

"This isn't yours," he observed. "But this one is."

I didn't respond. I was too busy listening. A sound like a small herd of elephants was fast approaching.

"Congrats!" Terry bombarded me in a bear hug, grinning insanely.

I choked, caught unawares. "For what?" I managed feebly.

"Ah… nothin'." She was instantly cool as she turned to Phineas with an obnoxious smirk. "He doesn't know, does he?"

"You know?" I stared in shock.

"It's nothin' really." She shook her head. "Deiunthel told me."

"Dei knows?" I felt thoroughly violated.

"But he heard from Maurice," Terry continued, obviously oblivious.

"Maurice!" I gasped, horrified by the mere idea. "Am I the laughingstock of the entire palace?" I demanded.

"What happened?" Phineas glared. "And why, pray tell… am I the only one who doesn't know?"

"It's nothing," I snapped.

Terry went pale. "You mean… you don't know?"

I took a step back, suddenly realizing that I had been mistaken. "No, apparently I don't."

127

"Artemis?" a voice wondered from down the hall.

It was Raphael.

He stood in the shadows only a few feet away, scratching his head nervously and carrying a purple rose that had begun to wilt a little.

"Oh damn…," Terry muttered, slinking off into a bedroom and pulling the door closed behind her.

"Raphael, what is going on?" I demanded, pulling him aside "I wake up this morning and suddenly…"

"It's not what you think," he began, wincing slightly.

"Now that I sincerely doubt!" I cut him off. "Somehow everyone in this palace knows we…"

"They don't," he interrupted. "But they do know something else I hadn't meant for them to find out about."

I fell silent.

"So what is it?" I whispered, almost afraid to ask.

"I have a confidant who isn't quite as trustworthy as I hoped he would be," Raphael admitted. "I sent him to run one little errand, and well… it isn't what you think. Can we go somewhere private?"

I nodded… overwhelmed by all of the thoughts that were racing through my head.

Following him upstairs through the empty ballroom, we stepped out onto the highest balcony, overlooking the second sunrise and the edge of the world.

After gazing out across the flickering waves for a few short moments, I turned back to Raphael and noticed something I hadn't before.

He had a ring in his hand.

"Raphael, if this is what I think it is…," I began, overwhelmed by all the troubling possibilities that had suddenly surfaced in my mind.

"I know it's a human custom but please let me explain." He smiled faintly.

I shook my head "no" but closed my mouth anyway. And he held up the ring, a beautiful, shimmering silver web of many-colored stones, obviously priceless.

"It's a family heirloom. My mother's. I sent Maurice to find it at Silver Point… and somehow word got out," Raphael sighed heavily. "One of the servants must have overheard us. I had planned to ask you over dinner." He admitted. "But I don't think we should go to Vespuccio's tonight. The press will be everywhere."

"You mean…," I began, though I already knew what he was trying to say.

"Now it's not a wedding ring, it's a promise ring." Raphael shook his head. "Think of it as a "maybe-someday-if-you-can't-find-anyone-else" ring."

"We've only known each other a few months! Think of how little time that is!"

I argued… though I didn't want to. The way I felt wasn't rational.

"Oh no," Raphael shook his head. "We've known each other many, many lifetimes."

I couldn't deny it. He'd spoken my exact thoughts.

"But the war…," I began. "I see what's happening, Raphael. There will be fighting soon."

"The war is a temporary condition. I have every confidence that it won't even last six months," Raphael finished. "And we do have forever."

"What if we don't?" I sighed, finally voicing my fears.

"Then we can't afford to waste a minute. Will you… think on it?" he whispered.

"Raphael…," I buried myself in his arms, fighting tears.

He closed his beautiful white wings around me in the biting cold, and I cried as I had never cried in all my life. A knock came at the door and Raphael pulled away gently, telling me to hush.

He disappeared through the archway.

And in my numbed hand, I held the ring. The small world of the palace suddenly seemed to be an overwhelming place.

Little did I know at the time, but, less than five-hundred miles away, the war had already begun. It was to be a war unlike any other, a single endless battle that would last fifteen years.

The High Commander

"Here is further proof for those who do not believe in destiny."

Twenty

The following morning, I departed for Ardra on The Hathor while Raphael stayed in Zenith, still attempting to deal the Republic as diplomatically as possible. As I had suspected, the Ardrans informed us that the ruins of Phoenicia were serving as a base for the I'Eloshir, who had resurfaced in the Chaos Realm virtually overnight. Our sources said that they were preparing to attack Orienca.

Knowing that it would be disastrous to allow them access to the Knight's Palace, the building that was home to the Armory of the Southern Isles, I positioned my forces around the city and waited for the coming battle.

I guessed that the demons would ride at dusk, as they preferred to do, enjoying the advantage they held over the humans who were fighting blind in the growing darkness. It was in that assumption that I made the first of my fatal mistakes.

I waited from sunset to sunrise with my soldiers, and still, the I'Eloshir did not show themselves. When morning came, despite the uneasiness that I felt, I agreed to let those who had stood watch by my side have some rest. Yet as soon as I gave the order for the men to return to their tents, the first of the army appeared on the horizon line.

In a flash they were upon us, tearing through our barricade and into the city. Even the men who were armed and ready to fight were no match for the phenomenal strength of the I'Eloshir.

Visions raced through my mind of past wars... wars that I had fought alongside the Warriors of Magog. It sickened me to know what would become of us, yet to be incapable of any action, to feel the fear that I myself had once caused.

"High Commander!" a voice shouted from a rooftop inside the city wall.

It was the Baroness. Gloria's fire-opal burned crimson against her chest, the flames of the gem trailing down her sword arm to the blade that she carried. Behind her crouched the black cat, its yellow eyes ever-watchful of its mistress. Beside her stood Xane, wielding a spear. As Gloria's gem radiated fire, his was caught up inside what appeared to be a small windstorm.

"We're losing ground. We've got to retreat!" Xane shouted, waving madly in my direction.

"Where?" I demanded, knowing he was right. The I'Eloshir would take the city. We had no choice but to leave it at their disposal and hope to save as many lives as we could. "Where?" I repeated anxiously, watching the dark sky.

"There is an underground passage inside the Armory that leads from Orienca to Celedon," Xane explained. "My brothers and I used to play in the tunnels when we were kids. It hasn't been used as an escape route in centuries, but it could be our last chance."

"That's madness," I argued, more afraid with each passing minute. "The I'Eloshir will follow us into the tunnels. They are more at home underground than above."

"But they don't swim very well, do they?" Gloria interrupted, patting her growling pet. At the mere thought of water deeper than a few feet, I suddenly felt sick. There was still demon enough in me to shudder at the thought of being submerged for more than a split second. Water was life-giving, but it was also cruel. It was one of the few forces of nature that could kill in either extreme, whether there was too little or too much.

"High Commander?" Gloria wondered, obviously sensing my distraction.

"Get the people out," I ordered, coming to my senses. "Xane is right. If there is one thing the demons hate more than sunlight, it is deep water. Take the tunnels to Celedon." I paused, waiting for them to run, but neither Xane nor Gloria so much as blinked.

"Go!" I pointed. "Evacuate your city, fool!" I ordered.

"But you...," Xane began, obviously sensing what I was about to say.

"I will hold off the army. I've done such things before," I replied, without waiting for him to finish his question.

"Alone? But that force is at least a five-hundred strong! And each of those beasts is like ten men... or more," Gloria stared, dumbfounded. "That's suicidal!"

"That is an order," I corrected. "Go now, and hurry!"

Without questioning me further, Xane fled, shouting orders... and Gloria followed close behind.

Trusting them to handle the terrified civilians, I climbed to highest point in the city, the tower of the Knight's Palace, and held my staff to the sky, crackling in purple flame.

"HEAR ME!" I ordered, glaring down at the demon ranks. I spoke in the Old Tongue as I commanded them, drawing all of their focus towards me, the small, seemingly insignificant mortal who knew, somehow, the language of the I'Eloshir.

The I'Eloshir stopped suddenly, their attention drawn towards my command. Despite my lack of practice, the order rippled across the battlefield in massive waves that sent chills down my spine.

At the head of the army, Zae rode... and I realized that my ridiculous plan had in fact succeeded. Even she remained motionless, awestruck and disabled beneath the power of those two little words.

The few citizens of Orienca, who remained thankfully unaffected, grabbed hold of those who were mesmerized and continued to run, my few remaining Imperial soldiers racing after their charges into the underground passage.

"HOW DO YOU DARE ATTACK THIS CITY!" I ordered for the second time, clenching my teeth to avoid losing control as a sharp pain wracked my body. Attempting to control such powerful magic without the strength of my true form was agonizing. "SHEATH YOUR SWORDS!"

In one motion, the army obeyed as all of the drawn weapons were lowered and returned to their carrying positions.

"NOW BOW!"

The I'Eloshir cowered, bowing in submission... but Zae smirked, and I realized in horror that I was losing my hold on them.

I would have to do something drastic. Without shifting, I leapt down from the roof of the tower and landed awkwardly on my feet, more pain shooting through my legs and my back in such a way that I knew I had broken something, and badly.

Humans are not well built to jump off four-story buildings, I realized belatedly, thankful that I hadn't killed myself. The hurt was remarkable as I continued to walk, hearing a cracking, grinding sound in my right leg and feeling a piercing sharpness in my left. But I was too stubborn to fall.

Arrogantly, I strode through the monstrous horde of frozen I'Eloshir, coming to a stop before Zae's horse.

She was precisely as I remembered her, ageless as all of the warriors of Magog and eternally hideous, though her left eye had developed an even more malicious squint than I remembered. It took me a moment to realize it was made of glass.

"DO YOU DEFY ME!" I ordered, staring her in her good eye.

She shuddered, pained by the force, and I stumbled, knowing I did not have enough energy to control all of the warriors for much longer.

Yet Gloria and Xane had worked quickly. Not far away, I could see Xane leading a woman and her children into the Armory. They were among the last.

I began to pull away from the l'Eloshir, lessening the force of my command and slowly backing into through the open city gates, hoping desperately that the demons would remain still for just a little longer...

It was then that my control snapped.

Zae shook her head furiously, escaping from the last ties of the magic and glared down at me, both of her eye suddenly focused, clear and full of hatred.

"I do not know who you think you are, Traverser," she snarled, drawing her sword. "But you will not order me again! Follow me!" She commanded, spurring her horse forward and charged with the rest of the army close behind.

And I ran, sprinting madly towards the doorway where Xane stood, escaping the hooves of the horses only barely as they struggled up the stairs of the Armory. Without a backward glance Xane dove through the door and I followed, barring the gate behind me and diving into the dark, cold water of the open pool.

I sank immediately, struggling furiously for something to grab onto, panicking, wondering why I had not chosen to die instead under the swords of the l'Eloshir.

Instead, I had chosen to drown.

"High Commander... Artemis!" Xane's voice wavered, seeming so far away. Strong hands pulled me out of the water and I gasped, breathing the stale air gratefully. I was drenched, freezing and terrified.

Xane and Gloria stood on the ledge with a few of my men, looking down at me uneasily. Though I had run from an entire army of demons and jumped from the castle wall without hesitation, I had nearly scared myself to death by throwing myself into a mere six feet of water, water I could very nearly stand in.

Further away in the darkness, a long parade of flickering torches lead off towards Celedon. So far, Xane's plan had been a success. If the lights were any indication of the refugees numbers, more than half of the city and a third of my troops had escaped.

"You cannot swim?" one of the men in front of me wondered.

I shook my head. "No, I cannot swim," I admitted, somewhat awkwardly. "Such a little thing," I sighed, attempting to seem unconcerned. "I'll be fine," I reassured the soldier, though I still struggled just looking down into the darkness.

"We'll have to carry you then," a second warrior offered. "Come on, you can trust us."

I paused, hesitating, unwilling to step back into the underground canal. Above, I could hear the demons hacking at the solid door.

There was no alternative. Terrified still, I slid into the chilling water, instantly tense although the two men held me safely afloat as they had promised to.

"No wonder you sink," Xane laughed. "You've got to loosen up and calm down."

"That's easy for you to say." I snapped, choking on yet another mouthful of the filthy sewage. Swearing viciously, I ignored the bewildered stares of the men who had heard me and recognized the origins of my speech.

With the grace of a dancer, Xane dove into the canal, surfacing with a smile.

"You're right," he admitted. "It's my second element. I've been swimming since I was two."

Hours passed as we continued through the labyrinth, sometimes swimming, often climbing or walking, though to me each second we were in the water felt like an eternity.

And then, finally, at long last, I saw sunlight in the distance. Pulling away from the men who held me, I struggled, grasping for the stone ledge.

"Hey, you're swimming," Xane joked.

"Thank the Gods... we've made it." I climbed out and raced up the stairs into the center of a courtyard where thousands of soaking wet figures stood, battered and bruised and waiting in silent fear for what might have followed them in the darkness.

"Is this Celedon?" Gloria wondered suspiciously as a group of green-cloaked Elvin clerics came running to our assistance.

"Celedon," I breathed a sigh of relief and collapsed to the ground.

Twenty-One

I awoke to find myself wrapped in too many bandages to count, warm and dry in a bed of my own. It was some hours later though I couldn't determine precisely how much time had passed. The memory of the swim was still fresh in my mind. Shuddering, I struggled to think of other things, and finally forced myself to my feet. The room I was in struck me immediately as being unique. Tapping the walls, I heard the faint clang of metal and the door itself, though unlocked, was unusually thick.

There were no windows. Despite its sumptuous décor, the room itself reminded me vaguely of a prison cell.

The pain of my injuries had vanished and I was thankful for that, though I was not in any particular hurry to meet the healer who had obviously done the mending. Though physically I appeared human, I still wore the marks of the I'Eloshir on my body… and so far as I knew, I was the only warrior in all of the history of our people ever permitted to wear the symbol of Inapsupetra's mask. That tattoo had been as notorious as my legendary name.

Dressing quickly in the soft robe that lay on the chair at my bedside, I left the strange cell-like chamber and headed down the hall, listening to the sounds of an obviously heated argument.

The door to the room I found myself standing in front of was locked. I knocked.

"Hello?" I demanded, but the voices inside ignored me.

"Open this door!" I snarled, slamming my fist against the wall, but there was still no response. With a small amount of concentration, I grasped the doorknob in one hand and snapped it off, flinging the door open wide and stepping inside.

I had entered a conference room. A crowd of nobles and soldiers, some that I recognized sat gathered around a long, oval table overwhelmed with hundreds of letters and maps marked with little colored pins. All eyes were on me, and on the door which was swinging faintly from its one remaining hinge.

"Don't worry, I'll replace it," I sighed, taking a seat at the table.

"Are you the High Commander?" a man whispered, almost awed.

"They told us you were unconscious," Gloria muttered, obviously a little frightened by my apparently instantaneous recovery.

"Someone healed me," I shrugged.

"The White Cross wouldn't go in your room," Xane shook his head heavily. "They said there was something unnatural in there."

"Oh?" I tried to seem unconcerned, though in truth I was beginning to feel uncomfortable. Fighting had taken its toll on me, especially facing Zaethe... and I was afraid that my weakness was allowing more of my demonic side to surface, perhaps too much more. I would have to be careful.

"Artemis?" Phineas's voice wondered.

Startled, I turned and caught sight of him standing in the doorway with Rosalind at his side. Her green opal flickered as she approached the table where Gloria and Xane were already waiting.

"Are you well enough to be here?" he wondered. "You don't look so good."

"I have just stood before an entire army and swam... mind you... through twelve miles of underground tunnel," I replied, tapping my nails on the table. "To answer your question, yes, I am well enough to sit at a table and listen to your bureaucratic gossip."

"Very well," Rosalind nodded, glancing at me with slight discomfort.

I stared back, realizing quite suddenly that she was the cleric that had repaired my broken bones. I knew not what she had seen and did not care either.

"Order of business?" I prompted, put off by the silence that surrounded me.

"The l'Eloshir are on their way here," Xane announced. "They seem to have stopped about two miles out of Orienca where the road breaks off to Aquara."

"Are you sure they won't head back to Phoenicia?" Rosalind wondered, wringing her hands as she periodically glanced in my direction.

"Highly unlikely," Phineas admitted. "They know that the people who escaped them in Orienca headed this way... and they're upset about that."

"So what do we do?" Gloria wondered, staring down at the marked map in front of her. "The demons can't cross the mountains that separate us from Orienca with their horses, but they could open up one of those Tears of theirs."

"Too much work," I shook my head. "And far too difficult," I sighed. "Few of the I'Eloshir possess any magic, let alone the ability to control a Tear. I don't imagine that any of the warriors we faced in Orienca could even cast such a spell. The I'Eloshir will simply continue back down the road to the west, and then they'll ride fast across the open plains. It will give us an hour or two at best before they arrive at our gates."

"They organize that quickly?" Xane wondered.

"Quickly?" I snorted. "Zaethe Eylchaur is an idiot. The warriors love her, but she's incompetent. If I...," I stopped short, realizing what I had nearly said and fought the chill that crept up on me. "If I were you," I corrected myself. "I would pray that she is the worst you'll face."

Footsteps echoed down the hall as a soldier raced into the room, clutching something glowing in his hand. Beads of sweat dripped down his face and his entire body shook as if he were about to have a seizure.

Gloria, Xane and Rosalind stared, all three of their gems flaring to life in an instant.

Whatever the man carried began to smoke in his grasp and he dropped it, shaking out his burned hand in pain. On the floor, the blue opal flickered faintly as the other stones grew dark once again.

"What is the meaning of this?" Rosalind demanded, her green gem sparkling. "Who are you and why do you carry the Stone of Aquara?"

The man smiled faintly and his features melted, slowly assuming a cat-like appearance. Though he still appeared utterly exhausted, he straightened himself out and bowed to the room three times, to the left, to the right and to the center where Phineas and myself stood.

"Panther?" Rosalind stared, her jaw dropped.

"Elhilom!" I gasped, ignoring the bewildered expressions of the gathered nobles. "What are you doing here? Where did you get that rock?"

"I stole it out from under the Count's nose," he grinned weakly, gesturing to the blue opal on the floor. "Didn't think it would be so hard to hold onto, but it burns like dragon's blood."

"You stole this from Octavian?" Phineas wondered, picking up the gem. The mad shuddering of the other stones quieted. For some reason, the blue opal did not react violently to his touch. "But why?"

"Your amigo Avencourt sold out his city to the IR," Panther explained, wiping his face with a towel. "Made a deal with them that when they won the war, he'd get the diamond mines in Accoloth."

"Impossible!" Gloria shook her head. "How could he..."

"A combination of greed and fear," Xane admitted, scratching his head as if he weren't entirely surprised. "The IR approached me too. They wanted to cut a deal for Orienca. I told them to go to hell. Never thought they'd sic the damn demons on me." He shook his head heavily. "But Octavian's purely a capitalist at heart. He'd sell his soul to protect his fortune."

Rosalind was silent. Her eyes drifted towards Phineas, who still held the blue stone.

"Master Merlin?" she wondered, using his formal title. "Doesn't it burn you?"

Phineas shrugged. "Not particularly," he sighed. "But I am a wizard."

"Someone must take care of the opal until we can find an Avencourt we can trust. And that might be awhile. Merchant pigs," Xane muttered. Gloria nodded appreciatively.

Phineas turned around to face the table and grew very pale.

"Oh no." He stepped back, pushing the stone away from himself. "I don't want that thing."

"Do you think I wanted The Staff?" I grinned.

The gem slid across the table on its own accord and stopped a quarter-inch from his grasp.

"You do have a point," Phineas smiled slightly and carefully slipped the chain over his head. "And it will be only temporary," he announced. "Temporary, you hear me?"

All four of the opals shimmered in the sunlight, and Phineas sat down heavily.

"This thing is a symbol of office, isn't it," he muttered. "Whosoever wears this controls one fourth of the continent or something?"

Rosalind nodded. Phineas groaned, burying his head in his hands. "Someone get me out of this room."

"Well, Panther...," I sighed, turning to where Elhilom had stood a mere second before. As I had expected he had vanished inexplicably.

I glanced around the room at the many astonished faces, weary and weatherworn. Unable to excuse my uncle's behavior, or his disappearance, I fell silent and left the table.

"Psst," Panther hissed as I stepped out into the hall. "Not feeling well?" he wondered, speaking in our own language and sounding somewhat amused.

"No," I shook my head. "It isn't so much bad as it is... unusual," I sighed.

"I am having a difficult time controlling myself."

"You don't have to tell me that, Ire'." He grinned. "I can smell the Emperor all over you."

"Elhil!" I glared. "It isn't funny. Nor is it what you seem to think!"

"I would keep this a secret," he muttered cryptically and then melted into thin air.

I had to think. There were still those who depended on me to come up with some semblance of a plan... after all, I was the great predestined "High Commander." But, despite my wonderful title and colorful costuming, I did not feel like a leader.

For the first time in my life, I didn't know what to do. I wasn't sure if the men of the Dynasty could defeat the IR and the demons of Magog at all, let alone how I myself would lead the Empire to victory. Though I knew that somewhere lingering in the back of my mind lay the strategies and tricks that had once made my armies invincible, I dared not force them to the surface, fearing that if I awakened my warlike side, I would lose control of myself, becoming once again the beast that I feared.

And if that happened... that would be the end of everything.

Seven hours passed and still the I'Eloshir made no move against us. I paced frequently and spoke less as the tense hours wore on, refusing to sleep until I remembered some weakness of Zaethe's that might save Celedon.

I thought of nothing, and that made me increasingly frustrated.

Finally, when Phineas and the others had reached the point where they were debating how they might knock me unconscious or otherwise force me unwilling into bed, The Spellcraft Orion arrived, with Terry and General Auderrauk on board, bearing awful news from Zenith.

Raphael had severely underestimated the strength of the IR. The Republic had successfully overrun most of Ranlain, though the Istarins were holding off their navy at Port Hope. In Accoloth, barbarians were forcing the I'Eloshir into the treacherous cliffs of the dragon's territory, and in Eldar the elves were picking off enemy soldiers one by one, while they themselves remained unseen in the branches of their beloved trees.

Aquara, however had fallen, as had the Badowin Isles where Maurice had been fighting, and the battle in the north had finally reached the point we had feared since the beginning of the war.

Zenith was under siege.

To make matters worse, we in Celedon were overwhelmed ourselves to the point where we could do nothing to help them.

We thought that things had reached their breaking point... that nothing could be more terrible than the helpless captivity we endured, isolated in a small castle with the population of two entire cities, desperately trying to remedy the shortages of food, weaponry and medicine that we suffered... all the while knowing that our capital was being attacked.

Then the demons came.

The Grand Vizier

"When given advice, consider the source."

Twenty-Two

The very ground beneath our feet rumbled as the I'Eloshir approached, Zae spurring her horse and holding aloft a burning banner that I recognized all too well. I couldn't imagine where she'd found it, but sure enough, the flag of a black mask on a red field was my insignia... or rather, that of the Ireval.

"Is she... that one?" an archer on the wall wondered fearfully. "You know, the Ireval?"

"No, fool," I snapped, perhaps more viciously than I had intended to. "If Zaethe Eylchaur was even half the strategist or one-tenth of the warrior that I… that Ireval was, we would all be dead in back in Orienca."

"We come to bargain!" Zae shouted as the clanking of swords armor and pounding of horse's hooves faded to a stop at the foot of the cliff that our fortress stood on.

Maurice stared. "Good God, did she just say what I think she said?"

"But I thought them demons didn't make deals," Terry frowned, peering down at Zaethe through a spyglass.

"They don't," Phineas shrugged, surveying the black and red field. "They kill, steal, burn and lie."

"Most likely, it is one of two things," I admitted. "Either Zae fears that her forces will be defeated, which is unlikely, considering her arrogance... and her numbers. Or there is something here in Celedon so valuable she does not want to risk damaging it when her army overruns the city."

"The opals?" Rosalind suggested.

"Possibly," I admitted. "Though I am inclined to believe that she would rather tear those gems off your dead bodies than receive them in a box."

"So what is it?" Terry asked, glancing at me skeptically.

"Perhaps she'll tell us." I shrugged.

147

Rosalind stepped forward, her green opal glowing. "As Duchess of Celedon, I, Rosalind Arbor, will hear your demands."

"We will spare your city," Zae announced. "On the condition that you release one of our people to us."

"We have none of your soldiers," Maurice argued. "The Errida Dynasty keeps no prisoners, especially not of the I'Eloshir!"

I, of course, had come to the obvious conclusion.

"It is me she wants," I turned to Phineas, who stood with his mouth open and a finger pointed at Zaethe as if he were on the verge of lapsing into childish babble.

"But you said it yourself... you know it's a trap!" Rosalind interrupted.

"A trap that I am setting," I grinned, attempting to seem as confident as possible.

Maurice stared, noticing that my gaze was drifting between Phineas, Rosalind, Xane and Gloria, all who looked equally ill.

"Those rocks of yours cause earthquakes, don't they?" I asked, though I already knew the answer to my question.

Xane nodded. "When we argue."

"But... that's dangerous!" Gloria protested, a small fire forming around her gem.

"I think I understand where you're coming from," Phineas agreed.

Tension between his blue opal and Xane and Gloria's stones caused a slight rumble beneath our feet.

"What are you mortals plotting up there?" Zaethe demanded, shielding her eyes from the glare of the suns.

Rosalind stepped forward, pushing the crowd around me apart.

"This is my city," she announced. "If you think we four may be able to save it... I will do whatever is necessary."

I explained the plan. It was classically not my style, being more reliant on sorcery than brute force... but I had a feeling that, if all went well, Zaethe would find it quite aggravating. There was hope yet for Celedon.

Below us, the I'Eloshir were growing agitated. Above them, where we stood, things did not look much better.

"Lunatic," Maurice snorted. "You don't know that it will work." Looking for support, he turned to Terry, who was grinning insanely.

"I gotta hand it to ya, Artemis," she laughed. "You don't ever do things halfway, d'ya?"

"Apparently not," Xane shook his head, whistling softly.

"Does everyone understand?" Phineas asked.

The group nodded, still marveling at the idea, and I sighed in relief.

"Then let's do it," Gloria agreed.

"Follow my lead," I whispered to the Duchess. "Ask Zaethe who she wants... as if you don't know."

"Who do you seek?" Rosalind turned back to Zaethe's army, apparently fearless. From the way her stone flickered uncertainly, I decided that she was an exceptional actress.

Zaethe laughed insanely and then stopped short, barking a few orders to her warriors, so quickly and harshly that I couldn't even translate what she had said.

All fell silent.

"Your High Commander," Zaethe glanced skyward and I felt as if her eyes could see me through the stone of the castle itself.

It was then that I realized the one fatal flaw in my scheming. After my escapade in Orienca, Zaethe almost certainly knew who I was. The others were likely baffled, but their state of confusion would not last long. Though Zae enjoyed games with high stakes, she would not be appeased indefinitely. Provoking her would give us time to ready Celedon's defenses, but it would also encourage her to reveal my terrible secret, both to her warriors and to the people of Ardra who were gathered within the castle grounds.

"Oh?" Zaethe surveyed the few defenders on the wall, almost as if she were contemplating whether to begin a speech or not. "Or does it surprise you mortals to learn that she is not your kind? Has she concealed her true nature so well? Do you see this flag?"

With that, she threw the flaming banner to the ground.

"Do you recognize the insignia?" she demanded. "Surely your fool Traversers have told you the tales of its origin. And yet you harbor in your very midst one of our most honorable legends!"

I could stand it no longer. Though I knew I was risking all of Celedon by making such a rash move, I had to show myself. The Dynasty would pay dearly if I did not.

How many good men would continue to fight for their homes when they learned they were serving under an evil that had once destroyed entire worlds? I had to preserve the illusionary reputation of Artemis Ravencroft in order to protect the one thing they still possessed when they were outnumbered and outclassed in every aspect...

Geruth's voice came back to me them.

149

"Humankind has a great love for legends... They must believe what is not true, for they find in their fantasies the strength their bodies lack."

"ENOUGH!" I flung open the doors, stepping into the light.

The power of my order rippled through the I'Eloshir army with a stunning effect, but I was weak still from our ordeal in the sewers and its influence did not last.

"Ah, so you have come,." Zaethe grinned. "You are not looking well, Cousin. Is it because your precious humans are throwing you to the wolves at the first sign of danger?"

"Never!" Phineas roared, pushing to my side.

"Silence!" Rosalind snapped, slapping him. "You do not have the right to make that choice! This is my city!"

"We cannot sacrifice the High Commander," Gloria argued. "The demons say they'll leave once they have her, but they also promised to spare Phoenicia."

"If they want her so badly...," Xane muttered, avoiding the other three and winking in my direction, his hand drifting towards his gun. "I say we kill her."

"And how do you propose to do that?" Phineas laughed, reaching out with his mind and snatching the weapon from Xane's grasp. "I am Lord Wizard of the Imperial Court! Do you think you could touch her while I stand in your path?"

I was amazed at his pompous attitude, but not as shocked as I was by the sight of Rosalind approaching from behind him with a staff in hand.

Apparently, simply "staging" a fight hadn't worked.

Without a moment's hesitation, Rosalind cracked him cleanly across the back and Phineas doubled over in pain. All four opals glimmered as Xane and Gloria stared in horror.

The foundations of the castle shook.

"God, Rosalind!" Xane gasped, shoving her aside. "Are you out of your mind?"

"What was that?" Gloria pushed Xane out of her path and grabbed the Duchess by the neck. "I thought we were supposed to be acting. That certainly doesn't look like you pulled your punch! The Emperor's not going to appreciate anyone beating up on his pet wizard."

"Pet wizard!" Phineas glared at her, insulted.

"I do what I must," Rosalind responded coldly.

"Egotistical bitch," Gloria slapped her. "We're in this together whether you like it or not!"

Further rumblings beneath the I'Eloshir caused them to back away from the gates, as I had anticipated. Nearby, where the sea met the land, white-capped waves were beginning to break on the rocks.

"What... was that?" Phineas staggered to his feet.

"Rosalind hit you with this," Xane explained, grabbing the staff from Gloria.

"But...," Phineas wondered.

"Look, get up!" Xane snapped impatiently. "She may have smacked you pretty hard but she's only a female. It's not as if you're crippled."

That did it. Gloria turned slowly to face him. "And just what is that supposed to mean, Tradewind?"

"Well, it's a known fact." He shrugged, apparently not sensing the foolishness of his remark, especially in the face of the Baroness. "You take the best female fighter and the best male fighter in the world... and the man will win. No contest."

"No contest?" Gloria hissed. Her cat snarled from the dark corner where it had been crouched all along.

"I can handle it, Dev," Gloria whispered to the cat. Xane relaxed, assuming, as I myself had, that he was about to be on the receiving end of a volley of insults.

Apparently, we had both underestimated Gloria's famous temper. She lunged at Xane, swinging madly with both fists. Xane caught her right arm, laughing, but it was hardly enough. Furious, she tore free of his grasp and kicked him between the legs.

Xane staggered back, stumbling over Phineas, who in turn reached out to save himself by grabbing the back of Rosalind's gown, effectively pulling her to the ground on top of them both.

"Hey hey hey! Break it up!" Terry pushed her way into the fight, catching Gloria by the hair, only to be tackled in turn by the Baroness's cat.

"Declaw that damn house-pet!" Xane cursed, as the cat raked her claws across his back.

I could feel the trembling in the air, though everyone else seemed distracted by the extended-family feud that was taking place on the battlements. Though I thought it childish at first that the four of them had gone completely insane over such ridiculous issues, I could not deny that it had been Rosalind's recklessness... not my own that had saved us.

There was a sickening lurch as the ground began to crack, tearing open in one single motion. The demons, on the far side of the divide, shrank back in horror as the ocean waves rushed to fill in the chasm, surrounding us on all sides with deep, impassible water.

The argument ceased immediately as Gloria and Xane realized what they had done. Rosalind helped Phineas, who was still rubbing his back, onto his feet.

"Oh." Maurice sat down rather quickly, shaking his head in wonderment. "Well... I confess."

"I don't," Lucy admitted, appearing quite suddenly between us. "Hate church," she paused, munching on the popcorn she carried under her arm and gazed out over the newly formed moat. "You know, this is what's supposed to happen to California."

"What...who?" Terry muttered, turning around for an answer. Of course, as soon as any of us realized who had been speaking, Lucy had vanished yet again.

"Traversers," Maurice groaned, resting his head in his hands.

"I don't know how you stand them, Phineas," Rosalind sighed. "I've met that witch three or four times and I've never said more than a word to her before she disappears completely."

"It takes some getting used to," Phineas admitted, glancing at me doubtfully and then turning back to the Duchess who blushed.

"Oh... and about the... stick," she smiled awkwardly.

"The deathblow to my back, you mean?" He grinned.

"Yes... that," Rosalind whispered. "No hard feelings?"

"It worked, didn't it?" Phineas shrugged, and then winced again. "But I think you broke something."

"How long do you think that river of yours will hold those demons off?" Maurice wondered, eyeing the army suspiciously.

"Indefinitely," Phineas admitted. "So long as the four of us stay here... we can always start hitting each other again." He paused. "Though next time, I think it fair that I should be the one with the weapon."

"Agreed," Xane nodded.

"The I'Eloshir won't want to mess with the kind of magic they've just seen," Gloria added. "They're not partial to water either."

"And they won't fly, even though they are able to," I finished.

All eyes were on me.

"They fly?" Terry groaned, shaking her head and blinking at me. "Like fly-fly?"

"They what?" Rosalind gagged. "Dear god, I thought the feathers were for show. You don't mean they can actually..."

"Why not?" Maurice wondered, cutting off the Duchess and interrupting Xane who seemed ready to speak.

I smiled slightly, thinking of Zaethe standing frustrated on the opposite shore, snarling and cursing me in every language she knew. "Because their leader can't."

"I can always work up a windstorm if they get into the air," Xane offered.

"Good thinking," I nodded, and then paused, wondering what else I could say.

"Raphael needs us in Zenith," Maurice announced suddenly. "If you're sure you can hold your ground here... Terese and I should be returning to Ranlain."

Raphael. It seemed like ages since we had last spoken. I tried not to appear overly distracted, but I guessed that I did anyway.

"You should go with them," Phineas tapped me on the shoulder and I jumped nervously.

"But...," I began.

"Give us some credit, will you?" Gloria grinned. "We're big kids."

"Fair," I laughed. "I suppose you're right."

Gazing out over the horizon, I searched for the silver speck that I knew was out there... somewhere. There was danger still before us... the news from Zenith proved that. Yet our victory over the I'Eloshir without a single life lost gave me hope. If four bickering nobles could hold off a demon army, though we had suffered much already, the war was far from lost.

Twenty-Three

"This is a wonderful ship," I commented, exploring the engine room of The Spellcraft Orion.

"Almost reminds me of The Dogma," Maurice admitted. "God, I do miss that one." He glanced skyward. "That one... now that one was a beauty."

"Hear you got yourself a Spellcraft too," Terry grinned, following us along on the tour. "But nobody seems to know where you came into the money. The Good Old Boys wouldn't even buy me one if I sold my soul. These things are sure something, Spell-ships," she sighed wistfully.

"Have you ever heard of the one they call Panther?" I grinned, enjoying her expression of shock immensely.

Terry and Maurice both stared.

"His Lowliness?" Terry wondered. "Of course, the guy's legendary! But why would he buy you a Spellcraft? Why would he buy anything?"

"He didn't," I shrugged, thinking back on the day we acquired The Hathor. "We stole it."

"That's insane," Maurice argued. "Even for a Traverser, it's impossible. I would have remembered if there was a Spellcraft reported stolen... it would have been all over the news." Maurice shook his head. "Do you mind my asking where you took it from?"

"Outside of Border-Town," I sighed. "It's strange though. The ship seems to be almost living sometimes..."

"Might I have a look at it?" Maurice asked, obviously intrigued.

"If my uncle ever brings it back. Look at this." I pulled a small scrap of paper out of my pocket and held it up for them to see. "I found this where my ship was docked the night after I landed in Orienca."

"Sorry no notice, borrowing ship, need to kill big monster/rescue in-laws. Damn woman threw me out until/unless when/if I bring them back. Love,

154

Elhil," Terry read. "So that's Panther, huh? He always like that?"

I nodded, sighing heavily. "Sometimes I wonder what to make of him myself."

"Traversers," Maurice snorted. "Thank God there are none in my family."

I knew better than to take offense at that remark. Though Maurice loved nothing more than complaining about any immortal that crossed his path, we all knew that he was loyal to the Dynasty. It was almost comical to see him advising and berating Raphael as if he were the father and Raphael the son, although in truth it was Raphael who was centuries older than Maurice.

We set sail at once, soaring off towards Zenith at a breathtaking speed. Hours passed uneventfully, and then, once we were far beyond sight of land... we received a distress call. As good and respectable people, we responded. We thought we were being honorable... even benevolent in rescuing the poor, marooned strangers who had begged us in the names of the Gods. We were fools.

"I'm picking up something, General," one of our men on the ship announced, waving to Maurice.

"So?" Terry gestured to the sailor's controls.

"Let's hear it," Maurice agreed.

A crackling sound I had learned to recognize as a radio transmission filled the cabin, accompanied by voices.

"Help... Imperial soldiers... 465678... stranded... need doctor, cleric... 56.4, 64.2... Spellcraft Porthos... wreck."

"They're right below us," I realized, peering out the window. "But there's no land for miles!"

"Lookit!" Terry pointed. "There! That's a sea-patch!"

"It must be the wreck," Maurice rushed to her side. "But The Porthos disappeared weeks ago!"

"What's a sea-patch?" I wondered, squinting out over the waves to where Terry had pointed. Sure enough, in the distance I could barely glimpse the silhouette of something that appeared to be a large iceberg.

"But that's ridiculous!" I argued. "We're much too far south for ice."

"Not that kind of ice." Terry shook her head.

"Spellcraft fuel doesn't agree with the environment," Maurice explained. "It'll freeze anything solid, even your hands if you touch it."

"You mean..." I was amazed.

"When a Spellcraft crashes into the ocean, it freezes the water around it. We can clean up the mess, of course, but it is a very time-consuming and expensive process," Maurice sighed. "Environmentalists… especially the elves and the Druidic Council go crazy about it. I'm surprised this disaster wasn't reported right away."

"I never knew," I stared. So that island of frozen waves was what remained of The Porthos. It was a frightening thought.

"Not many people do," Maurice admitted.

"What should we do about the distress call, General?" the helmsman asked.

"We're going in," Maurice announced. "By the size of that sea-patch… I'd say there's a good chance that there might be men alive down there."

"You sure, Maurice?" Terry wondered.

He shook his head. "Not entirely. But if there are sailors of this Empire shipwrecked here… we cannot afford to pass them by."

Without further discussion, we landed.

Stepping out onto the sea-patch, I felt instantly ill. Visions of ships exploding in midair raced through my mind, of armies racing across miles of frozen waves.

I shook my head and forced the dark thoughts away, knowing I had envisioned an impossibility. Even if every Spellcraft in Zenith were to crash… they would not be enough to cause that kind of damage. Still, the idea made me uneasy.

What was worse, was that there seemed to be no sign of a single living soul on the wreck. Buried in a pile of snow, the radio still buzzed faintly, though it must have been ages since it was touched by human hands. Or else… nothing was as it seemed.

"Chilly, ain't it?" A voice laughed. "Why don't chu'all freeze?"

I stopped short, feeling the cold barrel of a gun jabbing into my back and turned, raising my hands slowly above my head.

"Drop em', magic-user!" the man sneered. He was human, dressed in white camouflage and ski glasses, unshaven, stinking, and armed to the teeth.

And he was not alone. From behind every snowdrift and bend in the ice, soldiers appeared, all nearly invisible against the bleak white canvas of the landscape.

It was impossible to count how many there were, but they outnumbered us for certain.

"Chu, and chu' with the hat on, the two of you put those hands of yours behind yer backs, keep em' flat against yer own bodies and don't chu point em' at no'un." The man who held his gun to my head ordered again. "Don't chu think that we don't know what yer kind can do. The rest of chu'all keep reaching for the sky. Argus, tie em' up."

"Aye, Captain Ymir," the one who stood closest to Maurice nodded.

I could feel the man's breath on the back of my neck as he squinted at me with his one good eye, knowing that I was someone he should recognize. And then it hit him.

"If it ain't the High Commander!" the one called Ymir exclaimed, recognizing me quite suddenly. "The bloody High Commander!" He laughed triumphantly. "Boyos, search this un' good. She's not t'have anything she kin catch a reflection in, ya hear? Else we'll lose the lot of them prisoners an' mayhaps our lives as well."

"Aye, Captain." Argus nodded. "What t'bout the others?"

"Gen'ral Auderrauk and ..." Ymir grinned. "Madwoman Mack. The Chaos Knight, if I'm not mistaken. An' I know I ain't, when it comes to you!" he growled, slapping her across the face.

"What is the meaning of this?" Maurice demanded. I was equally baffled by the strange turn of events.

But Terry knew what we had run against, it seemed. "You all are Slavers, ain't you?" she hissed. "Should've smelled ya comin'."

"Slavers?" I was aghast. "Slavers... You mean... they'll sell us?"

"To the highest bidder," she nodded. "There weren't no more of them in this realm, not for a long while... I'd seen to that, till the Republic came."

"Which reminds me, Miss Mack." The captain grabbed Terry by the hair. "I have a dead mate who'd love to meet ye. That's if our Admiral imself' won't pay up... which methinks he will, considerin' how ye cut out is' eye."

"What do we do?" I whispered, nudging Maurice.

He shook his head heavily. "If I knew..."

"Getta move on!" the Slaver nearest me snapped, slapping me across the back with the flat of his sword. I staggered forward, into the darkness of what had been our Spellcraft, and down into the brig, where the three of us were chained to the walls. The other members of the crew, those who would not fetch a high ransom or were too loud for their own good... were brutally and unceremoniously shot.

Hours passed in the darkness where we lay, torn between our fear of both what lay ahead, and behind us. Though neither Maurice, nor I myself spoke a single word, Terry seemed even further withdrawn, scratching patterns in the dry rice piled at her feet and mumbling to herself as if she were attempting some sort of spell that continually failed to yield any result.

"Thanks Shaeruhl," she grinned faintly. "You're a gem."

Finally, she looked up, rubbed her eyes and turned to us.

"I've gotta go," she announced. "I got a "Get out of Jail Free" card from my Good Boys."

"Terry, this is madness," I argued. "There's no way to escape."

"Yeah." She shook her head. "That's what I told em'. But they says they're givin' me a Favor, so I gotta have faith they know what they're doin'... this is one hell of a Favor an' I hate to think'a how I'll hafta pay this one back, but I promise I'll bring the cavalry soon as I can."

The pure, clear sound of a ringing bell echoed throughout the ship, and in a flash of brilliant white light, Terry vanished.

"Impossible," I stared. "That kind of sorcery..."

"Damnit!" the captain roared from above. "Damn those Boys, they've taken Terry Mack."

"You sure?" another of the men wondered. "Shouldn't we look?"

"Y'hear that bell, chu fools?" Ymir snarled. "Don't chu know nothin? The knight's gone and she'll be back sooner then's good for us if she's got them Boys on her side! We gotta lose those other two nobles an' split quick."

"Maurice, who are they?" I wondered.

"Slavers," Maurice shrugged. "That we've discussed."

"Not them," I shook my head. "Terry's boys... the "Good Old Boys"."

"No one knows," Maurice admitted. "Though, with all the Favors they seem to request and distribute, many people believe that they must be powerful Etone. Very old Traversers, perhaps. Traversers," he sighed.

"That's a favor?" I stared. "How did they do that? She's vanished without a trace!"

Maurice nodded.

"And she said that then these "Good Boys" of hers … they would expect help in return," I muttered, beginning to understand. "But what kind of a favor might such a being demand from a mere mortal?"

"No one knows," he shook his head, "those strange few that have met the legendary Good Boys take the secret with them to their graves."

"Where to, Captain Ymir?" one of the Slavers asked, entering the cabin above us.

Maurice and I both fell silent.

"Set course for that island to the west. There's a few beasties there that ave' a fair supply of treasure," the captain yawned, reclining his chair.

"Safehaven Island," the helmsman announced, almost mechanically. "Full speed ahead."

It was a long time before I dared speak again, trying to make sense of all that had happened. After what seemed like an eternity, the ship began to slow, and finally stopped completely.

Sensing the darkness that lingered so near, I suddenly felt very ill. Above, on the deck, I could hear the distant sounds of conversation in a language I knew, though I made out few of the words.

"I think they've found a buyer for me," I muttered. "Kyul thuatha ire'aielu undyr su nys'kaa nyesh...," I muttered to myself, translating what little I could hear. "It's the l'Eloshir. They don't understand why their lord is giving up so much of his treasure in exchange for... the worthless traitor."

"Demons?" Maurice stared. "But I thought they were taking us west, towards Safehaven! There are men of the church on that island... Safehaven is a sanctuary!"

"Tell that to the l'Eloshir and they'll kill you for speaking the word." I shook my head, fighting off another of my dark memories. "The stories about holy relics and sacred space are just that… stories. The only thing demons fear from monks and priests is their white-light magic. They'll live in a cathedral and sleep around the altar if the priests are all dead."

"This place is a sanctuary!" the priest in my mind screamed… moments before I crushed his skull. Sick as it was… that thought brightened my mood considerably.

All at once, I returned to the present, disgusted with myself.

At that moment, the trap-door above us opened and two pairs of grubby hands reached down into the pit where we lay, pulling me to the surface.

Next, before my eyes adjusted to the light, I could hear them dragging up Maurice.

Across from us sat the Slaver's captain Ymir, and beside him, a man I did not recognize, a human who wore on his cloak the symbol of the Republic.

He smiled broadly when he caught sight of Maurice and myself, filthy, battered and helpless.

"This is excellent, Ymir!" The IR man grinned, surveying us as if we were horses, or perhaps simply meat. "General Auderrauk... and High Commander Ravencroft in one nice little package. I shall take them both. Name your price."

"I'm afraid I can't do that, Mr. Fairfax." The captain shook his head. "But chu're welcome to Lord Errida's Grant Vizzer. I'll take three million for im'."

Mr. Fairfax. The President of the IR. Often I'd pictured him, sometimes as a powerful warrior, other times as a wise and silent sorcerer... never as an ordinary human. So this one unimpressive mundane was the responsible for the hell we were going through. I could kill him in an instant. I considered doing it.

"Then I'll give you six for her. Make that seven. Seven million."

"Nohow. Can't take." Ymir shook his head. "Y'see there's some folk in pretty high places what're looking at settlin' things with Miss Ravencroft here. Real high places, boyo. Higher places than you even, Mr. Fairfax."

I shuddered, feeling a sudden chill, as a dark, shadow materialized slowly in the room, stepping silently out of a near invisible Tear.

Maurice stared, muttering prayers under his breath and lowering his eyes as if he'd just seen death and was preparing to go meet his maker.

I stood only very still and refused to bow, though the force of the shadow's will alone was nearly enough to bring me to my knees.

It had been a long time since we had come face to face, my father and I.

Fairfax paled.

"Geruth Ithraedol." He smiled winningly. "I should have guessed. You're a reasonable man, Warlord... we could work something out."

"This matter requires no discussion." Geruth ran his claws across the captain's desk, digging deep into the wood. "In any other case, I would gladly bargain with you, gold and gems in exchange for a useless mortal, but you see this one..." He grinned, relishing the words he knew I hated to hear. "This one is my daughter."

The Judge

"If they take to the air, he shoots them down. If they hide in the earth, he digs them out."

Twenty-Four

"OBEY ME!" The force of Geruth's order pounded over and over again in my mind as I felt myself being drug through miles and miles of worlds... and between worlds, gradually losing consciousness.

My body ached in every way possible as I struggled futility, unable to pull away from the Warlord's phenomenal power. Finally, when I had exhausted all of the energy I possessed, I fell through the other end of the Tear... fell gasping for air and sliding across the wet stone floor.

The water should have been cold, my skin should have torn and bled on the rough gravel... as it would have, had I still been human.

But I was mortal no longer.

Though I had felt no hatred, no lust, no evil emotion, somehow my demonic form had returned. I lay on the ground, digging my claws into the dirt and tasting the blood where my fangs had cut my own lip.

Even though it flowed from my own veins, the scent was marvelous... the blood, the air, even the mildew.

That sudden awakening was perhaps the only worthwhile thing that had come from the hellish shift I had gone through. I breathed as deeply as I could, grateful in a way, that, if I were to die, I would not meet my end without experiencing the world one last time with my powerful senses intact.

However, with the sight, and the smell, and the sounds, came also the revolting body of a beast. At first, my wings were too heavy for my aching muscles to lift, as if they were dead... yet slowly, as my heart pounded furiously, I could feel them again.

The hatred that I bore for myself, for what I was, at that moment nearly consumed me.

At any other time, repulsive as it was, I would have experienced an upsurge of power with the change, as I became stronger, faster, and nearly invulnerable.

But at that moment, with Geruth standing over me, I felt none of those things, only my weakness and inadequacy against such an ancient and all-seeing foe.

"I returned you to your proper form," Geruth announced, smiling slightly. "Do you feel better?"

"Bastard," I snarled, "I hate you."

He sighed, almost as if he were disappointed. "I thought you might say that."

"If you intend to kill me, you might as well now," I glared at him. "I have never feared death... and you know it."

"Indeed," Geruth sighed. "That amusing trait of yours did pose a problem, when I was deciding how you should be punished. You see, Ireval..."

"Do not call me that name," I muttered, refusing to look at him. "Call me Daughter, call me Beast, call me what you will... but do not call me that name."

"Why not?" The Warlord grinned. "I seem to remember quite well, a time not so long ago when you were proud of that title. You were glorious then... they all envied you. Even I... I envied you. You had a certain grace when you killed, you made each death unique… artistic. Remember those ages, Ireval. Remember the power, the freedom... the scent of smoke on the dying breeze. The feeling of holding a still-living heart in your hands, the taste of a single soul."

I remembered, and within me, something stirred. Furious at my own shortcomings... I hated myself for not resisting the temptation he placed before me, and it was that hatred, again, that reawakened my conscience.

"Times have changed." I shook my head. "I am not what I was."

"Times will never change," Geruth hissed. "And you will always be what you are. Do you know where we are, Ireval?"

I looked up in bewilderment at the ivy-covered walls, the bleached skeletons on the stairs and the granite altar in the center of the room. And I realized, with horrific certainty, that Geruth spoke the truth... that I did know this place.

Near the altar, in a hidden alcove, stood a masked statue of Inapsupetra, wielding a sword in her right hand and a rose in her left. Unlike all of the other idols I had seen in the depths of Magog, it was half-black and half-white, evenly divided down the center.

Upon closer examination, I realized that the sword was blunted, and the rose full of long thorns.

"I do," I nodded. "This is where you found me... this is where my sickness came from. This is the place where my memories left me."

"A lie," he grinned. "Perhaps one of the most marvelous lies that I have ever told. You never ran away. You were never cursed by the Sun-God... your mother never killed herself. You had no mother. You were nothing before that day, that day... that I created you."

"Such magic is beyond your power," I argued, though I could barely speak those few words. I wished desperately that Geruth was lying, only wanting to trick me, and turn me back to my old ways, but I knew I could make no such accusation, sensing myself that it was all true... all of it.

"I CREATED YOU, DO YOU HEAR ME!" Geruth roared, smashing the altar in two. "YOU ARE MINE!"

"No...," I sobbed, hating myself all the more. What redemption awaited such a creature? If Geruth had made my body... how had he gotten my soul? What other life had I been destined for, yet never known?

"Kill me now!" I cried, flinging myself at his feet. "I beg you, kill me!"

"Ah," Geruth laughed softly. "It worked."

I stopped short and slowly pulled myself to my feet, backing away, yet not daring to take my eyes off of him.

"What have you done?" I demanded.

"You have been tried, found guilty, and punished," he recited. "For your disobedience to my will, you are hereby sentenced to live... the rest of your immortal life within the confines of these walls in the body that I have given you. When all your mortal friends are dead, and your beloved Empire a wasted land of ever-burning flames, when I have destroyed everything dear to you, I shall return to you and let you know. And then, then I shall seal you within this place and leave you to your memories... forever."

No crueler words had ever been spoken.

"I will die," I argued, perhaps trying to convince myself. "I will someday die."

"No," Geruth shook his head, "you will not. Your blood is quite pure. You are a truer Immortal than you realize, Ireval. You will never die. But you will wish that you could, as you remember this day a thousand times over... and over... and over for eternity."

Without another word, he vanished.

"Geruth!" I screamed, pounding my fists against the walls, unable to open a Tear, unable to break free of that hateful place, that place that harbored no sound of life, save my own voice.

165

"Warlord!" I begged, knowing that he would not answer me. "Father..."
Still, there came no reply.

Furious, I ran to the statue of Inapsupetra, tore her sword and her rose from her stone grasp and pried at her mask, though it would not give way.

"What have you done to me?" I demanded. "Where are you now! How can you let this happen! I am your beloved, damn you. You were supposed to protect me..."

A cold hand reached down to caress my shoulder, and a soft voice whispered for me to hush.

Startled, I looked up, only to find the Goddess motionless. Yet the idol had moved, compelled, perhaps by its own desire, and it was her stone touch that I had felt on my shoulder. But the statue no longer breathed, and her eyes were emotionless, except for what appeared to be a single silver tear on her cheek. I caught it as it fell, amazed.

In my hand I held a tiny, moon-shaped mirror.

I had known it, somehow, always... deep inside, even at the worst of times! There were those above us, and those above them, and somehow, though far-withdrawn from the mundane world was someone... some power that understood this hell we fools lingered in and sought to make things right. The feeling was glorious for an instant, and then it was gone.

Without wasting a moment, I jumped, throwing myself headlong into oblivion. Water rushed up around me, wherever I had landed, cold, dark, and crushing to my already air-starved lungs.

In a way, I was thankful. Death, death at long last. A tormented soul such as myself could have asked for no greater gift.

Twenty-Five

And yet I did not die. I came to my senses lying wet and bedraggled, still in my demonic form at the foot of a tall waterfall.

Had I been human, the drop would have surely killed me. Again, I cursed myself. Even with all the power one could ever desire, I was unable to break so much as a single bone in my own body.

Voices approached in the forest. Not daring to ask for food, shelter or aid, such as I was, I simply lay still and closed my eyes.

"Hey!" a boy's voice exclaimed. "Everybody, hurry... you've got to see this!"

Footsteps surrounded me.

"A demon," the second voice belonged to a young girl; though from the way she spoke, one would have guessed that she was wise beyond her years.

I recognized her presence without even opening my eyes.

The girl was Brin Falchon... the young sorceress who had held the crystals in the Prophet's test of the Imperial Court... and the boy was her closest friend, Ira the Kid, the Etone child from Mad Mack's.

I was in Istara.

I knew well that many of the Empire's children had been sent out of Zenith and away from the coasts of Ardra, into the forests and mountains of Edgar's kingdom where they would be safer.

Still, though they were young, Brin and Ira both held great power, and Ira specialized in the particular brand of white magic that I myself found very difficult to fend off. I would not risk startling them, for fear that I might kill them accidentally.

Holding my breath, I continued to play dead.

"Brin! Ira! Get away from there!" Edgar roared, crashing through the underbrush. "It might be alive!" He stopped short. "It's a she," he observed.

167

"Damn, I didn't know there were any pretty ones."

"A demon? Here?" a second voice wondered, a very familiar one.

Startled, I opened my eyes and sat up.

Brin and Ira screamed in terror and Edgar tripped over a stone, sliding off the path and into the water.

I stared, finding myself face to face with Phineas. He dropped the sword he carried, recognizing me in an instant.

"All of you, run!" he ordered. "I'll deal with this beast!"

Ira and Brin nodded obediently, vanishing without a trace, but Edgar was too stubborn for his own good.

"Get out of here, you fool!" Phineas snapped. "Run!"

"I'll fight with you," he argued, drawing his blade.

"And what if there are more of them in the forest?" Phineas demanded. "Protect the children!"

Realizing quite suddenly what Phineas was plotting, I pulled myself to my feet and jumped into the air.

Feeling the wind in my wings, even for the briefest moment was exhilarating.

"The young ones!" I shouted, to my invisible allies. "Follow them!"

In a flash, Edgar was gone.

"Artemis," Phineas stared. "What happened? Where have you been? We heard you were dead!"

"I very nearly was," I sighed, descending to the ground again. "I wish... I wish I was." Not having the heart to lie to my old friend, I told him the entire story.

"But that was six months ago." He shook his head.

"Time passes differently between realms, I suppose." I admitted.

"This is fascinating!" Phineas contemplated the idea, scratching his head thoughtfully. "If one day in Magog equals half a year in our realm... and if the demon's year is two days less than..."

"I do not understand such numbers." I shook my head. "I cannot even count my own age."

"You're seven hundred... eighty-nine... or was it ninety eight?" He grinned. "Master Galwick and I figured it out once. Took us all night."

"I should have guessed the two of you would try," I laughed... and then stopped short. Phineas froze, as if he too had just realized that something was amiss.

"There's something wrong, isn't there?" Phineas asked, suddenly. "You're talking, you're being rational. Why... why haven't you changed back?"

I turned away.

"Because I can't," I admitted. "My father put a spell on me."

Phineas squinted at me. "What a strange magic," he muttered, awed. "I'm sorry, but it isn't anything I can remove. The enchantment is wound so tightly... I can't even see where it begins and ends," Phineas shrugged, "but I'm not the most powerful wizard in the world."

"Just in the Empire," I finished. "Geruth has been studying spell-crafting for centuries. He lead the assault against Raedawn... and his mother taught him virtually everything she knew... which was a considerable amount."

"What are we going to do?" Phineas whispered finally. "Edgar will be back soon... and I'm not so sure we need another fool in on our secret."

"Our secret?" I wondered, slightly amused. "The two of us and Raphael, you mean. And Panther... and Lucy, Deiunthel, Ordo, Beyoni... possibly Ruveus or Rosalind and at very least Maurice. How is that a secret?"

"You have a point," Phineas agreed. "But I still don't like the idea of Edgar knowing... well, everything."

"I don't blame you," I nodded. "Can you disguise me?"

"It won't look good," Phineas winced. "I'm terrible at that sort of magic," He explained. "If I wasn't... well, I'd be five inches taller, not to mention this hair...," Phineas sighed. "I could never make you look like yourself."

"This is myself," I muttered, clenching my teeth. "What I want to know is whether you can make me look different. Not necessarily human again, just different.

It's one thing if someone recognizes me as I'Eloshir...," I whispered. "It's another thing entirely if they recognize me as..."

"Say no more!" Phineas rolled up his sleeves and slipped a dragon-shaped pendant off of his neck, laying it to rest on a large stone before him.

"What happened to the blue opal?" I wondered, realizing suddenly that he no longer wore the Ardran gem.

Phineas shrugged. "Gave it to a little girl I ran into. About six years old. Student of Rosalind's sorceress."

"You what?" I stared. "You gave a magical artifact of that power to an apprentice mage... a thing you didn't even trust yourself with! It sinks continents and you gave it to a... a child?"

"I had a good feeling about her," he admitted. "I had a good feeling about you when we met. I think it's safe to trust my intuition."

"If you say so..." I shook my head and turned away. There were some things I would never understand about Phineas, and his logic was one of them.

Mumbling something under his breath, Phineas clapped his hands. In a shower of silver sparks, a large yellow shadow appeared, radiating from the necklace.

Almost as if he were afraid to see the results of his work, Phineas opened one eye hesitantly.

"Oh," he winced.

"Master Merlin!" Edgar shouted, racing back towards the river.

"Damnit," Phineas groaned, "Artemis, you've got to run."

"No time," I shook my head and grabbed the still-glimmering pendant from where it lay on the stone, slipping it around my neck, and not a moment too soon.

Edgar burst into the clearing, breathing heavily.

Upon catching sight of me, he sheathed his sword, still staring as if it hadn't occurred to him that he was being impolite.

"What do I look like?" I demanded, elbowing Phineas.

"Not... good," he muttered, shaking his head. "Human... maybe ogre."

"Ogre?" I glared.

"It would explain your strength," he whispered. "And your height, and your temper..."

"Temper!" I snarled, insulted. "I was the bane of entire civilizations! By the Gods, you have never seen my temper!"

"Friend of yours?" Edgar turned to Phineas, who sighed heavily. "I... oh. yes," he finished. "She arrived just in time to help me get rid of that demon."

"Trivial." I smiled as genuinely as I could, wiping the dirt off my hands. "Master Merlin could have handled the beast by himself, of course, but I happened to be walking by..."

"Well educated for a troll," Edgar shrugged.

I hissed for at him angrily for a split second and then fell silent, realizing what I had done. Apparently, the disguise did not change what I was, only what others perceived me to be.

Which meant that I was still very much a danger... to myself and everyone else as well.

"Are you all right?" Edgar wondered.

"Quite." I nodded.

"You seem familiar," he shook his head, "what was your name again?"

"Rebecca!" Phineas announced suddenly. "Edgar, meet Rebecca the

Wanderer."

"Rebecca?" I eyed him suspiciously, wondering just where he'd gotten the name from.

Phineas sighed, "It came to me, okay? Call it an epiphany."

"Very well," I sighed, shaking my head.

And thus, Rebecca the Wanderer, the first of my many aliases, was born.

Twenty-Six

Following Phineas, who watched me nervously, and Edgar, who kept his eyes on the sky, I soon found myself in a green clearing at the foot of an immense willow tree, its heavy branches creaking in the wind as the entire tree rocked back and forth, almost hypnotically.

The place had been beautiful and full of life once, I could feel it, but something had drained all of the color away from the clearing, leaving only the undeniable aura of age and wear.

"Kids!" Edgar shouted, waving to the tree where Ira and Brin were hiding. Two small faces peered out of the green curtain, eying us suspiciously.

"We're not kids," Ira argued. "I'm fifteen and Brin's fourteen."

Fifteen? I stared, knowing that I would have placed the both of them somewhere around ten.

"And we're both magic-users," Ira continued. "We'll take care of ourselves."

"As you took care of that demon?" I smiled.

"Hey, how do you know about...," Ira began. "Who are you anyway?"

"Rebecca the Wanderer," I replied.

"You Etone?" he demanded, climbing down a few branches.

"Maybe," I grinned, remembering the customary greeting. "What about you? Are you a brother?"

"Could be." Ira grinned, leaping out of the tree and adopting an almost gangster-like swagger. "Where you from?"

"Nowhere you've ever been to, Bro," Phineas interrupted.

"Master Merlin?" Ira gasped. "You're a..."

Phineas shook his head. "No... I'm not a member of the Brotherhood. I did live with one for awhile, though."

"Who?" Ira wondered.

Phineas winked. "Went by the name of... Silas Galwick"

"No way!" The boy grinned. "My bro' Germ met him once, back like a hundred years ago. Said he was wicked righteous."

"Master Galwick?" I shook my head. "Not the sorcerer I knew. He was tired more often than not... and old enough to be feeling his age."

"Oh," Ira sighed, sounding disappointed.

"But he was a good teacher. I bet you learned a lot." Brin slid out of the tree, her eyes focused on me as if she could see right through my disguise spell.

"I was never his apprentice." I turned away, though I could feel her eyes still on me. There was something about the girl that I had always found troubling. Though she appeared human, I wondered about her origins more often than not. I supposed that it was the age her eyes radiated that unsettled me. She was not merely a young animal as most children seemed to be, she seemed like a newborn immortal... somehow fully aware of her incredible potential without losing her startling innocence.

"I didn't say you were," Brin stared still.

I shuddered, stretching my invisible wings to the sky, trying to calm myself by focusing on the breeze. Without another word, we began to walk, headed towards civilization.

I kept towards the back of the marching order, avoiding conversation and savoring the strong north wind that blew through the trees. If ever there was a day for flying, a day such as that one would have been ideal.

What was worse than the temptation, however, was the fact that I had wings again. Though they could not be seen, I guessed that the vision of an ogre soaring through the air as if held by puppet strings would be enough to ruin my disguise permanently.

I planned to rid myself of the need for it, of course, but who knew when... or if ever I would be able to.

Still, even imagining that I was flying was pleasant to me, anything to take my mind off Geruth.

A black feather wafted on the breeze and landed at Edgar's feet.

"Look, there's a raven feather!" He grinned. "I thought the birds had gone from this part of the forest."

"They have," Brin replied coldly, once again turning to stare at me.

"Not all of them," Edgar argued. "There must be some left."

"Or perhaps our hunchback is not what she seems," Brin muttered.

The others frowned at her cryptic warning and continued down the path.

173

"What are you?" she demanded, gazing at me in such a way that I knew I had no choice but to be honest with her.

"You know," I replied, not daring to come any closer.

"I sense that you are not what you appear to be." Brin shook her head. "Nothing more."

"Hurry up! We've got a few miles to go before we reach town!" Edgar shouted.

"Let them walk at their own pace," Phineas advised. "Rebecca knows these forests well, she'll take care of Brin should any of those demons be lurking about."

"I'Eloshir!" Brin gasped, suddenly understanding our plot. "You were the one we found in the river! I knew it... but why... what would Master Merlin..."

"Quiet," I ordered. "I am a friend of his," I explained, with some honesty. "But as the times are... one cannot tell enemy from ally, let alone demon from Traverser."

"Look at me," Brin demanded. "I can tell."

Pulling me by the collar down to her level, she gazed deeply into my eyes as if prying for some information that I was not sure I myself possessed.

"Artemis?" she exclaimed, recognizing me instantly. "But what happened to you? You've been cursed!" she screamed, tearing off her cloak and shoving me away. "Cursed!"

"Brin, calm down!" I ordered. "Brin, they'll hear you!"

"They did it to my father!" Brin sobbed, falling to the ground. "They made him a monster... my mother tried to hide him! And then she met the t...teacher, but he wasn't what he... he made her k...kill them... my b..brothers, she killed them all!"

"Phineas! Edgar!" I shouted. "Help me!"

There was no response. They had evidentially passed beyond earshot.

"Brin, you must gain control!" I demanded, shaking her. "Whatever you think you see, it is not happening! Do you hear me! You must listen!"

All at once, with a piercing cry, the young sorceress vanished in an explosion of light, a fiery phoenix-form marking her passage across the sky.

So much for my protection...

Days passed in the wilderness before I finally stumbled into the city that Phineas had assured Edgar I knew how to find.

Though I had moved much more quickly without worrying about how foolish my disguise must have looked, and without any companions to protect,

I had failed to account for one thing... the sheer size of the forest I was traveling through.

Many times I had crossed my own path over, and after each circle I was left wondering why I didn't simply go running for the nearest Tear, until I reminded myself that, most likely, if I jumped, I would be seen... and the sooner I was seen, the sooner I would be caught.

So it was at noon of my fifth day in the forest that I reached the merchant's city of Port Hope. Wasting no time, starved and exhausted as I was, I headed directly for the tavern. Though Phineas and Edgar were nowhere to be found, it was there that I first heard talk of the Empire's failing condition.

"The entire Falchon House is dead. Lady Rose killed them all herself, then took a jump off the nearest cliff," a man muttered. "Bloody nightmare. Wouldn't have surprised me if her husband snapped, bein' how he was... you know, but she... my wife went to school with her." He sighed. "I always thought Rose was just fine, you know?"

"They say that General Auderrauk's been wounded," a sailor commented. "And I'll tell ya, that man may be the greatest there ever was... only now he's somewhat passed his prime."

"What if he dies?" another man, a knight in rusted armor, muttered. "What if he dies like the High Commander? Then who leads us?"

I had not fully come to grips with the fact that I was dead. It had been difficult enough accepting that I was immortal... and now, quite unexpectedly I was deceased.

"They ought to have some sort of list," The sailor agreed. "Ought to say who's next in line... and whatnot."

"What about Terry Mack?" the young boy who was sweeping the floor suggested.

"Nah, she's too young," The knight shook his head.

"Too young?" The sailor laughed. "That wench is a sight older than your grandmother!"

"She don't act it," he muttered.

"Does the Emperor act like he's eight hundred?" the sailor demanded. "Before the war, back when the Herichae Rangers and the Kingstown Paladins were going to the series... you remember how it was all in the papers how he got caught saying he'd rather play baseball than politics. That sounds like a kid thing to me."

I laughed softly. If only they knew.

'Say, what you laughin' at, Beast?" the knight growled, glaring at me.

175

"Forgive me," I apologized. "I just overheard your conversation. "It has been awhile since I've seen civilization."

"Been awhile since civilization's seen you," the knight corrected. "God, you stink like dragon dung. Take a bath!"

"Excellent advice," I agreed, though I was somewhat insulted by his remark.

But just then, as I was about to make my way up the stairs, a sound on the streets grabbed my attention.

Racing out the front doors of the inn, I saw that a sort of argument had begun outside in front of the Apothecary... an argument that apparently concerned three well-armed mercenaries... and a gangly, filthy boy I recognized immediately as Ira.

"Lemme go!" he demanded, biting the man's hand that reached for him, and kicking the mercenary's partner in the shins.

"I'll cast a spell!" he threatened. "I'm Etone! The Brotherhood will come after you!"

All the men laughed.

"Now hold up kid!" the leader of the men muttered, turning to glance at me through his strangely glowing green sunglasses. "We ain't afraid of none of your make-believe Traversers. And we're not gonna hurt you... we just want to talk to the wizard Merlin..."

He drifted off into silence as he stared at me.

"Men... you'd better have a look at this." He snapped his fingers and his two companions turned in my direction, all peering at me through the same greenish glass.

"Sweet Jeezus," one of the mercenaries gasped. "What'dya think that one's worth?"

It was then that I realized that I had been mistaken. The three men were not merely suspicious travelers... they were bounty hunters! More of Terry's damnable Slavers, no doubt.

"Ira...," I began, but the boy was nowhere to be seen. To make matters worse, the scum no longer cared what became of Phineas... now that they had a new target.

Me.

"She got that high of an MC standing still?" the leader wondered, still squinting at me. "Five-forty. What they hell kinda troll ranks a five-forty?"

"No troll."

"Now hold it Kef, you tellin' me that ain't no troll?" the leader snapped.

"I may be half-blind you dimwit, but my sense o' smell is just fine."

"Excuse me, ma'am...," the one called Kef began, stepping closer.

An instant before he even touched me, I threw my arm out. Not seeing me move, he walked right into it, the effect being somewhat similar to what might have happened, had he been stopped by running into a solid wall.

His sunglasses fell to the ground, not cracking as I suspected they might, but exploding into a mess of near-invisible circuitry, their glowing lenses fading instantly to black.

"What the hell!" the leader gasped. "What was that? Argus, did you pick that up?"

Argus only shook his head, bewildered. In his hand he held the exploded remains of what had been a second pair of green sunglasses. "MC went over six hundred."

"That's impossible," the leader argued, adjusting his own shades.

It was then that I guessed, with some amusement, what strange "levels" it was that they were attempting to measure.

Magic. Power.

"Now you three are going to leave my people alone," I ordered. "You are going to go back to wherever you came from and never bother this realm again."

"Oh?" The leader grinned arrogantly.

Concentrating, I snapped my fingers and his sunglasses exploded. Clutching the fresh burns across his face, the Slaver swore and peered at me from between his fingers... drawing a gun.

He fired three times, each bullet passing through my disguise with a yellow crackle, yet glancing off my skin as if they were nothing more than small, lifeless pebbles.

There were advantages to being what I was... sometimes.

"How'd she dodge that?" Kef wondered.

"She didn't dodge em'," the leader snarled. "They hit and bounced off."

"Could she be... one of them?" Kef grew very pale.

"Maybe." The leader shook his head. "One way to find out."

"Oh good, I was hoping I'd have something to do!" the third Slaver, Argus grinned insanely, flinging off his heavy black coat to reveal a white tunic with a very large red star on the front.

A cleric.

"Moving down in the world, God-Summoner?" I growled. "Doesn't your creed forbid you to use your powers against innocents?"

"You're not innocent," he replied coldly. "You've killed more than a thousand times. I can't even count how many deaths hang over you."

Stung by the truth of that remark, I did not respond. Bullets, swords and fire could not defeat me. But a cleric's spell... that was another thing entirely.

Glancing across the nearly deserted street, I caught sight of a large framed mirror wrapped halfway in packing paper and propped against what appeared to be a bathtub. Fate, apparently, had been at work once again. I knew better than to question such an obviously disguised blessing. And with Phineas and the others... safely on their way to friendlier places, I decided it was time for me to relocate as well.

Preparing to jump, I suddenly caught sight of Ira crouched behind a stack of shipping crates on the pier. He had hidden himself well, but he hadn't run far enough. From his vantage point he'd been watching the entire fight.

Still, the mercenaries hadn't noticed the boy... yet.

"RUN, RUN YOU IDIOT!" I ordered, though he didn't appear to be listening to me.

A bolt of white light shot over my head. Without wasting another second, I dove through the glass, hoping he had sense enough to listen.

The Slavers fled, horrified by what they had just witnessed. The legendary few, the powerful, immortal, worldly Traversers... were real. To make matters worse, I had proven that there was at least some truth behind the claim of every Etone. There were quite a few brothers ... and sisters out there, and they did look out for their own.

"Look! Traverser!" I could hear Ira shouting triumphantly, despite the distance of space and time. "Hey sister! Go sister, go!"

I ran... and ran like I had never run before, until after what seemed like an eternity, I finally caught sight of that silver star flickering on the horizon, its perfect light still burning strong, despite the darkness that threatened to put it out completely.

Zenith.

Twenty-Seven

In a shattering of glass, I was inside the palace, and, despite my condition, I was only too glad to be home. The Imperial council hall had become the city's refuge, soup kitchen and shelter for the ever–increasing numbers of homeless and destitute. It was not uncommon to catch sight of orphans in rags begging for a few coins where once only kings, knights and wizards had held their feasts.

But even these things gave me hope. Walking down the white corridors, I saw a young boy huddled in a corner, wearing what appeared to be one of Raphael's good robes, and another, a little girl wrapped in a green velvet cloak that bore the symbols of the massacred Falchon House. It seemed that the worst of times had at least brought out the best... in some of us.

I wondered momentarily if anyone recognized me, preferring to go unnoticed as I wandered the marbled alleyways of "Castle Sanctuary," as its new inhabitants had taken to calling the palace. The war had spared no one. Faces I recognized from high-end dinner clubs and street corners alike had fled the city proper, in fear of the increasing numbers of rogue demons and Republic soldiers.

I glanced towards the balcony on the second floor, wondering if Raphael would be in his chamber... wondering if I dared go see him, speak to him... anything. I knew the words I wanted to hear, but as I ran my hands across my own face, passing through the illusion I wore, I was repulsed.

Brin's haunting cry came back to me, again and again, echoing in my mind. Cursed... cursed!

Would Raphael understand, as Phineas had? No one could see me now, save the few who knew my secret. Artemis Ravencroft, who had never really lived at all was now dead... and there was only me. The last we had spoken was ages ago. In all that had come to pass since that day, would Raphael have forgotten what I really was? Though in the shadows of the library we were both l'Eloshir, I knew that publicly... no one outside of Raphael's family... not even Maurice had ever seen him as he truly was.

Raised a Traverser, he was so accustomed to his human form that oftentimes it seemed that he was more human than demon, while I was clearly the exact opposite. Was it only "Artemis" that he wanted, for her to share in his masquerade of humanity? Another noble immortal full goodness and hope, and all of his other beautiful, false truths? It was possible. Anything was possible.

The door at the end of the hall creaked and a feeling came over me. It was as if I had been living my life entirely in black and white, only to be submerged suddenly into a realm of vibrant color.

And I felt alive again, sorrowful and overjoyed all at once in that breathtaking instant... as I turned slowly around.

In the fading sunlight that trickled into the room, a man stood, wearing a long blue cloak full of stitches. Though the hood was pulled over his head, there was no mistaking the faint sparkle of his tired eyes as he looked up and saw me standing in the center of the hall, my clothes in shambles and a bundle of old newspapers under my arm, wearing a face not my own, hoping that the spell might conceal what I had become.

All at once, I felt that I had to be with him, to tell him everything, to confess how cold I had been, how terrified I had felt... and how lonely it was.

I had thought, foolishly, that I needed no one, convinced myself that I was destined to be eternally damned and ever roaming, a silent witness to the passing of the ages. That denial washed away in an instant, as I realized quite suddenly, that I could not continue as I was, that I could not endure another moment of existence without running to him.

I would have given a thousand years of my life for one touch, one word from him... and nothing more.

I stopped short, knowing there were tears in my eyes. Raphael, however, seemed distant, as if he had just seen a ghost.

Startled, I began to back away.

"You all right, Lord Errida?" a man near the door asked.

Phineas's enchanted pendant burned against my chest. I wanted to tear it off... I hated it then more than ever, but I dared not, knowing well what body I still wore.

Raphael nodded to the stranger, somewhat shaken. "It is strange that I should tell you this, but that woman reminds me of someone I once...," he admitted. "She looks nothing like her of course… but she carries a little of that spark. I only wish that I… never mind. It is not something that I should trouble you with."

"Lady Ravencroft." The man nodded, his expression very nearly matching Raphael's, as close as mimicry would allow. "M'pathy," he explained, wiping a tear from his eye. "You don't have to say nothing to me."

"But….," Raphael began, looking utterly confused.

"You forget that everyone knew," the man laughed. "The very first day that she appeared at court. Shame though, that she's dead now. The people would've liked to see her as Empress. And High Commander. Can somebody be both?"

Raphael turned away without answering the man's question.

"Did I say somethin'? The man wondered. "Forgive me, your highness…"

Raphael shook his head. "If only," he whispered, so softly that I even I could barely hear him.

I had suffered enough. To hell with hiding, to hell with everything! Fighting back more tears, I tore the pendant off and flung it across the room, not caring that I would be seen by everyone, not as a human… but as a demon.

Raphael believed I was dead, and Maurice had nearly been killed, riding where I myself should have been. If they would take me as I was, I would lead them once again, and gladly. And if they would not, if they demanded my death, I would go willingly as well. It was a far, far better thing to die knowing that those who were truly important still lived than to linger eternally in doubt and fear.

All around the room, sleeping bodies rose, feeling the surge of magic from the broken amulet.

"Artemis?" Raphael gasped, nearly falling to his knees.

"Raphael… I," I began, nearly choking myself on tears that would not fall… before I could even speak. Yet still, within me lived a warrior, a cold, terrible warrior who could say what must be said and feel nothing! I could play that part once more. I had to, standing before him… or else I was truly powerless.

"It is I," I nodded, bowing my head. "I am alive. I have been hiding because I am ashamed. I am… trapped, like this. He cursed me because he wanted the world to know what I was… they wanted you to see me as I am… a monster!"

Broken completely, I fell to the ground, sobbing, my hands pressed against the floor, searching for pain that I could no longer feel.

And I would have lain there indefinitely, drowning in my own tears, had

I not felt, quite suddenly, a hand upon my face, strong yet gentle, and as pale white and seemingly lifeless as my own. I looked up, very nearly disgusted by the creature that knelt before me, had it not been for his eyes, so knowing and full of compassion.

Though we stood before a hundred witnesses, so intense was his emotion, that Raphael had shed his human form.

"If you are a monster," he whispered. "Then I am one too."

"Raphael, why?" I begged desperately, bewildered. "The people need you, they need the Empire! They need things to be the way they were!"

"Not as much as they need the truth." He shook his head. "They are strong. They have outlived countless Emperors and Empires. They have each other, and their histories. I'm only a guide, and that's all I've ever been. The people have never relied on me completely... they've never needed me... the way you do now. You should have come to me. You should always come to me."

"Raphael, I was afraid," I argued, though it hardly sounded rational.

"Afraid of what?" he sighed. "Afraid that I would reject you because of... what we both are?"

I nodded.

"So old, and yet you have learned so little," he laughed softly, drying my tears. "I could never have turned you away, not if you were bloodied and scarred beyond recognition, not if you had been changed into a wild creature that none could tame. Not even if touching you would bring me my death."

"I could never lose you. I would sooner give up a piece of my heart."

"Raphael... I...," I began, searching for words.

The door opened again at the end of the hall and Maurice staggered in with his crutch, his jaw dropped at the sight of the two of us in the center of the floor, kneeling in such a way that we might have been stone.

Raphael stood.

"Hear this," he announced, in a loud, clear voice. The mumbling crowd fell silent. "You are confused, good people, and within reason. You are not certain of what you see before you. Is the Emperor a man... or is he a beast? Look well, citizens. What is here is no illusion. Touch these hands, if you dare... though I assure you that there is no warmth in them. See these teeth, and these claws, and these terrible wings. And listen, for I tell you now, as I should have long ago, that I am this creature. When I speak with you in the hall, when I bring you food, when I hold your children in my arms and tend to your wounds with my own hands... when I wield my sword in battle against our enemies, always this creature lives within me."

"But know you, countrymen, that I am no monster. A monster cannot feel shame or fear, a monster kills without remorse. A monster cannot have sorrow, nor joy. And though fire does not burn me, and though steel will not cut me, I am victim to all of those emotions, most importantly the one thing truest, that which separates our kind from them. Love."

"In the end, when the final lines are drawn, I shall stand against the forces of Magog, not because they will not have me, but because I reject them. That which I stand for is that which we all stand for, that which out enemies are trying to take from us, the rights of freedom and peace... the right to live our lives, not as what we are born as, but as what we choose to become."

Never had truer words been spoken. Forcing myself to my feet, I staggered forward and nearly collapsed again, had Raphael not caught me in his arms, drawing me toward him.

The pain that had been welling up for so long within me faded away like the last snows of winter, and as he held me close, I began to feel again something I had expected was lost to me forever.

Warmth.

Pain wracked through my body, though it was the pain, not of a wound, but of the kind that comes from healing.

We descended to the ground, Raphael and I, both human once more.

The gathered were silent with an almost solemn reverence, as they waited in anticipation and fear for what the Emperor might say next.

Maurice clapped faintly, an expression on his face that I realized I had never seen before. The Vizier was smiling.

And the crowd, the joyous, applauding crowd rose to their feet as one, embracing each other, sobbing, laughing and confessing fears and woes that had lain buried for far too long.

In a way, that triumphant hour foreshadowed what was yet to come.

The Dragons

"They live each day, not as their last, but as their first."

Twenty-Eight

The following morning was brisk and cool as I marched down to the marina, accompanied by Phineas... and Maurice, the stubborn fool, who insisted he was well enough to ride a horse.

Men stared as we approached The Spellcraft Hathor, which had been brilliantly repainted as the new flagship of the Imperial Fleet.

"I don't believe it," Lucy stared, turning to Jeo who sat beside her, the two of them dangling their legs in midair off the edge of the dock.

"Hey everybody!" another voice shouted, suddenly certain of what so many had been silently wondering about since I had donned my purple cloak, picked up my staff and left the palace. "It's the High Commander! The Commander's back!"

A deafening cheer rose from the gathered sailors and soldiers on the pier, many of whom I recognized, and some that I did not, though all knew me. The younger ones crowded around The Hathor, reaching to grab my cloak, or my hair, or anything else they could lay their hands upon, while some of the more disciplined veterans bowed or saluted.

I entered the cabin of the ship to meet with my commanding officers, all my dearest and most trusted friends.

To the right, Rowanoak stood, looking every bit as ancient and solemn as Raphael, who was seated beside him.

Lounging in a chair nearby, Edgar picked his teeth with a hunting knife, while Baroness Gloria seemed to be conversing with a large black-furred shadow under the table, her terrible "cat".

On the floor, Ruveus sat, humming to himself and plucking the strings of his mandolin in a meditative fashion.

To the left, Terry sharpened a brutal-looking dagger, accompanied by an empty chair and the cleric Sikara, who was grinning insanely, her normally flawless white robes splattered in black ink.

"I've written a speech for you," Sikara offered. "It's a little lengthy but I'm sure you'll present it beautifully."

I eyed the large roll of paper suspiciously but then took it with a smile. "I shall try to do it justice," I agreed.

"Welcome to "The-World-Hasn't-Ended-This-Morning-Breakfast," Ruveus announced, offering the three of us a pitcher of juice and a box of doughnuts.

Phineas and Maurice sat down immediately and lost no time in finishing off what remained of the food, but I had more pressing matters on my mind.

"How does it look out there?" I asked, turning to Rowanoak who closed his eyes and contemplated the question.

After a few moments concentration, the Elvenking shrugged. "Much the same as yesterday." He shook his head. "Two warriors ride in the lead, Zaethe and the one they call Orin Saede. They have two Tears ready to open at any moment, but the majority of the I'Eloshir army is still trying to find some way around the water."

"We're on an island." Edgar frowned, suddenly interested in the conversation. "There is no way "around" the water."

"I wouldn't be sure of that." Phineas shook his head. "They could tear down trees like they did in Celedon and build some sort of bridge."

"A bridge that spans twenty miles?" Raphael wondered. "Master Merlin, with their resources, how long do you suspect that will take them?"

"Thirty years," Phineas admitted. "There isn't a forest near here."

"But couldn't the IR fly them over in their aircraft?" Gloria demanded. "They bomb us every day for God's sake! How hard would it be for them to airlift some demons across?"

"It isn't a matter of 'could they'." Ruveus grinned. "It's a matter of "won't they"? The Republic seems to feel pretty confident that they can take Zenith without the demon's help. Why should they split the profits?"

"Merchants and tactics seldom mix well. Prince Ruveus does have a point." Maurice nodded.

"Drop the prefix, pal." Ruveus shook his head. "Just call me Ruveus. Just Ruveus."

I shook my head and tried not to smile, wondering what had come over me. I was riding into battle, possibly to my death... and I found it funny.

"I guess I un'erstand that," Terry agreed. "And I un'erstand why they can't all get over in a Tear... it takes a long time to make a big Tear and our clerics have been blasting all those little ones before they open, left n' right. But what I still don't get is… these demons have wings. They all got wings and I ain't never seen any of em' fly… and it can't just be cause' of that crippled one no more."

"They can fly, correct?" Maurice asked.

I almost answered but then realized that the question had been directed at Raphael.

Raphael sighed. "Correct."

"But they won't," Terry finished. "Not even to get here and kill us?"

Twenty miles? I bit my lip and glanced at Raphael, who rolled his shoulders and winced.

"Too far." We both shook our heads at the same time and then broke out laughing.

Everyone stared, and I quickly composed myself, but Raphael would have none of it. Still laughing insanely, perhaps merely for the sake of doing so, he slapped Rowanoak heavily on the back. Caught off-guard, the Elvenking staggered into the table, eyes wide in bewilderment.

"Do that again and you're liable to break him in half." Maurice grinned, despite himself.

Shortly after the preparations were made, our meeting adjourned and I went out into the field to address my troops, for the first time in ages, walking with confidence.

Our ship landed silently on a field of white tents outside the city wall. At the foot of the ramp, where no soul had been before, Dei suddenly appeared, sipping his red drink and petting a small brown puppy he held in his lap.

"You can rub his head," Dei offered, holding up the dog for my inspection. "He's good luck."

Though the concept was foreign to me, I smiled and gave the puppy a pat anyway.

Dei grinned. "Don't tell anyone I said this," he warned, motioning for me to come in closer. The Prophet winked. "Today... will be one of those days."

"What do you mean?" I wondered. "Those days? What days?"

"One of those days," he repeated, with more enthusiasm. "You know, one of those days that they write books about."

"Deiunthel...," I began, turning back to where he had stood only a moment ago. The Prophet, of course, had vanished.

Reaching the head of the army where hundreds of the realm's finest were gathered, waiting in silence for the attack they knew was coming... I closed my eyes and took a deep breath. Ever ominous, the black Tears flickered overhead, near bursting with the darkness they carried, while across the sea, another threat lingered, the anxious and frustrated I'Eloshir, still waiting near the edge of the water, searching for a way to bring their army to the city walls.

"A speech, High Commander?" Maurice suggested.

I unrolled Sikara's parchment and scanned the paper, trying to catch sight of a good opening piece, but all that I could make of it was that there were a far too many old-fashioned "For's" and "Thou's", not to mention other such words that flew well over the limits of my own vocabulary. Speaking the language of the I'Eloshir I was ridiculously eloquent, but my centuries of practice served little purpose. I had never actually had to inspire a defending force before… only my faithful warriors, who were usually already thirsting for blood.

"People of the Empire!" I raised my sword to the sky.

It had gotten the reaction I desired; the men were already applauding.

"Now what?" I turned to Phineas, who shrugged.

"Hello?" he suggested awkwardly.

I grinned. An introduction so thoroughly preposterous had just occurred to me, a speech so pitifully short and irreverent that it was perfectly appropriate for a day such as this. Rowanoak paled and I guessed that he had read what I was thinking.

"People of Ranlain, of Ardra and Istara, Eldar, Accoloth and the Isles! What is this day?" I asked of the crowd, not sure of what kind of answer I ought to be expecting.

"Monday?" a man suggested.

"Wednesday," his companion sighed, correcting him.

"My birthday," another volunteered.

A few of the soldiers snickered, but the rest were silent until, at long last, a man in the back raised his hand.

"Spring Equinox?" he suggested.

"Is it?" I wondered.

Phineas shrugged doubtfully.

"Then today shall be called the Battle of the Equinox!" I proclaimed. "Fight bravely men, and do deeds of honor.... for this day will be remembered in centuries to come. Today, the balance of light and dark that has weighed so heavily upon us, the siege that has crippled... but will never kill our realm... today the stars do align themselves in our favor! Today the tides turn, and they turn for the Dynasty!"

Almost as if on queue, the suns began to rise in a blaze of color. I grinned, relishing the arrogance of my last dramatic line.

"Because, as you see... today I have returned."

And what a glorious day it was, the greatest victory of the entire war.

The scourge that had plagued the interior of the city we obliterated, the lurkers that attempted to climb the walls we destroyed, and by the time the suns set, two of the Republic's most powerful and influential generals knelt before Raphael and I in the Great Hall, signing documents of complete and unconditional surrender.

Yet as I retired for the night, I was still uneasy. In my minds eye, I saw demons climbing the docks of the marina, dark and silent like so many spiders... seeking something... something they must never have, not at all costs.

Twenty-Nine

Weeks passed as we struggled, day and night to hold our ground. Months came and went, and still we fought. I moved into a tent on the battlefield, keeping watch myself for at least a portion of every night, and sometimes the whole of it.

There were days when we triumphed, and days when we lost all hope.

Days when I felt that the end had finally come... and days that I realized what still lay ahead. Yet I would never surrender. Even had I known then what would become of us, the possibility of giving up... of admitting defeat, would never have occurred to me.

I won respect and admiration, perhaps more than I deserved, for the simple reason that I stood by every order I gave. I was no coward. When I was not riding at the head of my army, I was on a ship, flying above it. If I demanded the men to move against terrible odds, I myself went in beside them.

Tall tales and rumors began to race like wildfire through the ranks of the Empire's brave defenders. Soon I had become more godlike than mortal, and though I was uncomfortable to say the least, my father had taught me the value of a good legend.

If believing that I could truly be in a thousand places at once would help my soldiers to win the war, I would let them dream of it.

Then, after who knew how precisely how long, the dawn that we had feared finally came, and with it, the alarm.

I raced from my bedchamber without bothering to dress properly and immediately ran for my ship. The Hathor, docked far away from the rest of the fleet, remained untouched, but from my vantage point, I could see the whole of the port, Spellcraft torn open and scattered, some half-sunken beneath the black water and others still dangling at the height of skyscrapers, balanced haphazardly on platforms that looked as if they had suffered the

192

wrath of a hurricane.

Worse still, was what had happened to the sea. I realized quite suddenly that my fear of the water, my fear of the ocean's darkness, and of the Spellcraft's ice... was hardly irrational.

It had been a portent, a vision to warn me, and I had dismissed the terrifying scenes in my mind as merely a few bad dreams.

Yet the nightmare had come to pass. As far as I could see, from the city walls to the edge of the world, the once beautiful waterfall cascading into space... all the sea had become a silent snow-plane, an icy white expanse of roaring white-capped waves permanently frozen in time, never again to crash against the shore.

I shuddered at the thought and then turned to Raphael, who stood beside me. "Why didn't they kill us?" he wondered, shaking his head. "However they got here to steal the fuel... they could have easily taken the city as we slept."

"That would have been merciful." I shook my head, unable to take my eyes off the scene. "They want us to fight... and to suffer as much as possible."

"They're coming!" a voice roared. "Oh God, they're on their way!"

Sure enough, the very ground beneath our feet rumbled, as the dark horde approached, a vast field of I'Eloshir beyond mere numbers... any one of them a match for five strong men.

In the lead was Geruth himself. I recognized him at once, for Zae and Orin had been stripped of their red-robes, as had the other generals, all of them reduced to mere fighters under the Warlord's command. Only he would not be humbled, wearing his mask of dragon-bone and his breastplate of red-painted human skulls, masquerading arrogantly as a God.

"DESTROY THEM!" Geruth roared, ordering his warriors. "DESTROY THEM ALL!!!"

I clenched my teeth and fought the power of the order.

"YOU WILL NEVER TAKE US!!!" I screamed in reply, desperate to buy even a few more moments of time.

Then, all at once, when it seemed that things had reached their breaking point, the sky ripped open into a horrific Tear, pouring out a stream of Republic aircraft, all firing upon us.

"How can we fight them?" I begged, tearing at my own hair, not knowing what power, if any, heard me. "Inapsupetra, our ships are destroyed! What do we have left?"

"The Accoloth Air-Force," a familiar voice snickered.

A large shadow loomed over me, and I traced its outline before turning around, just to be sure that I wasn't hallucinating.

Panther winked, and Ejora waved, with her arm over his shoulder, wielding a heavy axe. That sight alone would have been enough for my tired eyes, but there was more.

Behind the two of them stood creatures... so tall, wise and powerful, no demons... nor Traversers, but beings that were both completely human and utterly not.

The smallest of them stood at a height of sixteen feet, a long-necked, scaled beast of awe-inspiring proportions, glimmering gold like an ancient idol, and the largest rivaled the height of many of the buildings nearby.

There were six in all, remarkable, beautiful and almost childlike, were they not so unquestionably deadly.

Never had I been so close to a dragon.

The leader of the group laughed softly, lowering his head to my level and winking at me knowingly. "I'd rather play my mandolin."

All at once, I recognized him.

"Ruveus?" I stared. "I had no idea..."

Panther grinned, elbowing me. "I'm good?" he prompted.

I nodded. "Yes uncle, you are."

"After this, we go out for sushi," one of the dragons muttered.

"Raphael, look!" I shouted.

"Artemis, I've found ships!" he yelled back. "The demons missed the ones that were in for repair! I've got The Excelsion and The Adonis!"

"And I've got Ruveus! The dragons are here!"

"What?" Raphael flung open the door and raced out of the Spellcraft garage.

Ruveus grinned. "Anyone else for a good long stare?"

"I'm afraid that I have an army to lead," I interrupted, buckling on my sword.

"Wanna hitch a ride?" one of the dragons offered.

"You mean..." I looked up and backed away. It would be the ideal way for me to oversee the field, but I could not help feeling that riding any creature capable of reason, whether the service was offered voluntarily or not, was almost sacrilegious. "Is that really appropriate?" I wondered.

"Your protocol will get you killed HC," another dragon laughed. "Take a lesson from us. Somebody says, 'Hey, you wanna try this...' and you don't know what they're talking about, you just smile and say, 'Sure, I wanna try that.""

"Climb on," Ruveus offered. "I'll carry you. Just don't go covering up my eyes or nothing."

"If you say so." Somewhat uncomfortably, I did as I was asked and soon found myself sitting in an odd sort of position, uncomfortable but balanced on Ruveus's back.

"You 'fraid?" the little dragon inquired.

"Of course not," I replied stiffly.

"Hold on," Ruveus advised.

"I have exceptional balance," I argued.

The little dragon snorted. "Hunh, yeah, you think so, eh?"

"I... think...ahh." I lurched forward, nearly falling off.

"Ready?" Ruveus asked.

"Ready." I nodded.

"YEEHAWWW!!! Let's get em!" Ruveus roared, shooting skyward. A plane dropped from the sky in a burst of flames, forming a crater of black water in the middle of the ice field.

The battle turned in a mere fraction of a second. Many of the Republic's pilots fled, racing back towards the Tears that they had flown through. In their realm, I supposed, such creatures as they now battled were the stuff of fairy-tales.

Yet out of the corner of my eye, I caught sight of a suspicious-looking craft, built much like the fighter planes, only bulkier and slower.

"Bomber!" a voice shouted, as one of the dragons swooped over us.

"Do we blow it up?" another wondered.

"Heck no Evanshea!" the first snapped. "We don't know what sort of payload it's got! You seen what happens when we smoked those magic-explosives! Damn near took out half of Gelthar. We gotta have it crash into the water! The only thing that puts Mag-Flame out is good ol' fashioned $H2O$."

"You must stop that plane," I argued. "It's headed for the palace."

"No can do HC!" The dragon dove towards the sea. "I've gotta lose these three tail-biters first!"

"Ruveus...," I began.

"Got a stupid idea," he agreed. "You sort of fly, right?"

"No... Ruveus!" I groaned, suddenly understanding what he was about to attempt.

"When I say jump, you jump," he ordered, calmly... completely serious and collected.

I did not argue.

"Jump!" Ruveus shouted, skimming within inches of the bomber.

I jumped and caught hold of the plane, but only barely, heaving myself inside, breathless. The dragons were right in knowing not to set fire to the aircraft, I realized, surveying the heavy stock of magic-bombs and ammunition. Forcing my way into the cockpit, I drew my sword and prepared to take out the pilot, only to have him turn to face me with a grin.

"Phineas?" I stared, wondering how he'd gotten inside before me.

He grinned, jerking a thumb at a man who lay hog-tied on the floor, apparently gagged with his own socks.

"They were planning on using these bombs to take out the city wall," he explained. "But I've got a better idea."

Soaring over the battlefield, he dropped the explosives in the center of the advancing I'Eloshir, on the ice of the harbor.

"DYNASTY RETREAT!" I ordered.

Without question, the men ran.

"Isn't there supposed to be an explosion?" I demanded.

The moment I spoke those words, the blast I had anticipated came. In one horrific burst of flame, the ice gave way, cracking into a thousand pieces, sinking and drifting back towards the edge of the world, carrying with it the invaders who had dared use our own technology against us.

Though we were nearly a mile away, we could still hear the terrified screams of the demons were drowning... and worse still, we were near enough to witness those who had survived, hundreds of them... clawing their way out of the freezing depths and onto the still, silent waves of The Frozen Sea.

Thirty

Many more days passed. News of our struggle against the Republic had reached further than any of us had dared imagine, attracting small but heroic forces of rebels and offworlders, who were all eager to have a piece of the IR, all seeking vengeance for the systematic destruction of their own realms.

Still others flocked to our aid, holy warriors and clerics, who had been following in the wake of the world-destroying I'Eloshir. Though I was glad of their assistance, I still felt apprehensive each time a group of paladin passed by, perhaps fearing that they might see fit to grant me a blessing.

I had been showered with gifts as well; some things that I knew not what to do with, and others I was indeed grateful for, such as weapons and armor from sympathetic souls five-hundred worlds over.

Yet the war... the war raged on.

"FIRE!" I ordered from my post atop the icy ridge. "FIRE!"

That morning had begun on a high note, my spies informed me that Zaethe had been found dead, presumably poisoned by a member of her own company.

Still, she was not riding in the lead... and I knew her demise would slow the warriors of Magog very little, if at all.

"High Commander!" a voice shouted.

"GENERAL AUDERRAUK!" I ordered... not realizing how close we stood.

"You are in your nightdress," he reminded me.

"No time!" I roared back, though my bare feet were bleeding and numbed.

"I hereby relieve you of your command until you dress yourself properly," Maurice announced.

"The cause?" I grinned. This conversation had become a tradition between us.

"Temporary insanity," Maurice sighed. "Should last less than fifteen

197

minutes."

I returned to my tent, threw off the white shift and realized for a split second exactly how cold I was. A hissing sound from beneath my blankets warned me that I was about to step on the exact thing I'd been looking for.

My armor. A living, symbiotic creature that fed off of spell energy, kept me warm and allowed me mobility above and beyond what one could accomplish even in loose-fitting clothing. The Prophet, in his many travels had come across the creature, which he called an Ether-Raptor and had assumed that I would appreciate it. I did indeed… if only he knew how well.

I slipped on my boots, threw on my heavy velvet cloak and stepped back into the battle. A scout on a motorcycle skidded to a stop in front of me.

"High Commander!" He bowed.

"What news?" I demanded.

"Hey we got em' runnin' on the west!" Terry yelled from above, flying on dragon-back.

"Good! Show no mercy!" I shouted back.

"High Commander!" the scout begged. I turned back to him. "It's a trap," he blurted.

"What's a trap?" I stopped in my tracks, instantly overwhelmed by a terrible sensation of fear.

"They've given up the Republic!" He shook his head, coming to his feet. "The I'Eloshir are…"

A sharp, whistling sound shot through the air without warning. A crossbow quarrel appeared out of nothingness and struck the messenger in the back. He fell.

I dropped to help him. "What… where? Cleric!!!" I yelled. The dart was seeped with a green ichor that burned my skin where I touched it, a poison strong enough, not only to kill a human, but to destroy an I'Eloshir. It had clearly been meant for me.

"Hold on, help is coming," I whispered. "Now…"

"The I'Eloshir…," he coughed.

"The I'Eloshir are what!" I shook him, despite his grievous wound.

"Behind us…," he whispered… and breathed his last.

"Treason!" I roared. "Find that archer!"

My men raced off.

"REINFORCEMENTS! TO THE WALL!" I ordered.

"High Commander?" Maurice wondered.

"They're trying to get around us!" I ran for my horse, a black-winged creature I had found saddled and bridled the morning before, a gift from Panther, no doubt... and mounted up. "But now that we know they won't have that chance!"

I took to the skies. "Forward!"

The I'Eloshir had reached the perimeter of Zenith, the city under siege.

The defenders of the wall threw all they could over, sorcery, bodies ridden with terrible plagues, vats of boiling water and oil, small cars and hazardous exploding tanks of Spellcraft fuel.

But the I'Eloshir were merciless. They had given us the only thing we couldn't hope to control... a second front.

And high in the sky above the Imperial Palace, a third dark Tear was forming.

"Mages! Clerics!" I could hear Phineas's voice... wherever he was. "Destroy that before it opens!"

Cleric's spells flew through the sky, bleaching a track of pale death across the demon army.

It was not enough.

The third Tear burst with a sickening crunch, and the world itself seemed to quake in agony. More planes shot through the abyss, dropping bombs.

I dove out of their line and then regained my position over my army. The field appeared nearly completely black.

We were losing.

I clenched my reins in my teeth and waited for the first fighter plane to make a second pass, releasing a blast of fiery energy. The plane went down into the sea, and another patch of water froze, seeped in Spellcraft fuel.

If we survived at all, we would be cleaning for centuries to come. More planes flew over.

"CLOSE! I COMMAND! TEAR CLOSE!" I ordered, hoping it was still possible.

The Tear snapped shut near instantly, and a cheer rose from our side.

The damage, however, had already been done. A heavy magic-bomber shot towards the Imperial Palace.

"TAKE DOWN THAT PLANE!" I ordered, wondering how many more commands I could give before I fell unconscious.

If the palace were destroyed, the energy source would be cut off with it and our entire perimeter wall would collapse.

Spells and cannons fired... but all fell short of the mark.

I tried to push my horse further, but he'd taken a hit in the gunfire and could scarcely stay level.

I dismounted, threw myself forward and landed… somewhat painfully on the deck of The Spellcraft Adonis.

"High Commander?" The captain stared in shock.

"Follow that plane," I pointed. "We must stop that plane... at all costs."

We shot forward, almost within range, but then… stopped, suddenly rocked by an immense blast from below.

"Primary engines out," the helmsman turned. "Pardon me C'mander Ravencroft, but we're screwed."

"Any smaller craft on board?" I asked.

"Two speeders," the captain admitted. "But they've both been blasted quite a few times. If you take one, you could fall."

I started the first. "And if I don't take one the dynasty will."

I dialed up the wall on the onboard communicator. "Wall Control! Raphael! Pick up!"

A somewhat fuzzy image materialized on the monitor. It was Raphael. He had positioned himself in the control tower of the perimeter wall. Electricity crackled from the exposed wires that surrounded him, and his face was unusually pale, almost dead-looking.

"Artemis… what's happening?" he begged. "I've been working for ten hours and I can't seem to keep the energy fields stabilized. Damned technology!"

"Raphael, there's a bomber headed towards the palace and I can't stop it! You've got to do something or we'll lose the city!" I interrupted him, desperate.

"Can't." He shook his head. "There's only one thing I can think of, and it's locked away in the Vault."

"No. Stay out of the palace. It's too dangerous!" I begged, knowing what he intended to do.

"Kaora's scepter." He shook his head. "If anything can protect us now… that would be it. I've got to reach it."

"Raphael!" I protested, knowing he would not listen to me.

"Sweet Lord what is that?!" a voice screamed in terror. The screen went black.

"Wall Control! Wall Control!" I begged.

No response.

The airspeeder stalled and rapidly began to lose altitude. Gunfire from below struck the plate… and twice in my right leg.

But I scarcely felt my own pain.

I watched in horror as the Imperial Palace exploded in a flash of silver light, crashing into the sea. The ground cracked open, shifting hundreds of feet upwards and then downwards and apart in one single deadly motion.

The green aura of the wall short-circuited in one near-nuclear blast.

Gone.

The battle was over. Zenith had fallen.

The war was over.

The Chaos Realm was lost.

The airspeeder collapsed and I plummeted towards the sea of screams and death below, falling for what felt like an eternity.

I clutched my ring and begged for a swift end, knowing I'd lost all I had.

The Architect

"The greatest of designs are often the simplest."

Thirty-One

I could hear chanting… chanting in the darkness. I was so far away from my own body that I scarcely knew if I was alive or dead.

A bright light seemed to beckon, but as I approached it, and the wonderful white balcony where Raphael stood waiting, two dark guards of Magog slammed the shadows closed before my path.

I was caught, my arms tied by blue ropes of energy, ripping me across space and time. Summoned, by some greater force, flung through the limitless void betwixt countless dimensions. I fought back, tearing, pulling, and screaming in rage, but it was futile. Darkness overcame me and I lost my human form, bleeding, numbed, and terrified.

And then… I awoke.

I opened my eyes and saw a rather fat human woman in her early forties who was bent over a book, face-down and arms up as if she was attempting some sort of strange magic.

She looked up at me with a look of complete surprise and partial terror. The scream, when it finally came, was quite extraordinary.

"What's going on, Patty?" a voice demanded, and another human, a man of roughly the same age and build entered the dark room, turning on the lights.

The moment his eyes came to rest on me, he grew very pale. "How did… What did…," he rambling, staring.

I flexed my sore wings and pulled a shard of steel out of my neck with my claws, licking up the blood from the wound and marveling at its sweetness. Returning to the present, I stumbled forward and stretched, rolling my shoulders.

"Nahyoh'ysk," I muttered in the Old Tongue. No mortal words would sum up my terrific agony quite so eloquently. And though I was lost and bewildered by what I knew must have happened to the Chaos Realm, my fear was overshadowed dramatically by physical hurt. Emotionally, I wanted nothing more than to collapse and cry for centuries but physically... I was wounded. The mere idea baffled me, it was so ridiculous. I had never really been truly, permanently injured in all of my life. I would actually have a scar.

Touching the deep gash in my own chest, I looked up to face the woman who had summoned me.

It was apparent that neither the husband... nor the witch knew quite what they had conjured.

"What were you trying to do?" he finished.

"Call up a spirit," she admitted. "Cal's been having strange dreams again."

"Strange dreams?" The man shook his head. "I think you've meddled in something a little bigger than a seventeen-year old's nightmares. What did you really do?"

The woman, Patty, shook her head. "I don't know. Perhaps we ought to ask it."

It? I was offended.

"Please," I began. The two humans stared, amazed that I spoke their language, perhaps. "Where and when am I?"

"The year's nineteen eighty-nine," the man replied, with some uncertainty. "You're right around Brunswick, Ohio. I'm Bruno Fargrove and this is my wife Patricia. We're pleased... or I guess maybe we're honored to meet you."

"If you were honored, you would take my hand," I replied.

Bruno reached out, but Patricia pulled him back. "You just going to let it out of the circle?" She glared.

"Out of the circle?" I stepped across the green line without so much as a pinprick of energy attempting to hold me back. "You mean this line of chalk here?" I laughed, folding my wings back and shedding my demonic form. "That parlor trick could never hold me. I've known children capable of stronger wards." I glared. "I simply asked for a hand... because I have two bullets in my leg... and a spear, I think, between my ribs."

I staggered over to the empty chair and sat down, pried the metal pieces out somewhat awkwardly with my own dull nails and useless teeth, searing the wound closed with a flame in my hand.

Patricia stared in awe at the violet glow. "You heal yourself?" she wondered.

"Heal? Hardly," I snorted. "I have just cauterized the wound."

Bruno winced.

"It is apparent you have absolutely no training," I continued. "Nor do you appear to have the slightest knowledge of what you have done."

"What are you?" Bruno wondered.

There was something in his eyes I supposed I could forgive.

"I have always considered myself as a who, not a what. But if you must know, my name is Artemis Ravencroft, and I am a Traverser. High Commander of the Armies of the Imperial Errida Dynasty and the Chaos Realm. May I have one of your shirts?" I pointed to the closet.

Nodding, Bruno produced a white dress shirt. Though I could barely reach behind my own back, I managed to release my armor. The symbiote hissed quietly and rolled into a metallic ball under the chair.

Though both were obviously spellbound by the creature, neither of them said a word. Gratefully, I buttoned the loose shirt, knowing that... now that I was not dead, I had quite a bit of healing to do.

"Wine, water... whatever you drink here," I ordered. They had summoned me against my will, after all. It was only fair that I should receive some hospitality.

"Mountain Dew?" Bruno asked.

"Fine." I rubbed another spot on my back... a burn, I guessed, from a clerical spell. My behavior had become rehearsed, mechanical. Instinctively, I was pushing the memories of death deeper into my subconscious, breaking my world into simple patterns that allowed me not to think, not to imagine anything.

"I take it I pulled you out at a bad time," Patricia muttered.

"Moments away from death," I admitted.

"So it was a good time?" Bruno wondered, returning with a few cans of his beverage.

"Not so," I shot back. "My army was destroyed. I should have died as well."

"Maybe," Bruno mused. "But maybe not. All I know is that this is never happened to us before, and if what you say is true about Patricia's power... there has to be some greater hand in this."

"A greater hand... indeed." I caught sight of a strange painting on the far wall, one I almost recognized. "What is that?" I pointed.

"That?" Bruno laughed. "That's something Cal did, he's this kid that comes in our store. He said he saw the picture in a dream. Two people... kinda hazy looking on either side of this girl floating above the floor with these 'crystals'."

"Inapsupetra," I whispered, somehow understanding the power of what had happened to me… all at once.

The feeling was rather like being ill.

"How'd you know?" Bruno stared. "Ina…nas… what you just said there! That's no random word… is it?"

"No indeed. And that is no mere painting." I pointed, though I knew my hand was still shaking from all the blood I'd lost. It had just occurred to me what the Gods must have been thinking, sending me to this strange place. Whoever had painted the scene... had to be a Prophet... a Traverser... or both.

"Where is he, the artist?" I demanded.

Bruno and Patricia looked to one another doubtfully.

"This Cal you speak of… I must see him immediately," I muttered, not taking my eyes off the portrait on the wall.

"I can call him when he gets home. He goes to the high school... it's right down the street," Patricia offered.

"That will not be soon enough," I replied coldly. "I will fetch him myself. And as far as our relationship is concerned, I would advise you two to stay out of the demon-summoning business. If you think I am difficult, you will not like the other sorts of things you may call upon. Drink."

Bruno passed me another can immediately, yet in his eyes I could tell he was apprehensive.

"Miss Ravencroft... I'm not so sure you're going to want to be running around our town... you."

"I am aware of my appearance," I snapped. "I do not intend to pass for human. I simply will not be seen."

"Can you do that?" Bruno wondered.

"You may try to watch me." Concentrating on the mirror over the mantle of the fireplace, I jumped over the back of the couch where they sat, smashed through, and disappeared.

Racing through the short space between the two mirrors, I caught sight of an empty locker room and returned to the real world.

Almost immediately, I cursed myself. In my arrogance, I'd forgotten to ask what "Cal" looked like.

And then... I heard breathing. One of the locker doors creaked slightly. The room was not deserted. I had been seen.

"COME OUT," I ordered.

Still, nothing moved. Furious, I kicked the wall, breaking through the concrete. "Out! Do not make me find you!"

I pulled on the doors, only to discover that they all refused to open. Closing my eyes, I tore through them with my mind, throwing a wave of purple fire from my fingertips, sending a hundred of the little black locks clattering to the floor.

And then, one of the larger lockers burst open. Coughing and covered in white powder, a young boy fell to the floor in a pile of sweaty, filthy clothes.

I stared.

"Jeezus!" he swore. "Don't kill me, I swear, I didn't mean to see any..."

"I was careless," I admitted, realizing what must have happened to the unfortunate child. "It will not happen again."

Footsteps approached, tramping down the halls, followed by many loud voices.

"Farewell." I nodded, and prepared to jump.

"Wait!" the boy gasped. "Take me with you."

"Fool," I laughed. "You don't know where I am going."

"Doesn't matter." He shook his head.

"No." I shook my head. "You say that now, but you cannot imagine the places I have been."

In a flash, I was gone, and in another shattering of glass, I was back in the Fargrove's living room. I sat down on the couch, smiling at the stares I received from Bruno and his wife. "Let's talk."

Thirty-Two

Hours passed. I followed Bruno out of the dim room and into the kitchen of the home, where he produced a small stack of pictures.

"The kid draws mostly buildings," Bruno explained. "Objects really. But every so often he puts the pencils aside and turns out a painting. He's only done about six... so long as we've known him. He gave Patty the one in the den, but I suppose he's go the rest." Bruno held up a white piece of paper. "You recognize this?"

I did. The sketch was of the Library of Alexandria.

"It's a library," I admitted. "Possibly the best there ever was."

"That's what he says." Bruno shook his head. "What about this?"

"A pit," I explained. "They're quite common in most worlds... people fight and others bet on them."

"Like professional boxing." Bruno nodded.

"To the death," I finished.

"So it's not like boxing." He shrugged and finally held up a very large paper folded several times.

The Imperial Palace.

"Isn't it obvious? It's a castle, fool," I sighed and turned away. Here in a strange world, yet still reminded of what I'd lost.

Tears welled up in my eyes, but I forced myself not to cry. Not... yet. There were some things I had to understand first. And more importantly, I wanted to be alone.

Patricia came back from down the hall. "Cal will be here in fifteen minutes," she announced. "He's bringing the paintings."

The doorbell rang. I twitched involuntarily and braced myself for whatever wizard or prophet might walk into the home of the amateur summoners. He'd evidently been to Zenith. That alone proved he was powerful.

Patricia took the canvas from unseen hands, and the scrawny, red-headed boy from the locker room entered the relative darkness of the house, closing the door behind him. Upon entering the kitchen he stopped short and stared.

I recognized him... and he recognized me in that instant. All at once, the strange boy's begging at the school made perfect sense.

Meeting a Traverser was sometimes the only way a stranded mage could make it home. And of course, any magic-user, even a young one, would be anxious to escape such a dull, mundane realm as the one Bruno lovingly referred to as The Good Ol' US of A.

"You're..."

"Not human?" I supplied, figuring that was what he was getting at. The pause while he absorbed that little bit of information was too long for my liking.

"I'm a demon," I explained. "A Traverser. Dimension Traveler."

"Sorcerer?" Cal wondered.

"That too." I nodded.

Cal shook his head. "Have we... met? Before today?"

"I do not imagine," I admitted. "But my memory is not so good."

"I was told you wanted to see my paintings." He uncovered the first canvas. "They say you know where my ideas come from."

"The buildings I recognize," I agreed. "I must say... your detail is remarkable. Surely you have been to Zenith."

"Where?" he wondered... with startling honesty.

"Zenith," I repeated. "The city you draw."

"It exists?" He stared at me, wide-eyed.

"It did." I nodded. "Though I can't be sure how much of it is left now."

"What happened?" he wondered.

"A war." I refused to say more.

"I have dreams," Cal began. "In my dreams I see these places but without people. A few times I've seen people too, but each time it was almost like I was looking through someone else's eyes. The first was this one."

He held up a dark canvas featuring a laughing, drunken cat-man I knew all too well.

"That is Panther," I sighed. "Ah, Elhilom." I smiled despite myself. "He would be proud of that painting, I think. He is somewhat over-fond of his own face."

Cal squinted at his own work. "In my dream he was trying to get me to play cards with him."

"Not surprising," I admitted. "He's quite the gambler."

"You know him?" Cal was incredulous. "Really... he..."

"He is my uncle. Nothing you could say about him would surprise me in the least," I replied. "Now let's see the next one."

I was troubled by what I'd already realized, that two of the portraits seemed painted from my own memory. If the rest were to follow, I didn't know what I would tell him.

The third painting was of Phineas, in the tower where we had first met, sitting on the floor, staring.

"Do you paint these from your own perspective?" I wondered, though I already knew the answer.

"Yes." He nodded.

"Show me another!" I finished, somewhat sharper than I'd intended.

"Well... do you recognize this one?" he asked, though he must have known that I did. I said nothing.

The fourth painting, an image of Maurice troubled me all the more. My closest friends. I carefully lifted the tracing paper from the final canvas, an incomplete sketch of a man surrounded by wires and machinery, staring helplessly skyward, though he was several floors below ground.

He was a tall man, dressed simply as he preferred... shoulder-length dark hair and those haunting, compelling eyes. The shadow of pencil rubbed on the pipes and bricks behind him did not match his smaller, human figure, but the wings drawn there could not have been more painfully appropriate. One look at the drawing was all it took for me to know for certain, but I held the canvas much longer, clutching it to my chest and closing my eyes.

"Raphael," I whispered... and then loosened my grip, looking up to face the three virtual strangers who stared at me so helplessly, completely ignorant of everything... yet somehow aware enough to dig up my most painful memories.

"Oh Goddess, no!" I threw it across the room and stamped back towards the study. The likeness was so perfect it pained me to look at it, but I crawled towards the corner where I had thrown it despite how terrible I felt.

There was something I hadn't told him, something I wanted him to know, desperately, but for the life of me I couldn't remember what it was.

Cal stared down at where I lay on the floor, my gaze fixed on the eyes of the painting, wallowing in my own tears, furious at my inadequacy. What good was I now, to anyone? What value did my immortal life have, now that everything was gone?

"You know all of them!" Cal argued. "You know who saw those things too!"

"Go away!" I growled, lifting him clear off the ground with one hand. "I did not ask to be sent here, and I did not come to kill... but I will destroy anyone who defies me! Is that understood?"

The boy nodded, shaken, and took a step back. "But... who was it?" he mumbled, knowing doubtless that I could hear him. "I don't know why I dream those things... don't blame me!" Cal begged. "I just need to know... who was it? Who saw those people?"

"It was me," I stopped short and stared at him, "those people you have seen through my eyes and mine alone! I do not know how you got into my mind but I want to make it perfectly clear that you are not welcome!"

"Then you're the one," Cal whispered, sounding almost awed.

His surety startled me. "I'm the what?"

"If my dreams are true and you saw... those things... then you're the one who's supposed to find it." He shook his head heavily.

"Find what?" I stared, knowing at that instant that I had uncovered a great and terrible secret indeed.

"It," he whispered, holding up a small, lifelike portrait of himself.

The Cal in the picture stood clutching something against his chest, a thing I recognized all too well. Had he not spoken a word, I would have known in an instant what it was. Cal looked up at me, his eyes wide and pleading, his hands shaking... overcome by the nameless fear that had suddenly and mercilessly descended upon both of us. "The book that rewrites history," he explained. "The Archives of Teyme."

Thirty-Three

Lightning struck overhead... and the doorbell rang for the second time. No one answered it. The door shattered under the force of a phenomenal blow, and Ordo dunked in, swinging his war hammer over his shoulder.

"We're with the man with the hammer." Jedera pointed as Bruno attempted to stop her entrance. Bruno stepped aside.

"Thanks ol' pal." The Prophet grinned, bowing theatrically.

"Artemis!" Ordo gasped. Lapsing into the Old Tongue, he muttered and swore almost incoherently. "Panther will be happy to know," he finished. "He was... not well when he thought you were dead."

I had not known whether or not my uncle was alive, but it was a slight comfort to me to learn that at very least he... if no one else, would welcome my return.

"By the Gods, you are alive!" Jedera stared. She reached out to touch my hand.

"Told ya." Dei grinned.

"I'm a survivor," I admitted.

"And, Architect." The Prophet bowed to Cal. "Pleasure doing business with ya... but I'm afraid your time on this earth has come to an end."

"Am I going to die?" Cal shuddered.

"Of course not!" Jedera laughed. "We're just taking you home."

"Home?" Cal wondered.

"Well, the experiment was quite a success," Ordo admitted. "Except that last part... and that's why we've come to get you."

"I don't understand," Cal stared.

"Past lifetime." The Prophet shook his head. "And it gets messy, lemme tell you that! We'd intended to pick you up before you keeled off, but it was an accident and it really took us by surprise. We went all over this universe

214

and a couple other dimensions trying to find you…," he sighed. "And now we have."

"You mean…"

"You were, or rather are… or perhaps may yet be the Architect, apprentice of Teyme the Great. You designed… or maybe you're currently designing or will someday design the city of Zenith. None of us quite know how your cosmic threads worked so we can't repair the damage that's been done to the wall. The Republic may have won the war but they won't be able to keep Zenith if you can help us get the power back up and the Tears closed again," Jedera finished.

"But I don't…" Cal began.

"Sure you do!" Ordo argued. "Or you will, at any rate, once you're back in the Chaos Realm with your computers and Teyme's books. I've kept all the original drawings of the city. You'll see them again once we get you to Gelthar."

"In good time," I interrupted, bewildered by their mad… mindless rambling. "About the Archives."

"The Archives?" Both Jedera and Dei stared wide-eyed. "The… Archives?"

"A book I picked up at a pawn shop. I had a dream I was facing myself and asking for the book, and that I gave it to me… or … Artemis," Cal explained.

"The greatest power in the infinite universe." Ordo shook his head. "In a pawn shop… imagine that. Still, it's not surprising that you found it. Your old master was quite the practical joker, wasn't he?"

"We've got to go get Teyme's blasted book." Jedera jumped to her feet. "If you remembered where you put it and we remembered where we put you… it's only a matter of time until someone else remembers what might have already happened."

"I'm confused," Cal sat down rather quickly.

"Look kid, time travel sucks," Dei agreed. "Why don't you pack your things for now and we'll figure out all the future/present/perfects later?"

Sirens echoed, coming closer and closer.

We looked out the window. Across the street, Cal's house was surrounded by police. Cal raced out the front door.

"Too late," Prophet groaned.

"Mom!" Cal shouted. The woman on the front porch ignored him, almost intentionally, it seemed. "Mom… what happened?"

"Somebody broke into the house," she muttered. "The neighbors saw them running out…" She shook her head. The six of us listened, carefully creeping out the Fargrove's front door, where we stood safely behind the growing crowd, though we were still somewhat suspicious in appearance.

"What'd they steal?" Cal asked.

"Nothing, apparently," his mother snapped, "but for some reason they tore the pages out of every last book."

"We're too late." Jedera shook her head.

"But who was it?" I wondered.

Jedera pointed to a long, deep crack in the pavement that I hadn't even noticed before. To an ordinary mortal, it would have appeared to be nothing more than an extra line of tar from the road, but we all knew better.

"My guess is they came out of that Tear." Jedera shook her head. "Not long ago."

"We should follow," Ordo agreed. "As much as I hate traveling between realms, Jedera is right."

"You're… leaving already?" Bruno stared. "But there's so much I… we…"

"Read the book." Dei tossed a paperback version of *The History of the Realm* to Patricia. "Publish it if you want to. It's a crazy story and it ought to bring some interesting guests 'round your place if you happen to be looking for trouble."

"Are you sure that's wise?" I began.

"And if anything nasty shows up, you can use your demon-summoning gig to call on her." He jerked a thumb at me.

"Deiunthel!" I glared.

"You arguing?" The Prophet grinned.

"No," I finished, turning to Cal, who had rejoined our group, a red sketchbook and a strange metallic pen in his hands.

"Let's go," he smiled, a look that seemed fairly close to tears. "There's nothing else here for me."

I was genuinely moved. His entire world thrown upside-down in less than an hour… and still, he showed no fear.

"Remind me to introduce you to my friend Phineas some time." I shook my head.

Deiunthel was laughing.

The Etone

"A companion for a day, a friend for life, a brother forever."

Thirty-Four

The blackness of the Tear swallowed even Ordo's substantial bulk, but Dei glowed like a lamplight… finally leading us out to the other side. We stepped through the last of the mists between worlds and found ourselves in an even darker cavern.

"Where are we?" I wondered, sniffing the air skeptically. "Is this Chaos Realm?"

"Underground Zenith," Jedera nodded quietly. "I wish I could say I was surprised, but I'm not. Trouble's been climbing out of the sewers lately, I'll tell you that! All the good magic-users moved down here to escape the IR concentration camps. Unfortunately, all of the not-so-good ones were already running this trap."

"I suppose there were some messes," I guessed. "How long has it been since I disappeared this time?"

"More than six months," The Prophet admitted. "Less than a year."

I listened… and to my horror heard gunshots in the distance. "There's already fighting?" I couldn't believe it.

"Worse." Ordo shook his head heavily. "The Etone are at war."

I was shocked. As far back as I knew of, the highest caste of street mages… members of the Etone Brotherhood, had always left each other and their respective gangs alone, even when they crossed paths at Mad Mack's. Apparently, not anymore.

"I take it we're with the Good Etone," I sighed.

"You would think so," The Prophet admitted. "But the Nakhet Syndicate was the first to give in to the IR. A lot of people in Zenith even think that the Good Etone mighta sold the Dynasty out."

"And the White Cross?" As much as I hated them, I knew those clerics would never abandon a true cause.

219

"Mostly executed," Jedera explained. "The demons wanted them all killed, and the IR frankly doesn't have much use for any sort of religion. Those that are left went to help out the True Etone. Ira is with them, he's that kid who used to clean tables at Mad Mack's, and his two brothers... the one's a big-time art-dealer vamp they call Germaine the Skunk."

"So we're evil now." I shook my head.

"Indeed we are," Dei announced gravely. "Proves that everything depends on perception, doesn't it?"

I didn't reply to that. Bad... I could deal with.

"When are we getting out of this damnable nether-realm?" I heard a familiar voice muttering nearby, just behind the nearest wall. I ran my fingers across the cold stone and tried to guess its thickness, maybe a foot or two.

"Phineas?" I shouted, wondering if he could hear me. "Phineas! Can you hear me Phineas? It's me... Artemis!"

"Artemis? Impossible... did you guys hear that?" another voice I recognized interrupted. It was Ruveus.

"I heard it." Phineas pushed him aside. "Is that you, Artemis?"

"It's me!" I shouted through the wall. "Where are you?"

"In here," a third voice announced, one that I guessed was probably Ira.

"There's a wall between us!" Phineas yelled, as if it weren't incredibly obvious. "Want me to blast it?"

"And cause a caf' in?" Someone else laughed... very darkly. "Haf you lost your mind, magick-man?"

"Can it, brother," Ira ordered.

"I outrank you, brother," Germaine shot back. "Haf some respect."

"Respect where respect is due, man," Ruveus leered.

"Well if we aren't going to blow it up, what are we supposed to do about the rock anyway... just erase it?" Ira argued.

Cal stared, his eyes lighting up as if he'd just realized something perfectly remarkable. He pulled from his notebook an old drawing, obviously wrinkled... and sketched a doorway into the stone wall. A door materialized in front of us.

"Wow..." Dei stared. "Now draw me an Icee."

Cal shrugged and haphazardly scribbled two of Dei's peculiar red-ice drinks, one for the Prophet and the second for himself. He grinned insanely.

"Did you see what happened!" Cal exclaimed. "It appeared!" He laughed.

The rest of us ignored them. We were too shocked by the appearance of the door in the cave.

"Where'd the door come from?" Ruveus wondered.

"I drew it," Cal admitted.

"But that's ridiculous... you'd have to understand Teyme's Alchemy," Phineas muttered, opening the door.

The look on his face was somewhat mixed, and though I couldn't make out precisely what thoughts were racing through his head, I knew he must have realized what I felt. He looked old.

True, he was at very least thirty... but I had never stopped to really think what that meant for a human.

"Are you okay?" Ruveus wondered, squinting at me. He, of course, was unchanged, but his human form was even less real than mine was.

"You look like you're gonna drop," Ira announced, stepping into the light. He had grown a few feet and was beginning to need to shave, but his eyes were still childish. Armed with two guns on either side and a short sword slung across his back, he looked more like a mercenary than anything, except that he wore a white t-shirt which proclaimed "Yes, I'm a cleric".

The fourth member of the traveling party I assumed to be Germaine, Ira's older brother who had fallen through a bizarre Tear one morning and lived five hundred years as a vampire in Hungary before returning to his family in the Chaos Realm, only to find that he wasn't even late for breakfast.

His hair was done up in what looked like a poor mess of white and black dreadlocks, hence the name "Skunk". He wore small green glasses and a green suit-coat, which happened to look absolutely repulsive.

Still, the aura he carried was that of one not to be toyed with.

The nine of us stood in silence, evaluating one another almost suspiciously. Ira glared at Cal, Cal stared at Germaine, Ruveus stared at Ordo and everyone else looked at me.

"I got him!" a voice screamed, as Terese dropped, apparently through the ceiling and accompanied by the cleric Sikara.

The moment of tension broken, we all backed up and drew our weapons.

Terry and Sikara were both brandishing stakes. Germaine jumped up onto the wall like a spider and hissed. Ira loaded his gun.

"He's my bro!" Ira shouted. "Leave him!"

"What's going on!" I demanded.

"Oh c'mon... we're just doing our job!" Sikara whined, turning to face me. Her eyes grew very wide and she put a hand to her chest as if she were having a mild heart failure.

Terese gasped, noticing me as well.

"Artemis? Back from the dead?"

"In a manner of speaking, yes," I replied.

Cal stared at Terese, half in awe at her entrance, and half because of her revealing spandex and leather attire. The years had begun to affect Sikara as they had Phineas, but only barely. Yet... perhaps thanks to the efforts of her "Good Boys", Terese remained exactly the same as I remembered her.

Cal closed his gaping mouth and blinked, still shocked. I knew that look to be one for trouble, and I suspected that it would be very difficult to tell the boy that Terese was nearly a hundred years old and well out of his league.

"So what's going on?" I repeated.

"We're vampire slayers," Sikara admitted. "The job stinks, but we get paid and it keeps the IRP away from us. Everything costs money now."

"The IRP?" I wondered.

"Interdimensional Republic Police," Terese translated. "President Fairfax's goons."

"Know what IRP really stands for?" Ira grinned. "Think about it. It's why they're so pissed off all of the time."

"Stop now!" Phineas glared. "Grow up, will you?"

"Well, if Artemis is here, I'm on her side," Terry admitted, putting away her weapons. "If anyone can get the Dynasty back on its feet, you can."

I realized from the look in her eyes that she meant it. It should have been a comfort to me but somehow it wasn't.

"Where are you all headed?" I asked, glancing at each familiar face.

"Back to camp," Phineas explained. "Some of the men captured a Tear Soldier this morning."

"A what?" I wondered. I knew I should have expected to be somewhat behind the times, but I felt as if I had lost far more than just a single year of my life.

"Tear Soldiers have been around since the days of the Dynasty, but I doubt you've ever met one. They're a fairly elusive branch of the Chaos Knights that specializes in breaking down high-volume Tears," Sikara explained. "But they don't work for any government... so the IR couldn't shut them down like they did the rest of the Empire's peacekeepers. Most Tear Soldiers are a little bit crazy. They live between dimensions like the Etone do, but they usually ended up jumping around all of the nasty worlds instead of the nice ones."

"Sounds like fun," I sighed, wincing at the thought. I knew of quite a few terrible dimensions that even the I'Eloshir avoided, and I couldn't imagine living in any of them.

"The average career length is somewhere around two years," Ira continued. "And this sister they caught seems to have worked about seven."

"Impressive," I agreed.

"Well, let's get a move on," Ruveus yawned, scratching his head. "I hate to push everyone, but this part of the Underground isn't exactly safe right now."

"You said it, bro." Ira shook his head heavily. "I almost stepped on a Mag-mine ten minutes ago. I'll bet there's a whole IR hive somewhere near here."

Without arguing, we all moved to follow Ruveus and Ira, with the exception of Deiunthel who had disappeared inexplicably.

"Hold up!" Sikara waved from behind us. "I'm coming too!"

"Too dangerous," Terese ordered. "You should go back to the surface."

"I'd advise against you following," Phineas agreed. "Tears have been opening up left and right down here. Terese has got a hefty arsenal of mage spells, she can easily take on the Republic and a few monsters. Ira may be a cleric, but he's also a member of the Brotherhood. He's used to the… changes… that Tears cause in the way magic works. But nothing you learned from the White Cross will do much good down here, not with the dimensions shifting."

"I'm coming," Sikara finished, seeming considerably less than confident. "To the edge of the world."

"And back again?" Phineas wondered. Sikara did not respond.

Thirty-Five

The Tear Soldier, Lieutenant First-Class Rexhon Sidal, was a blonde Elvin woman who stood at barely four feet. When I first reached the tent where the Etone had her tied up, I fought the urge to laugh, unwilling to believe that such a small, child-like creature was capable of the sort of destruction the others feared she would cause.

I was proven wrong. Rex's remarkable healing skills were eclipsed only by her incredible speed and berserker attitude on the battlefield... and what a battlefield it was.

The day that I first stepped out into the underground war was nearly a religious experience. I remember standing in the middle of the chaos, swords sending sparks up into the air, guns and spells firing above my head, all in the blackness and the mists of the multi-dimensional cave.

Before my very eyes, men would dive at one another, ready to die at that moment, only to slip into unseen Tears and vanish before their swords ever clashed. Some disappeared indefinitely, while others would return seconds later, suddenly and inexplicably burning in flames.

Occasionally a soldier would vanish one day and return the next, twenty years older and baffled by the passage of time.

All in all, it was as horrific a conflict as might have occurred in the very depths of hell. As terrible as The Frozen Sea had been, it was nothing compared to the sheer magnitude of the... the thing I had suddenly found myself in the middle of, a war, not between humans and demons, but of Traversers and demi-gods.

"Your friend," Rex wondered, gesturing towards me from a distance. She seemed to avoid me with a particularly strong fear, as if she could somehow sense how near I was to my breaking point. "She has never seen a Tear-War before, has she?"

It took me a minute to realize that the elf was talking to Phineas.

"Is she going to be ill?" Rex asked, reaching for her medical kit.

Phineas shook his head, staring at me strangely. "No, but she may need to kill a few things," he replied. "Artemis is accustomed to bloodshed."

"She is more than accustomed," Rex corrected, whispering in a low voice. I heard her anyway. "I have never seen that expression on a human before. No sane man wears a face like that."

"She isn't insane," Phineas argued, though he seemed somewhat unconvinced himself. "And she's not human either. She's a Traverser."

"A Traverser?" Rex mused… and then gasped. "A true Traverser?" she demanded, pulling Phineas aside. "An…" Rex trailed off into silence, almost as if she couldn't bring herself to say the word.

Forcing myself back to the present, I turned to face those who were gathered behind me, overlooking the slaughter.

"I'Eloshir," I finished her sentence coldly, hating the sensation that had come over me. Though I knew that having some willingness to fight was beneficial in any battle, my desire went far beyond the simple instinct of self preservation. I was miserable. I wanted to kill. It would make me feel better.

"Yes," I continued, not looking at her directly, but instead at the dark rocks over her head. "How else could I travel through mirrors?" I demanded. "Don't act as if you didn't know that I once served the Warlord," I sighed heavily. A black rat scurried past my foot and I grabbed it suddenly, without thinking, holding it in my hand and very nearly crushing the creature until I remembered that I had an audience. I set the rat free.

Both Phineas and Rex took a step back, and I realized that it had not been just the two of them staring. The entire camp watched me in silence as I snapped the tie that held my hair back, letting it fly loose around my face as I lowered my eyes, taking a deep breath and trying to compose myself.

"You looked like something just then," Sikara stammered, perhaps trying to explain why she was still gawking at me. "Not human."

"I've just finished explaining that!" I glared. "Surely you know by now that I have never been human." I shook my head. "I thought everyone knew… after Raphael…" I drifted off into silence, sensing that my explanation had not improved the situation.

Cal bit his lip, his eyes wavering as he stared at me.

"It was scary," he admitted.

Sikara nodded quietly.

"Gods damn the lot of you!" I snarled. "I mean you no harm, you know

225

that!"

"What you mean to do and what you might do anyway are two different things." Ruveus shook his head. "I don't know, Artemis. Maybe you do need help."

"Doesn't anyone trust me?" I demanded, searching their cold, frightened eyes for some response.

"This isn't the first time you've returned from the dead," Phineas explained. "As a matter of fact, it isn't even the second time... or the third time."

"What are you trying to say, Phineas?" I whispered, suddenly very uncomfortable.

"It isn't natural," Ruveus finished. "It's almost as if..."

"As if I what? You know I wouldn't... I could never have... he would never have died, do you hear me? HE WOULD NEVER HAVE DIED!" I did not let him finish. "For now, believe what you must," I hissed, turning away into the shadows.

I was still numbed by the realization that not even those closest and dearest to me dared trust me, even after all of the terrible things we had been through together. The thought agonized me. All I had ever wanted was lost to me.

I stopped short, refusing to drift into my own web of sorrow and self-pity, drawing my sword. Without another word, I leapt off the face of the cliff and into the sea of death below.

A year passed in the darkness of the Tear, a lonely year, days drifting into weeks and weeks into months, all without sunlight and seasons, without rain or wind, silent and terrible to suffer through.

Perhaps what gave me heart in those dark times was seeing the change that had come over Cal, since we had met, so long ago in his world.

When he had first followed us, leaving behind all he had ever known, I had glimpsed only a bit of his extraordinary courage.

Though in the beginning I had doubted that he was truly the incarnation of Teyme's legendary apprentice, as time wore on, he grew more confident when the rest of us faltered, his bright spirit shining more brilliantly than Deiunthel's godly glow.

Yet, as his friends and teachers died and vanished, even he became colder and hollow. It pained me, knowing that the characteristics he had begun to assume had lead to his being nicknamed "Young Sir Ravencroft", after myself.

"'Do not become like me.' I warned him always. 'I alone carry enough bitterness to drive all sunlight from the world.' You must never become like me."

At times, he listened, something would give him hope and he would be reaching for the sky once again, imaginative and ingenious as ever.

That... that was before the quakes began.

When the situation had seemed as grim and awful as it could have possibly become, quite suddenly a rumbling started beneath our feet, revealing not one of the small Tears that might swallow a fighter or two, but a large, gaping maw of darkness that ripped across a line of fifty men... and threw them out again in an instant, nothing left but bleached skeletons.

With the utmost certainty, I knew then that I would have to end that war. If I could not... in a few short days, we would all be dead.

Thirty-Six

We met in a few off-hours at Phineas's tent to discuss the problem at hand.

"The Tear that we've been fighting in is collapsing," Rex explained. "It's suffered enough damage to the infrastructure. We're bringing it down."

"Any way out?" Ruveus asked.

"No." Rex shook her head. "You gotta have either zero-neutral MC or way over two-thousand MC in the environment to control a Tear collapse and get out alive. So long as the battle goes on between The Brotherhood... we're trapped. When the Tear goes down, we go with it."

"You sound like you're okay with this," Sikara muttered, shuddering at the thought.

"It goes with the job." Rex nodded. "All three of the men I was trained with died in Tear-Wars. It'll be good to see them again. Damion was my best friend, Luis... he saved my life once, and Jatrac still owes me money."

"And what about the rest of you?" Cal demanded, speaking up for the first time in weeks. "You're just going to give up?"

"Like most Traverser battles, the conflict here's been brewing for a thousand years," Rex sighed. "This cavern couldn't take a five-thousand MC blast, even if there was a mage in the infinite universe powerful enough to supply it. The only choice that leaves us with is to stop the fighting and go for the zero-neutral. But with how bad the Etone have always wanted to kill each other, nothing's going to scare them out of doing it. Not even the Demon Queen rising from the depths of Magog."

I smiled slightly, despite the grim situation. A solution had just occurred to me.

"And what if I could bring Ireval to you?"

For the first time in ages I saw a little of the childish hope I'd missed so

228

much in Phineas's eyes. Then it was gone.

"It's worth a try," he admitted, though he still glanced at me fearfully.

"What day is today?" I asked. It was the typical question that I always posed before going into battle, a strange, almost obsessive tradition that I had carried over from my time with the I'Eloshir.

"Friday the third." Cal checked his watch.

"Good. A good day to end things." I turned to Phineas. "I'm going to need your help to pull off this illusion," I whispered, hoping he would follow my true meaning.

"An illusion?" Cal wondered, instantly suspicious. "But I thought you said those red scanners the guys wear let them see past that kind of stuff. The green scanners are magic, the MC numbers, the red scanners are..." He trailed off into silence, still staring at me.

"Not this time." I shook my head. "Not this time."

I think Germaine knew then. Vampires can smell death. I positively reeked of it.

"Be careful, majick-man," Germaine warned Phineas. "Too much sunshine is good for nobody."

We stepped out into the war after a few minor plans, mostly consisting of how we would keep the "illusion" going, or rather, how Phineas would be able to keep me on the right side of the conflict.

I didn't want to accidentally kill any of my friends.

I stood on the top of the cliff in the center of the battlefield and reached for the sky, not even wincing at the bullets and spells that came flying at me.

In a moment, they would be irrelevant. I gave in. For the first time in years, I gave in completely to the sheer power of the darkness I carried with me, not to relish in the warped pleasure of it, but to save thousands, friends and foes alike.

I screamed aloud in rage at the terrors I had been through, at my loss, at Raphael's senseless death and Phineas's terrible mortality.

All the things I hated, all that was so wrong and despicable to me, came rising to the surface... and the change came.

The pain was terrible and wonderful all at once. In a world where so much was weak and dying, I was suddenly strong again. I could see for miles and hear the slightest whisper, smell the blood on a man's blade and know whether he had just killed a human or an elf, an ogre or an I'Eloshir. And then, as I felt my wings again, realized that I... I could fly, my demonic arrogance returned.

229

I was Artemis no longer. I had surrendered myself, my conscience, my sense of balance and my feeble desire to do good… surrendered it all in that instant, locking off the parts of my mind that felt guilt and fear, the weaker parts that thought things through and opened myself up to the power I had sworn off, not because I needed to… but because I wanted to.

My true form alone would have awed the Etone, but even that did not satisfy me. I wanted a release from my deeper pains, a comfort that I could not hope to achieve without closing off all my thoughts and memories completely.

Though I had lost control briefly before, once facing Maurice and another time with Beyoni, never before had I truly destroyed myself as I did in that instant.

Artemis was dead. I was Ireval.

At first, I had worn a mask, a skulled trophy Ruveus had kept from the Battle of The Equinox. But then, with my true self revealed, I no longer wanted to hide behind anything. My foes deserved to see who it was that stood before them.

One minute I was standing alone on the monolith, and the next I was hovering in midair, crackling with purple energy.

The temptation to destroy everything in my path rose to the surface. The battle hand slowed in places.

And that ridiculous mask, the mask I despised so much, I tore it off, throwing it into the field where it exploded into a column of purple fire.

"STOP MORTALS! BEHOLD!" I ordered, breathing in deeply the smell of blood and shuddering at the icy-hot chill that raced through my body.

The armies froze. I enjoyed the silence immensely. I was free.

And yet I couldn't fathom how I had found myself in my current place. The last thing I remembered clearly was a terribly long ago day when I had stood at the gates of Tirs Uloth and argued with Zaethe about whether or not we should spend the night.

"Look at what you have called upon!" a strangely familiar voice roared. "The Ireval, the death of five-thousand worlds, gone for decades… now returned to bring chaos upon you!"

"Who are you!" I demanded with a growl, wheeling about to face the speaker who had dared interrupt my dramatic line.

The white-armored humans approached the battle line more hesitantly, seeing that my aggression had shifted to their opponents, some even drawing their weapons.

"I will kill you, human!" I snarled, grabbing the first man who crossed my path. The green and red glass over his eyes shattered into a hundred pieces as I called fire to my hands, throwing him into the ranks of his fellow soldiers, a hole the size of my fist burned cleanly through his chest.

"Who spoke!" I demanded, sniffing the air and following my instinct. Another human in black stood on a rock and stared at me, the two of us nearly eye to eye.

I was furious… I was insanely furious without knowing why!

"Raphael," a voice interrupted, and my memories came flooding back to me, instantly and cruelly. I could not see who had spoken.

"Oh Goddess," I whispered, realizing suddenly that the man I had stared down was Cal. If someone hadn't snapped me out of my insanity, I might have killed him.

"It's going down!" Rex shouted. "MC thirty, twenty… wait! Something's wrong… it's rising again! Sixty, eighty, one-hundred…"

A low growl rumbled through the floor of the cavern, almost as if the Tear itself were a great beast, awakening from centuries of slumber.

"Caf in!" Germaine roared as a shower of boulders poured down from above us, immense rocks and slabs of concrete.

"We've got to get out of here!" Phineas grabbed Cal by the neck and flung him on the back of a motorcycle, revving the bike up and careening through the Etone's camp.

"No way out!" another voice screamed in terror as a boulder the size of a small house collapsed in front of the Tear's exit. "Help us God!"

I focused on the wall of the cavern, drawing my energy back to the point where I doubted I could control it. I didn't care. I had to blast something. I fired the spell, throwing out the entire stone wall.

The green MC scanners the Good Etone and the IR wore exploded, all of them simultaneously. Whatever power I had released was far beyond measure, but it had done the trick. I fell from above, cold, drained, senseless, maybe the closest to dead I had ever been. Daylight streamed in. And… how beautiful it was.

I shed my wings and lay motionless on the ground, vaguely recalling Ruveus picking me up and slinging me over his back. We stepped out onto what had once been a stretch of green fields, now a battle-scarred, frozen, scorched and Tear-ridden desert leading up to the city of Zenith. I scarcely recognized it, the silver glow tarnished by what seemed like centuries of filth, not only a few year's worth.

"The Tear closed," Phineas admitted. "We lost about a hundred. The IR lost more."

"You seen Sikara?" Terry demanded, clutching her battered arm. "Where's she gone to? Any of you seen her?"

None of us had.

"Rex went down." Ruveus shook his head. "I saw it... a Tear swallowed her up and she was gone. But she knew it was going to happen, with the way she always talked about those partners of hers... she knew."

Germaine staggered towards us, his clothes smoldering as if they'd very recently been on fire and had not been extinguished completely. But the flames were not enough to distract him. "Ira!" he shouted. "Brother!"

The man he was following turned and gasped at him, horrified by the burns on his face. It was not Ira. We'd lost a third of our group. Cal was crushed. It still seemed impossible to him that those he had talked to... flirted with and fought beside only hours before were gone... gone forever. I had seen too much and lived too long. There was nothing I could say.

The Apprentice

"A new generation will take up the sword when we have passed on."

Thirty-Seven

We settled back down at Mad Mack's Magic Users, myself in human guise, still being "wanted" in most parts of the city by those who believed I had in fact survived The Battle of the Frozen Sea by some unknown means. How right they were.

Business, however, was slow. People feared to be caught in a place that had been so much a part of the dynasty… a restaurant catering to Etone, powerful wizards and Chaos Knights.

It had been the place to go if you wanted to meet someone famous.

It became the place to hide if you didn't want anyone to know you were famous.

The upstairs rooms of that cold brick building became our sanctuary, where we few and scattered rebels met to tend our wounds and trade bits of information, futilely planning for an attack against the Republic that we knew we would never possess the men or the resources to initiate. There were too few of us left, and too many of the enemy.

Graffiti was drawn on the one tower of the Imperial palace that surfaced above the ice of The Frozen Sea. The famous library of Alexandria had become a headquarters for the hated IRP and all of the beautiful parks and gardens that had once made the city an Eden to behold were dead, rotting and overgrown with weeds.

Cal had recently returned to Gelthar with The Prophet, while Jedera and Ordo were out looking for another exiled relative, Ignatius The Bookkeeper, patron of lost manuscripts.

Ruveus had taken to "smoking" frequently and playing his mandolin for tips, fortunately competent enough in his shape-changing ability that he was even able to sleep in his human form, though he often complained that it gave him "a pain in his tail" that wouldn't go away.

I carried such a pain myself, comforted by the renewed trust of my friends, but agonized in the worst possible way every time I looked up to the sky, and each time my gaze drifted in the direction of the ruins of the palace, but especially when I witnessed the barren, shattered rock that had once served as the foundation of the lighthouse at Silver Point.

I had lost more than the one soul that I had ever truly loved... I had lost all of what might have been my future. For without Raphael, I cared nothing for life.

All in all, the situation was moving beyond poor and drifting towards destitute, which was not the way I'd imagined my return to the Chaos Realm.

"We're broke," Phineas announced one evening as we sat around a table in Mad Mack's, checking through our meager finances.

"So what do you want me to do?" I wondered. "They test people looking for legitimate work. At least the rest of you are somewhat human."

"Not you, Artemis, me. I'm working." Phineas shook his head. "It's about time I get a job."

"Doin' what, Phinny?" Terry wondered. "At least I've kinda done work before. Law enforcement in the Badowin's... before I ever met my Good Boys. You and Ruveus combined can't even come up with half of a resume that'll pass customs. First question. What did you do in the days of the Dynasty? Aristocrat? Mage? Bamn... shot down like that!"

"I'm not talking about doing anything legal," Phineas shot back. "I'm talking about taking an Apprentice."

"An Apprentice?" I wondered, intrigued by the possibility. There were few alive that rivaled my skill with a sword, and though guns were increasingly popular because they could combat magic, some of the braver wanderers of the street still carried traditional weapons as a mark of honor and courage.

Phineas was a brilliant wizard, of course, a natural magic-user. It hadn't occurred to me that he was nearly the same age that his master, Galwick had been when he took his first pupil.

"Sure." Phineas shrugged. "I bet there's lots of kids that still have a little family money left. Once the schools closed down, they all hit the streets, a lot of them with magical problems they still need training to control."

He was certainly qualified to teach, that much I couldn't argue... but the real question was whether of not we could find a student qualified to learn from the most powerful mortal wizard in a thousand years. And so, the search began.

At first, few replied to the somewhat vague advertisements we had posted around the city, but as word got out that the "Magic-User seeks Apprentice" was really an advertisement posted by the legendary Lord Wizard of the Imperial Court, hundreds of letters flooded us daily, not to mention the reckless and more street-savvy individuals who arrived at Mad Mack's to answer the ad in person.

"I'm really good. Honest," the forty-sixth candidate of the day claimed, as Ruveus ushered him out.

"I should just add "no humans" to that paper, shouldn't I?" Phineas sighed. "It's amazing what some people think qualifies as a magical gift these days."

"That's true," Terry admitted, cleaning her sword on the bar counter.

We all sighed in unison and returned to our various petty tasks. I tapped my pen on the table, shaking a little more ink into it and continuing my awkward sketch of a Spellcraft that was moving off the napkin I had begun it on and gradually working its way across the surface of the table.

"You're not drawing on my table again, are ya Artemis?" Terry wondered, obviously unconcerned.

"Does it matter?" I muttered, ignoring Phineas's amused grin as he leaned over my shoulder and glanced at the sketch.

"You really can't draw, can you?" He smirked.

"I've never had time to learn." I shrugged.

"No time in seven-hundred years?" He laughed. "That's saying something."

"Let's see you draw, Phinny." Terry threw him a pen.

"Draw?" Phineas stared at her. "Oh no. I'm a wizard, not an artist."

The bells that hung on the front door jangled as a young girl... perhaps thirteen, peered into the room. She was of medium height and not too slightly built, with her brown hair braided into pigtails. Her obviously worn jean-jacket sported a purple star-shaped patch on the shoulder, made of a strange fabric that seemed to glow almost magically.

"Are you Master Merlin?" she wondered, her soft voice full of a sort of awed fear. "Indeed." Phineas nodded, squinting at her. "And who are you?"

"My name is Tai Mariel," she whispered. "I found your advertisement." Pulling a rumpled paper from her jeans pocket, she unfolded the paper so that the three of us could read what was written there. It was not one of the fliers we had made.

It was on orange construction paper and written in black marker by an obviously childish hand.

"Magic-User seeks Apprentice," which had been our slogan, was vague yet effective in drawing a crowd, but the flier that Mariel held was much more specific in its details, incriminatingly so.

"Master Wizard Phineas Merlin seeks Apprentice 12-18 years old. Must have been apprenticed previously for 3-6 years, preferably in Ardra or Eldar. Find him at Mad Mack's Magic Users."

Terry squinted at the paper. "Where'd you get that, girl?" she wondered, obviously a little uncomfortable.

Coming upstairs in the elevator, Ruveus scanned the room, munching on a bag of peanuts. He glanced at each of us with a look that almost resembled pity until his gaze came to rest on Mariel in the doorway.

"The wizard isn't seeing any…" Ruveus began, but Phineas silenced him.

"Have you any previous training?" he asked. "As you must know, I do not intend to work with beginners."

"Some," Mariel admitted. "I know it says three years, and I've got just that," she paused. "I used to live in Celedon, so I'm from Ardra. And I was apprenticed before… to Mistress Wendy Vesper. She was court sorceress to Duchess Rosalind."

Phineas smiled faintly. If he had ever met a woman capable of holding him down, Rosalind was it.

"And how is the Duchess… these days?" Phineas wondered.

The girl shook her head. "Dead. Miss Vesper tried to protect her from the IR, but the Duchess wouldn't let us stay. She told us we had to escape and then used her opal to make us run. Miss Vesper could have fought the Duchess, but she always told me that a good wizard doesn't disobey her lady's orders. Miss Vesper died too. She got magic-poisoning."

"Dead?" Phineas stared, absorbing the information slowly. "But that isn't…"

"Half of Ardra is in the ocean," Mariel continued. "And the rest of it has become a testing site for synthetic magic."

"Synthetic… magic?" Ruveus rolled his eyes. "Of all the really… really stupid things in the universe…"

"The IR think magic is a science." Mariel bit her lip and clenched her fists. "They took three of the girls at my home and haven't brought any of them back yet. They might get away with that… with some of those girls… but I dare them to try and take me!"

She clutched in her hand something that flickered faintly, a glowing stone I barely recognized… not having seen it in so long. The blue opal of Aquara, the one Phineas had given to the little girl in Celedon on nothing more than a good feeling... fate had drawn her back to him, as he'd always suspected it would. I was amazed.

Phineas, still in a dark mood over the news of Rosalind's death, smiled slightly. I could tell he'd found the one.

Weeks passed, and Phineas was surprised to learn that almost every lesson he decided to teach Mariel had already mastered at some point.

"Third year?" Phineas guessed, checking off the record he had begun to keep. "She must have been a young talent."

"No younger than you were." I shook my head. "She's doing well."

"Better than I could have hoped," Phineas agreed. "I only wish we could figure out some way to pull her out of that orphanage."

"We'll come up with something," I reassured him, though I was doubtful. We had neither the magic nor the technology to remove the tracking chip implanted in Mariel's arm, and we could not take her legally, not with the background checks the IR ran. I sat down and sipped my tea slowly, watching planes flying past our window.

The republic's steel gray fighters hummed, shaking the foundation of the building as they shot over. In my mind's eye I pictured Spellcraft drifting past in the sunlight, wind billowing colorful sails, people waving from the open decks... the cold, blue-smoke breeze that followed in their wake, painting the sky itself with silver streaks of ice.

Yet there were few of those great ships left, and those that had escaped the hands of the IR were far away, hidden deep in the mountains and forests of Accoloth and Istara.

Just then, a violent explosion blew through the door of Phineas's office.

"My experiment!" Phineas gasped, jumping to his feet. A cloud of smoke poured out the door, followed by a faint crackle of electricity.

Mariel staggered out of the workroom, holding up a small red jellybean. Her hair was singed and her clothes spattered in a multitude of acidic colors, but there was no mistaking the smile on her face.

"What exactly where you trying to do?" I wondered, surveying the wreckage.

"It worked?" Phineas ignored me, standing with his hands planted on Mariel's shoulders as if he were about to hug her. Mariel nodded, grinning, and he lifted her off her feet, the two of them dancing around the room.

"My girl, you are brilliant!" he proclaimed, holding up the little red bean. "It worked!" he sighed, smiling.

"What worked?" I demanded for the second time.

"Alchemical candies!" Phineas exclaimed triumphantly, racing into the workroom and coming out again with an apron full of candy. "Jellybeans! Jellybeans with the power to make you fly… the ability to level small buildings and cure all ills!"

"You've gone mad," I stared.

"That's what you think now!" Phineas laughed, scooping up a handful of beans and offering them to me. "Here, try one!"

Tossing aside my better judgment, I chose a pale blue candy and ate it. The taste was sugary and somewhat unpleasant, as if the flavor of raspberry had been used to cover up something truly obscene.

"What's supposed to happen?" I wondered, suddenly feeling sick. I looked down.

I was floating upwards at an astonishing rate. Before I could stop myself, I hit the chandelier with my head.

"Phineas, this is ridiculous!" I argued, pushing off of the ceiling. "How do I get down?"

"You don't!" He applauded his own work. "That's the beauty of it! It wears off in about an hour or two!"

"An hour! Good gods man, haven't you anything better to waste your time on?" I demanded, dodging the light fixture for the second time.

A red jellybean floated past me. I caught it.

"Don't eat that one!" Phineas shouted, as if I were miles away instead of merely stuck to the ceiling of the room. "Never eat the red ones!"

Certain that I didn't want to know why, I wisely decided not to ask.

Thirty-Eight

Three weeks passed, three casual, uneventful weeks. I continued to decorate the table-tops of the bar with my sketches, while Phineas wasted the majority of his time causing explosions with Mariel, and Terry began to bring home packets of paper with titles like "Get Rich Quick" or "How to make $2000 today without using magic."

"Where is Mariel?" Phineas wondered, pacing the bar as we waited for his apprentice to arrive for her lesson. "It isn't like her to be late."

I had to agree. It certainly wasn't. Mariel often arrived at the bar a few hours early and almost never left until the sun went down. One of the girls in her class at school was a talented illusionist, the daughter of a famous Etone by the name of Ricardo the Shadow-Tamer.

Ricardo had been executed by the IR a few months back, and since then his daughter had been more than willing to help Mariel "get back" at the Republic. Teka Shadow-Tamer had created an illusionary copy of Mariel that would attend her classes at the public school while Mariel herself slipped out the back door and headed to her real lessons with Phineas.

The plan was brilliant and seemed to work flawlessly. It was almost impossible to believe that it had been thought up two girls who were barely in their teens.

The door chimed and Lucy sauntered in, accompanied by Igor the gargoyle and Master Jeo. They were all wearing matching black shirts over their usual clothes that read "Ozzfest" in scribbled red letters.

"Where's Mariel?" Phineas demanded.

Lucy shrugged. "I was out back waiting for her an hour ago. She didn't take my cab."

"That's ridiculous!" Phineas argued. "Lucy, she always takes your cab! She doesn't have money to pay anyone else!"

"Terry? Could ya' be a dear and get me a Tequila Sunrise?" Lucy asked, avoiding Phineas.

"Anything for you, Jeo? Igor?" Terry asked, mixing the drink.

"Sure thing, babe." Jeo grinned. "Bloody Mary."

"Vodka," Igor grunted, standing on his bar stool.

"Isn't it a little early for all of you to be drinking?" I wondered, glancing at the three of them suspiciously.

"Nah," Lucy sipped her drink. "With this dimension as it is… anytime's a good time to get hammered."

"Didja hear that Baroness Gloria landed herself in prison?" Jeo asked suddenly, stirring his Bloody Mary with a celery stick.

I hadn't.

"Turns out that the IR Bureau of Dangerous Familiars confiscated her black leopard," Jeo sighed. "Ammano loa, I saw that one coming… All that over a friggin' cat and now she's in Antares."

The room suddenly fell silent and I found my gaze drifting from Lucy, who was sitting on the floor tapping her nails to Phineas, who stared at me strangely from his favorite booth.

"A cat?" a voice growled. I looked up. Above the bar in the rafters sat crouched the large, black cat that had always been Gloria's shadow. As close as I stood to the creature, it looked much bigger than I had remembered it. "I am much more than a mere cat!"

"The cat talks," Phineas stared.

"I am Devonny de Phoenicia… Baroness Gloria's spirit guide… not her 'cat'," the beast snarled, digging her claws into the wood of the rafters.

"Any particular reason you decided to drop in here?" Jeo wondered.

"I was hoping I could convince the lot of you trashed semi-retired magic-users to help her escape," Devonny admitted, retracting her claws and then extending them almost methodically.

"Break into Antares?" Lucy gasped. "Are you insane, fuzzball? You do realize they keep gods in that prison!"

"I am aware of the fact." The cat seemed unconcerned. "I've been planning to get her out since I escaped from the labs myself, and if you'll listen for more than three seconds…"

The bells chimed again and Ruveus burst through the door. He was breathing heavily and he clutched in his hands a rumpled newspaper. His sunglasses slipped off his nose and broke on the floor, but he scarcely noticed them.

242

"They have her!" Ruveus pointed to the picture in the paper, falling to his hands and knees, utterly exhausted but thankfully unhurt. "The IRP took Mariel!"

"Mariel…" Phineas sat down heavily and Lucy took a bite out of her glass, crunching on the broken pieces thoughtfully in her mouth.

The cat clucked, almost as if she were chiding the lot of us for being so inept… so irresponsible that we couldn't even protect a young girl.

"Poor child," she purred. "Poor unfortunate child."

A few hours passed as we attempted to compose ourselves and put together the best rescue operation we could muster. With our current lack of resources that meant that Terry, Ruveus, Phineas and myself were planning on charging the police headquarters with swords and spells flying, hoping we would survive long enough in a frontal assault to find Mariel.

"Then we break in," Phineas sighed. "That isn't much of a plan."

"You'll rush into the IRP building head-on but you won't consider helping me infiltrate Antares," Devonny muttered. "Stupid two-leggers."

We all ignored her.

"It isn't hard." Cal traced the route on his blueprints as he entered the bar, talking on his cell-phone with Deiunthel and Ordo close behind him. He and Terry hung up their phones simultaneously and Cal unraveled the rolls of paper he carried under his arm.

"I've got the stuff you asked for," he announced. "It'll be simple to get into the IR building. Aside from the Imperial Palace, Alexandria Tower was my favorite project. I know that library like the back of my own hand." He glanced at Devonny and shook his head. "But Antares… I'm sorry I can't help you there. Antares is between-realms. It changes all the time. Even if I could get hold of a plan, I'd have no guarantee that the Tear that got you all in would be able to get you back out again. But this rescue should be simple, if they're holding her on the island."

"You say it'll be simple, but you can't account for security," I argued. "You drew the building… not its current occupants."

"And the High Commander is afraid of cops." Ruveus shook his head. "Who would have thought I'd live to see the day?"

"Do not fight with me!" I warned.

He fell silent.

"So we'll borrow a sub from Germaine the Skunk," Terry sighed. "He owes me a favor, so we won't have any trouble there… but then what?"

"And then you bust the doors down," Lucy repeated, shaking her head…

a grin breaking across her face. "You're all crazy."

"Are you coming?" I wondered, hoping that she might consider helping us. Her time-stopping talents would be invaluable in such a circumstance, but like her best friend Jeo, Lucy seemed content to be bystander rather than a participant in most of our endeavors, especially when the situation was potentially dangerous.

"Hell no!" Lucy frowned. "What... you think I'm nuts?"

"It would be a safe assumption," I shot back, turning to Ordo. He glanced at me skeptically and then sighed, defeated before he spoke a word. Taking Lucy by the arm, the two of them stumbled into a corner, whispering to one another and glancing at me sporadically.

"How is your daughter?" I asked Ordo, though he clearly preferred not to talk to me at that particular point. "I hear that my uncle's run off again."

"Artemis!" Phineas glared.

"Well, we are not making progress!" I muttered.

"Ruveus and I will go inside," Phineas explained, tracing the route on Cal's map.

"Not without me you won't." I took a final sip of ambrosia and then pushed my glass away. "If need be, I can pull the three of us out of there," I pointed out, turning a little mirror in the palm of my hand so that it would reflect the light.

"The three of us will go in," Phineas corrected himself. "Leaving Cal, Terry, and the cat with the sub."

"Spirit Guide," Devonny corrected.

"The rest of you hold down the fort here in case we run into any unexpected difficulties," Phineas ordered, clapping his hands together. "That settles it."

"Fair." Lucy nodded, popping open a bag of pretzels and situating herself behind the counter. "See you in a couple hours."

"You better hope so." Terry shook her head.

"I know so." Lucy grinned.

"Buh-bye girlfriend!" Jeo waved as Terry headed to the door. "Bring me back a souvenir!"

The six of us, including the cat piled into Terry's van and headed down towards the Shipping District. The area had never been particularly nice, not even in Raphael's day, and since the coming of the Republic, the few establishments around the wharf that used to be respectable had deteriorated somewhat.

Pulling down a narrow alleyway into the shadow of a gray building with a black-and-white barcode sign over the door, we reached Germaine's warehouse.

I had heard legends about the place. Despite our experiences in the Etone war, it never ceased to amaze me how many members of the Brotherhood Terry seemed to know intimately. Though she often blamed her wealth of information on the exploits of her brother Christopher who had died twenty years ago, I still couldn't help but look at her strangely as she opened the lock effortlessly and lead us towards what she referred to as "The Studio".

Inside the warehouse thousands of oddities from any number of worlds cluttered the space, everything from famous paintings and fine oriental rugs to modern technology and weaponry.

It did not take us long to find the Skunk. At the far end of the building, sitting atop a tall stack of packing crates, Germaine sat lounging in an oversize armchair, surrounded by bodyguards and women, watching a few musicians who were cleaning up their instruments.

Still, as simple as it was to track the Etone, it was somewhat more difficult to convince him to lend us an expensive piece of his collection without down-payment or guarantee of safe return.

"Hey Germaine!" Terry shouted, sliding down the banister of the stairs as if she'd had some practice.

"Ah, Terry!" the old vampire exclaimed, rising to his feet and almost gliding over to where she stood, bowing dramatically. "Velcome to ziz Kilmor's humble abode." He grinned winningly. "Can I get you a drink?" he wondered. "Something to eat, perhaps?"

"I'm fine, thanks." Terry shook her head. "I actually need a favor."

"A faf'vor?" Germaine paused, and grimaced, as if he were contemplating something exceedingly unpleasant. "Not a Good Boys faf'vor, I hope?" he hissed under his breath.

"Hell no," Terry replied. "I may be a sister but I'm not no dimension jumper and I ain't nowhere near the level of their interest yet. I met em', but I'm not their bill collector if you catch my drift. I don't want nothin' big, I just need to borrow your sub."

"Haf you any idea what you're doing?" he wondered. "It is… important to me for… business," Germaine muttered. "Smuggling is very profitable now, my dear."

"Don't you dear-me nothin' Skunk," Terry sighed. "I've helped you before. Add up all the favors I done given you and I'll take em' back in this one," Terese spoke slowly. "You owe me."

"I owe quite a few faf' vors it seems." Germaine stared at me. "You may take the sub," he finished, after a long and awkward pause.

"Thanks pal." Ruveus grinned, patting him on the back. "Here... have some jellybeans!"

"Ruveus!" Phineas warned. He turned to Germaine with a strikingly serious look on his face. "Don't eat the red ones."

I still couldn't fathom what Phineas meant, but I guessed he was quite confident in the power of the red beans, seeing as our entire arsenal consisted of our personal weapons and several small, carefully sorted bags of them.

"Ready?" Cal loaded his shotgun. I couldn't help but laugh at his appearance.

The gangly, library-lurking kid we'd pulled out of an average life had suddenly been overwhelmed by an entire lifetime of knowledge, and at the worst possible time.

Cal still carried with him the soldier's persona that he had assumed in the Etone war, and though he had begun to remember his training in the fine art of Teyme's Alchemy, he still seemed to me more of a warrior than a wizard, and that I respected.

I wore a heavy gray coat, but had done without most of my usual clothing. There was no point in disguising myself under layers when I planned to move quickly and strike viciously if I needed to. The sword slung over my back was the only weapon I needed, besides my own two hands.

Germaine winked in my direction as the others descended down towards the sub.

The sub was a black, egg shaped craft floating almost motionless in a green-lit rectangular pool, the perfect tool for a wily trader attempting to avoid the trade restrictions of the IR. It was much larger than it looked and moved with an impressive speed, though it seemed almost invisible when it stood still.

"They ever ask you who you run with, you tell them it's with me," Germaine advised, suddenly dropping his accent.

I couldn't fathom what he meant, or how he'd suddenly learned to speak properly, but nodded and got into the submarine anyway.

"If only there was some way we could avoid the water," I muttered, closing tight the hatch over my head.

"You scared?" Cal wondered, though he must have known that I was at least a little uneasy.

"Terrified," I admitted.

"Then why are you here?" he asked, searching my face for some betrayal of emotion.

"It isn't about being afraid," I muttered. "It's about doing what must be done. I have no purpose if I am helping no one. I accomplish nothing if I allow others to assume risks that I am better-suited to take myself."

"Do what you must, do all you can," Cal agreed. "It's a bit cliché, but I like it. Who told you that?"

I glanced to see if Phineas was listening... and said nothing more.

Thirty-Nine

The sub skimmed along below the surface of the dark bay, shooting towards the island that had formerly been the Library of Alexandria, now home to the IRP headquarters. We docked underwater and forced our way through the airlock with a secret entrance code that Cal had quickly scrawled on the original plans.

The tunnels beneath the tower were all white with vaguely rounded corners as if we were standing in a series of pipes. Water dripped onto the floor in places, and even our footsteps echoed as we headed down the corridor to the left, as silent as we could possibly be, just the three of us.

Despite Phineas's arguments that he knew the layout of the library far better than I could ever hope to, I lead the way, sword drawn and followed closely by Ruveus who sniffed the air every few feet and nodded quietly to himself, gripping up on the hilt of the blade he carried.

Finally, we reached the end of the tunnel, a massive metal door that closed across the end of the pipe. Peering through the smoky glass of the tiny window a few inches above eye level, we scanned the room it led into. Across from us were three elevators, but between the point where we stood and our destination, six IR officers were standing on their guard.

"Ok," Phineas whispered, motioning for Ruveus and myself to come closer. "Middle elevator. Ready?"

"Let's go." Ruveus nodded.

Concentrating, Phineas formed a tiny ball of fire in his hand. "Stand back!" he warned, and then loosened the spell. It took down the door in a tremendous burst of flame. Without waiting for the smoke to clear, I leapt through the still burning flames and brought my sword down quickly on the first officer that crossed my path.

Charging up another spell, Phineas fired a wave of ice that flung two more of the men through a wall.

The rest fled in terror, except for one fool who dropped his gun and stared at us in bewilderment as the elevator doors closed.

"Hot… Cold… Hot… Cold…," Phineas panted, shaking his hands furiously. "That was a terrible combination," he muttered. "I think somebody else ought to throw the next spell."

An alarm went off and a sickening green smoke began to fill the elevator.

"This isn't good," Ruveus observed, looking ill.

"Get us out of here!" Phineas begged. "Stop this thing!"

"No problem." I clenched my teeth and punched the control panel, electricity racing through my body and blood dripping from where the sharp metal had cut into my fist. The elevator screeched to a stop, the doors opened and we ran out, not sure what floor we were on, but only too grateful to be breathing again.

"Hands behind your backs!" an artificial voice ordered, holding his rifle mere centimeters from my head.

We had stumbled directly into a trap. Slowly, we followed the lead of the IR guards to the top floor of the building. "Any ideas?" Ruveus hissed.

"I'm working on it," I muttered, digging my hands deep into my pockets, searching for the mirror I had brought with me.

"Looking for this?" One of the guards laughed, holding up the sliver of glass. "Hey boys, this one think's she's a Traverser!"

"Give that to me and I'll let you live," I snarled, reaching out for the mirror which rippled faintly as my fingertips neared its surface.

"Break it!" the leader of the guards ordered, slapping the man who had taken it from me. The mirror shattered. I hissed faintly and lowered my eyes.

"She… is?" the man muttered in disbelief, staring at me.

"Move ahead, you three!" The officers pushed us towards a set of double-doors which opened on their own accord, rifles pointed at our backs.

The room we had entered was an office, white walls with wood paneling, a seating area of blue chairs and a massive desk off to the right, hidden in shadow.

"What it is now?" a man's voice complained from the dark corner.

In the center of the room, Mariel sat slumped over in an office chair, a look of incredible blankness plastered on her face. The man behind the desk turned around and wheeled his chair into the light. He stood slowly and bowed dramatically, looking up with a disrespectful grin. I growled, recognizing him instantly. Garret Fairfax, President of the IR.

And although I had only met him once before, face to face, I could sense in him even more of that terrible, mad power that I recognized all too well. It was in this seemingly ordinary human I had rediscovered a true nemesis. Geruth. The two of them were more alike than I cared to believe possible.

I found myself almost wondering if the strange man was I'Eloshir, as his very demeanor reminded me so clearly of Orin Saede, but my senses told me he was not. As much as I wished that Fairfax might be a demon, seeing that as an excuse for his senseless barbarism, the fact remained that he was only a horribly evil human being, something I had not imagined was truly possible.

"Mariel!" Phineas shouted. "Mariel, are you all right?"

"Let him go," Fairfax ordered. The men released him on command, and Phineas ran to Mariel's side. He shook her furiously, but she did not respond.

"Oh, Mariel!" Phineas stood, lifting her as gently as he could. "Thank God, at least she's still breathing! What have you done to her?" he demanded, pointing directly at Fairfax with a shaking hand.

"Cured her." Fairfax grinned, swinging Mariel's blue opal like a pendulum and then snapping it back into his fist, placing it in a small box with the green stone that was its twin. "I intend to collect them all." He grinned, obviously savoring the look of horror on Phineas's face as he saw Rosalind's stone. "And as far as your sweet little girl is concerned... apparently, she was developing some slightly unnatural reactions to ordinary stimuli."

"What in the thirteen hells is he talking about?" Ruveus scowled.

I shook my head. "I wish I knew," I muttered, increasingly uneasy as no one moved to relieve us of our weapons.

They had forced us to sheath our swords as we stepped out of the elevator, but Ruveus and I had both drawn our blades upon sight of Mariel and not one guard had attempted to prevent us from doing so.

"You!" Fairfax pointed, squinting at me. "I've seen you before!"

I said nothing and remained motionless in the corner. Attempting to control my breathing, I closed my eyes momentarily and prepared myself to lunge at Fairfax.

But before I had the chance, he sat back in his chair and Phineas stepped in front of me.

"I hope you know who you're toying with, Fairfax." Phineas glared. "Or this may be the last game you ever play."

"Threatening me, mage?" Fairfax sneered. "The walls of this room are packed with over a thousand pounds of Duricide powder. My scientists have assured me that it has proven quite successful in preventing the transfer of potential energy into what you call magic."

"That's ridiculous," Phineas argued. "You're a fool if you think there's a remedy for the power of the elements! It can't be measured and it can't be stopped!" He clapped, but only a few sparks of fire resulted.

Baffled, Phineas stared down at his smoking fingertips, obviously crushed by the horrific realization that had just come to him. He had believed for his entire life that magic was the one constant in the universe, the one force that could never be extinguished completely because it was the one power not drawn from an external source, but from within a person, the power... as he called it, of the mind and spirit.

"Impossible!" Ruveus stared.

I didn't feel so well myself, but as I am first and foremost a warrior and not a mage, I took the opening when it presented itself. The distance was considerably far for a sword thrust, but with a dagger or a smaller object I could kill Fairfax, or at least leave him unconscious. Yet Phineas and Mariel still stood in the way, and I had nothing to throw, save the bag of jellybeans.

Scanning the room quickly, an idea suddenly occurred to me.

I flung the jellybeans I carried at the guards nearest to the door; therfore, blowing the men through the walls and out the windows. The fire blazed violently for a moment and then contracted back inside the lifeless shells of the still-smoking red beans.

"Never eat the red ones?" Ruveus wondered, awed by the force of the explosion.

Phineas shook his head and lifted Mariel up onto his shoulder. Ruveus raced for the exit and Phineas followed, glancing back to see what I was doing. I motioned for him to go.

After all, I still had business to attend to.

Fairfax and the remaining guards moved to follow after Phineas and the others, but I blocked their path, standing in the doorway. Having no other options, I gripped up on my sword.

"I don't need magic to kill the lot of you," I snarled, feeling some of my old nature surface. I did not struggle to contain the power I felt rising within me. What they had done was unforgivable.

"I remember now," Fairfax's tone was slow and poisonous, "I saw you in my associate's mirror." I knew who his "associate" was. Forcing myself to listen... if only for a little longer, I kept my eyes fixed on Fairfax, snarling through my clenched teeth.

"You were the leader of The Dynasty's armies... weren't you? The High

Commander," he whispered, knowing he was right.

"The same," I replied coldly.

"It is an honor to meet you." He smiled winningly and I hated him all the more.

"What do you want?" I demanded, breathing heavily. The rising cloud of gray-green gas stung my eyes and burned my throat, but Fairfax himself seemed immune to the substance's poison.

"I have a proposition…," he began.

"No." I did not let him finish.

"My sources tell me that you have a remarkable talent, something that would make you a particularly deadly assassin…" Fairfax whispered. "And I suppose I need not explain what's in it for you… Ireval."

"Never." I glared, feeling a sudden chill. Though I struggled to contain my building insanity, I was quickly losing control.

"I was hoping we could talk," Fairfax sighed.

"I don't negotiate with the likes of you," I growled, knowing the change was about to begin. Then… all at once, my energy drained away.

"The likes of me? I am the supreme ruler of seven hundred worlds!" Fairfax slammed his fist on the table.

"And I am the last defender of this one!" I could see a thick vapor drifting out of the vents and I knew my strength was fading fast. I had thought for a moment that I would overcome the poison that had robbed Phineas of his powers… but I could not. Whatever it was… it was working. Weak as I felt at that moment, I knew I wouldn't be capable of holding my human form much longer. And yet, I would lose consciousness before I shifted. Not even my darkest thoughts would yield me strength enough to kill Fairfax…

"Duricide making you ill?" he wondered. "I actually think it smells rather nice."

The guards began to close in. I dropped my sword, dizzy and swaying unsteadily back and forth. And then I saw it… a sliver of a Tear on the far wall, glowing with an unnatural pale light, almost as if some strange benevolent God had placed it there for my use. I knew not where it led and I didn't care.

"We'll meet again Fairfax." I picked up my blade and pointed it at him. "And when we do… I shall have the pleasure of destroying you and your Republic."

Walking slowly, I approached the Tear. None of the officers moved to follow me… as if they somehow could not see the exit that I had found.

Still somewhat off-balance, I jumped and began falling slowly through space and time until I landed halfway on my feet in the middle of a golden field. In the distance, an immense flight of white marble stairs lead upwards as far as the eye could see. It was a place as beautiful as Magog was terrible... and I knew almost immediately, with frightening surety, that I had at last found my way to Raedawn.

The Sentinels

"They are the keepers of the most ancient of secrets."

Forty

"Looking for someone?" a voice wondered. It was a strange, all-encompassing sound, a sound that rippled the air around it almost like my Order.

Someone? I was confused. "I was summoned here," I admitted, shouting over the roar of the winds.

"Summoned?" The voice laughed. "By your own heart, no doubt!"

"Who are you?" I demanded. I couldn't follow even the faintest sign of motion as my eyes searched the endless wastes. "Why can't I see you?"

"You may call me Dakor. I am a Sentinel, Guardian of the Gate. Follow the stairs, Ireval, and we shall face each other soon enough."

"How do you know me?" I wondered, suddenly cold at the sound of that terrible voice, speaking my own hated name.

"You are a true daughter of Inapsupetra," the Sentinel's voice lingered on the soft breeze. "All of Raedawn knows you."

"I am many things... but certainly not an angel," I argued. "I don't belong in this perfect place."

"This is not heaven," Dakor sighed heavily as the winds that whipped around me calmed, settling into a small whirl of white and silver glass flowers at my feet. "And Magog is not the hell you imagine it to be. All will be explained soon enough."

"Soon enough?" I clenched my fists, looking for something nearby that I might break to pieces. "By what do you mean, soon enough!?" I demanded. "Soon enough, in good time... someday you shall understand!" I sighed heavily, shaking my head. "I have been waiting far too long to live without some answers, Dakor... if that is your name. Do you hear me? Far too long."

"Then, follow the stairs, Ireval. Follow the stairs." Dakor laughed.

Though I had not taken a single step, the distant staircase, drew closer spilling a path of liquid marble out before me. A second wave of glass petals came flying past, soft to the eyes but like tiny knives against my skin… as the turning world itself shifted to a slow stop.

I began to run up the stairs… and continued to do so for what felt like hours, though it never seemed that I climbed any higher. I stopped and my gaze drifted towards the steps in front of me. I had to think, if only for a moment, think and figure out where I was going instead of blindly pushing myself forward.

To my horror, I realized that I was no closer to the top of the stairs than I had been when I had started running.

"What is this?" I demanded, Dakor did not answered me. The wind was silent and the only response that came to my plea was my own echoing voice and the sound of silver bells. Suddenly fearful, I took a step back… but the moment my foot touched the step behind me, the ground beneath my feet began to move. At first it rumbled forward slowly… but then it shot out from beneath me at a blinding speed.

The sky around me became an endless streak of yellow and pink and gold as more glass flowers shattered against my skin. I closed my eyes and dug my nails into the stone, nearly blown away into oblivion by the force of the magic that surrounded me. All at once, everything came to a sudden and complete halt.

"Sometimes, in order to move forward we must retreat," Dakor's voice whispered, snickering faintly… presumably at my utterly horrified expression. Though the terrible flight had stopped, I dared not open my eyes for fear of the glass flowers. I was bleeding already from a thousand tiny wounds.

Worse still, I did not see the purpose of the "lesson" and refused to believe that I had just winded myself running up a thousand stairs for no reason whatsoever.

"Ireval," Dakor's voice sighed, so terribly close that I could feel the warm breath of some great beast mere inches from my face. It was then that I opened my eyes.

I looked up, and found myself face to face with two great stone creatures. The first, a lion, who stood nearest me, I knew to be Dakor.

The second was a wolf, somewhat smaller, lying a few feet away. It appeared to be sleeping.

"Vatra." Dakor shook his heavy maned head. "A mere child after all these centuries."

"Where am I?" I begged, though I instinctively knew.

"The Gates of Raedawn, child." Dakor laughed. "Look."

Gesturing with his massive paw to a wall of silver and gold rose vines, he bowed his great head until his shimmering eyes were level with my own, full of the white glow of a thousand stars.

"You said you would explain to me why I am here." I shuddered... feeling a sudden influx of power. The gates swung open.

"Taer kyurae mos Aryon, su kyurae mos Inapsupetra," Dakor recited, speaking in the language of the I'Eloshir. "I believe you know that little proverb. Order and chaos forever opposed, yet eternally connected. In another sense, one might assume that... if you had never seen light, you would not recognize darkness."

"Poetry," I sighed, unimpressed by the speech. Had I come so far and fought so hard only to be left with nothing but riddles? "How does it mean anything?"

"Balance," Dakor whispered. "The mortal world was not meant to be a place separated by such distinctions. The unnatural beauty of this ruined city chills those that walk here, because this is a realm that should not exist. Each choice a mortal being makes can create any number of realities, all of them a mere shadow of the greater truth. All that you perceive as dark and light... is nothing more than a spectrum of fading grays. Yet since the I'Eloshir and the IR have begun to interfere in the Fate of the Chaos Realm, things have become very black... and very white indeed. Dangerously so."

"What am I supposed to do?" I argued. "I tried to save the dynasty... and I failed."

"True." The Sentinel closed his eyes. "It is rather unfortunate when those who are most deserving of victory cannot achieve it. Raedawn was shattered in much the same way your Empire fell," Dakor explained. "You judge yourself more harshly than you realize. It is true that there are nobler souls out in the world, more deserving of the chance you have been given. Yet though others may well deserve your gifts, they were not granted them. For good or for ill, this power was given to you. Make of it what you will."

"I wasn't meant to be a hero," I argued futilely. "I don't want these... gifts, whatever you call them! They are not gifts... they are curses!"

"A gift and a curse are often one and the same," Dakor sighed. "Take Achilles for example."

"Who?" I wondered in bewilderment.

"A human legend," Dakor clarified. "Achilles achieved great power from a bath that he was dipped into full of a potion which covered all of his body

259

except for a small spot on his heel. Had his parents not held onto his foot, he would have fallen into the bath and drowned at that moment. That one small weakness saved him, but in the end it also cost him dearly. A normal man would have gone through life taking his sword-blows as they came and never achieving such glory as Achilles. Yet, a normal man would have also been far less likely to die from a prick in the heel."

"I fail to see your meaning." I shook my head.

"Your past is your tragic flaw," Dakor explained. "You possess a great strength... far beyond what most dare imagine, but you are also held back by an equally great weakness. You must accept that weakness and move past it."

"It is not possible." I shook my head, not entirely sure of what I was arguing.

"Not possible?" Vatra laughed, opening one eye. "A young man named Teyme once told me that, when I asked him to make me a star. And do you know what I said to him?" The sentinel paused. "If you believe as you have never believed before... If you dream far beyond what you dare imagine. If you fight with every last atom of your being... Then you will know what is possible and what is not."

Vatra smiled faintly, coming to his feet. "Teyme made that star. It was the last great thing he did before his death, so long ago now. Or so it is written in the Archives."

"Enter," Dakor ordered, gesturing to the path before me. "Go to the Temple. Perhaps there you will find the answers you desire."

I stepped through the open gates in a burst of silvery light and found myself instantly standing before Galwick's tower... the first place I had seen in the Chaos Realm. Stepping through a flock of chickens, I approached the door, and opened it.

Darkness surrounded me, the darkness of Magog.

I was standing amidst the wreckage of my own shadowy chamber, a place that did not frighten me as I thought it might, but still, I pushed myself onward... following the narrow, dank, stinking stairs upwards to some long forgotten goal.

I opened the door at the top of the staircase and stepped into yet another strange room.

The door vanished behind me, leaving me standing in a circular tower of nine identical mirrors, where a round pool of black water filled in the center of the floor.

Hovering above the pool was a book, an ancient text I recognized immediately.

Its pages glimmered as if they had been pounded flat out of solid gold, and the red binding of the book shimmered as if it had been made from some leather that held flames under the surface. The Archives of Teyme.

I reached for it. In my hand I held a feather pen, a fiery-red plume that had appeared in my grasp. Thousands of possibilities raced through my mind as I suddenly realized that I had indeed been granted a great power.

I could change time itself. I could write out the war. I could bring Raphael back. I could write out all the evil I had done and return to the night so long ago when The Grandmother had slain my grandfather before my eyes. I could live a different life, a life without such pain and such regrets.

I… I was selfish… and a fool.

The book slammed shut before me and I found myself staring into the bottomless silver eyes of Inapsupetra. They were so cold, in the still shadow of her mask, though her body was no longer that of a stone statue, black and foreboding. She was a woman standing before me, not of flesh and blood but of pure, ever-moving energy, dressed in a white robe that flowed in all directions as if it were submerged in water.

"You are not ready." The goddess shook her head heavily, as if she much regretted the action she was about to take.

I stepped back… but there was nowhere for me to retreat to.

A violent blast of white electricity sent me flying through the first of the nine mirrors.

Forty-One

"We gonna ea' ter?" a voice wondered.

I awoke somewhat painfully lying on the ground in the middle forest and far from any sort of beaten path. It had rained recently and from the shapes and heights of the trees, I guessed I was somewhere in the darker regions of Eldar, land of the elves. That was all I could gather from my blurred vision, but I figured it was a safe enough assumption.

"We gonna tie' er up den?" the voice pressed.

"No, stupid!" There was the sound of a second little voice, possibly slapping the first.

Realizing quite suddenly that I was surrounded, I leapt to my feet and drew the only weapon I possessed, a small boot knife. Fortunately, either that... or my sudden awakening from near death proved to be enough.

"Aieeeeeeeeee!" several small somethings screamed in unison.

As far as I could tell, they appeared to be three-foot tall mouse-eared humanoids, dressed in a variety of skins, bones and war paint, an entire herd of tiny barbarians. with raccoon tails and little furry bat-wings.

"Hold!" I tried to avoid kicking any of them. "I'm not going to hurt you!" I wasn't sure they believed me, but the blood-curdling screaming certainly died down.

"You sure?" One of the creatures wondered. I nodded.

"You fell off the mow-tan." Another pointed to a tall, snow-capped spire in the distance. "Gods live up there and they trow'd you down."

"In a manner of speaking," I admitted, surprised that they had guessed the truth. "It was an accident."

"You know Gods?" The mouse-people were in awe.

"Some." I hoped I wasn't getting myself into more trouble.

"Which ones?" they demanded, hopping around madly.

I bit my lip and sighed, figuring that they would probably view some of my Traverser friends as deities. "Well... I...Ordo, for one. Lucy... and Panther."

"Panther, hunh? We never heard of em'... never heard of no'un Panther, did we boys?" The tallest of the creatures turned to the others with her hands on her hips, grinning and bobbing her head.

"No ma'am!" The rat-people saluted and shook their heads, some saying yes and others no. They were terrible liars.

"Say you, what's he lookin' like?" the leader demanded.

"A cat, actually. Most of the time," I admitted.

"Black hair?" she wondered, squinting at me.

"Red shirt made outta shiny shiny soft-'tuff?" One of the other tree rats pressed, climbing up onto my lap.

"He is fond of silk," I sighed.

"He steal 'tuff?" the leader whispered in my ear.

"On occasion." I nodded.

The "mice" danced for joy. "She knowshim, she knowshim!" they chanted. I was confused.

The leader of the little people removed her rat cap. "They callsame Mouse." She grinned. "Chief of the fearsomeanaferoferocious TreeRats of Herichae!"

"That's us!" the tree-rats chorused. "Tee Watu!"

"Panther told us you would come," Mouse explained. "He'sour friend. He told us we oughta take you to the Green-King."

"Well then, I suppose we must go." I smiled winningly and tried to stand, but immediately fell, thanks to a piercing pain in my leg. Somehow the old wounds from the bullets I had taken in the Battle of the Frozen Sea had reopened themselves.

"You hurt?" Mouse wondered, poking at my leg. "Looksa like blood to me."

"I doubt I can walk very far," I admitted, shaking my head heavily.

"I'll carry you," Mouse volunteered.

"That's a kind offer but I really...," I began, and then stopped short.

The little creature had lifted me entirely off the ground.

"You're strong!" I laughed, scarcely believing what had happened.

"Sure am." Mouse grinned. "Chief Mouse the Mighty!"

Strange, to say the least... but I had seen stranger. Even pulling my weight behind them, the Tree Rats moved through the forest at a remarkable speed, finally coming to a stop in the center of what appeared to be an orange grove. Several small, round shelters, constructed from mud and twigs and slung between branches, the Tree Rat's homes, were the only signs of civilization, and even they seemed almost natural in origin.

The dwellings were of stable construction, though apparently their unused appearance was due to the fact that they often went unoccupied, as the little creatures seemed to prefer sleeping upside-down in the trees themselves.

"This's' far as we go now," the one called Mouse announced. "Sun goes down an' dogs'll be out."

"You're... afraid of dogs?" At first I was surprised, but then I considered the fact that the tallest of the little people stood barely three feet high.

"Dogs's bad mojo. But worse is ubiwuki. They follows the dogs."

"Ubi... what?" I wondered.

"Ssshhh!!" Mouse hissed, clapping a hand over my mouth. "They'll hear you!"

I fell silent, supposing that the Tree Rats were referring to either some larger animal or a sort of vengeful spirit, neither of which I feared.

Still, they had saved me from bleeding and hobbling across many miles of unfamiliar terrain. I would respect their superstitions, at least, for the time being.

The sun set and the Tree Rats gathered around a bonfire in the center of their village, singing and clapping in their nearly unintelligible version of the common tongue.

Though my arrival was obviously of great interest, especially amongst the younger ones, the main focus of the celebration seemed to be Mouse's recent acquisition, a large, unmarked wooden box.

"This is stole from ubiwuki," she explained proudly. "It had their magic on it, but I cuts their letters off and writes mine instead."

Squinting at the box from a distance, in the firelight I could make out a discolored patch where the paint had been hacked away with a small knife. Replacing what had possibly been the only form of identification on the strange thing, were five small characters marked in red tree-sap.

"What's in the box?" I asked.

The Tree Rats all stared as if I had just spoken some sort of blasphemy.

"We don' know," Mouse muttered. "We neva looked."

"Do you mind if I...," I began.

"No!!!" they all screeched in unison, immediately jumping to cover the box.

"You look in you don' come out!" One of the Tree Rats warned. "Things goes in. Things neva comes out."

The idea was intriguing, but at that point, avoiding an ambush at the hands of the Tree Rats was more important to me than solving the mystery of their box.

"You say that it had letters on it before," I prompted, hoping they were not too caught in their fear to respond.

"Ubiwuki letters," Mouse replied.

"Can you show me what they looked like?" I wondered.

"Nun-uh." She shook her head. "No how."

One of the smaller Tree Rats reached out to softly touch my coat, and I grinned, remembering their fascination with Panther's red silk.

"If I gave you something, would you show me then?" I asked.

Mouse's eyes lit up. "Give me what?" she demanded, inching closer.

Remembering one of the few bits of magic I'd actually mastered, I proceeded to draw a strand of silk scarves from thin air. My raw talent was much better for causing large explosions than forming more artistic creations, but there was some use in being able to produce bandages from nothingness. Phineas called it "spinning."

The Tree Rats gasped in delight, catching the silks as they fell to the ground and dancing about, waving the glittering colors in the moonlight.

And I smiled again, despite myself, simply watching them.

Only one of the little people seemed to realize I was still sitting at the campfire. Mouse approached me cautiously and rubbed the blue silk scarf she held in her tiny hands. "You really want to know about the box?" Mouse asked.

"If you would." I nodded.

"Go open it." She pointed. "Just don't get in."

"I do not imagine that I would fit," I admitted.

"You be surprised," Mouse warned. "Strange thing, that box."

With a sigh, I stood up and walked over to where the box lay. A peculiar feeling came over me, and I wondered for a moment if there was any truth in the Tree Rat's fear of the mysterious chest.

Still, I had to know... curiosity being part of my nature.

And so I opened it. The interior was dark and of unseen depth, but apparently empty. I reached inside, feeling for a bottom, my hand coming to rest suddenly on something that felt terrifyingly familiar.

Then... it was gone. I reached in again, focusing my energy on grasping what I knew lay somewhere within the box. Before I realized what had happened, I found myself dangling completely inside, hanging by my feet, knowing that it was only a little bit further.

"Lookashe!" the Tree Rats screamed, from what sounded like very far away.

"Hold on!" Mouse called. "We get you out!"

I reached further down... when quite suddenly my left foot slipped.

"Yaaahhh!" the battle cry echoed around the box as a rope lashed itself around my leg and the Tree Rats began to heave me out. "Rat pull, rat pull!" they chanted in unison, jerking on my leg every few seconds with another burst of remarkable strength.

I did not struggle. The secret of the box had occurred to me then. I cleared my mind and visualized the emptiness.

Expect... nothing.

And in my hands, almost at that instant, the thing that I had sought materialized.

Returning to the surface and slamming the lid shut, I sat and stared at what I had drawn out of the abyss.

My staff. For the life of me, I could not remember when or where I had lost it, but I could guess. On the inside of the box, the evil letters Mouse had spoke of were stamped in black... over and over again. IRP.

For people who did not believe in magic, they certainly seemed to use it often enough. From developing spell-resistant armor to magic-depleting drugs, the IR had caused more chaos than any of the dark mages of old... myself included.

"What issat?" One of the Tree Rats wondered, pointing to my weapon. I tore the packing paper away, and they stared, awestruck, at the purple light that quickly filled the grove.

The energy faded. Stunned by the sudden light, those who stood closest to me, slumped to the ground, snoring softly. I was amazed at the strange effect and turned to my host, who blinked sleepily.

Then, perhaps directed by my own desire to rest, the remaining Tree Rats instantly stumbled off to bed.

Some time after the little people had departed, yet before I closed my eyes completely, Mouse crept up to my bedside, still staring at my staff.

"Is shiny," she commented. "Strange thing, it make everyone s..weepy." She yawned.

"Yes, it is." I nodded in agreement. "I can never be quite certain of just what it will do. I guess that somehow... it depends on how I feel."

"You think there's another one of them things in the box?" Mouse wondered. "I like the shiny stick."

"I wouldn't go looking for it," I advised.

"Me neither," Mouse agreed. "I'm Chief. Chief protects people. Chief is too m'portant to get eaten by ubiwuki box. Chief sends som'body else."

Shaking my head at her backward logic, I sighed and went to sleep.

Forty-Two

Morning came.

Though I had gone to bed a little after midnight, I still rose before dawn. All around me, the sleeping Tree Rats hung upside-down in the branches of their grove, looking like some sort of strange fruit.

Gathering my things, I had intended to sneak away before the little people awoke... but, as usual, my attempts to be secretive were immediately noticed.

"Leave wit'out breakfast?" a voice demanded.

I looked up. Directly above my head, a little Tree Rat grinned. "Is bad manners. You get where you going when you s'posed to get there," he explained.

Ah, the irony of that.

I sighed to myself and dropped what few provisions I had been carrying, my sword, my rolled-up coat and the staff which I had wrapped again in brown cloth and was using as a sort of a crutch.

"Fair enough," I agreed. "Why don't we eat then?"

Breakfast turned out to be more of a chaotic affair than the dinner celebration of the previous night. Quite possibly, I will forever be scarred with visions of small creatures scampering about covered in flour at the mention of the word "Pancake".

Still, there were no deaths and few fatal injuries. After eating, the Tree Rats fumbled their way into marching order, and we headed into the forest once again.

Hiking over miles of rocks and undergrowth, they never slowed, though even I myself grew weary. Finally, at long last, we reached the foot of an immense tree, towering into the clouds. It seemed to be a sort of palace.

"This is the Green King's city." Mouse gestured to the tree. "Herichae Delamaer."

"Does the Green King have a name?" I wondered.

"Rowanoak." One of the Tree Rats grinned. "King of the Elves."

I was amazed to hear that the old man had survived the devastation of the wars… but not as amazed as I was by the sheer ingenuity of his livable tree.

"Who goes?" the guards at the gate demanded. They were dressed in armor that might have fit them once, but the men were thin and pale-faced, even for elves. The legendary city of Herichae had avoided any major battles during the war, being so difficult to reach and virtually self-sufficient, but the draining of the Chaos Realm's life sustaining magic had begun to take its toll, even in the middle of one of the most sacred and secluded places in the world.

"Artemis Ravencroft." I stood as well as I could manage and unwrapped my staff.

"The… Artemis Ravencroft?" the first soldier wondered, though he must have recognized my weapon, if not my face.

"Is there another?" I brushed the dirt and leaves out of my hair and did my best to assume my most standard pose, stern and focused with my nose held somewhat higher than what would have been considered polite.

"Fyeris," one of the elves whispered in awe, recognizing me then. "You are alive."

I smiled faintly, though I was unsettled by the look he gave me, his eyes full of respect and admiration. I felt deserving of neither. I, after all… had lost the war.

"Welcome to the Grove of Herichae, High Commander Ravencroft." The guards bowed and parted their spears. Stepping onto a sort of man-powered elevator, I rose into the green canopy of the trees.

Crowds of elves, humans and Tree Rats, most of them apparently refugees, parted as I made my way towards Rowanoak's palace, voices all whispering in awe as the word spread.

"Nice city, hunh?" Mouse grinned, loping in front of me on all fours just to keep up with my walking pace. Surrounded by a crowd that recognized me, I forced myself to march proudly, despite my dehabilitating injury. Rowanoak's city was truly beautiful, that I had to agree with. Yet the settlement in itself was nothing compared to the castle.

Squirrels raced in and out between the constantly growing branches of the cathedral-like Great Hall, and at the end of the chamber, on a throne formed of four intertwining white rosebushes sat Rowanoak in his crown of leaves, still looking regal, if not a little worn by the past years.

His silvery gray hair glimmered in the sunlight as he stood. Sweeping aside his heavy green-velvet cape, he bowed to me, despite my ragged condition.

Though the Empire no longer existed and I had long since lost my rank, Rowanoak was still a king, not yet dethroned by the IR. I couldn't imagine why he would offer me assistance, let alone show me any sort of respect.

"I was told you would come from the Mountain of the Gods," Rowanoak announced, returning to his throne.

I shuddered, sensing immediately that something strange was going on.

"Lord Elhilom was expecting you, when he was here last. Have you come in search of him?" Rowanoak wondered. It surprised me that he used Panther's true name.

"Hardly," I admitted "I had not intended to visit. I simply arrived and met up with these..."

I stopped. The Tree Rats had vanished.

Rowanoak smiled. "They do that," he admitted. "It is their way."

"But I understand if things seem a little... odd," he continued, obviously sensing my confusion. "My mother was Sitri Elundriel of Sidrufen, one of the founders of the White City, sister of Teyme himself. Though she never had the opportunity to bring me there, I too, have visited the Tower of Raedawn."

"How...," I began. "When..."

"Never ask how." Rowanoak held up his hand and I fell silent. "It only makes things even more complicated. But to answer your second question, it was three hundred years ago on a terrible, unfortunate night that should have been my first wedding. I saw a white light in the distance... a Tear, of course... except that I was so horribly drunk that I thought it was a unicorn." He laughed softly. "Imagine my surprise when the unicorn I was petting so happily revealed itself to be Dakor the Sentinel. Of course, no one believed me when I returned three days later, as no one will believe you now. To mortal men, elves or humans... Raedawn simply does not exist. It was destroyed nine centuries ago."

When I thought about it, I realized that he was right, and wisely resolved to keep silent about what I had seen.

Night fell and the city of Herichae drifted off into a lazy state, small parties here and there, a few campfires burning, and an overall aura of timelessness encircling all of the wood. I fell asleep, quite full and almost drunk, enjoying once again the simple pleasure of having servants to do one's bidding.

And once again, morning came.

I awoke on the cold, hard ground, wondering if the previous night had been a dream. My staff lay by my side.

"Poor hosts," I muttered, climbing to my feet, somehow completely healed.

My empty pack was stocked with provisions and my worn coat had been exchanged for a fine green silk robe, not the best for traveling, but warm with a sort of inner magic.

"You there," a voice announced, cold and calculated. "Good morning."

I turned, squinting at the sunlight that reflected off of four blue-visored heads behind me. The white uniforms with the navy stripes across the chest I recognized all too well. The IRP.

"Good morning?" I cursed silently, jumping into the tree cover despite the bullet that whizzed dangerously close to my head.

I leapt over fallen logs, occasionally feeling gunfire break through the air behind me. The IRP had stopped chasing me, I realized... and then discovered why.

"Ubiwoookieeeeee!!" the Tree Rats hooted and screeched, swinging down from the trees, armed with nothing more than daggers and slings. Still, to the unsuspecting IR they were formidable opponents, fast and strong for their size, everywhere and nowhere all at once.

"Run Artemis-su!" Mouse yelled.

I ran... and then stopped short. The few soldiers to escape the Tree Rat's ambush were marching towards me at a slow and measured pace, peering through the scopes of their rifles.

Panicked, I looked to what lay ahead and cursed myself for being so foolish. I was about to run off a damned cliff.

"Control, we have a UI," one of the IRP muttered into his headset. "MC level... six-thirty seven-twenty eight-twenty?"

Knowing I had no choice but to fight, I turned back to the men... walked towards them and their guns, calling up a sphere of dangerously crackling purple flame.

"Nine-twenty... nine f-ffifty? That can't be right... that's too hi...Aaaghh!" the man screamed. Whatever instrument he had been using to estimate my power exploded in his hand.

"Backup!" the IR shouted. "Backup!"

Backup? It was all I needed, at any rate. My spell fizzled suddenly as something blue shot over my head, causing a very large explosion amidst the

IR ranks.

"Need a ride?" a familiar voice wondered from above me. A huge shadow blotted out the sun, wavering faintly as whatever it was drifted slowly up and down, hissing like a steaming tea-kettle.

The sound was familiar. It was the rumble of a Spellcraft engine.

I looked up. Phineas waved from the deck of the Hathor with Ruveus and Panther at his side. I swung onboard and we disappeared over the horizon before the hunters managed to fight their way out of the brush.

"So where is everyone?" I wondered, sipping some ambrosia with Panther. He, Phineas and Ruveus were the entire crew.

"Don't know," Panther admitted. "From what I hear they're still working on a way to break into Antares with the cat… what's her name?"

"Devonny," Ruveus supplied. "Her name's Devonny. And I wouldn't keep calling her a cat. If you can imagine a sarcastic vampire with six-inch claws and a taste for hot sauce… you get the idea. I like her less than my mother-in-law and I think she's more dangerous too."

"I didn't know you were married." I laughed, amused by his embarrassed grin.

"Married with five kids," Ruveus admitted. "I'll be King of Accoloth if the Empire ever comes back," he sighed. "Gotta have an heir."

Though I was glad for my friend and his family, the thought of Ruveus's wife and children agonized me. He was so fortunate… I wondered if he even realized that.

Germaine had lost Ira, Terry had seen both of her brothers killed, and Brin's entire clan had been slaughtered. Phineas would never marry Rosalind… and I had failed to save Raphael.

"Yeah, Devonny," Panther sighed, abruptly changing the subject. "She's a crazy fool."

"I could say the same for you," I admitted, glancing at him skeptically. "What brought you out of Gelthar anyway?"

"Boredom," Panther admitted. "My damn woman won't let me do anything… she thinks I'm gonna leave her or something."

"Are you?" I wondered, though from the expression on his face, I gathered that he wouldn't consider such a thing.

"Maybe," Panther winked. He shook his head. "I don't mean that Ire'… but sometimes … you know how it is. That's amore'."

"Amore," I echoed. The thought made me uncomfortable, stirring up too many old memories. "You know, Elhil, there's something strange about this

Spellcraft," I mused, hoping he had sense enough not to push our previous conversation. "No matter what rendition of hell I get myself into… this ship always seems to come to my rescue. It's almost as if everything chaotic in this realm somehow leads back to the Hathor."

"Madwoman," Panther snorted.

I didn't respond.

Forty-Three

Fleeing Eldar and not about to return to Ranlain, I found myself working in a wayside "Flotsam Ironworks" off the coast of Ardra. My job consisted of forging weapons and shoeing horses while Phineas continued to give magic lessons, although he refused to take another official apprentice after the fiasco with Mariel.

She'd lost all memory of her mage training and become completely convinced that magic did not exist. That had cut Phineas deeply, down to the point where I was doubtful that he would ever recover.

Still, we were more fortunate than we might have been in those dark times. We both had a place to hide where the magic was still strong enough for Phineas to maintain a continual disguise spell on the both of us, a place where IR were few and far between... and signs still occasionally read "Etone Welcome"... or more often, "Etone Please".

Needless to say, I despised it. I had grown too comfortable in my position while the dynasty still reigned, and I was certainly not about to step back and "lurk in the shadows" for awhile as Panther had suggested. I wanted to be myself. Was that so much to ask? We ran for two human years... a mere eye-blink in my time.

Still, I am not patient by nature, and I can only lower myself to the level of working wench for so long.

It had been an average day, which was exactly what I hated about it. The same drunken mule had been harassing me every morning since he floated his raft into town six days before. I had reached my breaking point.

"Keep pushing it," I warned, glaring at the man... the Slaver called "Kef". I lowered my visor and turned up the torch, showering him in sparks of red-hot metal. Foolish, arrogant mundane.

"Jest why do you hate humans anyway?" Kef demanded, bringing his hand dangerously close to my tools. "Heard some pilot over there say you hate humans. Hate yer own kind."

"My own kind," I repeated. It would have been wise to ignore the comment completely, but instead, I simply stopped working and stared. "What would you know about my kind?" I demanded.

"Yer a human, ain'cha? And I'm a human. I'd say I know pretty much about ...our kind." He winked. "At least everything worth knowin'."

It was the final straw. I had been listening to the narrow-minded fool ramble for hours... and besides, from my perspective it was high time for me to leave. I didn't know where I would go, so long as it was anywhere but the Aquarius Flotsam.

"You, human, had best watch your tongue," I growled, rubbing the dragon pendant in my hand, seriously debating smashing it with my hammer. I was tired of my artificial face, at any rate.

There was a certain dry stench that it filled the air with, wrapping me in a blanket that seemed to filter out any outside energy that I might touch. I had worn it continuously, even as I slept... and the longer it was near to me, the more I hated its yellow glow.

"And you, wench, had best to... stop hatin' your own kind. Else they might not treat you so nice," Kef slurred drunkenly and tripped down the steps. We were face to face.

"Is that a threat?" I countered.

"You want to take it like one? Look, wench, all I was sayin'..." He drifted off into silence.

"Jest what are you gettin' at anyway?" Kef's new partner, Benjae demanded. He turned around from where he stood at the leatherworker's booth across from me, his attention immediately pulled by the potential sounds of a fight. I wasn't the least bit surprised to find that the fool's friends were getting involved. Slavers never minded their own business. I cursed silently. A pestilence on the lot of them.

"I say... you gonna look at me?" Benjae snapped in front of my face. I fought the urge to break his fingers.

"Hey Smithy! What in Hellsgate is wrong with your whore?!" Kef yelled.

"It's her shop, idiot. There ain't nobody else here but that skinny kid she feeds," Benjae corrected, but it was too late. I was already fuming.

"Whore? Me? I think not." I glared.

"Look, all I was...," he began.

"HOLD YOUR TOUNGES!" I ordered.

Benjae stared at me blankly and I was satisfied… until Kef pushed me from the side. "You tryin' to order us around, woman? Like we's some sort o' lowborn peasant-swords?"

I was a little shocked, wondering if my power had gone defective from long disuse, but then decided that it must be the liquor in the man's system, making him ridiculously reckless.

"That is what you are," I replied calmly, though I could clearly see on their cloaks the symbol of the IRP, which was all the more reason for me to hate them.

"You don't exactly look like a lady of quality yerself. Betcha hate us home-bred mortals cause you're part freaky. Ogre maybe? Or Troll!" Kef sneered.

Terry Mack had given me the one of the only attractive disguise spells I had ever worn. Though Phineas tried his hardest, and though I would have been caught a thousand times over without him… sometimes his work was slightly inadequate. I was tired of jokes and slurs. Though my father was by all means a bastard, and though I had never met my mother, there was one thing I was certain of. I was a member of the Ithraedol clan. We were brutal, and cruel… and arrogant, yes… but we were not fools, nor servants, nor whores. I leaned over the wooden railing and stared the Slaver in the eye.

"If it's a fight you're looking for…," I hissed.

"Don't fight with wimmen," Kef muttered drunkenly.

"But I suppose a bawdy wench like you can hold your own against any man," a voice interrupted. I turned, knowing I recognized the presence I sensed behind me, a shadow that blocked even the roaring heat from my fire.

House of Aquara. My eyes met his chin. I recognized the dark eight-foot giant immediately.

"Octavian Avencourt," I muttered.

The years hadn't changed him a bit, except that he'd lost his opal, and that he'd ceased wearing his Imperial robes in favor of the sort of suits the men of the Republic were fond of. The gray coat made him look even taller, though it did not fit him as well as his Aquaren blue and silver had.

"You know me?" He squinted, obviously shocked that someone so beneath his notice would recognize him. Surveying my shop, he fell silent for a few short moments and then turned back to me. "Your pieces are exceptional. Were you a member of the Ardran league?" Octavian wondered, glancing at my work. The weapons I forged were of superior quality, but only by human standards. The sword-makers of Magog would have laughed at my pitiful attempts and told me to practice with horse-shoes for another few centuries before they would even consider letting me touch the legendary black metal, but in the mortal world… I was a master of the craft.

"No. I've heard of you, but we've not met," I lied.

"Who are you?" he wondered, perhaps fancying himself a prophet or seer. "Are you sure we've never been introduced?"

I would have loved nothing more than to drown him in the horse trough outside and let him have a closer look at my true face... but instead I shrugged innocently and fell silent.

"Count Avencourt?" a tinny voice announced.

A man in a white magic-resistant suit stepped inside the garage, wielding a rifle. Three other IRP officers accompanied him, stepping out of my back door and I froze. The door opened to a narrow dirt alley behind the shops of Aquarius Flotsam, a place the locals fondly referred to as "Mage Street"

I winced, hoping they hadn't caught Phineas training the neighborhood's children in the fine art of spell casting. Though he only taught them smaller works, nothing too destructive, his practice was enough to put him behind bars even if he wasn't the wanted "criminal" that he happened to be.

"We've caught a UI," the officer announced.

That was it, of course. I knew in an instant that my worst fears had been realized. A UI was an Unregistered Illegal. In this case, Phineas.

"Well, let's see then." Octavian motioned to the men by the door, snapping his fingers impatiently.

They drug him inside. Phineas was bruised and battered... not much of an enemy when he was rendered incapable of casting twenty-foot walls of fire, exploding things with a flick of the wrist and freezing enemies in their tracks with nothing more than a concentrated glare. The whole room reeked of Duricide spray.

"Don't recognize him." Octavian shrugged. "Probably just small-time."

Hardly. But of course, the last time Count Avencourt and Phineas had met, Phineas had appeared in his true form, a man with brilliant blue hair and a fondness for leather, not as a measly looking blonde "child". The dragon pendant that he wore flickered faintly from exposure to the gas and finally died. The illusion of the skinny boy faded away and Avencourt gasped.

Phineas stood, brushing his hair out of his eyes, adjusting the collar of his worn Imperial robe and pulled his monocle out of the breast pocket, placing it over his eye and glaring at the IR officers with a cold and arrogant expression.

A few other men in the shop recognized him as well, and the small crowd gathered in the "Mage Street" alley applauded and cheered insanely... until they found themselves staring at a dozen gun-barrels.

"Lord Wizard Phineas Merlin." Octavian smiled slightly.

The Slaver Kef reached for his gun but then dropped it, his hands shaking uncontrollably. "Them Traversers look out for their own boss, they look out for them...," he rambled insanely.

"Get a hold of yourself, fool," Octavian snapped. "The Etone are all either dead or locked away in Antares!"

"You... think you've caught them all?" Phineas grinned. "And those that you have... do you really think you can hold them, as long as they live? They're faster and stronger than you can imagine, and they have very good memories." Phineas smiled faintly. "What happens when they get out?"

"They won't escape," Octavian argued, though even he himself did not sound convinced. "And you won't either."

If any time was a good time for me to lash out against the IR and the Slavers on the Flotsam... it was then.

"LEAVE HIM!" I ordered. "He's done nothing to you, your House, or your damnable President."

It didn't work... again. The entire room ignored me.

"Go back to your mel'work'!" another fool snarled, pushing me away from Phineas. "This bus'ness disn't concern you, wench."

"I SAY IT DOES." I touched the pendant then and lifted it a fraction of an inch off my skin.

Octavian felt it then, the change in the air.

All his years of magic school amounted to very little, he simply shrugged the sensation off and near continued out.

"Did you hear me or not?" I repeated. "You're free to leave but my friend remains with me."

"He does?" Octavian frowned. "And just how do you expect to enforce that on us?"

It was the perfect response. I couldn't have scripted it better if I were writing a play.

"Do you challenge me?" I asked. All eyes turned.

"Challenge you? To a duel? Like a Chaos Knight? Like a bloody Etone!" Octavian winced. "Are you out of your mind, woman? I may be tall, but I'm not a Traverser!"

"No, you're not." I paused, savoring the fear that rippled through the men at that instant. "But I am." Snapping the chain of the pendant, I let the illusion fall as if I'd stepped out from behind a cloud. Only a fool could mistake me for anyone but the High Commander. Octavian stared. He was no such fool.

"You're ....," one of the other regulars began, as if he knew he's seen my face before. I wouldn't let him spoil the introduction.

"High Commander Artemis Ravencroft," I replied. Sensing the sudden influx of magic, my symbiote rolled out from its corner near the forge and latched itself onto my body. I tore off the tattered and stained shirt I had been wearing, revealing the more impressive glimmer of my living armor.

The crowd that had begun to gather around us cheered insanely, and the IR began to back away, scanning the streets as well as the sky for any possible route of escape.

"You're the one! The...ssister from Ppport Hhhope!" Kef stammered. "You're the one the IRP is after!"

"IRP and everyone else on the six continents." Panther stepped out of the back room and shook his head. I recognized him, despite his human form, though I had not been expecting him to show his face on the Flotsam after the last time he'd gotten us in trouble.. "You've gone and ruined my business, Ms. 'Rebecca the Wanderer.' And I believed you too."

"Elhilom, you damned trickster!" I muttered, speaking our language. "Are you trying to get me in more trouble?"

"What are they saying?" Octavian demanded. "Who speaks the Traverser's tongue?"

Panther laughed. "I suppose when you're finished picking up the pieces of these egotistical mortals, we l'Eloshir will have to have a little battle ourselves. It seems like aeons since we last fought with one another. I wonder if you still have your remarkable skills."

"Law 462," I replied, switching back to the common speech. "Duels of any kind are expressively forbidden."

Panther snickered. "Ah yes... so I see. My young apprentice."

"You know the IR laws?" Benjae wondered. Evidently he was too drunk to realize exactly how much danger he was in by simply being in the same room with myself, Phineas and Panther, His Honorable Lowliness.

Yet the moment I looked over my shoulder, Panther was gone. Only his voice lingered, whispering faintly, "Run, Ire'," he hissed. "Run now, you arrogant fool!"

I ignored him.

"Of course I know the IR laws," I snapped impatiently, turning back to the room, wondering why no one had even begun to panic. "I've made it my mission to break every last one of them."

The shop was oddly silent. Evidently the IR didn't believe that I was who I claimed to be or... I was not the threat that I seemed to think.

"We have you surrounded," a voice boomed over a megaphone outside. Four helicopters lowered into the street, scattering the terrified crowd. Many of the other citizens of the Flotsam were also wanted criminals of the Republic, Etone, former Chaos Knights, wizards and Imperial soldiers. I did not expect them to make a stand, but watching the men flee still pained me. Our once-proud people had been reduced to a pack of helpless, screaming filthy little rats.

"High Commander Ravencroft, come out with your hands behind your back," Octavian ordered, grinning broadly.

I had no choice, I realized, as they drug Phineas away. They had cornered me in a place where I would not dare use my full power, for fear of killing hundreds of innocent people. Resigned, I stepped into the street as I had been commanded. My eyes searching the windows of the shops along the road and the alleys between them. Silently and fearfully, men and women watched as I obediently lowered my hands.

"I will be back," I announced to all of those who might be listening. "I will return."

Cold, cleric-fire cuffs snapped around my wrists, burning my skin. I winced but refused to bow my head, marching into the waiting transport and stepping heavily on Octavian's foot as I passed him by.

"I am glad that you survived the war," I hissed in his ear.

"I'm sure you would enjoy putting a bullet in my head," he responded, unphased.

"A bullet to the head would be merciful," I replied. "I would prefer to see you suffer as much as possible."

"Is torture something they teach you noble servants of the Empire?" Octavian countered.

"You forget, mortal," I glared, snarling through my clenched teeth. "I was not trained by the Errida dynasty. I was trained by the Warlord Geruth. I'm sure you've seen what he does to traitors. Neneviej, Octavian," I whispered in the Old Tongue, winking at him with a vicious grin and nodding towards the image of a black mask spray-painted next to a devil's head on a nearby wall. "Ask your friend Fairfax who I really am."

Obviously making the connection, Octavian looked visibly ill as the door between us closed, the helicopter lifting off into the sky in a whirr of blades. My strong front had been entirely useless. I had terrified Octavian and inspired the populace but I could do nothing to remedy my own situation. I had been reckless, I had ignored my uncle's warning… and I had been caught.

And so, I went to prison.

The Exiles

"The greater the legend, the further his enemies pursue him."

Forty-Four

Antares is quite possibly one of my least favorite places in all of the infinite universe. The name alone is suggestive of all kinds of miseries, "Antares Interdimensional Tear Containment and Rehabilitation Center." The "recovery" process, as it is so named, is a series of brainwashing and magic-depleting experiments most often done on humans and other less powerful mages.

Those deemed unfit to be assimilated into society are simply left alone for an indefinite amount of time without food or water until they eventually die.

For most, it only takes a few weeks. For others, it can be very long time indeed.

Trapped inside a small room with a strange machine that sped up time itself, I spent the equivalent of thirty-five years in that hell-hole.

My symbiote died... and still, I lingered on, wondering what was keeping me from simply fading away.

It is almost impossible to describe the thoughts that went through my mind as I lay there on the floor, motionless for years at a time.

No human could survive such an ordeal, and for demons, the ritual punishment of being confined eternally in an empty chamber is the most extreme form of torture imaginable.

Geruth had been right when he had guessed that I would not die, not when starved and abandoned, not even without water or light.

A sword blow or a spell could still kill me, as could suffocation, but without the aid of an outside force I was truly... horrifically immortal.

According to the I'Eloshir, if I had survived even five years in untouched solitude, I would be considered worthy of a third moon on my shoulder, the mark of a god. And yet somehow, though I much desired death, I tripled that time, and then tripled it again. The part of me that was Artemis Ravencroft faded into grief and daydreams, but my demonic side, my great weakness survived, not on the fragments of my somewhat broken will but on the faint flicker of an inner emotion that I almost failed to recognize.

Though I did not know when, or how, I knew that I would someday be freed.

Then, after who knew precisely how long... the door opened.

A sliver of light flickered in the impenetrable darkness and I gasped, awakened suddenly from my deathlike sleep.

That feeling was revolutionary. After imaging light for over a decade, I suddenly felt a sensation completely foreign to me... one that I remembered vaguely from some long ago day when there had been sun. It was, I suppose, in mundane terms, the will to live. It was not quite optimism... but it was enough.

"She's still alive?" the voice wondered, awed. "The machine workin'?"

"It's working," a second voice agreed, leaning into the room and tapping the buttons on the wall. I could hear every motion of the man's fingers against the panel, his breath, his heartbeat.

"Knew she was immortal," the first voice whispered. "Perhaps we ought to move her upstairs."

"Don't matter how much time you put on em' if they're those crazy Etone bastards," the second sighed. "We got one Traverser up there we been running on three hundred years... per day. Says his name's Zeuks or something. Rambles a lot."

I smiled slightly, feeling a strange well of strength opening within me. It had been awakened by the light.

"She just smiled at me." The first man pointed. "I mean... Goddamn... that was freaky."

"She's almost dead," the second argued. "She doesn't know we're here."

I knew. I could smell their sweat and taste their fear already. It was like a drug... a dangerously addictive drug that one could go without indefinitely... yet never truly lose the desire for.

I was willing and ready to succumb to my darkest, most barbaric urges for the extra strength I so desperately needed.

The door was open. If I killed them, I would be free.

Aside from the fact that I was ... starving.

I stood up, snapping my chains and stretching my long-crushed wings as far as the low ceiling would let me.

My body, overcome by exhaustion and filth, suddenly felt new again.

"I though this cell was supposed to be the High Commander," the first man stammered, staring at my shadow rather than my face.

"That ain't the High Commander." His partner staggered back in horror.

"What are you?" the man whispered, his hand shaking nervously near the trigger of his gun.

I smiled again, knowing consciously that I was going to kill the both of them... and that I would enjoy it. It is one thing to run your sword through an enemy on the field of battle... and another thing entirely to rip his throat out with your teeth.

"There was a saying once," I began, drawing closer, though my own voice was dry and harsh from disuse. "I am the thing that devils fear. I am war... and pestilence... and that unnamed dark creature that lurks in the back of your mind and threatens to devour your soul when you sleep. And I... I am the death of five thousand worlds."

"Irevaaalll!" they screamed, trying to flee. My cleric-cuffs shattered as I willed my magic to the surface.

I jumped and snared the first of the men by the neck, snapping his back and tearing my claws deep into his soft skin, breathing in the smell of blood.

Nothing would stop me. I would kill anyone who crossed my path. A decade in silent darkness can have that effect on you.

Prisoners banged on their cell doors, begging and pleading, angel or demon, to set them free. And... I ignored their cries.

I wanted something else to kill. More guards came running and I crushed them, all of them with my bare hands. Their bones were only twigs in my grasp, and their blood was weak, but their meager souls had some value to me.

I held a man's heart in my hand, breathing in the smell and remembering the drums in my mind. Sensing another presence behind me, I leapt onto the ceiling and then dropped down on the fool's back, crushing him.

"Lord God... what is that?" the sole survivor demanded of the man beside him... one of the few that I had torn apart but not quite finished.

The fool looked me in the eye... and I stared at him back for a moment, listening to his furious heartbeat before reaching out, slowly and purposefully to take his gun.

He shot me in the chest. I paused, picking up the lifeless shell of the bullet.

The man knew then... knew with a frightening certainty that he and his allies had not been mistaken. "I…reval?" he stammered.

"Yes," I replied, one final word before I crushed his skull. The white power rushed through my veins and I stood again, energized, ready to destroy whatever might remain. Sheets of blood dripped from what remained of my ragged clothes as I pushed my way through the bodies piled in the narrow corridor, seeking any who still lived.

The perverse ecstasy of that destruction… the memory itself is sick.

I had killed forty men before I slowed a pace, and still, the bloodlust lingered. I could taste it.

"Artemis?" a feeble voice whispered.

I turned, hissing, and found myself face to face with Phineas, thin and obviously beaten…. peering through the bars of his cell.

I snapped the bars and strode towards him, towering over his wasted form, though in my eyes he was only another weak and insignificant mortal, no one that I knew. A human with a brilliant, glowing wizard-soul, the single brightest light I had ever seen in one body.

"You're alive?" he whispered, awestruck.

I paused, and then realized what I had nearly done, collapsing to my knees and shedding my wings.

"I'm alive," I replied. The power in those words.

I touched my own human face, still tasting the blood in my mouth and fell silent, dropping completely to the ground and tearing my nails into the dirt… I had intended to kill the guards… in order to escape, but in the end… what I had done was far, far worse. I remembered little of the details, save that I had killed at least one man with my teeth alone. There were several souls stirring restlessly within my veins as well. I could not… would not go back so far… never again!

"It's been some weeks," he admitted. "But it feels a lot longer…"

"Weeks for you, perhaps. I had stopped counting the years in my cell." I shook my head, still unwilling to believe what I had done, yet equally unable to deny the horrific truth of it. The blood… that was proof enough. Turning away from Phineas, I squeezed some more from my sodden clothing, drinking it down, hoping desperately that he would not see me with the red in my mouth.

"I believe it is high time we get out of here," a voice announced.

I turned suddenly. His hand on my shoulder, Panther passed me a vial of ambrosia and held up a silver key. Beside him stood Ruveus… and Gloria, looking thoroughly abused. With them was Devonny.

Panther put the key into the lock of Phineas's door and turned it, though the door itself was already torn from the hinges. Every cell in the hall opened… and from the cheers I heard both above and below, I assumed every cell in the prison had as well.

"Elhil, where did you get that?" I wondered.

Panther shrugged. "You know, I actually can't remember. I think I was on my way to…"

"Save the story," Gloria advised. "I for one, would like to see some daylight."

We followed the mob out through the already open exit doors at the end of the hall and into the pitch dark betwixt.

Some of the stronger prisoners had already broken their way through weak points in the shadows, but our small party remained, trying to regroup. An older King Edgar and Brin Falchon, forever childlike, joined Phineas, Panther, Gloria, and Ruveus while I tested the Tear for a break, and then found one.

"This way." I pointed, helping the others through and then jumping myself.

The Tear closed behind me with a pop, and I climbed up a ladder and out of the closed file cabinet aboard The Hathor.

"Coincidences," Phineas muttered.

"Aieh," Panther groaned. "You were right. Ire'. Everything does lead back to this damnable ship."

Forty-Five

We returned to Zenith, despite the fact that the IR were combing the city regularly in search of the four thousand prisoners that had escaped Antares. Constantly watching, ever alert... ever in danger with each breath we took, we lingered in the shadows, waiting. Yet after what had felt like so long in captivity, I was only too glad to face a little turmoil.

Phineas told me I was getting out of control when I bought myself a motorcycle and began spending my nights roaming the streets as a sort of vigilante.

But... I merely wanted to do something...

How could I have known then what destiny still awaited us?

It was an early, somewhat misty morning after a heavy rain the night before. I was sitting at the bar inside Mad Mack's Magic Users, reading The Chronicle with vague disinterest.

"How's your morning been?" Jeo wondered, handing upside-down from the rafters. He took a shot of some vile-smelling alcohol and then reached for the gallon of orange juice sitting on the stool beside me.

"Breakfast is the most important meal of the day." Jeo grinned. "You should really have some."

"Not hungry," I muttered, annoyed by the wizard's ridiculous antics.

"Suit yourself." Jeo swung down from the ceiling, kicking the toaster and catching the flying pastry in his teeth. He sat down on the pool table and munched contentedly, still staring me down.

I sighed, knowing I would never convince him to leave me alone and reached for the pastries still in the box.

It was then that Terry walked in. She was deathly pale and staring into oblivion with a look I recognized as an expression of "apocalypse upon us."

"What is it?" I wondered, though I knew it had to be something awful.

"They want me," she whispered. "They called me and now I hafta go."

"Go? Go where? Are you insane?" I demanded, shaking her.

Terry shook her head and pushed me away with a limp hand.

"Well, who wants you?" I asked. "I'll kill them... mortal or not, you know I will..."

"They," she repeated, as if it had some cryptic meeting. "You know, them. The Good Old Boys."

Often I'd heard her refer to the mysterious organization from which she had gained her near-eternal youth. Sometimes as The Good Old Boys... and sometimes by specific names... most often "Shaeruhl" who she referred to almost as a sort of favorite sister, though I could never guess whether the person was male or female. Yet Terry never spoke more than a few words about her "Good Boys," which gave me the impression that whoever "they" were... they were not appropriate for polite dinner discussion.

"And they want you too," she muttered mysteriously. "Though they're not sure it'll work out, cause of who you are an' all."

Terry brushed past Jeo and disappeared into the elevator.

"What got into her?" Jeo whistled. "Goddamned loony."

I honestly couldn't answer him. The door bells chimed, and Phineas raced in, breathless and followed by Cal and Mariel.

"Is she here?" he demanded, scanning the room nervously.

"Who?" I wondered.

"Terry!" he snapped. "Who did you think I was talking about?"

"She's here." I nodded. "She just went upstairs."

"She what?" Phineas gasped.

"No." Cal shook his head. "She wouldn't."

"I'm inclined to believe she would," Mariel admitted, very matter-of-factly. "After what that man said..."

"Did she say anything to you?" Phineas asked. "Before she left?"

"Something about her 'Boys' again," I sighed. "Would someone please enlighten me? What is going on here?"

"Terry believes she's been called upon," Phineas explained. "Mariel and I ran into this stranger down by the hospital. He and Terry went off to talk. A few minutes later we ran into Cal, and then Terry came back ghost pale and wouldn't speak to any of us. She seemed considerably shaken up."

"I know. Another recent development in her relative madness, I suppose?" I shrugged and poured myself some juice.

"According to that man, whoever he was... Terry's "Good Old Boys" want their favor. Apparently it's a big one... seeing as they've done a lot for her... and I guess Terry thinks she owes them more than she can ever repay," Cal whispered. "She thinks there's only one way out."

"Declare bankruptcy?" Jeo suggested.

And then it hit me. The kind of favors that seemed to circulate between Etone were not the kind that involved anything so simple as cold hard cash... "She's going to kill herself!" I choked.

"No." Cal shook his head. "We're going to stop her."

We raced up to the top floor, threw open the doors and stared in awe. Even Phineas... and I myself were speechless when faced with such an incredible power.

An immense dark shadow loomed over Terese where she stood on the ledge, a blue-robed entity of some unimaginable magical force. The ghost removed its hood... looking so much like Terese, young and old at the same time. He appeared to be human, but his eyes were full of a wild, magical glow as if he knew far too many things to comprehend. Two more tall shadows appeared on either side of him, both dressed in the same shifting blues and grays.

Cal grew very pale. "Teyme?" he wondered in disbelief.

A bright light hovered on the horizon line, a supernatural lantern leading into the black tunnel of space.

Then, a sound like a freight train screeched, and the blue ghosts scattered, fleeing from a furious comet-like creature, a silver-scaled, almost invisible serpent, some powerful, immortal, demonic beast that soared over our heads before disappearing into another faint Tear in the distant sky.

I couldn't move. I was frozen in time, watching the entire scene from within a dream.

The ghost rematerialized, hovering almost nervously, and Terese jumped.

Free of the spell, Cal threw himself forward and dove for Terry. Phineas caught him, only barely, and I caught them both.

We were all too late, but we had seen beyond a shadow of a doubt that our realm, our petty battles and foolish quests, indeed, all that we had ever known and feared and loved had moved to a level beyond mortal comprehension.

I remembered Raphael, long ago reassuring me that the Chaos Realm, despite its name, was really quite stable. He had been referring to the Traversers and the Etone... and I had assumed that meant we were safe. Neither of us had been comfortable discussing the possibility of beings greater than ourselves, truly infinite. The ability to do... anything at will... seemed too large a power to entrust in a single source... but there were those who truly possessed it.

So much depended on those shiftless deities. If only they knew.

But now... Terese's self-sacrifice proved what we, in our mundane arrogance had overlooked.

The few of could not save our world. Not so long as there were Gods still at war.

Forty-Six

The funeral was like a dark dream. I kept hearing Terese's voice, denying the existence of an afterlife.... of a God. Her Good Boys had been wandering the mortal plane forever, eternally unresting... and for what purpose? She doubted the reality of a release after death... and yet she threw herself headlong into the unknown.

I wondered over her actions... Phineas's and my own. I wondered why I did not die in Antares, and why I did not die at the battle of the Frozen Sea.

Phineas and Panther were the only two living souls that I remained close to, Panther on a pure drinking and gambling level, and Phineas less and less as he grew older and I remained the same.

I needed some time alone to dig up what little remained of my own life. We all did.

For days, none of us spoke and then we decided it would be best if we went our separate ways. Phineas decided to follow Lucy and Jeo on one of their self-proclaimed "misadventures", and Ruveus went to see his wife and children in Accoloth.

Panther took the Hathor with his wife and Cal headed to the Badowin Isles to find Terry's estranged family.

I began to walk... heading south towards Ardra.

I knew not what I expected to find there, or even if it was "there" I was trying to reach, but I continued to put one foot in front of the other, wandering the continents for a year's time.

I had many small adventures, made friends and foes, was hunted, arrested... never quite successfully, and found myself ignored and stranded on several near desert-islands.

I went to see Bruno and his wife, found them quite rich, and then grew tired of their world, longing for my home.

Thus... I returned to the Chaos Realm.

The IR lingered, as if they were closely akin to leeches... drawing forth whatever light or life remained in the land. Tears spread like wildfire through the ever-darkening sky. My world was dying, slowly and painfully, and there was nothing I could do. The thought sickened me to the point that I almost left again... perhaps I would have gone forever.

But then one night... I awoke to my fire burning out of control for no apparent reason. In the darkness, I heard voices that I still recognized, though I had not seen the speakers in ages. King Edgar, Brin Falchon, and Baroness Gloria.

"We're still being tracked," Gloria sighed. "I wish I knew how to lose those pigs."

"I'm tired," Brin complained. "I've been walking for thirteen hours... and before that, they were going to burn me at the stake."

"We know, Brin," Edgar sighed. "We were there."

"I hate fire," Brin muttered. "And they called me a witch, all because I was wearing... pants."

"Brin, you are a magic-user," Gloria reminded her. "And even if you weren't, those dirt-wallowing mundanes would have pulled you out and named you one anyway. They fear anyone smarter and less-primordial than the lot of them. Overbearing, ignorant, self-centered energy-blind... quasi-emotional males!"

"That is a discriminatory statement!" Edgar grinned, pretending to take offense.

"Males," Gloria groaned. There was a rustling sound, as if she was searching through a knapsack or purse of some kind. "Where is my mirror?" she demanded.

"In the middle of the woods and the Baroness wants a mirror!" Edgar laughed. "Females!"

"I know," Brin yawned, apparently ignoring them both. "But pants... really... it's... so... ridiculous."

"Don't fall asleep," Edgar warned. "I can't carry you with my shoulder dislocated and we've got a helluva lot of walking to do before we're in safe country."

"I wonder if Devonny's all right," Gloria whispered. "She did save the three of us back there."

"Dev can take care of herself," Edgar reassured Gloria. "If anyone can escape those nutcases... she can."

"Poor Devonny," Brin began, sobbing faintly. "I hate them."

"Come on, Brin." Edgar slung her over his back and they continued through the forest. Gloria sang to herself, softly, an old Ardran song, and Edgar joined in on occasion when he remembered the words.

I listened as they whispered to one another, for hours it seemed, but when I at last looked up… they were gone.

"Head west," a shadow that looked suspiciously like Deiunthel advised. "Head west."

Without waiting for the suns to rise, I did.

Forty-Seven

It was in the small farming village of Elmwood that I found myself some days later, exhausted both mentally and physically but still unwilling to rest.

I'd forsworn my old habit of drinking ambrosia… perhaps hoping that my unmanaged stress would manage to kill me once and for all.

It didn't.

I walked for some hours past fields of wheat fields and apple orchards before reaching what could almost be referred to as the center of town. There was a tavern, at any rate, and that was good enough for me. I wondered what was keeping Edgar, Brin and Gloria, but then reminded myself, they were only human.

Horses, motorcycles, caravans, whatever mode of transportation the three of them had adopted after running all night would take them a few hours at very least to reach civilization.

I sighed and let myself in to the bar, despite the sign over the door reading "Newcomers Most Unwelcome" and beneath that "No weapons, no magic".

So they didn't like offworld entrepreneurs or troublemakers with sunglasses and airboards. I couldn't blame them. Despite my exterior Zenith-clothes, I was hardly "new" to the Chaos Realm.

They could throw me out if they were able.

"Who's that man over there think he is?" Some gifted soul at the bar pointed, evaluating my battered jeans and filthy green winter coat.

Man? I squinted through my disguise spell and wondered for a moment if it really looked that bad. It probably did.

"Thank you Phineas," I muttered, throwing off my scarf. "Barkeep! A drink!" I shouted.

"Didn't you read the sign?" the bartender pressed, obviously displeased by my appearance. Though his face wasn't one that I recognized, his smell…

strangely seemed familiar.

"Yes, I read the sign!" I sighed, ignoring the turmoil that had already started behind my back, and thought of Phineas.

I wished I knew where he had gone, but it required too much mental stamina on my part to find out. Perhaps I was finally getting old, or perhaps I was just sick again. I was about to start a fight in either case, and I relished the prospect. I hadn't beaten anyone senseless in a long time.

Just then... as I was developing my next insult, Gloria walked in. Shocked, I spilled my mug on the floor. I didn't particularly like beer, but it was still a waste. Centuries of drinking ambrosia had made it almost impossible for me to get nicely drunk on anything brewed by mortals but I still tried, regardless.

"Gloria!" I stammered, mopping up my mess. "What are you... how did you?"

There were too many questions, most of them involving transportation.

"Never mind," I finished. "Is Edgar with you?"

It took her a moment to recognize me, but when she did, she gasped.

"Is it...," she began.

"Yes," I hissed under my breath. "I heard you on the road last night. Where are the others?"

"Edgar's outside. I don't know where Brin went," she admitted, rubbing her Fire Opal.

I wasn't sure what Gloria Etharel thought of Edgar "Excalibur"... but I much preferred his alter ego, Edgar the Village Idiot.

Edgar entered with his customary swagger and brushed the road dirt from his face with an equally filthy handkerchief.

Gloria motioned to me, jabbing a finger at my dragon pendant and Edgar's jaw dropped. Fortunately, the considerably bounty on his head had made him slightly adept at recovering quickly from a slip.

"Goodevenin'..." He waited for my current name.

"Miranda Fargrove," I supplied, adopting a name I'd used in the past, and forgetting whatever I had been going by earlier. Aliases kept me out of IRP hands. The more the better.

"Goodevenin' Miss Fargrove. It's a pleasure." He kissed my hand.

I scowled and held back the sudden overwhelming urge I had to pitch him through a wall... reminding myself that he had not done anything to me that might have earned him a broken neck. "You two go upstairs," I ordered. "I have to do something."

It was dusk... night was falling. I needed to get royally drunk or physically exhausted if I didn't want to hurt anyone. So, being somewhat low in funds, I decided to run. Two steps out the door I stopped, shot down by a mind-numbing flash of white light.

Brin and her lovely entrances. I opened my eyes dazedly and looked up to see her standing over me in her Zenith clothes, a yellow jacket and a pair of patched jean shorts.

"Hello, Brin." I smiled weakly and climbed to my feet... just in time to catch her as she passed out. I drug her inside. "Edgar! Gloria!"

They both raced down the stairs.

"Oh my God!" Edgar crossed himself. "Is that Brin?"

"I'll get her," Gloria volunteered. "It's all right Artemis!"

I winced, hoping no one had heard the mistake. There was only one Artemis in the known realm, and that was me. No sane mother would name her daughter after a demonic soul-thief who also held the dubious distinction of leading the losing army in the last great war.

"Hold up," one of the men pointed. "Didju just..."

"YOU'RE DRUNK," I ordered him, and he fell silent.

Edgar and Gloria drug the swooning Brin upstairs and I went outside, kicking off my boots and removing my disguise spell once I was beyond tree cover. Breathing through the yellowish haze of the spell made me increasingly irritable. Unlike food, oxygen was something I couldn't live without. I jumped over a small creek and looked back behind me, reminding myself to stay hidden, especially since I wasn't under an illusion any longer.

I found a rock somewhere in the middle of a glade, about a mile or so from the village and sat down. I sighed and undid the gold clasp of my leather shoulder bag and produced Cal's red leather-bound notebook and silver "Alchemy Pen", the two items that Phineas had entrusted into my somewhat unreliable care when we last crossed paths in Celedon.

Gelthar had been raided and Cal was on the run. He wasn't sure how the IR were tracking him but he was more afraid of them confiscating his "tools" than capturing him alive.

I didn't know why I bothered to hide the two artifacts. Only an experienced eye would know what they were anyway. The original drawings of half of the buildings in the city of Zenith... and the damnable enchanted pen that would write in the damnable Archives if and when I ever found them...

The same went for my staff, returned by Panther after my escape from Antares. I carried it with me at all times, wrapped in layers of burlap. Most often, people left me alone. A seven foot stick, even a non-magical one, was a formidable weapon.

I sighed and closed up my things. Cal's possessions, twelve small glass mirrors and a few vials of ambrosia. That was all. I tended to travel light.

I unbuckled my sword and leaned back, halfway deciding to take a nap, when I was struck by a sudden chill. My hand instinctively went for my staff as I jumped to my feet. I was being watched.

"GO AWAY!" I ordered.

Nothing moved, rustled or breathed. It could be a Tear, part of my conscious warned.

"I hate Tears," I muttered aloud… and then smiled. If it was a Tear, odds were that it would be carrying something strong, and hopefully something evil that I could justify destroying.

Then, in one of the most horrific crashes I can clearly recall, a Tear opened above my head… and an old green station-wagon dropped from the sky, plummeting into the branches of a nearby tree. I had seen Tears bring strange things before, but never a car.

"Oh Lord, lord!" a voice exclaimed from inside the vehicle. I jumped back reflexively and tore some of the burlap from the staff's blade.

"Hello out there? Hello? Someone get me outta here… please!" the voice begged.

"How did you get here?" I demanded, knowing that the driver of the vehicle, whatever it was, would have needed some quite powerful magic to open a Tear from its home dimension to the Chaos Realm.

"I don't know, I was just drivin' home… didn't realize there was a tree between thirty-second and Calgary!" he stammered.

"Who are you?" I snarled. I didn't know precisely what I looked like, but the reaction I received from the poor man was astonishing.

He blinked, not in fear or surprise, but more in bewilderment as if he were wondering whether I really existed or not.

"Name's GW… GW Campbell… now you gonna help me down please?" The man smiled, his eyes focused on the blade of my staff.

Seeing no reason not to grant him the simple request, I lowered my weapon and wretched off the car door with one arm.

"My, that's some strength you got there," the driver muttered in disbelief.

"It was loose already," I lied, feeling a faint burn on my hand from the effort.

I evaluated my intruder as he evaluated me. He was, of course, more troubled by my appearance than I was by his… yet he did not scream

"I'Eloshir" or "Traverser" nor back away a single pace.

Still, was he brave? Or simply foolish?

All in all "GW" was an unimpressive man. An ordinary human, nice enough... probably near forty with a wife and children to come home to.

"Well, it's been a pleasure to meet you Miss...," he began.

"Ravencroft," I supplied.

"Thank you for pullin' me down." He scratched his chin and glanced up at the car in the tree. "My, my." GW shook his head.

"No problem." I slung my sword over my back and slipped on my boots, wrapping up my staff in its customary sheet.

"So... is this some kind of Renaissance Festival? Is that why you're all dressed up?" the man wondered.

"A what?" I was baffled."Oh yeah." GW smiled weakly. "I forgot... you're pretendin' it's real, right?"

"If you say so." I shrugged.

"Could you show me to the nearest town?" He glanced around. "Seems we're in the middle of nowhere."

"A mile from anything," I admitted. "I was actually going back that way myself, before you... dropped in."

"Think there's anyone that might help me unload the trunk?" GW asked. "I figure the car ain't goin' anywhere but the trunk is full of stuff for the church picnic."

"Church? Which church?" I wondered, a little more paranoid.

"Atlanta Assembly o' God," he announced proudly. "You've heard of it?"

"Not exactly," I sighed in relief, only too thankful that he wasn't a White Cross priest.

Thusfar, I had learned one thing. Whoever this GW Campbell was... he wasn't the one who had opened the Tear. That kind of mischief reeked of the I'Eloshir. It wasn't a comforting thought.

We reached town and the poor preacher seemed even more alarmed by his surroundings.

"Not a pay-phone or a trash can in sight," he muttered in disbelief.

"Let's go to the tavern," I advised. "They might have a phone you can use."

I listened carefully as we approached the run-down building. In addition to the strange sensation that I felt, it seemed that there was quite a bit of commotion going on upstairs.

It sounded like it was coming from Gloria's room. Ready for anything, I threw open the tavern doors and marched upstairs, followed by GW.

Eyes followed me.

"Ouch! You're hurting me! Let go!" Brin cried.

I smashed through the solid wood door with my fist, snapping the hinge-pins. The room immediately fell silent.

Brin was lying on the bed squeezing Edgar's hand while Gloria proceeded to give her stitches. There was no crisis… and no emergency.

Still, I couldn't comprehend why they were staring. I stepped into the light, my gaze drifting across every face in the silent room, until at last it came to rest on the one pair of eyes that were not utterly horrified by whatever it was that they beheld.

Reflected in the small mirror over the chest-of-drawers was a thin, pale world-weary face too distinct not to be recognized… by every bounty hunter and lawman on any of the six continents… the face of a woman whose features might have been chiseled from stone, who seemed in every way too cold to have possibly been human. It took me a moment to recognize my own reflection, and then I realized, all at once what had happened. A mile back, in the middle of the woods… sitting on a rock next to a car parked vertically in a tree was a pendant shaped like a dragon that carried with it a faint yellow glow.

I had forgotten my disguise spell.

Forty-Eight

"Artemis?" Gloria gaped. It had been awhile since she'd seen me without an artificial face, and I supposed, after all of here cushy, quiet years bounty-hunting bandits across Southern Ardra, she was still having trouble accepting the fact that she was standing face-to-face with a "real" Traverser.

What I wouldn't have given to be back in Zenith, sitting on a silver chair and delegating responsibility.

"Is that a question or an expression of shock?" I asked.

"Any particular reason why you dropped your disguise?" Edgar whispered, almost too slowly.

"I forgot," I admitted truthfully, as ridiculous as it sounded.

"You… forgot?" Brin glared, despite her wounds. "You're wanted across the Chaos Realm for escaping Antares… and you forgot?"

"I am nearly a thousand years old. I have forgotten more than any of you have ever experienced. Perhaps my memory is failing me," I countered.

"There's no reason it should. You don't age," Gloria pointed out. "You're a demon."

"A demon?" GW's eyes were wide. "A real… demon-demon?"

I shrugged, nonchalant. It did beg repeating.

"A Traverser to be precise," Edgar added. "One of the last surviving in the known dimensions."

"Frankly, I don't care," I admitted. "And by the way, King Edgar of Istara… thank you for reminding me that I should be extinct."

"Where are all these... Hold on! This is another world?" GW shook his head heavily and looked up, adjusting his glasses.

"There she is!" A man had reached the top of the stairs and he pointed. "Burn the Etone witch!"

He fired a shot from his gun and we all hit the floor. I reached for my sword but I'd evidently lost it somehow… and I wasn't about to whip out my staff in the middle of a hallway that was neither tall enough nor wide enough for me to wield it effectively.

"I didn't want to do this," I muttered, firing a streak of purple fire from my fingertips, throwing one of the men over the banister.

"What the hell was that!" GW gasped.

"We call it magic." I nodded to Gloria as a second posse raced up the stairs.

Without a word, she lowered her eyes and concentrated. The fire opal flared brilliantly and formed into a pair of six foot long red-energy claws.

Edgar dunked over Brin, sword in hand. "Tell me when the spells stop flying!" he shouted, over the roar of the oncoming mob.

I didn't have gold enough to pay for repairs to the tavern. Hopefully the men who'd started the fight would realize they were severely outclassed and let us sleep.

That, of course, was wishful thinking.

"No weapons, no magic!" the bartender roared.

The drunks kept coming. On the whole, the human race is extraordinarily persistent.

"Need a little cover-fire?" Phineas blinked into existence in a cloud of black and white smoke… dressed in a pinstripe suit with a machine gun on each hip.

"Phineas?" As relieved as I was to see him in one piece, his timing was terrible and his costume couldn't have been more ridiculous. His typical insanity had multiplied three-fold since he had begun traveling with Lucy, Jeo and Igor in the devil's yellow cab.

"Mess with one Traverser, you mess with the whole Brotherhood." Edgar grinned.

"No weapons, no magic!" a voice… quite literally roared.

The onslaught stopped instantly. A very large shadow loomed over the lot of us.

"Holy Jeezus it's a friggin' dragon!" One of the men gasped.

I smiled, not entirely surprised, and recalling the one tavern rule honored by scum in any dimension. Never… never, under any circumstances do you provoke the bartender.

"Who started it?" the bartender demanded.

The men pointed at me… and I shook my head heavily with a smile. The dragon laughed. I knew he'd smelled familiar.

"Hey Ruveus! Long time no see!" Phineas waved.

"Dude! I had a feeling you were around this part of the woods!" Ruveus grinned.

"A dragon?" GW looked ready to faint.

"That's the least of what you'll see here in the Chaos Realm," Edgar pointed out.

"The Chaos Realm, hunh? Like that damn videogame all the kids are playing?" GW wondered.

"Videogame? There's a videogame?" Gloria stared at me wide-eyed.

"Mr. Fargrove has apparently chosen to take his chances yet again." I smiled slightly. "Perhaps he'll make another million at our expense."

"That place is real?" GW looked even more confused. "Really... real?"

"Not any time to explain now." Ruveus glanced out the window and reverted, not to his bartender guise but his standard human form. Pulling a pair of pants out of the cabinet behind him, he dressed quickly and was somewhat embarrassed by how many eyes were fixed on the lot of us. Ruveus shook his head heavily and took his worn jacket off of a peg on the wall, not bothering to find a shirt or shoes. "I've been IRP'd so many times, I'd better make a run for it before one of my loyal customers calls the cops."

Gloria and Edgar were already halfway out the door.

"Hold on!" I shouted. "Where are you off to?"

"Anywhere but Antares," Gloria snapped. "If the rest of you don't get moving, you'll get caught... and if any of us are put before IR court, it'll be straight to The Party."

"The Party?" I stared.

"You missed it." Phineas smiled weakly. "Prisoners down where we were used to call third floor... where you were... The Party."

"Inapsu... In god's name why?" I demanded.

"Well, we figured it had to be fun up there. You know, music, caterers... hot tubs and everything. Why else would no one ever come down?" Brin explained.

"Amusing." I frowned.

"Hey Imperial Court!" Ruveus snarled, gesturing towards the window with a dramatic "I don't like what's out there" wave.

Despite our attempts to blend into the new society, at the mention of the word "Imperial", all of us turned, instantly at attention.

"What is it?" Phineas was genuinely intrigued.

"If it isn't obvious," he sighed. "The Baroness's 'caterers' have come to us."

Déjà vu struck then. Horrified by my own stupidity, I realized that I had been successfully tracked by the IRP six times… and three of those times, the chase had ended at a tavern. One would have though that I might have learned to save myself the pain of running so often by practicing a little temperance.

Then again… I am what I am.

Still, it was almost pathetic. In order to catch the most wanted exile in the realm, all the IR really had to do was find the nearest bar and pay a couple of fools to keep their eyes open.

We raced outside and barreled directly into the front line of three police cruisers, myself, Gloria, Edgar, Phineas, Brin… and Ruveus.

The IR seemed startled by our running out to greet them, but that was nothing compared to their reaction as something very large and glowing with magical energy shot down from above and came to a stop, hovering a mere ten feet over their heads.

"Tag!" a familiar voice shouted, throwing a rope ladder down to us.

I looked up in disbelief at The Spellcraft Hathor… Cal and Igor sitting in white plastic pool chairs while the incurable Tai Mariel stood, near vomiting over the rail.

"Excellent timing Cal!" Phineas waved, blinking onboard the ship in a burst of smoke, dragging Gloria and Edgar with him. I wished desperately that he'd never learned the obnoxious trick but said nothing.

Ruveus heaved Brin on his back and jumped straight onto the deck, rocking the ship with remarkable force. GW stared, wavering a little at the display, but still breathing. I had to confess, he was remarkably resilient for a priest.

I grabbed the rope Igor had thrown to us and pulled the Reverend after me as the Spellcraft shot off, leaving the IRP in a dazed blur.

The police hadn't been coming for us. They'd arrested two petty thieves from the Badowin Islands and expected to go home… unwittingly overlooking virtually all of the Interdimensional Republic's most wanted.

After we covered a reasonable distance, we brought down our speed and flew higher, above the open ocean.

"So where are we headed, mi amigos?" Cal asked, leaning on Phineas's shoulder to his left and Ruveus's to his right… standing slightly lopsided.

"Border Town." Phineas stared at the console. He'd known the ship was near enough to make a fly by in case of an emergency, but he had hoped we wouldn't have to call upon it. The IR seemed to be fairly good at tracing seven separate wanderers across the continents. Finding the lot of us gathered together on a single ship, and one of the few remaining Imperial Spellcraft at that... would be child's play. We were as good as caught.

"Any particular reason?" Edgar wondered.

Everyone fell silent, waiting for the explanation of exactly why fate had chosen to reunite us... the unfortunate "Defenders of the Realm" once again.

"A book," he replied bluntly.

It was the last of the great and legendary artifacts. The vault of the palace had housed many treasures, but nothing that paralleled the power of the book.

We already possessed Cal's plans and I'd long since recovered my staff from the IR's mysterious pan-dimensional box. The only thing that remained was a single manuscript far too deadly to be included with the rest of our wonders, the last surviving relic of Raedawn and the Errida Dynasty... the one thing I'd been obsessed with for years... ever since I'd first imagined of its existence.

The Archives of Teyme.

"You don't mean..." Ruveus began, though he well knew that what he was thinking, what we were all thinking, was exactly what Phineas had meant.

With the exception of GW, who was sitting very still and staring dazedly, the rest of us had been in on the conspiracy for quite some time.

I turned and surveyed what remained of my once-great armies. A group of legends who would not call themselves heroes, tossed together in pursuit of the long forgotten ideals of honor and equality... all impatiently wielding their weapons.

Cal wore two shotguns on either side, and carried a mammoth machete across his back. Mariel, when she wasn't denying the existence of paranormal force or sitting with her head buried in a book, was a capable enough spell caster, even without her blue stone.

Gloria had the red opal, and Phineas possessed his heavy arsenal of spells. Edgar carried nothing of value, nothing to show for his once powerful kingdom, save his signet ring and enchanted sword...

Ruveus, of course, bore only his mandolin... and his natural ability to transform into a thirty-foot long fire breathing monster.

"Music is the key," he muttered... plucking the strings dazedly.

"So where is it?" Cal wondered, without actually naming the book itself.

I shrugged and Phineas winced, knowing somehow that whatever he intended to say would not go over well.

"Probably somewhere in the underground," he admitted finally. "The City

Below."

"With Orin Saede! I've been tracking that l'Eloshir scum for months! I should have figured he was on his way back to the sewers…" Gloria glared. She'd hated Orin with a particular passion since she learned about how he'd orchestrated the massacre of the Falchon family and manipulated Brin as a child.

I myself still owed him several painful deaths.

"But what if Orin isn't involved… and what if he is and what if he's bluffing… what if he doesn't have it?" Brin pointed out.

Ruveus shrugged. "The girl's got a point. You got any other leads Phineas?"

"We could search the Tears," Phineas muttered, looking at the ground.

In silence, Cal slumped down, his face in his hands. The last time we had gone down into a Tear intentionally… that had been the Etone War… a year in the darkness of the space between worlds that had come crashing to an end with the deaths of Rex, Ira and Sikara. Rex had been a Tear Soldier at one point… and was possibly still living, somewhere in the depths of space and time, and Ira was more of a true Traverser than any Etone I had ever met... but Sikara never should have gone with us.

It pained me to think of how Cal had lost three of his closest friends... all in one horrific day. The final stage of the Etone War had come close to only one other historically scarring event... a battle where the death toll had numbered in the millions.

The Frozen Sea. Instantly, as soon as my mind made the connection, I turned away from the group.

The silence behind me was unnerving.

I paced the deck and the others went inside, somehow sensing my agitation.

Not all of them knew the truth about my origins, but they knew me as High Commander… and they knew it was best to let me alone.

The Demons

"Like fire and ice, yet flesh and bone."

Forty-Nine

The sun rose and still I paced, finally slumping down and slipping into a sort of reverie. The Hathor cruised through the skies until at last we reached the sandy gates of Border-Town, a city on the edge of the great wastes that seemed vaguely like something Bruno had shown me in a movie once.

I wondered briefly if the director of the film had ever been to the Chaos Realm, and then the alarms rang, waking the others up.

We had a canned breakfast of egglike mush… which I refused to touch, guiltily pouring a few ounces of ambrosia into my coffee instead. Everyone stared at me, though it was impossible to tell whether the reaction was based on envy or apprehension.

"You haven't eaten in days," Gloria observed, stirring the yellow-white slop with her fork.

"I've told you before, I don't have to eat," I sighed.

"That's pretty weird if you ask me," Ruveus muttered between bites of breakfast. "Something that never eats shouldn't be alive, let alone unkillable."

"Vampires can't eat," Edgar added. "What about them, hunh? What about vampires?"

"Thank you for that observation Ruveus," I sighed. "And for your information Edgar, I am not a vampire. I am not dead and I can also eat. I can simply choose not to eat, however… when what is being served does not resemble anything once living."

"Got aristocratic taste?" Phineas winked, and I smiled slightly.

"Living?" Edgar frowned. "Oh. You like meat then?" He grinned. "Like really bloody steaks and stuff? Should have figured with those teeth you have."

"What teeth?" I wondered.

"Well, you don't have most of the time, and you don't have them right now." He shrugged. "Only when you're pissed."

"There's a brilliant comment," Phineas groaned.

"Oh c'mon Master Merlin, you've seen her teeth before," Edgar sighed. "Don't look at me like I'm some kind of frickin' idiot."

"So… if you could have anything you wanted for breakfast, what would it be?" Cal wondered, changing the subject. I was thankful for that.

"I like sweet things especially," I admitted. "I spared a man's life once for a sugar cube. I had never tasted such a thing before, and he was in a barn full of horses, giving them sugar. I was going to kill him when he gave it to me, a mere treat for horses… but it surprised me so much that I forgot entirely about what I was doing. Mostly I like things with strong flavors. I prefer foods with very … distinct tastes."

"Like maple syrup?" Gloria suggested. "On a stack of waffles."

I was insanely tempted to flash out of view, break a few mirrors and return with pancakes but I didn't. It was entirely too risky and I had to protect my companions.

"Like blood?" Edgar smirked. "Like Kentucky-fried people parts?"

"Shut up you ass!" I growled, glaring at him.

Completely unintimidated, Edgar grabbed my lip and pointed, still smiling. "There. Those teeth."

After breakfast, we all went about preparing ourselves for our mutual return to society.

Phineas landed the Spellcraft in a junkyard, not far from the place where Panther and I had originally stolen the ship. Everyone stumbled out, muttering curses, their weapons close at hand.

We entered town, a veritable army of suspicious characters. Fortunately, in a town build on the blood of demons and other pitfighters, suspicious was ordinary.

"I've got to find someone who can fix this gun," Cal announced. "Brin and Gloria are coming with me."

"Not unless I'm coming too." Edgar smirked.

"Spoilsport," Cal shot back. "Can't a man have two women to himself?"

"Meet us at Lady Mercy's, the tavern around eight o' clock," Phineas explained.

"I'm going to set three of us up to fight in the pit, which ought to catch everyone's attention at least long enough for the rest of us to search for the book."

"Me!" Gloria begged, waving madly.

"Gloria... and Ruveus." Phineas smiled. "You up for it, old friend?"

"I'd rather play my mandolin," Ruveus sighed wistfully, though we all knew well that his magical instrument had been bashed over plenty of heads it its day.

"Und du, Artemis? You wills fight, no?" Igor asked.

I snapped back to the present, realizing I'd drifted off watching the newest unfortunate member of our crew... the Reverend, who was, as fate would have it, trying to argue logic with Mariel. "I am in no mood." I shook my head.

"Artemis...," Phineas pried.

"What about Igor?" I pointed.

Igor's jaw dropped. "Was?"

I took another discreet sip of ambrosia and wondered why I still felt as if we were being watched.

Igor agreed. Since Lucy had pulled him off the roof of some cathedral he'd only two loves... alcohol and battle. A perfect addition to the rest of the Yellow-Cab groupies.

"I'll take care of the priest and amnesia-mage," I offered.

More glares and expressions of bewilderment followed, but I didn't care. What I needed was to be around people who would not believe anything they saw.

"The two of you are shopping with me," I announced, butting in between Mariel and GW.

Mariel stood with her hands on her hips and glared at me. I was something she couldn't explain... and I wasn't friendly enough to pass by her "poor genetic misfit" stereotype.

"Why do you always act like you're in charge?" she demanded.

"I am in charge," I countered.

"I believe that." GW nodded readily. "Those other fellas seem pretty scared of you , girl. I don't know what you did to em' but I'll bet it wasn't pretty."

"I'd say that it was magic," I leered... waiting for Mariel's reaction.

"Magic is one part coincidental and..." Mariel began.

"Two parts hallucination," I finished.

Mariel fell silent, and I supposed GW thought that was the best course of action as well. We drifted in and out of several stores until we came to an abandoned monorail stop.

It was quiet... and still, more silent than a cemetery. Thankfully, I'd brought my staff with me off the Hathor. I sensed I would need it soon enough.

313

Carefully, I began unwrapping the flannel sheets and tape from blade and waited, expecting an ambush.

Mariel's crossbow was poised. "Who do you think it is?" she wondered. "Snakes... Blades, Wolves?"

"Etone," I muttered.

Mariel took a step back. "You're sure of that, are you?"

I nodded. "Just watch."

The filthy glass mirrors of the station rippled slightly, and then shattered. Ten men, all dressed in black and armed with swords... all wearing faintly flickering green sunglasses jumped through the glass and rolled across the pavement, instantly leaping to their feet, eternally on guard.

The black and white barcode patterns on the back of each of their jackets revealed my assumptions to be true.

They didn't possess the true magic of moving Tears. They were not immortals... not Traversers... and yet, at the same time every bit as egotistical and insane as the realm-wanderers they copied.

It had been awhile since I'd seen a member of the Brotherhood.

"Hey look!" One of the men pointed. "Locals!"

"Wait! None of you punks move a muscle!" the leader warned, adjusting his black vinyl cap and shuffling out a deck of cards in each hand, ready to throw. "One of them's not human."

He scanned me through his sunglasses, looking for a clear reading.

I almost pitied them. The Etone lifestyle was especially harsh, living between dimensions for years at a time, stealing, fighting, and retreating into the shadows of a Tear to avoid capture... with no guarantee that the place you would jump into was any better than the place you had just run from.

Still... if they attacked first, they would regret it.

"Hold," I began, trying to seem diplomatic. "I'm a friend."

"Sure, ya'r," the leader slurred.

"That's a crock of sheeyah," another brother muttered.

"No, believe me." I shook my head. "I have never been... nor will ever be loyal to the Republic."

"Lying tramp." The leader slapped his cards. I knew how dangerous a "Poker Player" could be.

The Etone were somewhat famous for their television addiction. Fictional shows from offworld satellite waves gave them all sorts of ridiculous ideas, near-impossible plans they always seemed to make feasible.

The cards were one of those ideas, inspired by some cartoon their hackers had picked up, no doubt. And like most Etone toys, they were far more brutal than they appeared.

Fortunately, I only had one deck to watch out for. The other members of the gang carried chains, baseball bats and short swords.

"Who'd you run with... hunh, ex-Etone?" the leader demanded.

"Germaine the Skunk," I shot back, more or less honestly.

"The Skunk hunh?" the one with the cards muttered, with no small amount of distaste. "We don't run with the Skunk. Get em' boys!" The Etone rushed at us.

GW ran... but not fast enough. One of the gang members caught him around the neck with a chain and flung him to the ground. Running to pull him free, I tripped two men and narrowly dodged a flaming, razor-edged ace of spades.

Another man came up on my left and caught my staff with a metallic whip, tearing it out of my hands. I leapt over to the second platform, dodging a chain of exploding hearts only to be caught directly in the back with a baseball bat.

I fell on the tracks, scarcely breathing. There were quite a few not-so good things about being human... pain, for example.

The leader snapped a row of clubs at me, spinning lightning fast and trailed by energy wire. I was caught.

GW, fortunately, was not attempting to struggle.

Two of the punks were pulling his driver's license out of his old-fashioned wallet and biting it experimentally. They'd never experienced anything like inorganic identification before.

I was still trapped. A train whistle echoed... not far away, and out of the corner of my eye I saw the rail coming. I had thought the station was abandoned. Evidently not.

I twisted my right arm slowly out of my energy cocoon, reaching for my staff.

The monorail rushed at me at a near two hundred miles per hour and I lay frozen, trying to reach the weapon that lay a mere three inches away.

"Mariel!" I shouted. "Do something, will you? Cast a spell!

There was no response. I realized quite suddenly that she couldn't hear me. Perhaps it was for the better. What she didn't hear, she couldn't argue with.

A roar of flames shot over my head with a sound that rivaled the approaching train.

315

Mariel, flung by a fireball, landed on her knees beside me, shaken but still conscious. She glanced at me dazedly and then looked to the train. "Is that... the train?" She grinned.

"MARIEL, DO SOMETHING!" I ordered.

She looked at me for a moment, eyes wide, completely shocked by the force of the order. For a moment I thought that I had overdone it... and that she would never move at all, but then, all at once there was a hideous shriek as Mariel leapt into the air, glowing supernaturally. A flash of white light followed, and then, as she drifted back towards the ground, still dazed... I was almost certain that a herd of giant spiders had invaded the station.

Webbing was everywhere.

The train stopped, the doors only opening halfway. There were no passengers to unload... and, remarkably enough, no driver.

The Etone seemed relieved, knowing it must have been running a programmed course like most monorails they knew. And I smiled slightly, despite myself.

I touched my staff and the energy wires melted away. In my frantic terror I had reached far enough. I stood, tore the remaining fabric from the blade and jumped back onto the platform.

"I imagine your day hasn't gone all that well." I glared, evaluating the group. "So you decided to leave the Tears. Not that I blame you for taking a vacation... but attempting to kill us... that was a mistake."

The gang members stepped back and dropped their weapons.

Fifty

They weren't afraid of Mariel, although she'd been the only one casting spells.

And they certainly weren't frightened of GW… as he lay there on the verge of losing consciousness, beaten possibly worse than he had ever been in all of his life for no other reason except that he had been in the wrong place at the wrong time.

What was more… was not only were the Etone terrified, they were awed. Evidently, at least one of them had recognized my face.

"Ammano loa," one of the punks whispered, crossing himself and praying to his god. "It's impossible."

The card player removed his visor. "You're still alive?" he whispered.

There was a scar running across his left eye… and I realized, in the new light that he was considerably older than his teenage followers, maybe even forty. I did not know him, but he recognized me, all too well.

"You're Ireval," he breathed a sigh of bewilderment. "My oh my."

Mariel hadn't heard… and neither had GW. I was grateful for that.

"In this world, the name's Artemis Ravencroft. Also known as Rebecca the Wanderer or Miranda Fargrove," I explained.

He nodded respectfully. "I'm Heathcliff the Badger. You probably don't remember me, but I ran with Ira the Kid and Germaine the Skunk back in the Wars. I remember the day you showed up. Bad Friday… they still call it. Like a fricken' apocalypse."

I smiled slightly. I remembered too.

"What are you doing here in Border-Town?" I asked.

"Fighting. What else?" Heathcliff admitted. "My pack is running low on good mages. I need to buy some and I hear that there's a Traverser in this area who's got a killer stock of spell-slingers."

317

"He's my uncle." I nodded. "I wish you luck, though I wouldn't bet on winning any men from him. Elhil used to gamble with a group of bored astral powers, demi-gods, demons, immortals…"

"No lie." Heathcliff nodded, impressed. "Does he cheat?"

"Of course," I agreed, laughing. "But what would you expect from His Honorable Lowliness? Half the games people play Panther invented himself."

"No, no that ain't the guy," Heathcliff argued. "I met him before. We're cool with each other, y'know? He's great fun for an l'Eloshir. Showed me his real teeth once as part of a bet. Damn near pissed myself I did."

"But… he's the only pit lord in this area," I muttered, perhaps trying to convince myself of it.

"He used to be the only one in this area. But then he went to Accoloth for some reason… nobody knows why." The card player shook his head. "The guy I'm talkin' about is named Lacchuss somethin'."

"Orin," I snarled.

"I'm pretty sure the bookie said he was called Lacchuss." Heathcliff frowned.

"It's Orin. Trust me." I glared. "He's someone I owe a bad turn to."

"Holy hell," one of the Etone who'd been listening in on our conversation gaped. "You're the real thing aincha? A real sister. Traverser."

I nodded. If I had a cent for every time I had heard that.

"Tell ya what." Heathcliff put his cards back into their nearly bombproof case. "Just cause of who you are and all, I'm gonna do you a favor. You tell us who you want to win and my guys will get the bets going around the pits tonight so you and your crew can really cash out. Then, once I get back to Boss Umeoth, I'll send word around to all the old Etone and Tear Riders I know. Pretty soon you'll be up to your elbows in volunteer vets for whatever crazy quest you're plannin'."

"So what should I give you in return?" I asked.

He shook his head. "Nothin'. You ended the Bad War. And you were friends of my little brother Ira, you and Terry Mack," Heathcliff sighed. "God, these days… don't you feel so old?"

I nodded, silently. If only he could imagine.

"I'll tell you what," I stepped in. "After this whole business is over, granted, it could be awhile… I'll find you, wherever you happen to be. I may not be much of a mage, but I am fairly good at killing people."

"You'd train my fighters?" he stared. "That's one hell of a favor!"

"Take it for Ira," I replied, helping GW to his feet and picking up Mariel.

I walked off without another word.

Memories. I would have stayed longer, but it was already getting dark, and I still had one place left to go.

I left GW nursing a black eye and Mariel with him in the cleric's shop on the corner nearest the rail station and set off alone, towards the desert.

I remembered when the field of tumbleweeds hadn't possessed a single stone, and now it was full of names I knew all too well. Monuments to heroes whose bodies had never been found. Remnants of blasted helicopters from the Republic and shards of Spellcraft.

A white pillar stood in the center of the abysmal terrain. Border Town was the only place in the Republic that a monument to an Errida would be safe. It was a marble column from the palace itself, towering over the rest of the junkyard. Burned into the stone by some unknown means, probably Etone magic... was a short poem and a dedication:

"that which I stand for is that which we all stand for, that which out enemies are trying to take from us, the rights of freedom and peace... the right to live our lives, not as what we are born as, but as what we choose to become–Rest in Peace, Lord Errida."

Yet nothing lay beneath that marble slab. Not even a photograph. Years of living amongst humans had made me nostalgic in a dangerous sort of way. In Magog, when one died, they were gone. They had never been, they were irrelevant, their bodies disintegrated. And yet though I was still physically I'Eloshir, I could no longer see things as I once had. I found myself wanting to remember, wanting something to cling to, despite the fact that I knew nothing remained for me.

In all the time that I had lived, I had never experienced such a passion for the past. Never had I felt so completely at a loss...

Still...

"Raphael," I whispered, wondering if he could hear me, wherever he was.

I'd been from Raedawn to Magog itself for the Empire and in neither realm had I found him.

I wished desperately I could see his face again. Even in so short of a time, I had begun to forget what he looked like.

I could almost see him, vaguely. I pressed my hand to the white marble, brushing away the dust and drawing with a piece of charcoal on the stone. I finished my drawing, pulled away, and cried.

The face was perfect... as if carved by some ancient sculptor with a chisel, but the eyes were all wrong.

"DAMN YOU POWERS!" I ordered, feeling the air crackle around me like an oncoming storm. "I didn't ask to live this long!"

It was true, wasn't it... and I'd finally admitted that much to myself.

I was on this quest, fighting wars and taking risks because I wanted to die. My life was one of eternal weariness. There was no place for me in the new world.

I pulled the ambrosia from my bag and sniffed it... about to drink, but then, like a condemned alcoholic, I threw it at the pillar, its acid changing the surface a pale blue.

No more... no more wallowing in my own miseries! There were still those alive who depended on me. Though I myself remained unfulfilled, alone and dead to the world around me, so long as I still breathed... I still had a purpose.

I headed back into town. It would be a long night.

"Where have you been?" Mariel screeched, upon my return to the clinic. "Leaving us with the White Cross!"

"You're fine, aren't you?" I replied, ignoring her hysteria. "We have an hour until we meet Phineas at the tavern. I suggest we start on our way."

She snorted at me and minced outside, reading while walking. I turned to follow.

"Wait a minute." GW stopped me. "I got something to ask you, since you're the only one that seems to know anything about what's goin' on here."

"That would be a safe assumption." I was listening.

"Am I ever gonna get home?" he wondered.

I sighed, shaking my head. "I wish I could answer that question."

"Is that how this world got so crazy?" he asked. "A bunch a people tryin' to get home?"

"It is something like that." I admitted. "This place used to be better for a lot of us, but things have been falling apart for the past few years."

"You're tellin' me," GW whistled, looking out over the wreckage of the desert. "I think I can picture it... how it might have been," he admitted. "That white column out there. Looks like something from the Greek temples... but bigger." He paused momentarily and turned back to me.

"What world are you from? Everybody seems to know you, but I guess I just get this feeling that you ain't happy here. You're not like the rest of them. They're fun and loud like a bunch of kids... but you're different. You seem... old. I don't know what's happened, and it's okay if you don't want to tell me, but if you do, I'm listenin' and God's listenin'. You can tell us both and neither of us are gonna judge you."

I stopped short. I was tempted to blurt out my entire story... the entire story. We had a little time, and there was something about GW that I couldn't quite place. I knew if anyone could listen to me, and not judge... he'd promised true.

"I don't expect you to believe me." I lowered my eyes.

GW grabbed my hand and pulled me to face him.

"Honey, I believe you. I believe in a lot of things now that I never believed in before. I have seen some things... Good Lord, these past few days I've seen things I never even imagined! I fell from the sky into a tree, I saw people throw fire at each other and then I get a ride on this big ol' sailing ship that flies in the air... if that ain't impossible, well then, nothing is! Maybe I even believe everything, I don't know. I'm just not going to doubt what God comes up with any more, cause as I see it, he's sure a whole lot more creative than I ever thought he was."

He shook his head heavily. "I believe you no matter what you say. I wouldn't have asked you to tell me if I wasn't gonna believe you."

"It's a long story...," I warned.

"I'm a good listener." He nodded.

I sighed and began. "I don't think you realize what you're getting into. I may not look it, but I am... I suppose, somewhere around eight hundred years old."

"That's old," he sighed.

"It is." I nodded.

"How did you live so long?" GW asked.

"I don't know. But I can't seem to die. I tried to kill myself. I did things no human, no mortal being could survive... I fell off a two-hundred foot cliff onto a rock and walked away uninjured. I've been hit with a battleaxe that didn't even break my skin. The place I came from... it's difficult to describe. There's very little light there, and almost no water. Everything is dead from a terrible weapon that was activated centuries ago. Sometimes it's unbearably hot, and sometimes is freezes so cold..." I shook my head.

"I wish I knew what you're talking about," GW sighed. "It sounds... awful."

"You do," I explained. "War happens everywhere. You know what a bomb is, I presume?"

He nodded.

"They made one with magic," I explained. "It tore a world in half. This

321

world we are on is in all actuality… completely flat. The other half of the original world drifts further away all the time. Like the two sides of a moon, they are complete opposites. This side almost always faces the sun, that side rarely sees it."

"That's awful." He shook his head.

"That was only the beginning. After Raedawn was destroyed, what survived was changed… and we began to rule. My people are known as the I'Eloshir." I went on. "You would call me a demon, I suppose. I sometimes look as you see me now, but when I'm injured or … thinking dark thoughts, my exterior changes. I travel to different dimensions through mirrors and Tears. I can summon storms… but not control them. I can create fire with a thought and run so fast that people can barely see me move. I can lift a small car and order others to do things that they have to obey."

GW seemed more than a little frightened.

"But I'm not evil," I promised. "I did terrible things for hundreds of years… and then I changed. I didn't want to be what I was anymore."

"You… saw the light?" GW wondered.

"I guess you could call it that," I admitted. "But this… it isn't really about me. I'm just another piece in this puzzle. A few years ago, there was a war on this world. A good Emperor was killed by the warriors of Magog… the world I came from, and armies from another realm. The people in charge now call themselves the Interdimensional Republic. As evil as the I'Eloshir are, they come and go… killers, perhaps, but quick killers… not parasites.

"The Republic is even more corrupt. They burn cities and massacre thousands like the I'Eloshir, but they also destroy the land and do terrible mind experiments on human beings, throwing them into Tears to fight against the monsters that the IR cannot control. All they want is power… they don't care how dark it is, or what it costs. I know this because…" I choked on the words, but finished despite myself.

"Because they wanted me to join them. Not the me you see now, but my other side. In the days before I became Artemis Ravencroft… I was known as Ireval."

"Why do I think I know that name?" GW muttered.

"The Fargrove's books," I explained. "I am… I was the villain. Terrible as the story is, every last word is true. I believe he says in a chapter, that "The darkest, basest, most foul beasts of hell fled to their masters at the sound of her name." I paused, wondering what else I might say.

"I deserve every last word of it," I admitted. "Even if the tale were his fantasy, he could not have made it more awful than the truth of what I have done. Sometimes people use my name as a curse word now. I'm a story that frightens bad children. Not many know this," I warned.

"Phineas is the only person still alive who has heard my whole tale... the real truth behind what I have only begun to tell you. Bruno Fargrove knows most of it, but other than the Gods and I'Eloshir... it's just the two of them, and now you. Three."

I muttered to myself on the significance of the numbers and waited for GW's reaction.

He was silent for a long while... and then at last he picked up what he'd been clutching in his hand. It was one of the few things he'd salvaged from his car and his mauled wallet. A picture. A picture of two children and a woman in front of a church... his wife, his family.

"You got all that power and you're not even sure you can get me home?"

"I'll try," I promised. "If I could identify exactly where you're from, I would take you now, but searching..." I shook my head heavily. "There are too many worlds and I cannot waste so much time, especially not now. Maybe you should be asking your God. He knows more than I."

"I will." GW was resigned now. "I'm gonna ask him every day. But until he delivers me... I don't know enough about this crazy place to run off on my own. I know whatever you and your friends are doing has got to be dangerous, but you're my next best chance out of here, and I'm not afraid of much."

I didn't respond right away.

A stranger from another world, a stranger who was everything I never was... in all my years, was the person I least expected to understand me.

"Well I suppose we ought to get going." I muttered, picking up what was left of my things. GW closed his wallet and followed me out.

Fifty-One

We entered Lady Mercy's… and GW hadn't still said a word. I couldn't blame him. Phineas had nearly suffered a heart attack, and Raphael had paled considerably when I was through, admitting that the whole of my history was somewhat disturbing.

Yet suddenly, I had a new respect for the preacher. He had a purpose in this quest too, although Inapsupetra hadn't been kind enough to reveal it to me… I would learn for myself soon enough.

At the tavern we regrouped. I told Phineas what had happened at the train-station and Cal and Ruveus announced the bouts.

"Igor, we've got you against a mage," Cal explained. "He's well-loved around Border-Town, but he'd never make it in the door at a place like Salt City."

"You worried bout' that pal?" Ruveus asked. "It's okay to admit it, Igor… your "day" was about five-hundred years ago. Are you sure you can handle a real fight?"

Igor shrugged. "Ich weiss nicht," he admitted.

"Then there's Gloria," Cal continued. "She's pitted against another human, he's a big bastard… a drop-out Tear Soldier they say. I saw him working out at the gym, he's about six-four or so. Weapon of choice is broadsword, and from the slow way he talks, I'm guessing he's a little bit of a berserker."

"Piece of cake," Gloria sighed, sounding almost disappointed.

"Make it last as long as you can, babe," Ruveus advised. "We won't have much time."

"Why not?" Mariel wondered.

"Because Ms. Mariel…," Ruveus muttered. "The rest of you here wouldn't last ten minutes… except maybe Artemis, and "They" won't let me fight."

"They won't?" I frowned. "Why is that?"

"Because I used to be a slave," he muttered. "Some new law about that now. They won't have anyone who was ever "bound" by magic fight in the ring."

"That's ridiculous," GW interjected, though I doubted he knew what we were discussing. "What kind of place is this that still has slaves?"

"It isn't exactly an acceptable practice," I explained. "You saw the dragon in the bar."

GW nodded.

"That was me," Ruveus announced, rather bluntly. "Something the wrong, brother?"

"I thought you said you were a slave," GW admitted. "And I just don't see how anyone could hold you against your will if you're so big and powerful."

"That's where the whole "bound by magic" part comes into play. A minor wizard couldn't hope to control a dragon, but a powerful mage or a Traverser could," Phineas explained.

I immediately bristled, until I realized the remark hadn't been directed at me.

"That was more or less what happened," Ruveus explained. "I was really out of it at the time… and there was this woman, she's called Beyoni… well, anyway, she's a real, you-know-what. She bound me with a tough spell and locked me up in a little box, occasionally having me sing or dance for her guests. Then I busted out with Artemis."

No one said much after that. The realization had hit us, at any rate.

We had less time now than before, since Ruveus wouldn't be fighting, and we were about to match wits with Orin Saede himself… an I'Eloshir practically worshipped for his craftiness. And if a mad sorceress could bind a dragon prince, a God of Magog could certainly destroy a party comprised for the most part of nearly powerless humans.

Darkness fell… and not the shadowy darkness of near-night but the true blackness of the moon-hours. The time when strange things began to happen.

Finishing our meager supper, we headed down into the sewers. I remembered the place, the scent, the shadows. This was where I'd made my debut, so long ago now.

The loudspeaker roared to life, announcing the night's matches and catching GW and Cal off guard.

"Tonight… The Original Dark and Deadly, Pit-Lord Lacchus Aroth, welcomes Pel Lugana and his associates to Shadow Alley! Shadow Alley also welcomes special guest fighters Levru Odo and Mark Jefferson from the Salt City Major League! Ladies, gents, Tear-Runners and blood-lovers extraordinaire, have we got a show for you! First match of the night, Heathcliff the Badger, pack leader of the Southwharf True Etone… straight outta Hellsgate with fourteen years experience against the Shadow's own number-one card wielder, Majicka Frash!"

The music started. I pushed aside a grate above my head and Cal entered a quick security code.

The wall slid open and we entered the pit itself, splitting off in different directions. Phineas lead Igor down the stairs, acting as the gargoyle's manager and Brin followed, playing a very convincing hooker. She looped a towel around Igor's neck and winked in my direction.

Ruveus and Cal disappeared, presumably to cut off the alarms and possibly the electricity as well.

Gloria and Edgar shot me a cold look before heading to place their bets… and I was left alone once again with GW and Mariel.

It wasn't that I really minded GW, I would say that I even somewhat enjoyed his company, but any magic-user submitted to a long exposure of Mariel the Non-Believer tended to get a little edgy.

I tracked down a bookie and passed him twenty Phoenicians on Gloria.

I would have given him the rest of my savings, as the fight was a sure thing, but I didn't want him to think I was too certain.

I found a seat ringside and watched the cards fly, while Mariel, scowling and muttering, went to go get a drink.

GW didn't move. His eyes drifted between the fight and the first aid station where a cleric and a doctor were busy reattaching a Roman gladiator's arm.

"How do they do that?" He pointed. "They're just putting him back together piece by piece. How's that possible?"

I shrugged. "Magic. Advanced technology. A little bit of both. An arm's nothing. Wait until someone gets half of their face sewn together."

"Could they help someone who was … born without?" GW wondered.

"I imagine so," I shrugged, looking back to the pit.

"Next round!" the loudspeakers roared, as Heathcliff and Majicka staggered out of the ring.

It had been a draw, which was disappointing, but not unusual. They'd both run out of cards.

"Nuk Halmut, standing at six foot six and straight from the famous

Hellsgate Tear-War… vs. Ardra's Best-Loved Outlaw, The Baroness Gloria Etharaaal!"

"Impossible!" a voice gasped, and I felt … I guessed that someone had spit ale on the back of my neck. But I recognized that accent. Hidden behind the common tongue, was a hint of a language I knew well, one that wasn't spoken in any sunlit realm.

It had to be Orin. He was somewhere behind me… close.

I kept my head down. I didn't dare disguise myself now, knowing it was too late for that, but I didn't dare let him recognize me either.

Gloria and Igor could very likely have made a return to pit-fighting on their own.

Let him think that, I prayed, tapping nervously.

Hopefully, it would all go as planned.

The fight ended quickly, Gloria sauntering out without a scratch, leaving the Tear Soldier lying unconscious on the floor looking like a very large, very bald child in armor.

"Mercy for Halmut," the announcer called, and the crowd booed. Gloria bit her thumb and shot the front row an obscene gesture. The Etone gathered around the bettor's table applauded and laughed.

"Fight Three!"

Three.

I shuddered involuntarily and pushed closer to the rail.

"Igor Gunther, Salt City's legendary Wall-of-Stone versus Shadow Alley's hardcore Etone… Dadwero the Jackal!"

The gates creaked open and Igor stepped out, still looking strong and arrogant despite his age and chronic cough.

The crowd booed and hissed, but somewhere behind me I heard a faint applause.

"I recognize that one," Orin laughed softly, whispering to the woman next to him. "Saw him fight not so long ago. He's a little old for the business now, but you see some of these men, they fall in love with the pits... Five years pass, then fifty... it doesn't matter. They always return for just one more... last great battle."

The sirens blared and the fight began.

Igor usually fought with his claws and strength alone, but evidently he'd felt the need for extra security. A little bit of enchanted chain-mail and something in a belt pouch that I assumed one of the Southwharf Etone had given him, completed his ensemble.

He couldn't afford to get hit, even with half of a good spell. His magic wasn't what it used to be, I realized, biting my lip, and suddenly understanding why he had wanted me to fight.

Igor's claws clashed with Dadwero's spelled steel, the energy pushing them both back across the floor, though neither budged. Struck squarely in the chest by a burst of flame, Igor leapt into the sky and fired a handful of thin, razor-edged disks.

The mage wasn't fast enough to block so many sharp projectiles at once, and one imbedded itself in his shoulder.

Dadwero screamed like a wounded wildcat… and I was suddenly very afraid. I recognized his gestures, and I knew what kind of spell he was casting!

"Run, Igor, run!" I yelled.

It was useless. He couldn't hear me. Frantically I searched the crowd around me, looking for something, anything I could throw into the ring. GW was drinking a can of soda.

Out of options, I stole the drink and hurled it with all the force I had, the thin metal crackling with energy. The flaming mess of boiling soda and energy-charged can, struck the mage squarely in the back of the head, leaving a quite visible dent. Dadwero fell to the ground with a heavy thump. Only the faint rise and fall of his back revealed that he still lived at all.

"Interference," the referee announced from his place near the ceiling. The crowd booed... and then fell silent as the cameras zeroed in on me.

"Artemis?" Igor stared in disbelief, picking up the still-smoking soda can. "Es ist a... a Pepsi?"

An all too familiar hand reached around the back of my neck, sharp claws digging into my skin. It was Orin. He turned me to face him.

"Yes, 'Artemis'," Orin hissed. "Since when has your chosen weapon been a beverage can… and what, pray tell, are you doing here?"

"Nothing that concerns you, Orin," I shot back, pulling away. "I'm here to watch the fight."

In another instant, our voices were projected throughout the arena to match with the scene that was playing itself out on the video screens.

"That I sincerely doubt." Orin scowled, knowing he couldn't force the information from me as my father could. "You are a warlord, not a spectator."

A warlord, not just a mere warrior? I wanted to ask him, though I held my tongue. Wasn't I merely a worthless traitor, destined to be exiled? After all this time, why would any of the I'Eloshir address me with respect? Where was their contempt, the contempt I knew that I so richly deserved?

"How should you know… ass," I replied, avoiding his eyes.

"We ought to have a fight, us I'Eloshir. The show would be quite profitable. I'll split the winnings with you… if we fight to a draw." He laughed.

"Challenge, challenge!" the spectators chanted in unison, obviously intrigued with the idea.

"Shut that recorder off!" Orin ordered and the screen went dark. The crowd sighed in disappointment now that no one could hear our conversation.

"I won't take you up on that." I turned away. Though I desperately wanted to kill him, I knew I had to get more out of it than a little money and simple satisfaction.

"For a wager then, won't you?" Orin asked, switching into our language. "Eh, Ire'?"

"A wager of what?" I glared. "I already possess everything there is to be had, except this pit… and the mark of a God and you know I don't want either," I muttered. The words were like acid as I spoke them.

"What about the Archives of Teyme?" he pressed.

"As if you have the book," I sighed and shook my head.

"Oh, I do," he grinned, "or perhaps I don't. Can you afford to doubt me?"

I hated him all the more, knowing he was right.

"I accept your challenge." I lowered my eyes, avoiding his already triumphant smile. My face appeared on the video screen and the words echoed throughout the pit. If my instinct was right, this fight would bring me the closest I had been to returning to darkness since my escape from Antares.

"Go get ready," Orin hissed, whispering something to his aid. "We're next."

I turned down the hall and headed for the sewers to prepare away from prying eyes. On my way, I ran into Brin at the bar. I pulled her aside.

"Listen to me," I ordered. "Find the book. It's somewhere close, I know it is… It doesn't matter who sees what anymore. Orin knows we're here."

She said nothing, or at least nothing I heard, because as she opened her mouth to speak, I smashed the mirror I held in my hand and was gone.

Racing across a short amount space to my room on The Spellcraft Hathor, I shattered the mirror above my dresser, and began searching for my armor. Dei had explained to me how he baited Ether-Raptors while jumping between realms, and I had practiced the technique endlessly until I had succeeded in capturing a second symbiote for myself. The snake-like creature was sleeping inside an orange juice pitcher, which spilled over the edge of the table. Apparently, in addition to spells, they also had a certain love for most citrus.

With no small struggle, I coaxed the beast close enough to snap it around my neck.

Scaled armor, stronger than the hide of a dragon and faintly warm, raced down my arms and legs and up across the sides of my face and the back of my head.

I looked in the mirror, donning my Imperial colors.

If it was a show Orin wanted, it was a show he was going to get. I gathered my things and jumped, making a royal mess of my glass-filled bedroom.

Breaking through to the other side, I found myself in Shadow Alley's "stables."

It was then that I realized that the two of us were about to start something considerably messier than a mild fencing match.

I paced up and down the aisles, evaluating the beasts, drakes, horses... things I didn't know the names of, and wincing as I tried to remember the last time I'd actually fought on horseback.

It was the mark of the I'Eloshir, one of the things that had made me unique and legendary amongst my peers. I could ride, of course, but I could also fly with more coordination than most. When closed in upon, I would wield my sword, and at a distance my magic. I had combined each and every skill I possessed into a terrible dance of death, sword, claws, fire and teeth. Orin had studied my techniques well. To defeat him... I would have to fight as I once had... as if the very act of killing, the thing that I now abhorred... was unquestionably beautiful to me.

A tall black stallion stamped angrily in his stall, and I paused, for a moment almost believing that he was Erudite, Panther's winged horse that I'd ridden in the Battle of the Frozen Sea.

It was impossible... and yet.

I brushed aside his mane and gaped, half in awe, half in horror, at the quicksilver Imperial brand. His wings were clipped to make him controllable, but there was no doubt about it. This was my horse.

"What have they done to you?" I shook my head.

Eru snorted. Horse wisdom. What is... is.

I took him out, brushed him and saddled up. It did not matter that he could not fly. Whether I wanted to admit it or not, I had my own wings to contend with.

Remember what the I'Eloshir do. I thought quietly to myself. They kill, ride and hunt. Hunt... ride and start wars for no reason. Do not... lose control.

"You are better than that," I reminded myself, though it hardly felt convincing.

Was I really? Was simply recognizing a sin enough to atone for centuries of horrific crimes? Were my efforts even worthwhile at all? Regardless of how many lives I saved, I could not turn back time... not yet. But soon. Soon I would be able to erase it all, to end everything.

With a slow, even walk, I entered the ring on horseback, carrying my staff and a whip.

Opposite to me, the loudspeakers screeched to life as Orin showed himself riding in on the back of a dark bay, and dressed in red and gold silk robes. He unrolled a scarlet flag marked with a triple moon and donned a skull mask, arrogantly showing off his "god" status.

I took a deep breath, willing up as much energy as I dared and cracked my whip in the air. The alarm sounded... and we charged full tilt.

Fifty-Two

I caught Orin's lance in my blade and snapped it, unseating him on the first pass by bashing my elbow into his face. He fell.

"You call yourself I'Eloshir!" I snarled, unimpressed. "You ride like a mortal!"

"Mortal, am I?" Orin quickly rose to his feet... shedding his human form, and then off the floor altogether, firing bursts of ice. The energy struck the ground and Orin drew a gun, firing at the sky.

My horse reared and I dismounted, covering my head and rolling through the searing remnants of his Orin's spells.

The bullets had missed, thankfully. Even my symbiote would have been useless against those.

I looked at where the gunshots had struck the wall and smiled at what they revealed.

I cracked my whip, snapping the lever in the far corner. The walls shot upwards into the fly gallery over the pit. Mirrors. The surface underneath the wood façade was a room of mirrors.

Now the audience would get what they paid for.

I jumped through the mirror nearest me and then out again behind Orin, before he had a chance to recover and follow, catching him around the legs and stealing his sword.

He pulled a second scimitar from his back and our blades met in a shower of sparks. The power was exhilarating.

I was keeping up with him, blow for blow, pace for pace, and there were those who called him a god. I jumped again, and Orin followed, a mere fraction of a step behind.

It was enough.

As he soared into the physical realm, I faced the shower of glass and jabbed him in the chest with the pommel of his own sword. His claws tore across my back, reopening old scars, and I swept him onto the floor, striking him in the shins.

My sword pointed at his throat, I tasted his blood on my own lip and lost control all in that one instant.

Every bone in my body screamed in agony as I shed my human form. The wings brought a gasp of awe from the crowd, but to me, they were only a whole new hurt.

I tasted his blood again, cutting into his face with my claw. If nothing else... he would have a new scar to remember me by.

"Tastes human," I smirked, speaking in our language.

"I am not... human," he spat.

"Well, if you are certain you are not, then you must be I'Eloshir. Are you really a god?" I glared at Orin, raising an eyebrow and grinning slightly.

"I am," he stared back, still arrogant, though he must have known by then that he was helpless against me.

"If you are a god, you can do anything, is that true?" I pressed.

"Anything," Orin smirked.

I kicked him hard in the ribs and the egotistical grin vanished from his face.

"Can you die?" I pulled him up to face me, eye to eye... lifting him a few feet off the ground.

He did not respond.

"Five... four... three..." The announcer counted.

The fight was over. I wanted not simply to kill Orin, for some sick, perverse reason... but I wanted to steal his soul as well.

I knew if our roles were reversed he would have relished taking mine.

It didn't matter that he was immortal. I held in my hands his weapon... a God's sword, not my own.

An ancient black-blade of Magog, forged in the fires of...

"Inapsupetra," Orin whispered, his gaze drifting skyward.

It was final. He dared call on my goddess to defend his worthless body!

I threw him to the ground and brought the sword down in one fluid motion. My arm scarcely felt the shock as my blade cut off his head. In an explosion of silver light, Orin was no more. The crowd was silent in their reverence for the fallen I'Eloshir... terrified by what they had just witnessed, but I knew better than to simply hold my breath. A god's death never goes unnoticed.

I stepped back. There was a presence I felt... and it wasn't Orin Saede.

"DAUGHTER!" a voice ordered, pounding within my mind. "I HAVE COME!"

It was not my own conscious... it was the thing... the thing I'd been worried about all along.

I fought back. "LEAVE ME ALONE!"

Those nearest the ring in the crowd staggered, and I realized I'd screamed aloud, releasing the power of the order. Many of the gathered fled for the exits, taking the command quite literally.

A fanfare of trumpets rose from somewhere below and a dark entourage, a full company of Warriors materialized through the walls. Mirrors reflected a gray, grim battlefield not far from Tirs Uloth and before me stood thousands upon thousands of demons on horseback, every mirror reeking of death and destruction. And then, in the lead, a symbol that anyone who had fought in the past wars would recognize immediately.

A lone, dark figure in red armor, overshadowed only by his own immense wings. A creature whose eyes were burning pits to the onlooker, whose every movement was like a wave of fear, and whose cold, ancient voice could even wake the dead and draw them to arms against one another.

Geruth the Warlord... my father.

His grim form in itself would have been enough to break me on a weaker day, yet at that time I sensed he had somehow become more than I remembered. I recognized his stench, but not his power. The aura that radiated from his dark form was more than his own evil, it was the terrible magic of The Grandmother, the blessing of the Dark Gods.

With the Warlord rode the essence of death itself, all to defend the spawn of pestilence that I had destroyed.

"You cannot touch me!" I screamed over the crowd, already knowing why the demons had come. "I WILL NEVER AGAIN RIDE WITH YOU!"

Lightning struck overhead... outside. The oncoming storm far above ground shook even the walls of the pit and I fell to my knees, letting the rumbling, like the beat of drums and horses' hooves... overwhelm my body.

The Chaos Realm was dying, and we could not prevent it. We had begun the war that was brewing, as we had begun every conflict in the history of a thousand worlds... but we could not control it.

It was time for us... the children of Inapsupetra... time for us to leave.

But I would not give in. The Empire, this realm... it had shown me something no other world had.

I was not damned to roam forever in the shadows of Magog, manipulating minds and collecting souls simply to feel alive.

I had... Free Will.

I faced my father in defiance and almost died as my body was slammed by his phenomenal fist, crushing the bricks of the wall behind me.

Still, I forced myself to hold onto that crumpled mess of pain.

The world swirled and faded around me for a moment and then I lost consciousness, still cursing myself.

Why take Orin's challenge? Teyme's Archives were irrelevant.

Why not leave this world... leave before it dies?

Why not ride... ride and forget about everything?

Why linger in the stench and ruin of the civilization of man... when you could be an immortal?

I was vaguely aware of being moved, carried to a room. Though far from awake, I recognized the smell of the liquor that was being offered to me.

Ambrosia.

It was not what I wanted. As terrible as it had seemed to me in Elmwood, I wanted to go back to pretending I was human.

Miranda Fargrove wasn't such a bad name. I could move in with Bruno and become an instant celebrity. There were other stories I could tell him, things I had left out of my own memoirs, secrets so old and so powerful that they would shake the world.

I could tell him everything that "The History of the Realm" hadn't known about the legendary Demon Queen.

I could live well without those darker magics, I thought to myself, imagining a realm where I would see no more deaths, and suffer through no more wars.

I wished I had never revealed myself at all.

Ah, the lures of artificial mortality.

I drifted back to consciousness and found myself in an apartment, lying on a brown patterned couch, staring at a fuzzy black and white television, while strange little robots with arms and eyes missing... washed towels in the kitchen sink.

Brin, GW and Gloria all hovering over me like a pack of vultures.

"I'm awake!" I sat up almost too quickly and hit my head on the ceiling.

"Ow," I muttered, and then realized what I had done. The ceiling was only a few feet high. Brin, GW and Gloria were all on their knees.

It was they called in Zenith a half-apartment, designed specifically for occupants under five-feet, dwarves, gnomes... or gargoyles. Igor entered suddenly, his arms full of brown paper groceries.

"Igor, your place is a pit," I reminded him, recognizing the room.

"Ja, ja… Ich weiss," Igor sighed, passing Brin a cardboard tray which balanced a few paper cups of steaming coffee.

One of the housekeeper droids sputtered and Igor gave it a swift kick.

"It looks like you're writing a letter. Have a nice day," The robot chirped. "You've got mail."

I sipped the ambrosia that Gloria had left on the table and leaned back slowly, trying to avoid blacking out.

"It's been nine years since he lived here," Brin pointed out. "Thankfully, with a landlady like Ruthless Bearkiller, no one ever wanted to move in."

I smiled at the thought of the near insane barbarian-woman swinging her deadly broom at tax-collectors and firing rounds of ammo at the solicitors who came to the door and the bums who'd been dumb enough to loiter on her fire escape.

A few doses of jellybeans disguised as a thank-you gift had straightened her out as far as the rest of us were concerned… and of course, there was always the threat that we might reveal to the world the whereabouts of her "dead" brother who worked at a nightclub in downtown Zenith where he went by the name of "Shirley".

"Where's Phineas?" I asked.

Gloria shrugged. "Said he went to refuel The Hathor. Could be awhile."

"Alone?" I wondered.

Brin nodded. "Wouldn't take anyone with him."

It wasn't surprising. Phineas had always been a stubborn one.

Still, he was one of my dearest friends. I had met Phineas when he was young… only thirteen. Watched him grow up, age… and someday, I would see him die. Despite what I knew could not be helped… I couldn't stand the thought of losing anyone else as I had lost Raphael.

"What is the plan?" I asked.

"Concerning the Archives?" Brin shrugged, turning to Edgar, who was on the phone.

He mouthed a slight "I don't know" and resumed dialing.

I scowled at him, finding his preoccupation somewhat strange. Who did he know that wasn't in the room… and why would he bother to call them under the current circumstances?

I wasn't sure I liked him, or trusted him for that matter. Still, he and Gloria were close enough, despite their differences and I was sure that she would keep her eyes on him.

"I was thinking we should probably head down to Orin's apartments anyway," Cal announced. "I didn't draw Shadow Alley but I did create Salt City, and there are a lot of similarities between the two."

"Plenty of places to hide bodies, you mean," Brin sighed.

"I was going to say books," Cal admitted.

"I agree," I announced, sliding off the couch and onto the floor so that I could sit up straight.

Everyone stared.

"But Artemis, I thought…" Edgar began.

"I'm well enough." I glared at him. "And we'd best search the pit while there's still daylight on the surface. Once the suns set, we'll be in danger again. How many hours have I been out?"

"Seven," Cal counted.

"Not enough after what just happened… and not enough for the rest of us to get any sleep," Edgar mumbled.

"I require around three or four hours per night," I reminded him. "Seven hours to me is the equivalent of you sleeping two days straight."

"I'm not tired." Cal grinned.

"Well I am!" GW sighed. "And besides, I don't even know what I'm s'posed to be helpin' you people find. I figured I'd stick around here and help Mister Gunther with the spring cleaning, y'know."

"A reasonable request." I nodded. "Someone ought to be here until Phineas gets back anyway."

"I'll stay too," Edgar added. "I'm having lunch with a friend."

"Xane?" Gloria grinned. Sir Tradewind was known to frequent the south quarter of Zenith. From there, Border-Town was hardly ten miles.

"That's him." Edgar nodded.

"In which case, I ought to come along with you," Gloria explained. "He used to be in love with me," she admitted, as if it should be obvious. "I might be able to convince him to help us."

"I shall go with Artemis," Mariel replied stiffly. Cal and Brin each shot me an expression of pain.

"Four is a better number than three for a search party," I admitted. "Gather up your weapons… and be prepared to kill some rats."

"Feeling a little metaphorical, are we?" Cal asked. "You mean rodents… or demons?"

I looked out the window. From the top floor of the building, I could almost see in the distance… a faint flicker of gray. That direction was Zenith. Further north, Accoloth. West… Port Hope and Istara. Below us, however, lay centuries of unfinished business.

"Take your pick, Cal." I shook my head heavily. "There's plenty of both."

The Prince of Thieves

"Count your gold, your fingers, and your relatives."

Fifty-Three

We opened the doors to the pit and stepped inside after not seeing a soul the entire way down through the sewers. After Orin's death and Geruth's unscheduled appearance, I figured that most people with any sense would be avoiding Shadow Alley like a plague.

But no sooner had we entered the room than the gate slammed shut behind us and the lights went out.

"Trap," Brin commented.

"Thanks Brin," Cal muttered.

"It's dark," Brin continued. "Really dark."

I went for my flashlight. It was not the best illumination, but it was a good deal more reliable than magic when it came to places rigged with traps and most likely Duricide gas.

"Homey, isn't it." Cal blinked owlishly in the sudden light.

Somehow the four of us were inside a perfectly spherical room. A few lopsided bunks hung on the walls and the floor was three inches deep in sewage.

"How did we get here?" Mariel wondered. "And where did the door go?"

"Magic!" Cal and Brin shouted at the same time.

Mariel fell silent.

"This place is a dump." Brin shook her head.

"It looked better once," a voice sighed heavily. His left arm hanging limply at his side and a black ring around his right eye, Panther stepped out of the shadows.

"Panther?" I stared in shock, though with Geruth's return I was not surprised that he had been beaten senseless. Aside from tormenting me, my father's favorite pastime seemed to be abusing his younger brother. "What are you doing here?"

S.E. BELLIAN

"Sleeping," he admitted.

"But...," I began.

"You've walked into a trap, Ire'," he replied, speaking in our tongue, as if what he had to say concerned only the two of us. "It's the same one I walked into four months ago."

"I know that language!" Brin screeched in terror. "It's the demon's speech! Artemis, we've got to get out of here... he's a demon!"

I did not turn to face her.

"Four months?" I demanded, ignoring the pain I knew was reflected in Brin's eyes... as I too spoke the tongue of the I'Eloshir. "And you, of all people... you didn't break out?"

"I did." He didn't look at me as he spoke.

"So why are you here now?" I asked, and immediately regretted speaking. Something was wrong, and terribly so.

"It cost me." Panther shook his head. "I'll set your friends loose... he doesn't want them. I'm sorry."

"Elhil!" I demanded. "Tell me, now! What?"

Panther rolled his shoulders, assuming his demonic form, the one he so seldom wore. "Ire', I'm turning you in."

Brin wailed in terror, collapsing to the ground. Manacles snapped around my arms and legs and my neck, glowing white-hot with cleric's fire... and I shifted, despite myself. It was not as painful as the transformation had been the previous night, but with Brin so close... her expression agonized me, and there was nothing I could do.

How could I possibly apologize for being what I was?

"Bastard!" I glared, struggling to break free. "I'll get you for this Elhilom!"

Panther remained calm. "That's exactly what he wants."

And then it hit me.

"You did what you had to," I hissed, though I wanted to tear him to pieces. "I will find a way back."

The chains pulled towards the somewhat insubstantial wall, it was then, for what peculiar reason I will never know... it was then that I remembered Dakor's words at the gates of Raedawn.

"You must go back to go forward."

I ceased struggling. It was high time I paid the "gods" a little visit.

The dark hall of Magog was low lit and quiet when I entered as I was still drawn by the chains of Panther's trap. The chains around my arms melted into ash as I touched the ground. Drums rumbling faintly the warm, still-

342

familiar stone slick with blood and oil under my feet. Hopefully the risk I was taking would be worthwhile.

"Well, well," a voice snickered. "Been awhile since YOU fell from grace, hasn't it?" The shadow of a woman materialized... almost living, but not quite.

"Zae," I muttered under my breath.

"Well, Ireval." She evaluated me with the same critical eye. "Tired of our pet humans, are we? Tired of playing mortal?"

"Leave me alone," I shot back. It sounded shallow.

"If you're looking for Geruth he's not here." Zaethe grinned.

"Don't you dare read MY thoughts!" I spun around to face her. "You KNOW that YOU are no match for me!"

"Maybe I wasn't," Zaethe whispered. "But I'm dead now, and being dead has certain advantages... believe it, Cousin." She paused, as if she were afraid to say too much. "Besides," she continued. "I've been training all this time while you've been gallivanting around the Chaos Realm pretending to be some sort of mortal heroine."

"I never claimed to be a hero," I countered. "And I am mortal."

"A mere fraction. Half-mortal," Zaethe sneered.

"The better half," I sighed and turned to walk down the corridor and out of the darkness. Talking to Zaethe any longer was pointless.

Her shade bobbed along beside me, grinning like a Cheshire cat.

"Where are you going?" she asked, though she knew perfectly well.

I didn't reply. Without so much as turning to look her ghost in the eye, I shocked the projection with a small bit of half-concentrated energy, shattering it to bits.

Zaethe returned, melting out of thin air in front of me.

"That wasn't very nice." She frowned. "Destroying someone when they're trying to have a polite conversation with you."

"I tire of your games... now LET ME PASS!" I ordered. I guessed that it surprised her... a little.

"I don't have to listen to you anymore," she snickered, sticking her tongue out like the child she was. "I still have my title and you gave up your title when you became High Commander of the Traversers."

"You are dead," I replied, walking directly through her.

In the distance, I could see light, but I knew that my trial was far from over.

Orin was the next to appear, and he picked up right where Zaethe had vanished.

"Was it worth it?" he demanded.

"It was worth it." That I could say honestly.

"But Raphael is dead now and it's your fault." Orin smiled.

I felt suddenly cold… clenching my teeth and closing my eyes. "I lost a battle," I argued, knowing he had struck me where the pain was greatest. How dare he make such an accusation?

"You lost a war." The Grandmother materialized beside him. "A war that ended an Empire."

"The dynasty lost the war," I whispered, wondering if I even believed it myself. "It was not all my doing."

I could feel her slimy psychic fingers prying in my mind.

"The Falchon-girl knows what you are," The Grandmother whispered. "But she's too smart to say anything. And the Emperor knew, but he's dead. And Elhilom knew… but he's ours again. And your pet human knows… only he'll die soon anyway. Old age. Who will you talk to when there's not a single soul that still knows your name? Do you want to be alone in the mortal world for eternity? What are you going to do, Ireval?"

"DO NOT CALL ME THAT!" I was in a high rage.

"Know why the Traversers lost the Battle of the Frozen Sea?" Zaethe continued. "Know why the dynasty came to an end? Know why the Archives of Teyme are going to destroy everything?" She paused, and then grinned maliciously. "Not because no one can do anything… but because someone won't do anything. If you'd never run from your duty we never would have had to destroy the Chaos Realm at all."

"That is a lie," I replied coldly. "And you know it."

"You won't, Daughter of Geruth." The Grandmother stared at me. "You flee because you deny what you are… because you don't want to be a …"

"ENOUGH!" I cut her off before she could speak another hateful word. Yet knowing full well what body I wore, I made no attempts to conceal the inadequacy I felt. Twice I had lost control, in a mere two days.

The Grandmother was right. I was not strong enough to stand alone for all eternity. It had only been a mere decade since Raphael's death and already, the cold pangs of loneliness were tearing me apart.

I loved my friends dearly, but I needed… something, something more.

The Grandmother reached out, clucking softly and patted my shoulder, running her hands through my hair as she had… so long ago.

"Let me braid it for you," she whispered. "I will give you something gold to put in it."

I shook my head heavily, nearly giving in... anything simply to stay, to step out of time... back to a world where I was not a strange and impossible beast, older than civilization itself... but merely myself, as real as the cold stone that surrounded me.

Where I could be, neither hero nor monster... but merely a woman.

A strange burning raced across my arm where the Grandmother's ancient claws had touched my skin. I tore off the sleeve of my shirt, staring in horror as the black tattoos on my arm pulsed supernaturally, and a third dark crescent of blood formed... a third moon on my shoulder.

The mark of a god.

"No!" I snarled, tearing at my own flesh with my claws. The mark would not go away, I realized, but a simple tattoo meant nothing to me. It was the symbolism behind it that I hated.

"I will not take part in your game!" I snarled. "However long we may live, we have no right to name ourselves immortals! We did not create the world! We... we don't even understand it! A newborn human child knows more about the greater truth than any of us!"

I paused. "The three of you." I shook my head. "You should all be dead, but yet you remain! Why? Because you are cowards! You dare not see what lies beyond your current state... because you fear... you fear that I am right! You fear that maybe... you will find that none of us, not even Geruth himself are really gods at all!"

I knew I had uncovered a great secret then, for the Grandmother looked at me with the same pure hatred... the face I had seen only once before, on the day she had murdered Ardain.

"Traverser!" The Grandmother howled. "Wretched, wretched! They've gotten to you, haven't they? Poor Ireval, you have lost your very mind! Become what they wanted you to be, have you? A Traverser! Bastard of Raedawn! Wretched, wretched mage, cursed, despicable Traverser!"

"SILENCE!" Orin ordered. "It is not our place to interfere further."

The Grandmother closed her eyes and collapsed to the ground... tears in her eyes that struck me as strangely foreign. For a moment, I even felt... guilty, I supposed... for hurting her so deeply.

"You must leave now." Zaethe's hideous laughter fell silent. I had proven, to them and to myself, that they no longer owned me.

It would be far more difficult from that point forward. Now, the I'Eloshir would not merely be tempting me to return to them, they would be focusing every last resource on destroying me… and my legacy completely.

And if that meant three worlds had to be thrown into oblivion, that was what it meant.

"Gods save everyone," I whispered, pulling a mirror from my belt.

The ghosts faded into nothingness and I jumped.

Fifty-Four

Brin was nearby... I could hear her sobbing. I didn't know what sort of ordeal she had been through, but I could imagine that it wasn't something she wanted to relive. Cal looked equally ill, but our goals, as well as Panther's promise had been accomplished. We all sat, physically free from harm... on the floor of the pit.

How much blood had been spilt in that black sand? I wondered, picking up a handful of rocks.

Phineas appeared then, flanked by Gloria, her "spirit guide" and Ruveus.

"You're here." I was relieved, though I didn't know exactly why. "But where's Mariel? And GW?"

"Panther sent the Reverend home," Phineas explained. "Mariel went with him. Adventuring isn't exactly her strong suit anymore."

"I understand," I admitted, though it saddened me to hear that they had already gone.

"We've got to go, Artemis," he said. "The book's in Zenith."

Gloria shook her head heavily. "I met with Xane today, and just about twenty minutes ago he called me back. A few Chaos Knights broke into the headquarters last night and they say the IR have the Archives locked up in there, on the twenty-second floor below ground." She paused. "Six people died."

None of us spoke, at least not right away. I knew well enough why the IR wanted the book, and I could guess where they had gotten it from. But the only thing I could not understand was how the Archives of Teyme had remained in the grasp of a meager group of humans when there were several highly powerful Immortals very much interested in it.

Returning to the streets above, we headed for my ship. The Spellcraft Hathor rippled into visibility. There were seven of us aboard. Gloria, Cal,

347

Brin… Ruveus, Edgar, Phineas and myself. Seven versus all the evil and darkness in the cosmos.

Seven… seven is a powerful number. I knew then, despite everything… that we still had a chance.

The sound of my own footsteps as I boarded the ship was like thunder to me. I stopped short, staring up into sky above us. Almost as if summoned by my mind, a great light blinded me then, more powerful than either of the suns in the sky. I could hear the clash of steel against steel… and then a tremendous roar, loud enough to cleave the very earth in two.

"Artemis?" Phineas wondered. "Do you hear something?"

"No." I shook my head. "Why do you ask?"

"I guess you seemed a little distant," he muttered. "And your ear was twitching right then."

I shuddered, trying to clear my thoughts. "It must be stress."

"Or clairaudience." Phineas shrugged. "You could have a sixth sense. It isn't uncommon and I've always thought maybe your hearing was a little too good."

"What was that you just said?" I grinned. "I think I might have missed it."

"A bit of advice," Ruveus whispered, tapping me on the shoulder. "Stick with the giving orders. Leave the comedy to us professionals."

"Fair. You want orders, you have them," I announced. "I don't foresee that we'll reach any confrontation between here and Zenith, but if we do happen upon anyone, especially an IR ship, we are going to blast all thirteen hells out of them. As of right now… as High Commander, I declare unrestricted war on the Republic and the I'Eloshir of Magog. They've taken enough of our lives, and by the gods, they shall have no more!"

"Yeehah!" Edgar cheered, and then composed himself. Phineas smiled faintly and clapped.

I sat down in the captain's chair and the ship flared to life. The ceiling above the pit tore open with a mechanical rumble, and in a flickering of the eye, we were off, rocketing across the fire-scarred sky. The city of Zenith still glittered faintly across the dunes. Brin stood on the bow of the ship and raised her hands to the clouds.

Ruveus swiveled around in his chair and began to play, on his single instrument sounds that would rival an orchestra. But the song, however soulful, was not a happy one.

A strange, unsettling feeling came over me. Cal was enjoying his newfound toy, one of the big guns we'd had installed on the ship during the war, but everyone else had left the deck.

It was unnerving.

I scanned the horizon for any signs of a threat. Squinting, I noticed that there were four specks of white in the distance. I pulled out my binoculars from the cabinet under the controls.

The IRP.

"Cal, we've got four cruisers coming up at two-twenty," I explained. "Wait until you see the blue flare of the engines and then shoot them." I grabbed my sword. "It's time I woke up the rest of the crew."

I raced downstairs and threw open the first door I came to, running in on Gloria, Brin, and Phineas who'd obviously been having an important discussion.

Whatever it had been, it would have to wait.

"We're being chased," I announced. "We can't outrun them... so we will have to fight, and fight to win. I am not going back to Antares."

"Now this is more like it." Cal gripped the triggers of the guns.

"Great fun." Gloria grinned insanely, her fire-opal sparkling.

Then, quite unexpectedly, Lucy materialized onboard the ship with twenty boxes of pizza and a rocket launcher, followed by Jeo who carried a very large, snarling box.

"What the..." Edgar began, and then sighed.

The rest of us had grown accustomed to the completely random appearances of Jeo and Lucy... not to mention the somewhat less spectacular arrivals of their sane counterpart, Deiunthel, that we scarcely even blinked.

"What the hell did you catch?" Edgar stared at Jeo, attempting to seem in control. Edgar Dunharrow wasn't much of a fighter when he was ready for battle, and at that point he appeared fairly unprepared.

"Best toy ever." Jeo grinned, tapping the box and then shaking it viciously.

"It isn't poisonous, is it?" Phineas wondered, seeming almost paranoid.

"It might be," Jeo admitted. He poked at the box.

"I notta toy addamnit damnit notta toy! You letta me go! I notta toy!" a voice rambled from inside the box, sounding suspiciously familiar.

"Am I the only one here that realizes we are being attacked?" I demanded.

Everyone immediately jumped to attention. Two cruisers shot over our heads.

"Hold on... we're going underneath them!" I punched the controls and threw it into the old ship for all I was worth. The engines flared.

"Fire!" I gave the order. Two of the IR ships exploded on contact and a third spiraled into the sea. As the last of the ships plummeted into the water, an eerie silence overwhelmed those of us who stood on the deck of The Hathor. The fourth ship had vanished completely.

"IRP" A mechanized voice behind me announced. I turned around slowly.

The officer in the lead grinned. I didn't recognize him or any of his crew. There were about twenty of them… they had teleported aboard in their Duricide-coated armor and we hadn't even noticed.

"High Commander." He drew his gun with a smile. "What a surprise."

The agents laughed.

"Hands behind your back on the ground," the leader ordered. "The rest of you… hands up. No spell casting. We've got a magic resistant shield up. I'm sure you can't see it but it'll reflect anything under three-twenty."

Three-twenty? I turned to Phineas… who seemed about ready to laugh.

Over our years in exile, I'd grown accustomed to the IR's "MC" numbers, supposively an estimate of a magic-user's power. A mage who ranked around three-twenty was powerful in his own right… but Phineas had the habit of throwing spells that exceeded six-hundred, three or four at a time.

And as for myself, I was never quite certain how I scored, though I guessed that by the way their scanners spontaneously exploded in my mere proximity, it was some number that would make three-twenty look like child's play.

The agents fired. I dropped to the floor. The bullets stopped flying and I leapt to my feet, running the leader through with my sword as he stopped to reload. With all the armor he wore, it was the equivalent of punching through a cement block with an unsharpened pencil, and my arm went a little numb from the shock. Still, even with their commanding officer dead, that left twenty agents on board, all armed to the teeth.

I hit the deck for the second time.

Phineas held something in his outstretched hands… some spell I did not recognize but I guessed would be fairly messy.

"Throw it!" I winced, knowing I was still in the line of fire. I wouldn't die, of course... but I imagined I would be very badly burned.

"Hold it!" Brin ordered. She grabbed my arm and drug me out of the way.

"Relax, babe." Lucy grinned, munching on a piece of pizza. "Pretend they don't exist."

Admittedly, it didn't seem like much of a plan, but somehow I started to think that perhaps…

Phineas rubbed his hands together and grinned, firing an arc of green energy that washed over the IR ranks, electrocuting the first few men and throwing a couple overboard. It was remarkable to say the least, but unfortunately, not enough.

A low growl echoed from behind the pack of white IRP.

"Bowlingggggggg!" a high-pitched voice screeched as Devonny ripped through the IR ranks, claws bared.

Mouse... the Tree Rat saluted, grabbing one of the men by the neck and jumping off of the cat's back. She spun him above her head and flung him overboard effortlessly. I did not see how far he flew.

"Frisbee." Mouse grinned. "Don't you jus' love sports?"

"What about swimming?" Phineas glared at the Mouse.

"Just you try'n get close'nough big guy!" Mouse sneered, putting up two little fists.

I had never heard Phineas referred to as "big guy" before... and I must confess that I laughed. "Do you two know each other?" I wondered.

"She stole my jellybeans." Phineas pointed with a childlike pout.

"So return them." I shrugged, suddenly understanding the point of the charade.

"Can't." Mouse shook her head. "I ate em'."

"All of them?" Phineas stared, instantly turning green..

"Rowanoak had some too," Mouse admitted. "He grew a tail an' got reallyreally mad. Said something bout messin' wit' the line between nice magic and rotten magic. Then he had some a' those... those reeed ones!" She took a deep breath and shook her head heavily, still awestruck by the memory... before continuing. "And now he wans'ta kill you."

"Kill me?" Phineas frowned. "How do you know that?"

"Cause he hired me to do the job." Mouse grinned. "Assassinashun's one'a my spesh'eealities."

"Among other things." Jeo laughed.

"You got it." Mouse winked.

"Who would've guessed," Ruveus muttered darkly.

"Excuse me," one of the IRP agents interrupted, and turned to the other men who had quickly and wisely decided to stand behind him. They muttered amongst themselves for a few short moments... and I laughed softly, shaking my head in disbelief.

Finally, the new leader came to some sort of general agreement with his soldiers. He turned and drew a sword, glaring at me. "We are taking you to prison."

"Later." I grabbed the blade in my bare hand shoved him aside, ignoring the cut I had given myself.

Another of the men moved forward to arrest Phineas. Phineas flung him off the ship with a well-placed fireball. By then it was apparent that we were being merciful by not taking them seriously.

"So do you think that maybe if I fixed things..." Phineas wondered.

"I dunno." Mouse shrugged. "What would you do if you woke up with a tail?"

None of us could answer that, but Ruveus smiled slightly. "I'm a dragon, remember?" he replied. "It wouldn't surprise me."

"This isn't how an arrest is supposed to work," an officer whined.

"We're going to have to try this again," the new leader added.

"Six to teleport off," he announced, and they were gone.

"I can't believe it!" I sighed, slumping down in my chair. "The lot of you have completely lost your dysfunctional minds... and you still got rid of them all!"

Jeo and Mouse struck a high five. "Friends?" Mouse wondered. "No more of acatch'in me in ubiwuki boxes?"

"Friends." Jeo nodded.

"What about me?" Lucy asked.

"I still hatechu," Mouse shot back. "Ebbbleeeergghh!" She stuck her tongue out and rolled her eyes wildly before dodging behind a barrel.

"And I still want to duel with you!" Jeo added, pulling a whip from his side and cracking it dramatically.

"Why thank you both. You've brightened my day." Without further ado, Lucy disappeared.

"Wait for me, Lucy! I've got your keys!" Jeo shouted, unzipping a pocket of thin air and racing after her. Other than the rocket launcher, still smoking, and the stack of pizzas on the deck, there was no evidence that the two of them had ever existed at all.

"On to Zenith?" Gloria wondered, glancing at Mouse who looked up innocently, sitting inside the lid of one of the pizza boxes, a pepperoni hanging halfway out of her mouth.

I smiled despite myself. "Anyone up for pizza?"

Fifty-Five

I slowly brought down our speed as we neared the harbor. Skyscrapers and ruins of greater things loomed before us, and to our backs, gray-green clouds of pollutants drifted over the frozen waves… where once the Imperial Palace had stood.

I hailed the harbormaster. "Spellcraft requesting permission to dock."

"Spellcraft?" the harbormaster wondered in disbelief. "You're flyin' an actual Spellcraft?"

"Look out your window." I grinned. There was a faint pause as he set down his microphone and then I could hear the shouting on the other end of the line.

"Ammano loa, boys, lookit that!" the harbormaster shouted. "S'the most beautiful thing I've seen in years!"

"Is that a Spellcraft?" One of the men wondered. "My god, it's a real Spellcraft!"

"That ain't just any Spellcraft!" a woman's voice exclaimed. "Phrelic, look, read that number!"

"That's one hell of a flashy ship! Could it be…" The man's voice whispered, awestruck.

"003… that's The Hathor!" The harbormaster was truly amazed. Our ship had become as legendary as Phineas and myself.

"Permission granted!" the harbormaster announced and Phineas and I could see him saluting repeatedly with his two assistants from the window of the control booth.

The gate opened, crackling with green energy.

It was almost as if you could hear the phones ringing from office to office inside the compound, buzzing with the news. Despite the IR, Zenith remained a city that still loved the dynasty and everything about it.

353

And besides... I thought smugly to myself, even with her battle scars, the Hathor was a beautiful sight to behold.

Yet I had not realized until precisely that moment what kind of power the Empire still possessed. In the streets below, people purposefully rammed their cars into IR cruisers and blocked traffic, preventing the police from getting anywhere near the port.

A virtual revolution was in action, which was precisely what we had intended.

I switched off the ship and took the key for myself, handing Cal his notebook and pen. A crowd was already forming. The gangplank was lowered.

I turned to the gathered on the deck. "This is it, you know. The end of any normal lives you might have had, any identities you might have adopted since the end of the war. As of now... live or die, you are all legends."

I turned to face the mob, cheering, screaming, waving... Live or die... I was doing what must be done. If we would go out, we would enter the pages of history with a literal "bang". Hopefully just seeing our return would give the people strength enough to rise up against the IR themselves.

"Two hours, back here!" Phineas shouted as the crowd pushed us all our separate ways.

I shoved my way through the gathered and hailed a cab.

"Somewhere," I sighed, jumping in the back seat without even glancing at the driver.

Lucy winked. "I got just the place."

The cab screeched to a halt in front of what remained of Mad Mack's Magic Users. Mouse was already sleeping on the curb, having arrived with her unparalleled Tree Rat speed. I decided not to wake her and slipped inside the deserted building.

The bar was torn apart. All of the ambrosia and most of the alcohol had been stripped from the shelves by thieves, drunks and gangs... either partying or looking for some quick cash, and most of the artwork wore a thick coat of spray-paint.

Some of the floorboards had been ripped up too. I walked back towards where the elevator had been and stepped on a weak panel that moved beneath my feet. It was supposed to move, I realized, tapping it a little.

I had discovered a trapdoor.

I pushed the panel aside, coughing in the dust and lifted out a black film box with a few small words scrawled on its dusty gray lid.

"Phineas Merlin. Summer 3663." Without hesitating, I opened the box.

Photographs spilled out onto my lap, hundreds of them. I couldn't imagine when Phineas had found time to take so many when I'd never even seen him hold a camera. They were somewhat faded from the past years but still, in my hands I held what was quite possibly my last link to the life I'd only just begun to love before the war. The life I might have had.

I smiled faintly at a picture of Phineas and Ruveus sleeping in front of the television in Igor's apartment, and another of Panther and Ejora's wedding when the bride had clubbed the groom over the head with her bouquet after he had made a shameless pass at the priestess who had presided over the ceremony.

A somewhat questionable photograph of the Duchess Rosalind was signed with her name and "call me". Along with the picture was a small sketch of Galwick's tower. Phineas had the bill of sale there in the box. With money from Raphael, he'd bought back his beloved home from the Ardran Court and was planning to move there when he retired. Then the bombings had started.

I pushed the paper aside and refused to dwell on the terrible wrongness of it all.

At long last, I noticed that, amidst the scattered pictures, there was a black envelope embossed with the seal of the Emperor... a letter addressed to Maurice from Raphael. I almost didn't read it, the mere idea seemed disrespectful to the dead, but then I gave in. For Phineas to have kept it in the box with all of his other happy thoughts, I knew it had to be important.

I opened the letter and three more pictures fell out. They were all of me.

> To: Gen. Maurice Auderaukk, Grand Vizier,
> The Spellcraft Dogma
>
> From: CRSE Raphael Errida, Emperor of the Realm
>
> My dear Maurice,
>
> I suppose you will enjoy gloating over the fact that you are right. I am not entirely immune to a woman's charms, and it is "one" woman in particular. Fate has it that I continue to run into her, though I doubt she notices me, which is perhaps for the better, considering my reputation.
>
> Enclosed are some photographs I found in my study,

though I do not know who took them. I was hoping perhaps, that you and your "intelligence" might be able to find out who has been snooping around my palace these past few nights. It is a petty task, I know, but for some reason I sense that we should meet.

Eternally Grateful,

Raphael

I smiled despite myself and turned to the next page. The date was almost a year later, and this letter was addressed to Phineas.

To: Lord Wizard Phineas Merlin, CK 1443 E. Gandalf

From: CRSE Raphael Errida, Emperor of the Realm

Dear Master Merlin,

To you… I shall give all the titles I can possibly make up along with all the non-existent duties they encompass. I owe you more than I can possibly repay.

Not only have you replaced my completely incompetent poof of a Lord Wizard, the infamous Master Jeo, but you have also managed to save my face after that ugly press incident. I am glad to hear that you were able to get that "bit of land" you were after. You know, if the Ardran Land Council had given you any trouble, I would have gladly gone down to Phoenicia and roared at them all myself.

I can roar, you know. It is a rather amusing talent, and further proof that we "of Raedawn" are not so far removed from the l'Eloshir as we might prefer to think.

And then, there is the matter of Artemis. With the legends attached to her name, I admit, I was a little apprehensive. Still, legends are simply that… legends. And as far as her past goes, if she has moved beyond it, as you say, then it is irrelevant to me.

In the so many years that we Traversers live, we all have some regrets. My years in Ardra may have been quiet, but, as I believe you already know, before I went into hiding down south, I stirred up quite a bit of trouble for my parents and my dear Aunt Kay. When my brother and I ran away from home, I was scarcely thirty years old... but even that is not an excuse for the kinds of things that we did to survive when we were lost in the deserts of Magog.

Artemis has done nothing more or nothing less than I myself would have done in her place. It is frightening to admit, but I have no delusions of grandeur, and I know quite well the sort of things... unimaginable things that I too am capable of.

It was not until I met her face to face that I knew why I felt I needed to seek her out. We are perhaps the last two of our kind in all the worlds. Both having lived for so long, both surrounded by loving subjects and loyal friends, yet both completely alone, as she herself did say.

Yet it is not our loneliness that binds us so much as our desire for continual improvement. She is always reaching for greater things, a passion of mine that I have never found anyone to share so completely. We have common interests and emotions, and most importantly, common ideals.

Maurice argues that there must be some element of physical attraction between us, and he is not entirely wrong, it is just that there are so many more valuable things that I see in Artemis. She is not merely an object as some women are, but an asset in every possible way. Being with her inspires me to strive for things I had once felt were beyond my reach. I find it ironic... you knew from the very beginning, didn't you?

Still, I can't help but feel that we are running out of time. I have already had more than my share, I suspect, after eight-hundred and fifty years, but even immortals may fear death.

Does this sound rational?

I think you are right, Phineas, after all. What need I fear? I will send Maurice for the ring in the morning.

Your Friend,

Raphael

The ring.

I still wore it, though its glow was somewhat tarnished. I closed the contents back into the box and hid it under the floor, except for one picture, a photograph of Raphael on the balcony of the palace, looking out towards something only he could see… or perhaps merely admiring the view. In either case, it was more valuable to me than any of my worldly possessions.

"Artemis?" Cal's voice wondered, sounding so close and yet so far away.

I didn't answer. I was lost in my own thoughts, remembering how the sunsets used to be.

"Artemis!" Cal shouted, sounding a little more apprehensive. I snapped out of my trance-like state and returned to the dark bar.

"Forgive me," I sighed, recovering somewhat awkwardly. "Hello."

"Hey to you too!" Mouse grinned, saluting. "I's just gonna throw thisa punk out so me and you can talk."

She lifted Cal into the air.

"Mouse, put him down!" I ordered.

Mouse set Cal back on his feet, folding her arms and sighing heavily. Cal nearly fainted.

"I usta' be a bouncer," Mouse explained. "Afore I got my own tribe and all. People beatings and door slammings is two o' my spesh'eealities."

"Among other things," Jeo finished, stepping over the wreckage at the door, followed by Lucy at a distance. "How ya doin' my ladies?"

"Well enough," I muttered.

"So long as we can say "This is the worst"… The worst it is not. Or something like that." Cal quoted.

"Don't tell me it gets messier." Jeo frowned. "Cause' I am not breaking any nails to save this dimension! Any peppermint schnapps left in that bar over there? I need to mix me a drink."

"Why?" Mouse wondered. "Nothing bad's happened yet."

Just then we heard a scream.

"Something bad just happened." Lucy brightened visibly. Grinning, she sat down at the bar and kicked up her feet.

"Outside… that sounded like Gloria!" Cal pointed out, obviously shaken. Bullets fired.

"And that sound like ubiwooki," Mouse added.

"I wouldn't…," Lucy began, sensing what I was about to do. Her casual façade faded instantly and she looked genuinely concerned.

It was too late. I was already out the door. I scanned the streets for any possible mode of transportation and then caught sight of two horses outside of the convenience store. Without turning around, I vaulted onto the back of the first.

"Hey, that's my dad's horse!" a man shouted.

I glared at him. "I'll bring her back in one piece," I promised.

"Jesumachrist, it's the High Commander!" he whispered in disbelief, and then turned to his father who had just walked out of the shop, munching on something that smelled repulsive.

The skinny, rat-faced old man looked up at me for a moment and then collapsed, sitting on the pavement and staring into space with his hand over his heart.

"The High Commander's stealing my horse!" He smiled triumphantly, as if he'd been blessed. I galloped away.

The Warlord

"Wherever the pain is the greatest, there you shall find the mark of his claws."

Fifty-Six

I raced down the sidewalk to the scene of the disaster. IRP were everywhere, and Xane, of all people... was handing Edgar over to them. As much as Gloria didn't like her former fiancé, she knew that if he were sent back to Antares it would be an open-and-shut death penalty trial. Edgar didn't deserve that.

Though he was irritating more often than not, and though I constantly suspected him of causing mischief, he was unfailingly loyal to his companions, his subjects… and my beloved Empire.

I couldn't believe what I was seeing. In the days of the dynasty I had considered Sir Tradewind a friend. I would never have betrayed him. Evidently, he had no such love for the rest of us.

It was high time to give the police a more interesting target. I swung from the back of my borrowed horse onto the traffic light over the street and balanced on the bar, directly above the IR cruisers. Gloria saw me, and at that moment so did everyone else. I threw off my cloak.

The IRP stared.

"Make a break for it Edgar!" I shouted, as they raised their rifles to shoot. They fired.

"Get out of the…way!" I warned. Edgar dunked under a car. I closed my eyes and braced myself, running across the metal framework over the street, bounding across the wires and sliding down to a lower level via the nearest street lamp. The bullets missed. Gloria elbowed one officer in the face, hacked her chains on another's sword and fled.

The wires beneath me snapped and I leapt into the air, defying gravity for a moment before landing soundly on my feet on the hood of a car below, nearly flattening it and setting off the alarm.

The officers fired a second round.

I was hit, once or twice… enough to make me wince but not enough to slow me down. Without hesitation, I scooped up a handful of stopped bullets and flung them back towards the men who had fired them with the addition of a magical charge.

The end result was somewhat sloppier than I had expected, with bodies scattered everywhere. The man whose car I had destroyed only stared, baffled, and retreated back into the alley he had emerged from.

"Think about what you've done." I stared Xane down until he turned away as well. The remaining agents weren't stupid, quietly laying down their weapons, they let me pass.

"Fools," I muttered. I despised the lot of them, and knew they deserved punishment, but I could not find it in my heart to kill another person, not even a traitor like Xane.

I started walking back to the bar. A wave of sickness washed over me as an eerie howl echoed in the distance. I thought back to my so-called "premonition" in Panther's pit, and I began to run, past Mad Mack's, and on towards the harbor. A figure waved at me less than a block away.

"Artemis!" Phineas yelled.

"Phineas!" I shouted back, starting to feel the effect of the four bullets I already had in my body.

There was something terribly wrong. He was out of breath, and more than that. Wounded. I raced to his side and caught him a split second before he would have hit the black pavement.

Phineas fell.

"Phineas… what's going on?" I demanded. "Breathe, damnit, talk to me!"

He shook his head heavily but did not respond. "He has her."

"Who?" I demanded. "Fairfax? What happened?"

I lifted my hand away from his chest and gasped at the blood. Phineas had been run through with a heavy sword.

If I didn't get him to a cleric or a doctor right away… he could die, I realized.

"Help, someone!" I screamed futilely. But no help came.

"Cal! Gloria! Edgar!" I begged, my own echo mocking me cruelly.

We were alone on the near-dark street, the street that was steadily growing colder as the second sun began to set.

"Hold on… I'll help you," I muttered, wondering if I even could. Too many times I'd had people die in my arms, friends, strangers… old people, children. There had to be something I could do, something I wasn't doing. I only wished I knew what.

"Artemis, I have to tell you something," Phineas whispered.

"Save your strength," I ordered, though I was already crying. I had seen enough wars, enough wounds and enough deaths to know it was hopeless. So much blood from such a large wound... "Help is on the way."

"This can't be helped." Phineas shook his head, coughing.

"Don't say that," I argued.

"I have to tell you," Phineas pressed, grabbing me by the collar and staring into my eyes in such a way that I knew he was quite serious. "Geruth attacked us," Phineas explained. "The Warlord himself... He killed Ruveus and he took Brin."

"Ruveus?" I gasped. "Ruveus is dead?" Horrified, I shook my head heavily, fighting the wave of cold terror that overwhelmed me. "Ruveus," I repeated for the third time. "But no... Brin?" I wondered. "What does he want with Brin?"

"Only someone of royal blood can write in the Archives of Teyme," Phineas whispered. "You've done research, you know that. From ... what you've said about how politics work in Magog... even someone with a royal title runs a fairly good chance of not having any noble blood at all. You... you might, I think you... must, but Geruth... killed to earn his place as king."

I nodded. "But Brin..."

"She's not an Errida, no. And neither was Raphael. Errida isn't a name, it's a title. A word that... It means light... or something like that. The Emperor is the "light" of the people." Phineas smiled. "God, I love the elves. They make everything so beautiful."

"Phineas...," I whispered, wiping one of my tears off of his face.

"The Empress Kaora had no children," he continued, despite his obvious pain. "But her twin brother, Garth... his sons, Raphael... and Kieran Falchon, Brin's father."

"That means...," I began, suddenly understanding the enormity of what had happened.

"A princess," Phineas whispered. "She is our best hope and he knows it."

"How are you?" I wondered. "Does it hurt?" It was a fool question, but I felt compelled to ask it.

I knew there was more. Phineas smiled, despite his obvious pain.

"I am Galwick," He announced.

"Snap out of it," I ordered. "Don't talk like that, you're scaring me."

"If only… you could see!" Phineas shook his head. "It's so simple."

"What do you mean?" I wondered.

"One day you'll understand." Phineas smiled, clasping my hand with as much strength as he could. "We are all our own best teachers," he whispered… and then closed his eyes.

It was over. Our grand adventure had come to an end.

I willed the life back into him, I begged and pleaded and cursed the Gods. I would have gladly thrown myself to the hells for all eternity, if only… if only he would breathe again. But… that is not the way of such things.

Gloria and Cal approached, followed by Mouse at a distance.

"It's just the four of us. We're the only ones left." Gloria was pale. She clutched Edgar's signet ring and I knew without a word that he was lost as well.

We boarded The Spellcraft Hathor after leaving Phineas at the White Cross hospital. As much as I desperately wanted to wallow in my own dark memories until the pain went numb from time, I knew I did not have that option. I would not allow another of my friends to die.

Sailing west towards the edge of the world in the darkness, I stood overlooking The Frozen Sea.

If only I could turn back time. I had to find the Archives now more than ever. Once we rescued Brin and destroyed my father… what remained for any of us? I was heading into almost certain death with a young man, a mere boy really, a woman who followed her own path… and a creature I knew almost nothing about.

All those I had ever… loved were dead.

Ardain was wrong, I thought to myself, warming Phineas's cold dragon pendant in my hand. Being good was rewarding in itself, but goodness alone could not save a tortured soul.

As with light and darkness, love was simply a thing that could not be given indefinitely with nothing in return. Putting aside one's own desires was sufferable for a time, but not forever. Without something… someone to believe in, I was alone. And alone, I was nothing more than a bitter immortal with too much power and too little purpose. I wanted more, not just for myself… but for all the people of the Chaos Realm, an end to this agonizing cycle of death and loss and fear. They deserved better.

We pulled the sails and coasted onto the snowdrifts just outside a circular ring of stones. I knew not how I had found myself in Raedawn the first time, but I had been told that the ancient World Gates would reveal to me the path.

I stepped inside the circle and the doorways opened in a blaze of fiery light.

Gloria and Cal shielded their eyes, and Mouse latched around Cal's neck. I took both of their hands and stepped forward across the bend of time and entered the realm of Raedawn.

This... was it.

Fifty-Seven

"Here we are," I whispered. "Raedawn."

The golden fields had faded to gray and a sense of overwhelming wrongness hovered over the entire plane. I felt weighted down by a thousand pounds… and apparently Cal and Gloria were not faring much better. I took the first step of the staircase and then moved back, expecting to be fired upwards, but it did not work.

Something far more terrible than the deaths of my dear friends had indeed occurred.

"Follow me!" I ordered, running as fast as I could manage, and then finally slowing to a walk.

The others were far behind, and though I knew I had to protect them from whatever dangers lurked in this powerful place, and especially from my father, I could not force myself to wait too long.

I had to save Brin, and I was running out of time.

No more of my companions would die at Geruth's hands… least of all Raphael's niece. Phineas and Ruveus had already lost their lives guarding her. I owed that much to them, and especially to Raphael. I would protect Brin as they had done.

And then, at long last we reached the gate. The sentinel Dakor still stood guard, but Vatra was nowhere to be seen.

"You, mortal beings!" Dakor growled. "How dare you come here!"

"What has happened Dakor?" I asked, chilled by the fierceness in his voice.

He didn't answer, still bristling at the sight of the motley crew I'd dragged with me, two humans and a Tree Rat.

An old, old dream came flooding back to me then, of three riders on horseback. Though they had been cloaked in black making their bodies and faces unrecognizable, I had seen their eyes.

Mouse gazed up at me, uncertain yet fearless. Her eyes were a pale, unusual blue-gray like an oncoming storm. She, out of the four of us was most clearly out of her element, having followed not because she knew what we were up against, but simply because she could. Her innocence was startling, overshadowed only by her remarkable courage.

Cal would not look at me directly, but his eyes were brown, calm and calculating. He could analyze things down into their tiniest components without losing respect for even the smallest particle of life. He was a builder, a creator who regarded every element of every plan with equal respect. He was firm without being harsh and confident without thinking too highly of himself.

I turned to Gloria, seeing in her green, fierce eyes the soul of a coolly arrogant woman who would not take no for an answer. Sometimes too stubborn, she nevertheless set the standard for those around her, living the life that she preached.

They were the three riders who had carried me like the wind, the three horsemen who had brought me to the place that held... the secret.

"Dakor," I whispered. "I dreamed this once! Why?" I begged him, though not a flicker of emotion crossed his stone face.

"Proceed, Ireval," he responded stiffly.

"DO NOT call me that!" I ordered.

Cal and Gloria were visibly pale, but only Mouse dared to speak.

"You mean it's true?" she whispered. "You're really..."

"It's true." I shook my head. "And I suppose I should have admitted that long ago."

"No," Gloria interrupted, "you were right not to tell us. We wouldn't have understood."

I was amazed at her response. To admit such a thing... the Baroness was wiser than I had ever given her credit for.

"Proceed, High Commander," Dakor repeated.

"If I go in... so do they," I announced, standing firm.

"Be reasonable." Dakor shook his head heavily. "If the Mother learns that I have..."

"The Gods can have their fight with me," I replied. "This is the way it must end." I would not budge.

"Proceed then," Dakor cursed silently... I could tell from his eyes. And yet his power so completely overwhelmed my own that I could not fathom why he would not simply strike me down and return me to my proper place.

The gates unraveled, and I noticed for the first time that the gold and silver roses had begun to wilt.

"But be forewarned," Dakor interrupted.

I paused… and then noticed the body of Vatra lying dead within the courtyard. I knew who had slain the reckless sentinel, but I had never imagined that he possessed the power to destroy one.

Geruth.

I turned back to Dakor. A great silver tear in his chest made me wonder for a moment if he was hurt as well.

"Be forewarned," Dakor repeated. "For though you may possess the power to alter eternity, Ireval Ithraedol, Lady Ravencroft the Demon Queen… you may not possess the wisdom to change it for the better."

The great Dakor collapsed then, on those final words, the white light gone from his eyes. If I had not known better, he would have simply appeared to be a lifeless stone… but as it was, I was overwhelmed with a horrific sense of loss.

I knew not what the sentinel's cryptic warning meant, but I knew also that I had no choice but to proceed. Followed by Cal and Gloria, I made my way through the eerie gray courtyard. The tower I saw was not the one that I had seen on my first journey to Raedawn. It continued straight into the shifting storm clouds overhead, hundreds of feet high and completely smooth, a pale silver-white without the smallest ripple in the solid stone.

This was the true Raedawn, not the dreamscape I had imagined… and although it was beautiful, it was also terrible in its ancient coldness.

"The doors won't open," Cal announced, the look in his eyes revealing that he would very much like to go back already.

"They will for me." Mouse pushed him aside and heaved, sliding the first open a mere crack. The door slammed shut again with a sound like a gong and Mouse staggered back towards us.

I turned to the brass plate on the wall. "It says knock." I shook my head at the madness of the thing. The four of us knocked… all as one, and the doors disintegrated into grains of sand.

"Strange," Gloria stared.

She had spoken my thoughts exactly. We entered the dark hall, and at that instant, the piles of sand behind us melted back up into a solid wall.

"I don't like this," Cal muttered.

"Me neither," Mouse admitted.

The ceiling had begun to drop, and the corridor was becoming increasingly narrower. I remembered again the dream that I had... so long ago. Before us on the far wall of the trap was a mural of an immense dark tree, the painted surface pierced with swords.

I knew what had to be done.

"Wrap something around your hands," I ordered. "We're going up."

I threw Cal my gloves and Gloria a few strips from the back of my cloak. Mouse clung to Cal's neck and we climbed.

Despite my precautions, my hands were cut, raw and bleeding by the time I reached the second floor, pushing aside a tile and stepping out into what appeared to be a corridor of the Imperial palace.

White marble surrounded us and blinding sunlight filled the room, radiating from some unidentifiable source.

A pillar in the center of the space bore a short inscription, carved both in the language of the humans and that of the I'Eloshir.

"From darkness. Through war, Through peace. Through fire, wind and rain, fate, chance, time and ..."

The last word had been rubbed off magically. I couldn't begin to guess what it had been.

"Sounds like we've got a few more trials before us." Gloria shuddered. "And there's the first one."

The apparent daylight was coming from a white burning flame.

"So we walk through it and it doesn't hurt us?" Cal wondered. "Is it like a leap of faith?"

"The swords cut." I shook my head. "The fire will burn."

"But we've got to go anyway?" Mouse asked, obviously hesitant.

I nodded, collected myself and jumped through the fire, rolling on the ground to put out what I could of the flames... and then realized the danger the others were in.

Cal was lost, coughing in the smoke.

"Follow the sound of my voice!" I begged and then jumped back into the inferno. My armor nearly melted; hissing and red-hot against my skin until finally the symbiote released itself and slithered away. I led Cal through and then went back into the white fire for the third time after Gloria

The three of them were burned some, but not badly. My clothes were destroyed to the point where they were almost nonexistent, and my armor had set itself free, but my body was unharmed. It seemed that nearest to me the flames were the hottest, as if it somehow knew I could withstand the most.

Could such magic tell human from demon?

I did not know.

Gloria coughed, looking up at me with tears in her eyes from the smoke. She had never been one to fear her own element. "Never... never...," she stammered madly.

"We won't have to." I looked down the corridor. "The next challenge is wind."

A roaring hurricane pushed us back towards the flames. Every step forward flung us another three back, but finally we reached a turn in the hall and stepped out of the storm.

"Rain," Cal muttered.

I looked up to the sky... and then ahead to a large, deep pool that loomed before us. Cal put a hand in the water.

"It's not so cold," he admitted. "We can probably swim."

I took a step back, unwilling to go further. The ripples in the black pond terrified me. Harsh winds and fiery pits I did not fear, but a lake, an ocean... that was something else entirely.

"What's wrong?" Gloria wondered, holding her clothing and her weapons atop her head as she pushed away from the wall. "The water's almost nice."

"I... can't swim," I stammered, staring at the depths.

"I can. I was a lifeguard one summer. I'll help you," Cal offered.

"No! No!" I stammered, staying as far from the edge as I could.

"Artemis, get in the water!" Gloria ordered. "We have to go on!"

"GET OUT!" I ordered.

Something moved in the darkness below them

"GET OUT!" I screamed for the second time.

Mouse surfaced for air. "Jeez," she winced. "All that over me?"

The shadow in the water hissed and the leviathan rose to the surface. Mouse scrambled out onto the opposite bank, shrieking in her indistinguishable mix of languages and Gloria leapt after her, and accidentally dropping her crossbow, but Cal was caught in the serpent's coils.

"Snake!Bigfishafishsnakeafish! Kill it! Kill it!" Mouse rambled.

Gloria cast a fireball, her opal sparkling dangerously, and struck the creature in the head. The leviathan thrashed, drenching us with a wall of water and dunking Cal.

Snatching Mouse's dagger, I jumped swinging onto the serpent's neck and fighting my way to some point soft enough to kill the beast. I slipped, losing my grip, and the leviathan submerged, dragging me with it.

I choked, desperately trying to worm my way free. I was drowning under the dark waves, when suddenly I heard a piercing scream. There was blood in the water. I struggled futilely for the surface, still sinking, until all at once, a hand from above drug me out.

I gasped, so glad to breathe air once again.

The four of us still lived. My staff harpooned through the dead leviathan appeared to be the only source of bloodshed. The creature's body sank slowly under the surface.

"Your dagger." I offered the knife back to Mouse.

"You keep," Mouse sighed, gesturing to the legendary staff. "I lost your weapon."

"We've lost all our weapons," I muttered in disbelief, surveying what little remained of our gear. "If there are more creatures like that, I'm not sure what we can do."

There was a sickening crunch as Gloria forced Cal's shoulder back into place.

"You saved my life." I shook my head, resolving not to consider the possibility. "I don't know how…"

"I told you I was a lifeguard." Cal grinned. "Besides… we're even."

"Even?" Gloria sighed. "At a time like this, it doesn't matter who comes out even, so long as everyone comes out."

"Baroness is right," Mouse muttered. "Keepa'moving."

Wading through what remained of the flood waters into yet another dark cavern, we came to a white platform hovering over what appeared to be a bottomless abyss.

Another irrational fear, the terror of heights. Gloria seemed vaguely concerned, and Mouse shrugged, unimpressed, but for the first time, Cal winced.

"Oh god," he muttered. "How deep is that?"

I took a running jump and dropped onto the platform, helping Cal and Gloria pull their way up and catching Mouse when she very nearly fell short.

"Where do we go from here?" Cal wondered.

I pointed to a white statue of a horseman, floating disconnected from anything above our heads.

He faced the west, and a second white platform.

"There's no way to get there," Mouse argued. "I got a rope, and this thing sways n'ough that I pull it… but we's got to get over there an' tie up."

"I'll see if I can fix things." Cal quickly sketched out the platforms and attempted to draw a bridge.

Nothing happened.

"This is beyond our control." Gloria shook her head. "I might be able to move the rope over there... I could try to levitate myself out with my fire opal so that..."

"You will do no such thing," I cut her off. "Give me the rope."

Mouse nodded, cinching the end she'd already tied around the post.

"I'm jumping," I announced.

"You'll never make it," Cal argued.

I didn't care. I had to prove that I could. I ran and jumped, falling short a few feet and began to drop. Sliding down the rope as I fell, I had to fly. Had to... or I would never make it back again.

Yet at the same time, I resisted my desire to change, gritting my teeth and clinging to the rope for dear life.

Above me, something snapped.

"The rope's breaking!" Mouse screeched.

I couldn't see them, I was too far down in the darkness for that, but I could hear their panicking and screaming.

I pushed out and then swung forward, realizing there was a lever on the underside of the platform.

"There's some sort of machine down here!" I yelled. "I'm going to try to reach it!"

I grabbed the lever and pulled it down, wrapping my arms around the bar just as the rope snapped. The platform began to move.

"Hey... we're going!" Mouse shouted. "You did it Artemis!"

I pushed up through the floor tiles and flopped onto my back, scarcely breathing. We moved towards the second platform slowly, passing another two frozen white riders floating in the sky.

"More stairs?" Cal groaned, and I looked up from where I lay.

Sure enough, the platform had hovered to a stop and we were faced with a second flight of apparently limitless white marble steps.

Sliding down from the moving platform on Mouse's rope, the four of us stood before an open archway. Above the gate, a sign made entirely out of scissors read: "Beyond."

An immense thirteen-hour clock hovered in midair directly before us, its hands spinning madly in all directions... and the floor we stood on was scattered with hundreds upon hundreds of rainbow-colored dice.

"This symbolism is fascinating," Cal observed. "Scissors... that would be fate, cutting life's threads, and dice would be chance... and what better than a clock to signify time?"

"Three in one," Gloria snorted. "Why do I get the feeling that we're not going to like what's at the top of these stairs?"

"We've got no choice," I replied, shaking my head. "We have to go on."

"Onward." Cal grinned, walking up the first few stairs. "Beyond time and chance and fate." He laughed, presumably at his own obscure humor.

I stepped forward and slammed into nothingness.

"What's wrong?" Cal stared from where he stood, already ahead of me.

"Take off your coat," Mouse advised. "That's what the sign says."

"What sign?" I wondered.

Mouse pointed. Posted over a lonely park bench that I had not seen before and beside a black coat rack, a small paper sign read: "Please leave your hats and coats here. Many Thanks – The Cleaning People"

"I can't get through either," Gloria admitted. "And I'm not wearing a coat."

"A disguise spell!" I realized. "It must be!"

"Is that it?" Gloria wondered. She rubbed her face in a handkerchief and instantly gained twelve years. "Someone certainly has a peculiar sense of humor."

Though the dragon I had taken from Phineas possessed no illusion currently, it had been the subject of considerable spells in the past. I looped Phineas's pendant around the arm of the bench where Gloria had left her handkerchief and I slipped off what remained of my burned and tattered coat as well.

I tried the stairs again and fell backward, pushed violently by the invisible force.

"What now?" Cal wondered.

I rolled my shoulders anxiously, tasting blood in my own mouth. "There's only one other thing I can think of," I admitted. "And I'd rather not do it."

"It looks like you may have to." Gloria shrugged. "Honestly... how old are you?"

"Age is irrelevant." I shook my head. "I want you all to be careful," I explained. "I may not recognize you when I am through with this, and if I do not... you must all run as quickly and as far away as you possibly can."

I closed my eyes and forced myself back, continually reciting over and over the names of my friends, imprinting their faces upon my mind and

whispering my own name, lest I forget why we had come. The change came…
but like never before.

I wasn't surrendering to the darkness, I was harnessing it.

I didn't belong to it, I owned it.

If only I had known how simple it was.

Bones cracked and reformed, and the sound itself sickened me, although
I was amazed at how aware I was… aware of the world around me and even
of the remarkable expressions on Cal and Gloria's faces.

I stretched, leaning back a little and adjusting my balance.

So much for my… "hat and coat".

I sighed, not speaking a word and began up the stairs.

Fifty-Eight

A door at the top of the staircase swung open as we approached, revealing a familiar space… the mysterious room of windows and mirrors between worlds.

The Archives of Teyme hovered open over the central pit and Cal's mystical pen floated out of his backpack. The shimmering red feather stopped, poised above the page with a drip of gold-white ink glimmering at its tip, almost as if it were waiting for someone to pick it up.

Despite how exhausted I already was, I knew that it could not be so simple as that.

I glanced around the room at all of the shimmering gateways. Geruth could come out of any one, at any time. Another being might use the passages as well… a more terrible beast from any number of unknown worlds.

But the book was there, and I had the pen.

It seemed almost dangerous in and of itself, yet I reached out.

"Artemis, don't touch it," Cal warned. "This isn't how it's supposed to happen."

I stepped back. "I… don't know what came over me," I admitted, somewhat truthfully. I bristled as I sensed another presence entering the room. Thrown through the third mirror in a splash of silver water, Brin hit the floor.

"Break it!" she screamed, dunking. "Smash it, someone!"

Brin scrambled to her feet and turned, wrenching an iron bar from one of the mirror-like windows with strength that I had not known she possessed… and smashed the glass of the gateway that she had come through.

The mirror burst in a flash of purple energy… but yet another door across the room had already begun to ripple.

"Break all of them!" Brin screamed. "Break them all!"

Gloria fired bursts of flame from her fire opal and Mouse tore the ancient glass from the walls, smashing the mirrors with her bare hands. Cal dug through his knapsack, producing a slick, soaking wet baseball. He wound up and pitched.

Only I remained motionless, though I could have easily shattered all the mirrors in an instant. I watched in horror and stared at what remained of the glass on the floor. We were truly, truly trapped. There was no way out, no stairs, no Tears, no mirrors to traverse. We were trapped… And we were not alone.

A dark shadow began to rise out of the central pool, but it was not Inapsupetra.

I recognized his face in an instant, though the sight of him wearing a hooded black robe disturbed me far more than his blood-red armor ever had.

Geruth held in his hands the pen, the book, and was about to write.

He was capable of writing the Chaos Realm itself out of existence. He could transform all worlds into his image of perfection… and recreate me as a slave under the power of the darkness I had once led.

There was nothing I could do.

All it would take was a single word.

But somewhere, I found that ounce of strength and forced my eyes to meet his.

Spurred by a sudden influx of power, I dove forward and threw him to the ground, stabbing him in the chest with Mouse's dagger. His claws cut deeply into my shoulder and I returned the slash across his face.

Blow for blow, we fought, rolling through broken glass. Dodging the two of us, Cal, Gloria and Mouse all cowered in the shadows as we struggled for the book.

It was wise of them to keep their distance. Never in all of my life had I fought so hard, desperate not to lose my ground.

And each time I lunged, each time my wild attacks connected with Geruth's body… each time he hit me in return, visions flashed before my eyes of the past… the present… and the future, not as it was, but as it ought to have been.

Our claws locked, Geruth brought his knee into my chin, throwing me into the wall. I slid underneath him, ignoring the blood that welled up in my mouth and swept him to the floor, his colossal bulk sending a shudder through the entire room.

The Archives flew from his grasp and I threw myself forward, jumping on his chest in a vain effort to reach the book before it hit the ground.

Cal caught the Archives.

"Take it!" Cal screamed, pushing the pages at me.

I grabbed the book, but Geruth was already back on his feet.

He threw me against the wall and reached for the Archives again. I slid across the floor and seized the manuscript, tearing from his grasp the pen.

I pulled back in my haste and terror and realized that I had accidentally scratched a line across the golden paper. I had written in the book not a single word... but a line.

The light was so brilliant I couldn't tell to read what it said.

It was simply one motion.

Passion.

Fear.

Pain, Regret...

Love.

Hope.

The second I put ink to paper the room itself shattered into a million pieces of white light. A heavy shadow descended then, still, silent, foreboding. Figures surrounded me, faceless, moving in all directions, like ghosts made of black smoke, all whispering to another as they passes by, laughing softly. Utterly bewildered, I dropped the book and it vanished completely in a sudden burst of flame.

The mists of darkness cleared and I found myself no longer bloody and bruised on the floor of the tower, but seated in a high-backed silver chair... in a room of many columns and balconies, human again.

I was dressed, somehow, in my Imperial colors.

Two Republic generals knelt before me, surrendering what was left of their pitiful armies... after the Battle of the Equinox.

It was a stunning victory for me, but it would not last. Soon I would be called back to the front, to The Battle of the Frozen Sea.

I remembered that day.

Though I could scarcely believe it, I knew where, or more precisely, when I was.

Years in the past... in the days that had become legend, when gods walked amongst mortal men. Anything was possible then...

Before the fall of Errida.

The Immortals

"They, like their swords, are forged in the fires of the stars."

Fifty-Nine

My gaze drifted from the floor to the ceiling and then to the balcony where a young Brin sat, her mother brushing her long, red-brown hair. I stared, not only because I realized then that I had somehow stepped back in time, but because Brin's mother had killed herself long before the first army surrendered. History hadn't simply been reversed; it had been changed.

I couldn't imagine what Brin must have been thinking at that moment, but in her eyes there were tears. My mind whirled with possibilities. Brin was a child again, and her mother was alive. I did not know about the rest of her family, but I knew that simply being reunited with even one member of her entire massacred clan must have been her dearest wish. But how had I done such a thing when I was still unsure of what I had written in the Archives? It was preposterous.

Gloria on the floor, sobbed with her arms wrapped around Devonny's neck, and Cal and Mouse stood beside her, where they could not have possibly been... where they had not been, not the first time.

It wasn't a dream, or an illusion, I realized.

It had actually happened. I had a second chance to see Phineas and Raphael... a second chance to go back and un-make the mistakes I had made, but more than that, I now possessed a second chance to save... or destroy the world.

I had never meant for such a thing to happen.

It was wrong, an impossibility!

It should never have been.

At that instant, as I found myself there, in my chair before council and a hundred prisoners of war...

I fainted.

I awoke in my chamber with a slew of servants hovering over me, and almost panicked, before I remembered.

I was crying uncontrollably; I was so cold, so shocked and horrified that I had alterd the course ofhistory without ridding myself of my horrific memories. What I had desired, more than anything… was to erase the pain of the empire's people. I had hoped, perhaps selfishly that I would be allowed a release myself.

But no… that would have been merciful. And now, the five of us alone, Cal, Brin, Mouse… Gloria and myself would bear the knowledge of what had come to pass the day the Dynasty failed.

I brushed the servants away and sat up, perhaps a bit too quickly. Someone passed me a glass of ambrosia… and I drank deeply, closing my eyes.

I could smell the familiar scents of my quiet room, lavender, soft suede, the faint smoking of incense and even the dogs, where they had been. So many little, subtle things that I had never truly appreciated.

"Let us through," a voice demanded, out in the hall and I gasped in recognition, sitting up suddenly. The servants all jumped back… and he came to my bedside.

"They told me you fainted," Raphael whispered softly. Seeing the tears in my eyes, he took my hand and clasped it tightly as he sat down beside me, exactly how I had remembered him. "Are you all right?"

I could not respond. It had been so long since I had felt his touch, and ages since I had seen his face. So often had I wished, desperately that we would be reunited…

Yet I had known the truth; he was dead, and with that knowledge came the emptiness, the cold that had gripped me for so long… until that moment.

All at once, the wave of emotion swept through me and I closed my eyes, falling helplessly into his arms, expecting to pass through Raphael as if he were a shadow and nothing more.

And yet… there he caught me. Our eyes met the way they had that very first day in Ardra; I saw in his face the same expression I had missed most. The way that he had always looked at me with his eyes speaking volumes wordlessly.

I shook my head furiously, not facing him but holding him close, stubbornly… unable to speak, scarcely knowing how to breathe and desperate not to lose him, never again!

Phineas touched my hand uncertainly, but I could not bear to open my eyes. Without looking I saw him sitting there, waiting for a response, but what pained me more were the thoughts that rushed through my mind. Phineas slowly stood and left the room, glancing towards Raphael who nodded.

I would have begged him to stay a little longer, if I had found my voice… but no words would come to me.

I couldn't bear to think that I would have to live through both of their deaths over again… unless I could somehow change things.

"Raphael?" I murmured under my breath, attempting to compose myself slightly.

"I'm here," he promised, lying down beside me. The terrible pain that overwhelmed me was a combination of joy and deep, profound sorrow at the fate that I knew still awaited us.

Yet even for so short a time, we were reunited. "There is something I must tell you," I whispered, now that I had the chance.

A knock came at the door. One of my servants opened it from the outside… and I thought I saw Cal.

"Be on your way," someone said.

"Let him in," I ordered, sitting up. Cal stepped into the room.

"Artemis?" he wondered, obviously shaken.

"Yes." I tapped anxiously and glanced at Raphael. His expression was mingled with mild concern, and nothing more.

"Can I talk to you?" Cal asked.

Phineas frowned, stepping in from the corridor. "You know this boy?"

"He's a friend of The Prophet," I explained, somewhat truthfully.

"Is it all right if we leave?" Raphael wondered. "I'll be back as soon as I can, of course… but if you are well, Phineas and I should go handle the rumors."

"Good idea." I nodded. "Thank you."

Raphael and Phineas left together, whispering as they headed down the hall. I couldn't help but feel as if they were disappearing out of my life forever.

Gloria entered, followed by Mouse.

"Dogs." Mouse glared.

One of Raphael's wolfhounds growled from his place under my bed.

"He won't hurt you." I shook my head.

Mouse frowned. "All dogs is out to get me," she argued. I supposed I had to take her word for that.

Brin squeezed into the room and slammed the door behind her. "What's going on?" she demanded, hysterical. "What is going on!"

"That's what I came to find out," Cal explained. "It evidently has to do with whatever Artemis wrote in that book, so what did you write?"

"Nothing." I shook my head. "A line."

"That... hasn't happened before," Gloria stared.

"Obviously not," I sighed.

"So what do we do?" Brin wondered.

"Whatever we can." I forced myself to my feet.

"Is it right that we even try?" Cal asked. "Teyme may have created the Archives, but I'm sure that he never suspected that this might happen..."

"I'd rather not worry about that now." I took a sip of the ambrosia on my nightstand. "All I want to know is if it is possible. Can we do it?"

"Do what?" Mouse wondered. She was still staring at the dog.

"Save the world." I took a deep breath and glanced at each face that surrounded me. The room fell utterly and completely silent.

Sixty

The Frozen Sea loomed across the horizon line; massive waves of ice overwhelmed with thousands upon thousands of soldiers. Below me, a purple sea of Imperial troops joined the fast moving green of King Rowanoak's calvary. The Spellcraft Gemini raced overhead, firing on a Tear that seemed to be on the verge of opening, trailed by a flock of dragons, our incredibly fast, destructive and maneuverable strike forces that challenged even the best of the Republic's fighter planes.

Charging down another snow-covered hill and into the fray was a force of Barbarians from Accoloth, their swords and axes held high as Ejora herself led the attack.

"FIRE!" I ordered the three dragons that crouched on the stone outcropping below me. "FIRE!"

Spellcraft raced across the frozen waves towards the never-ending flood of planes rolling out of the steadily increasing black Tear.

A little Déjà vu? Perhaps.

"High Commander!" a voice shouted. "You're dressed this morning!"

"General Auderrauk." I smiled, turning around, well aware of how close we stood.

"News from the spies!" he announced, rubbing his snow-goggles clean on his red scarf.

"Let me guess," I sighed. "Zae's been poisoned?"

"No." Maurice laughed. "Orin has. Though I would dearly love to see that wench follow her husband. I'll lay my life on it, she murdered him. Probably found out he wanted to kill her."

That troubled me. Yet another little difference could mean the end of everything. A scout on a horse slid to a stop in front of us.

"High Commander!" He bowed, dismounting.

Though the scene had played out somewhat differently than I remembered it, an eerie familiarity struck me then. Some things… some things were very much the same.

"Down!" I demanded. The scout hit the ground.

"High Commander! We've broken the western line!" Ruveus shouted from above.

"Good! Show them no mercy!" I waved back.

"High Commander!" the scout begged.

"STAY DOWN!" I ordered.

He cowered in the snow.

"What's the meaning of this?" Maurice wondered, glancing at the bewildered scout.

"Watch." I scanned the sea. A crossbow quarrel shot towards me and I dunked, the bolt bouncing harmlessly off of the side of a tank of Spellcraft fuel.

"Ah. Now shoot him!" I pointed to the cliff edge where the very surprised assassin stood. My men fired, and the would-be killer fell.

"How did you know there was an archer up there?" Maurice asked, raising an eyebrow as he stared at me.

I shrugged. "Clairvoyance, perhaps." I paused momentarily, gathering strength for my next command. "REINFORCE THE CITY WALL!" I ordered.

"High Commander?" Maurice frowned.

"DO IT," I countered. He did not argue.

"Artemis!" Cal yelled.

I turned. Cal staggered through the snow, lugging a heavy book.

"What is it now?" I wondered.

"I know what's going on!" He gasped for breath. "I ran all the way from the Library… I know why things aren't the same!"

"Well, say it!" I demanded.

He shook his head. "It's a time machine, that's the way it works. Everyone in the tower went back."

"Everyone…" I fought the sickening sensation that was creeping up on me.

"Including Geruth." Cal opened the book, revealing a diagram that meant absolutely nothing to me… but his certainty, that was proof enough.

"That means he's one step ahead of us," I muttered.

The third dark Tear was already forming; I could sense it, but not directly above the palace. It had been too close last time.

Geruth had intentionally set it farther back... on the edge of the world.

"Mages! Clerics!" I could hear Phineas's voice. "Destroy that before it opens!"

Cleric's spells flew through the sky... and I knew what I had to do. I ran to the airfield and jumped aboard The Hathor, firing up the engines.

"What are you doing?" Cal demanded.

"What has to be done," I shot back.

"I'm coming too." He threw his backpack aboard.

I threw it off. "This may be a one way trip."

"Artemis!" Cal begged, gazing up at me with a desperate, weary expression.

I ignored him and rose slowly off the ground, firing skyward, arcing towards the Tear at top speed. The third Tear burst, and out came the planes, dropping their payloads.

"CLOSE!" I ordered. The Tear snapped shut.

I took a deep breath and concentrated, searching the skies for the dark shadow that I knew carried our defeat with it. A door opened behind me... and all at once I was distracted, knowing I had unwillingly brought some other unfortunate soul onto my suicide mission.

I slowed the ship in midair and turned slowly, half-expecting to see Phineas... or stubborn Maurice... Cal, any of my fool companions, all who were fearless enough to laugh in the face of death.

Yet the man who stood behind me was Raphael.

"What are you ...," I began, turning to face him. "Raphael?"

"I know what you're doing." He smiled faintly, interrupting me, putting a finger to my lips.

"Then you must know you can't stop me." I shook my head and pulled away.

"I'm not here to stop you," Raphael sighed. "Brin told me last night... she collapsed and confessed everything."

"You... know?" I shook my head. "But goddess... why are you here?"

"The fabric of time is a tricky substance," he explained, shaking his head heavily. "Your friend the Architect said that... well, it honestly wasn't what he'd meant but..."

"You know Cal is the Architect? Is there nothing she missed?" I sighed, on the verge of tears once again.

"Not much, I imagine," Raphael admitted. "And as far as Calvin is concerned, that was obvious. After all, Deiunthel only has so many friends."

I shook my head. "Raphael, I cannot let you do this!"

Yet, despite how wonderful it felt, knowing that, once again I had been accepted... forgiven and absolved, despite my shortcomings, it was then that the desperation hit me. "You shouldn't be here!" I begged him. "Go... go somewhere! Raphael... I..."

What could I say at that moment? The things that I had done, the battles I had fought since the end of the dynasty, from the Etone War to Raedawn... they had all been... not for myself, no... but for the Empire.

Raphael's Empire.

"Raphael, listen to me!" I finally whispered. "I have tempted fate and scorned death... battled through heaven and hell, only so that this realm might be saved, not because it is mine... but because it is yours, because you loved it. Because what you love... I love." I turned away. "You must go."

"And let you chase down those planes on your own?" Raphael laughed. "How could I possibly consider it?"

"But you could...," I began, though I couldn't truly argue with him, not then. I sat down at the controls and stared at the bewildering mess of buttons before me. Everything I thought I knew, everything that I was sure I understood, it was all meaningless and foreign to me. My world had been turned upside-down once again. "Raphael, you could...," I whispered.

"We could die." Raphael shook his head. "And imagine how ridiculous that would be. An adventure most worthy of our efforts."

"So." He sat beside me, steadying my trembling hand. "Let's "save the world", shall we?"

In all the years I had spent reliving the final days of the war, I had never once imagined that it would end in such a way.

Raphael fired as I composed myself and flew the ship, trailing after the planes. Two of the fighters went down and a third cut sharply across the edge of the world.

We were hit with a sudden burst of fire from behind, a massive explosion that had come from some unseen source. The Hathor plummeted from the sky, scarcely level and then struck the waves, coming to a stop... still almost afloat, yet motionless, her engines fizzling and freezing beneath the surface. I scrambled to my feet and stared in horror as I realized that we were done for, trapped in the center of a ring of ice. The bomber shot overhead, towards the palace and I concentrated my energy, focusing on a spell.

The wall would not break. The city would not fall. The war would not be lost, not so long as I lived!

And yet I could not reach it, slow it down or command it to stop. We were too far away. I turned, unwilling to believe that giving everything I had would still not been enough to save the dynasty. But then… quite suddenly, I felt a power behind me, Raphael… passing along his own energy.

The spell that formed was like none I had ever before cast, no violent purple flames, but a steady sphere of white light, light of a thousand colors… a light so pure and good and whole I could not believe that I held it in my own filthy hand.

"Why…," I gasped, turning to face him, looking into his eyes. He had surprised and amazed me once again. Was there truly nothing that we could not achieve?.

We were two sides of the same whole person, completed in one another, unified and strengthened by a power beyond all imagination.

"I love you," Raphael whispered.

I closed my eyes, yet saw it all… the power we released, shooting through the sky like a falling star, the last plane exploding into shards of silver… raining down on the battlefield where soldiers stared in awe.

And all the Tears contracted at once, closing and drawing their darkness with them. The demons shattered like so many mirrors, leaving only their bloodstained weapons and their shadows behind.

The war was over.

The battle was won.

A cheer of joy rose from the gathered, thousands of voices all crying out in unison. They had saved themselves from a force that threatened not only their lives, but their futures, their legacies… a power that would have destroyed all it was that they stood for. But now… they had been victorious!

They were… Free.

But we, we were already caught in the currents of the edge of the world, the ice shattering and the waterfall drawing us out into space… Raphael and I.

Nothing mattered anymore, save that I was not alone. At last, I was reunited with the light in my life… a man whose very soul burned with a rainbow of a thousand colors, a man I could not help but love, and who saw in me the things I most wanted to create in myself… and in his own way, made everything possible.

There was a flash of brilliant white light, and then blackness.

I felt no pain. No a single moment of my life flashed before my eyes, and

I heard no chorus of singing angels.
    Yet somehow… I knew that something had changed.
    It was then that I truly awoke.

Sixty-One

Suddenly, I found myself within the council hall of the Imperial Palace, standing in the center of the shimmering mosaic floor.

Nearby, where none such monument had ever been before, stood a tall marble sculpture of The Hathor rising above a rejoicing army. So many familiar faces were gathered together, engraved upon that stone, with their swords and banners raised skyward as the ship hovered above then all. My gaze drifted towards a plaque at the monolith's base, which read quite simply "Dedicated to the Heroes of the Battle of the Frozen Sea." It was followed by a long list of names, many that I remembered well...

A trickle of light passed through the shifting yellow-gold clouds of the sky above, and the memorial sparkled in the glow of sunset. That blessed sign alone should have been a comfort to me, but I still felt that something was incomplete.

The room was empty.

I heard voices down the corridor, echoing almost surreally, and the tall doors of the hall opened slowly, letting a new ray of sunlit brilliance into the now-shadowed room where I stood.

My eyes quickly accommodated the change, and I recognized the two figures in the doorway.

Brin Falchon, an adult once more, attired in a beautiful ceremonial gown, embroidered with the symbol of the House of the Phoenix... gazed at me with a troubled look and then turned slowly away.

Beside her stood an old, old man in the robes of a Master Wizard whose pale, knowing eyes gave me no doubt as to his identity.

"Phineas!" I laughed, so thankful that he lived... though I couldn't imagine how he had aged so. I paused, wondering why neither of them had spoken so much as a word to me.

"It's been twenty years," Brin sighed. "And still I think that I can hear her in this room."

"Not Raphael?" Phineas wondered.

"Raphael was always happiest in the kitchen," Brin laughed, "but Artemis was a born leader."

Was? Was I truly dead?

A blonde man in blue and red robes raced past me without so much as a glance, and bowed before Phineas and Brin.

"Master Merlin. Empress." The man grinned.

Brin blushed. "Bennet... please call me Brin."

"As you wish, Empress Brin." He kissed her hand.

I nearly fell to the ground, but then didn't, suddenly realizing I had no physical form to speak of.

Brin... the Empress?

"I'll hunt you down King Bennet of Istara, God help me I will! Don't you dare miss another session of court!" Phineas shouted. "Young fool, he's worse than the prince!" Phineas sighed.

My two friends vanished, and somehow I found myself in the center of the chamber once again.

This time it was Geruth who stood in the light of the hall, his black shadow glaring at me, full of hatred and anger.

"Daughter... you are mine!" he roared.

I walked directly through him. Everything had seemed so important then, I realized, smiling despite myself. And what was it really... truly? A small hidden fragment in the depths of infinity.

I turned away from my old life and followed the stairs, though they were not the stairs of the palace. I knew where I was headed.

The Temple... of Raedawn.

The steps ended abruptly, leaving me before the open doors of the sacred chamber. There was no longer any broken glass, and the Archives lay undisturbed.

That foolish god-book that had ruined, and at the same time saved ... so many, many lives, lay unguarded, open for all to take, as if in this particular plane of existence no being had ever given a second thought to its extraordinary power.

I looked to see what I had written, amazed.

"Hope."

I hope... there can be peace. How unlike me it sounded, and yet at the same time, how perfectly right.

The water beneath the hovering artifact rippled invitingly, and I descended into the unknown. Beneath the surface of the flickering pool was a room... a room I recognized all too well as my wicked grandmother's chamber within the dark halls of Magog.

Why such an evil place awaited me after all that I had been through, I did not know, but nor did it seem to matter.

Inapsupetra was waiting there for me, tall and serene... her mask and robes divided cleanly down the center, between black and white, while her blunted sword and her deadly rose lay quietly at her feet.

She stood as I came forward. "So, you have come at last?"

"Why am I here?" I wondered. "If I am dead," I added.

"You are an Immortal. Like all living things, your soul remains indestructible..." Inapsupetra laughed. "Even if your body may be killed. It is memory that preserves you."

"But I am still myself," I argued. "I find that strange."

"Why so, Artemis?" The Goddess wondered.

I shook my head. "I... don't know. It simply is. I don't wish to linger with the memories I have. I would rather be on my way... to another life."

"And so you are. At this very moment." Inapsupetra shook her head. "I am amazed it has taken you quite so long to understand... when your friend Phineas revealed the secret to you at his death."

"What secret?" I wondered.

"Look into my eyes," she ordered.

The sensation was unnerving. Inapsupetra's eyes were mirrors... reflecting so many worlds. I felt as if I were flying high above the many places I had witnessed in my life, the Imperial palace, Safehaven, Galwick's tower... the Fargrove's home, Gelthar, Phoenicia... and Magog.

But the Magog I saw in the eyes of the Goddess was not the Magog I remembered. The sky was clear, the forests were green, and the oceans... yes, the oceans... crashed against the rocks of the long-dry shores.

"What vision is this?" I whispered, awestruck.

"Balance," she replied, as we stood together on the windblown fields of Raedawn.

"What humankind perceives as perfection is merely an illusion. Not a single soul in all the infinite space and time is perfect. But there are many souls who hold great, unknowable potential. They are not fated to live and die by the limits that they place upon themselves. Every born creature possesses the power to create his own destiny. Yet those free souls are not without ties. They are connected, not to heaven nor hell, but to one another, like the silken threads of a spider's web. What begins with one individual soul moves throughout the entirety of creation, becoming a ripple... a ripple that spreads from a single drop of water throughout the vastness of all the seas in all the worlds."

Inapsupetra removed her mask.

And I... I faced myself.

I remembered everything... days, years... centuries and millennia. I saw a new star forming in the shadows of brilliantly glowing nebula, and stood witness as it grew old and faded, only to rise again from its ashes, a celestial phoenix reborn.

And all around I could see a great web... a web of the most perfect white light, its ties stretching out in all directions, touching each and every life.

The Goddess smiled.

"We are one," she whispered. "We are all our own teachers, our own guardians and mentors... our own saviors. All of us, everywhere are one, many reflections of the same whole being. Knowing this when we die, we do not so much return to our gods as we return to ourselves... and our source."

Epilogue

"You're free," a voice whispered as a pair of strong, cold hands shook me out of my reverie. Suddenly knowing where I was... and who I was, I sighed in relief.

Opening my eyes, I saw the face of a woman looking down on me with a faint smile, but then, as the clock on the wall chimed midnight, she vanished inexplicably in a shattering of glass.

Still shaking from the ordeal that had felt so terribly real, my hand brushed a piece of paper on my desk. It was a page torn from an encyclopedia of mythology, but the picture was worn and faded enough that the words could be read.

Written on the paper in flowing, elegant script was what appeared to be the closing lines of a book.

> My friend,
>
> I am sorry for any pain that I may have caused you, but someone had to know the truth. I have done terrible things, yet still, I have no regrets. I was born in darkness, and having never seen the light, I did not recognize it when it first revealed itself to me.
>
> I saw the light, brother GW, wherever you are... and I found that I could change.
>
> I thought that I had failed when my world crumbled beneath my feet, I thought that I was damned and cursed to wander eternally... but then I saw that I had brought the oceans back to Magog.
>
> Still, I am not a hero. I merely defend that which I believe

to be right.

I am not a God. No man is.

I am not good... but nor am I evil. Perfection is an illusion... and in the scheme of things, true contrast was never meant to exist. We are all just fragments of imagination, different shadows of gray, capable of great evil, yet also of salvation.

This, that you have just lived, is my story. A story of a thousand years, three wars, two exiles and hope amidst chaos.

Hope. Hope for all of us, everywhere. Your future is not set in stone.

Your failures are not shackles. Your dreams may one day indeed change your world.

Sincerely yours,

Artemis Ravencroft

Printed in the United States
54112LVS00001B/131